MAN MADE
GOD 002

By Brandon Varnell

Art by Lonwa

Man Made God 002
Copyright © 2020 Brandon Varnell & Kitsune Incorporated
Illustration Copyright © 2020 Lonwa
All rights reserved.

To see Brandon Varnell's other works, or to ask for permission to use his works, visit him at www.varnell-brandon.com, facebook at www.facebook.com/AmericanKitsune, twitter at www.twitter.com/BrandonbVarnell, Patreon at https://www.patreon.com/BrandonVarnell, and instagram at www.instagram.com/brandonbvarnell.

If you'd like to know when I'm releasing a new book, you can sign up for my mailing list at https://www.varnell-brandon.com/mailing-list.

ISBN: 978-1-951904-15-9

DEDICATION

This page is made in dedication to my amazing patrons. Without them, my characters would never get lewded by so many wonderful artists:

Aaron Harris; Adam; Alarinnise; Alexander Rodriguez; Armando Pastrana; Benjamin Collinsl Benjamin Morgan; Brendan Smiley; Brennan; Bruce Johnson; Bryce McClay; C.L. Holgrahm; Catcrazy9; Chase Corso; Christopher Gross; Cody Woodard; CosmicOrange; Dane Smith; DeseriDan; Dhivael; Dominic Q Roddan; Edward Grindle; Edward Lamar Stephenson; Edward P Warmouth; ElJako98; Emery Moore; Feitochan; Forrest Hansen; Forrest Hansen; Ine Airlcana; IronKing; Jacob Flores; Jacob Wojno; Jake Fedor; James Leon-Moore; Jeremy Schultz; Jesus; John Patton; Joshua Garrett; Kevin; Lane Watkins; LarC85; Lgikito; Lucid Fayt; Lupus Umbras; Mark Frabotta; Matthew Wallace; Max A Kramer; Michael Moneymaker; Nathan; Nathan S; Nex; Omegapudding; Patrick Burns-popieniuck; Peter Barton; Philip Hedgepeth; Rfael Eriksen; Raymond Tatton; Red Phoenix; Red Viking; Repooc Ilahsram; Riesenhuber Christian; Samuel Donaldson; Sean Gray; Seismic Wolf; Slim; Smudi Corp; Starwarscout Jon; Thomas Jackson; ToraLinkley; Travis Cox; Victor Patrick Bauer; Vigil Gardner; William Crew; XY172; Yuriy Snyadanko; Zach Strickland; Zenn Barger

CONTENT

TITANIA

A mysterious fairy who Adam meets in a dungeon. Guardien of the spear. She hates it when people talk about her height.

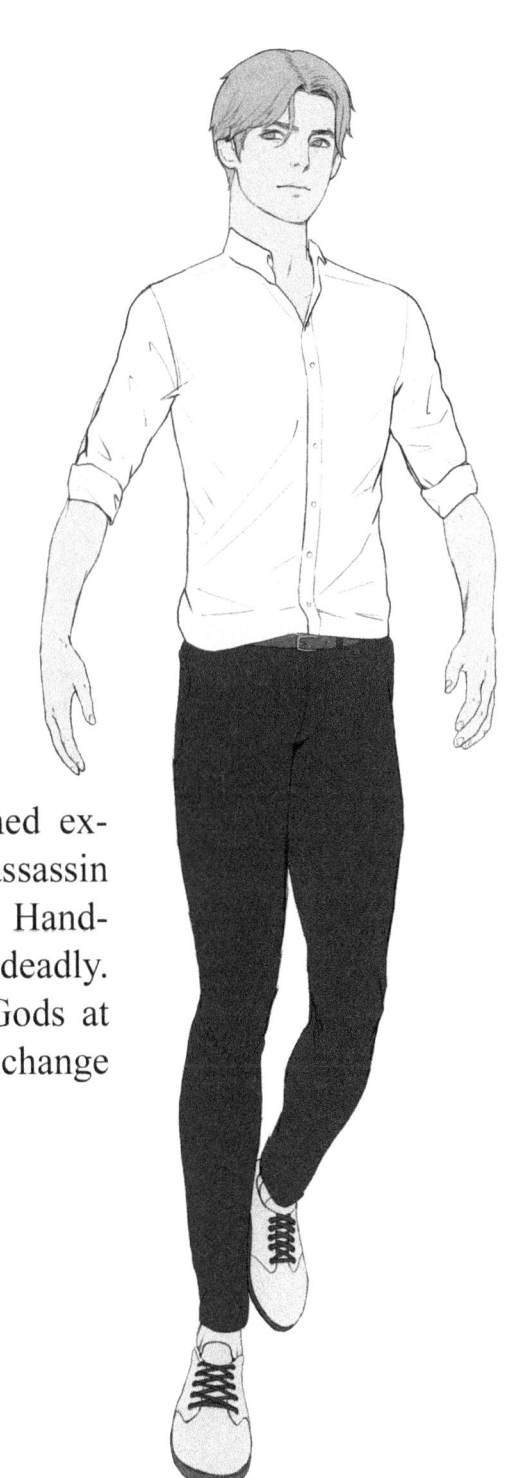

ADAM

A young man trained extensively as an assassin since childhood. Handsome, confident, deadly. He enters Age of Gods at Fayte's behest in exchange for her curing Aris.

SUSAN

Fayte's best and only friend. Genius hacker. Incredibly shy. Has trouble telling people no.

FAYTE

Daughter of the Dairing Family. Fayte is intelligent and determined to fight against her fate. She is the one who pulls Adam into Age of Gods.

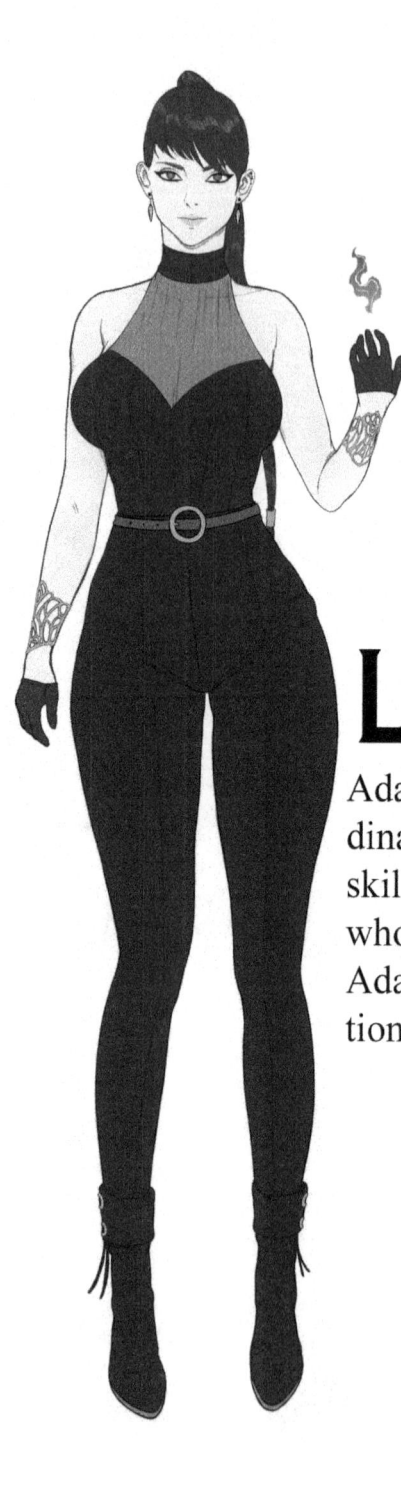

LILITH

Adam's most loyal suborddinate. She is a highly skilled and quiet assassin who will do anything Adam asks without question.

ARIS

Adam's lover. She used to
be rambunctious and wild,
but she became a cripple
after contracting mortems
disease. Currently in stasis.

LEAVING THE VIL-
LAGE OF BEGINNINGS

Adam had not realized there was a dock south of the village. The scent of wood mixed with the salt of the ocean as he followed the old mayor onto a wooden platform elevated above the ocean with simple wood posts.

The dock was not very big. In fact, there was only one ship, and it was probably only fifty feet long from bow to stern. It looked like one of those classic vessels that used to exist during the early fourteenth century: a wooden vessel with a sail, a mast, and no engine.

Adam watched as the boat rocked and wondered if this was really going to take him to the mainland. How would that work? Would he get on the ship and suddenly find himself magically standing in the next village on the mainland? Would he actually have to travel across the ocean? Most video games always skipped moments like that so they could place you right at your next destination.

He could not deny that he was curious to know how travel in this game worked.

"Well, here it is," the mayor said with a proud smile as he gestured toward the ship. "This is the ship that will take you to the mainland."

"It has been many years since I rode on a boat," Titania said with a nostalgic smile. "We fairies rarely travel on ships since we can just fly. However, there have been a few occasions where I traveled across the sea to the other three main continents, and I would always take a ship during those times."

"When was the last time you rode on a ship?" asked Adam.

"About three thousand one hundred years ago."

"… So old."

"I heard that!"

The mayor escorted them onto the dock and spoke with the captain of the ship, a grizzled man who wore no shirt. His bare chest was covered in thick black hair, he had a gnarly beard, and there was a cutlass swinging from his right hip. He looked like a pirate, but his eyes held a surprisingly gentle expression. They seemed rather jolly. It created an intense dichotomy between his appearance and demeanor.

"So these are the two who are gonna be traveling with me to the mainland—holy mother of Davy Jones! It's a fairy! And she's so tiny! Why is she so tiny?!"

"Would you people give it a rest already?!"

Adam rubbes the back of his head as Titania glowered at the man for calling her tiny. He seemed like an okay guy, but he had the same problem everyone else had with regards to Titania's presence —and her height in particular.

In either event, everything had been taken care of. The mayor informed them that this man would be taking them to the mainland, and the pirate-like captain asked them to climb aboard. He was particularly kind to Titania, who was still upset about being called tiny and ignored him. This caused the man to shed tears and profusely apologize over and over again.

Ding!

[Warning: You are about to leave the Village of Beginnings. Once you leave, you will not be able to return. Do you still wish to leave? Yes or no?]

The warning message appeared in front of Adam the moment he was about to board the ship. He paused for a moment but only a moment. There was no need to hesitate now.

He pressed "yes."

Ding!

[You have decided to leave the Village of Beginnings. Please be aware that you are the first person in the history of Age of Gods *to leave one of the Village of Beginnings. An international announcement will be made to let everyone know about your accomplishments. You will also be given a reward for being the first person to leave.]*

Adam read the message, and Titania, who had taken to sitting on his shoulder once more, also read the message with a perplexed look on her face.

"What does this mean?" she asked.

"It's telling me that all the other players are going to become aware of what I've done," Adam said. "I am the first player to leave a Village of Beginnings. That's a pretty big thing."

"Is it now?"

Titania didn't look like it was that big of a deal, but she was an NPC. She might have been the most realistic NPC Adam had ever seen, with an intelligence beyond any program generated personality he had ever met or heard of, but at the end of the day, it didn't change the fact that she was made of polygons and programming. He didn't think she'd understand even if he tried to explain this, and he was loathe to break the fourth wall to explain it to her.

They finally boarded the ship, and Adam was shocked when several waves caused the boat to rock. He stabilized himself, but he was still surprised. Waves lapped against the boat, a salty spray hit his face, and he could taste saltwater on his tongue. No matter how many times it was presented to him, the sheer realism of this game never failed to astonish him.

The captain was not the only person on the ship. There was a helmsman, the chief mate, the second mate, and several sea monkeys. All of them were burly men with no shirts and cutlasses strapped to their waists. They also acted the same way the captain had done when he saw Titania, right down to calling her tiny, which pissed the woman off so fiercely she flew up to the crow's nest and refused to come down even when Adam called for her.

He'd never met a fairy more sensitive about her height.

Then again, this was his first time meeting a fairy. Maybe they were all like this?

"All hands! Prepare for takeoff! Weigh anchor! Set the sails!"

Everyone except Adam began working, running about the deck as they followed the captain's orders. Several men used a crank to pull up the anchor, another group were unfurling the sails, and one had gone to the wheel and was preparing to steer them away from the dock. The captain stood near the helm as he shouted at the group.

With nothing to do, Adam moved off to the side and leaned against the railing so he wouldn't be in the way. He leaned forward, placed his forearms against the rail, and looked out at the sea.

How many years had it been since he'd gone to the sea? Before Aris contracted Mortems Disease, traveling to the beach had been one of her favorite activities. He remembered the cute bikini she had worn back then to show off to him. How old had they been when she did that? She was fourteen when she contracted Mortems Disease and she was seventeen now, so it must have been… over three years ago at least.

"So much time has passed," Adam said with a depressed sigh.

"What are you thinking about now?" asked Titania as she chose that moment to flutter down from the crow's nest. He hoped that meant she was no longer angry. It was no fun dealing with an angry woman, especially when her anger wasn't even his fault.

"Just thinking about the reason I began playing this game," Adam said with a wave of his hand.

Titania frowned, but she did not say anything more.

At that moment, the preparations to set sail were finished and the captain ordered his helmsman to steer them away from the dock.

The ship finally moved, slowly pulling out of the dock and the little inlet it was located in. Adam watched it all. He didn't say anything, but he was honestly kind of excited. He couldn't help but wonder what new adventures were waiting for him.

***

Fayte chanted under her breath as a level 10 [black bear] released a ferocious and hair-raising roar. Even though she felt goosebumps on her skin from that sound, she continued to chant as Susan fired arrow after arrow into the monster's hide. The Archer was using the [Deadeye] skill, which increased the accuracy of her shots.

-45; -45; -45; MISS; MISS!

Two of the arrows missed as the [black bear] charged at them, but in that moment, Fayte released her spell. Bluish energy swirled around her staff as she thrust it forward like she was planning to impale the [black bear] with it. She could feel the energy being pulled from her body, like something was tugging her soul out of her chest. Then the energy congealed into a small sphere at the very tip of her staff before it was launched forward like a rocket.

[Energy Blast] was a non-elemental spell that gathered magic toward the tip of a Mage's staff and fired it at extreme speeds. The sphere she shot forward and slammed into the [black bear], striking it on the face and sending it stumbling backward.

-124!

"I did it!" Fayte shouted in excitement. "Now is your chance, Lilith!"

At her shout, a figure shot forward like a bolt of black lightning, traversing the distance between it and the [black bear] in less time than it took Fayte to blink. Before she could even register what was happening, a rather large number appeared over the head of the [black bear], signifying how much damage had been done to it.

-450!

At that moment, the figure leapt backward, body flipping around like an acrobat. When the figure landed next to Fayte, it revealed a stunning woman garbed in all black. Black leather pants and a black sleeveless shirt covered her body. The pants showed off the wonderful curve of this woman's generous hips and her shapely butt. Her shirt, on the other hand, possessed no back and even showed off a good deal of her sideboob. She wore black boots, had a black sash wrapped around her tiny waist, and a black assassins mask covered almost all of her face. The only thing Fayte could see of this woman's face was her intense, dark eyes surrounded by beautifully unblemished white skin.

-45; -45; MISS; MISS; MISS!

Immediately after Lilith leapt away from the [black bear], Susan notched arrow after arrow into her bow and fired them. Three missed, but two hit. Likewise, Fayte began chanting for another spell, which slammed into the [black bear] like a powerful plasma bullet. Meanwhile, Lilith dealt damage by attacking from behind, using her powerful Assassin class to pull most of the monster's agro. Not even five minutes had passed before the [black bear] was defeated.

Ding!

[Congratulations! You have defeated the enemy [black bear]! Items dropped: [brown adventurer boots] and 300 gold coins! +400 experience!]

"We did it!" Fayte cheered.

"Y-yes, we did," Susan said with a soft and timid smile.

Fayte gave her best friend a vibrant smile, even though she knew Susan couldn't see it past her veil, before looking at their newest companion. She clasped her staff in both hands and bowed to the woman.

"Thank you very much for your assistance, Lilith. Leveling up would be a lot harder without you here."

"There is no need to thank me," Lilith said in a quiet voice. It was like a whisper, and yet, despite how softly spoken the words were, Fayte and Susan could hear them perfectly, like they were being projected directly into their mind.

Lilith had joined them just the other day. Neither of them knew who she was or why she had offered her services to them, but they did not regret accepting her offer. Had it not been for this woman and her incredible skills as an Assassin class player, they would have never been able to reach level 8 so quickly.

Fayte could not help but smile as she thought about the look on Adam's face when he discovered that she was at level 8 already. She was certain he would be shocked.

Ding!

[Attention. This is an international announcement to all players. As of 9:33 am Eastern Standard Time, the player known as Adam has reached level 10 and left the Village of Beginnings. He is

the first person to have done so, and as such, he has gained the reward of +100 status points, +500 ability points, and +5,000 Reputation. We hope this knowledge will encourage other players to try harder and reach greater heights as you explore the mysteries of the Forgotten Realm. Thank you all for playing Age of Gods.]

Fayte froze when she heard the announcement. It felt like a bolt of lightning had descended from the heavens and struck her, electrifying her and frying her brain. She simply couldn't fathom it.

Adam was at level 10.

Adam had already left the Village of Beginnings.

How was this even possible?

Fayte knew, of course, that Adam was an incredible player. Back when he first appeared in the gaming world, he had taken it by storm. He fought in tournaments against some of the greatest players of the time and left them humiliated. But even though she knew of his strength and gaming prowess, she was still completely shocked by how quickly he had reached level 10. According to the forums, only Lin Akamine and the Spear God were close to reaching level 10, and it was estimated they would need at least two or three more days.

"F-Fayte?" Susan called out timidly. "Do you think this is the same Adam you convinced to join our guild?"

Fayte took a slow, shuddering breath, then smiled. "Yes, I'm pretty sure this is the same Adam. There can't be two people with the same gamer tag, after all."

"He's pretty amazing, isn't he?" said Susan in awe.

"Yes. Yes, he is."

Now that she had begun talking again, Fayte calmed down and allowed herself to think rationally. Adam had already reached level 10. Meanwhile, everyone else was still stuck at level 7, where the experience points required to reach the next level became utterly ridiculous. She and Susan had just reached level 8 not long ago. It was suspected that it would take the more powerful guild masters at least several more days to reach level 9.

"This is going to shock everyone," Fayte said, finally allowing herself to smile. "I wonder what the forums will say about him?"

"Heh heh."

"What's so funny?" asked Fayte.

Susan blushed a little when she realized she had just laughed out loud, but then she gave a bashful smile as she said, "It's nothing really. I was just thinking about how long it's been since I've seen you smile like that. I've missed that smile."

Fayte didn't know what expression she was making at Susan's words. She didn't even know how Susan could tell she was smiling behind her veil, nor did she know or even understand what she was feeling. Guilt mixed with joy. Happiness congealed with sadness. She was feeling so many emotions as she looked at Susan that her face could not adequately express how she felt.

"I am sorry," she apologized. "I've caused you to worry about me. You have suffered because of me."

"N-no! Not at all!" Susan waved her hands back and forth. "I-I'm not the one who is suffering right now! I know how much your current situation is weighing on you! I'm not blaming you at all."

"Thank you, Su." Fayte reached out and tenderly brushed the younger girl's bangs away from her head like an older sister giving affection to her younger sibling. "Thank you for always sticking by my side even though I know you're dealing with your own problems right now."

Susan had her own hardships to deal with, but even so, she continued to support Fayte and her fight against Levon. Fayte didn't think she'd ever be able to adequately express how much Susan's continued friendship meant to her.

"You're welcome," Susan whispered as she looked down, her cheeks and ears turning red.

Since they had already killed the [black bear], Fayte decided it was time to move on. However, just as she was leaving, she noticed their other companion was not by her side. She looked behind her and noticed that Lilith had not moved at all. The young woman garbed in black assassin's clothing looked up at the sky, her face hidden by that mask.

"Lilith? Is everything okay?" she asked.

Lilith snapped out of her distracted state and walked over to them. Even though Fayte could not see her face, she thought there was a small change in the woman's eyes. She looked… happy? Yes, she seemed happy for some reason, though Fayte couldn't begin to guess why.

"Yes. Everything is fine. Let's go."

"All right."

With her two companions in tow, Fayte journeyed deeper into the forest in search for more enemies.

***

"Urk… I hate my life…"

"Ah ha ha ha ha! Aha ha!"

"S-shut up… stop laughing… hurk!"

It had been a very long time since Adam traveled via ship… and the last time he had done so, his life had been hanging by a thread. He hadn't even been aware that he was on a boat until after the ship had already docked in the American Federation's Rhode Island, since he was unconscious for most of the trip.

That was probably why he didn't know he could get motion sickness.

Which explained why he was half-hanging over the side of the ship, vomiting the contents of his stomach.

The constant rocking, the way it distorted his sense of sight, and the feeling beneath his feet made his stomach convulse. The world was spinning. It was truly unpleasant. He would have never agreed to travel by boat had he known this would happen.

On that note, he had no idea he could get motion sickness in a game. Weren't there settings to get rid of this sort of thing? He really wanted to turn off the motion sickness setting. Why did this game have to be so realistic?!

"I cannot believe… the most unconventional human I have ever… ever met… could get motion sick!"

Titania was floating above him, tears of mirth pouring from her eyes as she held her hands to her gut, laughing at his expense. She looked like she was having the time of her life. Adam, on the other hand, had never felt more humiliated in his life.

"It looks like yer having trouble," the captain of the ship said, voice sympathetic. "This happens to people sometimes. Don't worry. After a few days at sea, I am sure you'll get used to it."

The status screen that appeared above his head showed that his name was Red Beard, and he was at level 30. Adam didn't know why his name was Red Beard. His beard wasn't even red. It was black—hurk!

"Oh, God. I want to die."

"Aha ha ha ha ha!"

"Damn fairy."

On the captain's suggestion, Adam went with Titania into his cabin near the bottom of the ship to lie down on the bed, but even that didn't seem to help. No. It just made matters worse. The rocking down there was even more intense, and he felt like something was screwing up his equilibrium.

Because Adam couldn't sleep and still felt sick, he decided to log off. The world around him faded. Then the familiar ceiling of his bed appeared over his head. He blinked several times, then felt his stomach rebel and shot out of the bed, rushing to the bathroom, where he began throwing up his breakfast from that morning. He spent nearly five minutes just hovering over the toilet.

He'd never felt so disgusted with himself.

It was around noon when he logged out, so it was about time for lunch. Adam went into the kitchen after rinsing out his mouth with mouthwash. He decided to make a grilled beef sandwich, which he did by adding beef, provolone cheese, bell peppers, and onions between two pieces of bread that he slathered with butter and fried in a pan. The scent of frying butter made his mouth water. It also attracted the attention of someone else.

"What is that heavenly smell?" Fayte asked as she wandered into the living room.

"Lunch. Want some?" asked Adam.

"Yes, please."

Since Fayte seemed to be hungry, Adam made her a beef sandwich as well, then emerged from the kitchen carrying two plates in hand, which he set on the coffee table.

"Thank you," Fayte said.

She was wearing pajamas that day. It looked to him like she had only just gotten out of bed. Her pajamas were pink and cute, and they seemed to create an interesting contrast with her buxom figure. Her hair, long and golden blonde like threads of honey, flowed from the crown of her head in very gentle waves... though a few ends were sticking out here and there. While her hair was a bit messy, he thought it made her look prettier somehow.

Fayte Dairing was someone he had only met recently and yet, despite this, he felt shockingly comfortable around her. He'd never expected to feel this way around anyone whose name wasn't Aris. It made him a little worried since he wasn't sure he wanted to become personally invested in Fayte... though perhaps it was already too late for him to concern himself over such matters.

They ate in silence, both thinking their own thoughts, but once they were finished, Fayte smirked at him.

"So… level 10, huh? You realize that you are the first person to reach level 10 and leave the Village of Beginnings, right? Not even Lin Akamine or the Spear God has achieved that feat yet."

"I am aware," Adam said with a slow nod. "But this is good. I'd like to keep ahead of everyone else in the game since becoming more famous will make helping you win your bet that much easier."

Adam was working for Fayte to help her win a bet she made against Levon Pleonexia—the heir of the Pleonexia Family, which was the current most powerful family in the American Federation. The bet was that she needed to earn half the Dairing Family's annual income, increase her reputation to match or exceed the least powerful among the top ten most powerful families in the American Federation, and create a guild in Age of Gods that ranked among the top five guilds.

Anyone of these would be hard to achieve. Together, they were basically impossible. Despite this, Fayte refused to back down and continued to try. It was for this reason that Adam felt such a great amount of respect for Fayte—and perhaps why his feelings for her were stronger than they should have been for someone who was just a client.

Fayte looked like she was touched, but she didn't dwell on that topic for long and instead asked for tips on reaching level 10. Adam told her about how he had reached level 10. Fayte was shocked when he explained how he ended up in a dungeon and faced off against several 2- and 3-star monsters that were over a dozen levels above him. She didn't think she could do that, which caused Adam to shrug when she intimated as much.

In return, Fayte told him about her new companion, praising Lilith's strength and abilities. There was an odd look on his face as she talked about the woman. This caused her to ask about it.

"It's nothing. I was just thinking about how impressive Lilith sounds," he said with a smile. "You should definitely stick by her side. I'm sure she'll prove to be an asset in the future."

"I agree," Fayte said with a nod.

After lunch, Adam went into Aris' room to check on the girl and tell her stories about his time in *Age of Gods*. He noticed that the gauge, which showed how much Mortems Disease she had left to cure, was about three-fourths covered in blue. That meant she was nearly 75% cured. This shocking development made him incredibly happy because it meant she might be able to leave that cryochamber early.

He wasn't sure how long he spoke with Aris, but it was about 2:30pm by the time he ran out of topics. Adam wandered into the bedroom, grabbed some medicine meant for motion sickness, and swallowed it. He didn't know if this would help him in-game. At the same time, he had no desire to begin puking the moment he entered *Age of Gods*.

Once he logged on, Adam again found himself in the familiar *Age of Gods* world. The rocking of the ship still made him feel mildly uncomfortable. Oddly enough, however, he did not get sick nor did he feel a strong desire to vomit. Did that mean the medicine he took in the real world was working in the game? How did that even work?

"ADAM!!!!"

The shout startled Adam so much that he nearly fell off the bed. Leaping to his feet, he stared in shock at Titania as she flew in through the door. Her face was pale and panic stricken. He'd never seen her like this.

"There is big trouble! Come quick!"

"What is it? What's wrong?"

"We're under attack by pirates!"

Adam's mind nearly blanked at the mention of pirates, but then he hurried out of the cabin, up the stairs, and onto the deck. Just like Titania said, they were indeed under attack by pirates. There were currently ten people dressed in red pirate-like outfits on the deck and more coming via boarding planks. They wore cotton shirts with puffy sleeves that showed off their burly chests, their faces were covered in sweat and looked greasy, and they were all swinging cutlasses with reckless abandon as they attacked the panicking crew members of the ship he was on.

"Damn. We really are under attack!"

"I told you that already! Now hurry up and help them!"

Adam didn't need to be told twice. He gripped the [Rusted Spear] in his hand, activated [Blood Sacrifice], and charged into the fray.

The pirates were all at level 15. They were called [Black Beard's Pirates] in the status display screen when Titania used [scan] to help him see what levels they were. They had several attacks, but all of them were sword techniques like [thrust], [slash], and [swashbuckle]. The only one Adam really needed to worry about was

[swashbuckle], which was a debuffing skill that had a 25% chance
of causing the [fear] status effect.

Name: Black Beard's Pirates
Description: Pirates sailing under the flag of the infamous Black
Beard.
Class: 1-Star
Lvl: 15
Health: 10,000/10,000
MP: 500/500
Strength: 100
Constitution: 200
Dexterity: 100
Intelligence: 10
Speed: 50

Skills:
Slash: A slashing attack that does 200% damage and has a
100% chance of causing bleed
MP Cost: 50
Cooldown Time: 0 Seconds

Thrust: A thrust technique that causes critical damage
Damage = Strength * 3
MP Cost: 100
Cooldown time: 5 seconds

Swashbuckle: A taunting skill that has a 25% chance of casting
the fear status effect
MP Cost: 120
Cooldown time: 30 seconds

After casting [scan] on the pirates, Titania flew behind Adam
and began singing [Song of Vigor].

Adam flew across the deck and swung the [Rusted Spear], activating the [slash] skill. The blade of his spear tore through the pirate who was attacking one of the crew members. Adam was surprised when the man squealed like a gutted pig.

-3,640!

"What the heck?!"

Even Adam was shocked when he saw the amount of damage his attack had caused. That was a ridiculous amount of damage, but Adam didn't let his surprise stop him from using [slash] five more times, whittling away at the pirate's health until the man went down. He did notice every attack after that first one only did -1,320 points of damage, so that previous attack must have been a critical hit.

Adam's shockingly powerful attack caused all the pirates to lock onto him, and he soon found himself being trapped within a whirlwind of cutlasses. He was fortunate. These enemies might have been at a higher level than him, but they were not trained fighters. All of them telegraphed their moves like a bunch of rank amateurs.

Taking advantage of their lack of skill, Adam wove through the hailstorm of attacks. He spun the spear around in his hand and carefully parried each and every attack with a dancer's grace. Not only did he not allow himself to get hit even once, but he protected Titania as she sang behind him.

-1,320; MISS; -1,320; -1,320; MISS; MISS; MISS!

Despite the fact that this was a video game and this body of his was not real, Adam still felt his limbs growing heavy as the battle continued. He danced across the deck, spun his spear, and used [slash] multiple times in quick succession to cut down one of the pirates. This must have been the fourth one he'd killed. Adam didn't know how many more he had to defeat because it seemed like two more pirates replaced each one that died. To make matters worse, [Blood Sacrifice] ended and the cooldown time appeared.

"Adam! The ship! Let's take this fight to the pirate ship!" Titania shouted.

A glance at where Titania pointed revealed the pirate ship that had attacked them. It was much larger than their own vessel by at least fifty feet, making it around one hundred feet in length from bow to stern. Several boarding planks attached the two ships together. The pirates kept running across the boarding planks and landing on the ship he was on.

With a grimace, Adam leapt onto the nearest boarding plank and began swatting off the pirates attempting to walk across it. He didn't use an actual skill, so the amount of damage he did was only -1, but they were all knocked aside and fell into the water with a loud splash.

Adam landed on the pirate ship and was immediately attacked by at least ten pirates. All of them were at level 15. He gritted his teeth hard and began dancing across the deck, shuffling his feet along the floorboards as he spun the spear around his body to both attack and defend. His movements were swift like a rabbit hopping back and forth. While he managed to avoid letting himself be hit, he couldn't really attack either, and since he wasn't using [slash] or [thrust], it meant his attacks were still only doing -1 damage.

With a snarl on his face, Adam leapt back and thrust out the spear, then spun around to avoid being struck by an incoming pirate and thrust his spear out again. He caught the man in the chest. However, he did not remain there for long and kept dancing around his enemies while also unleashing a flurry of [slash] attacks.

-1,056; MISS; MISS; MISS; -990; -990; MISS!

Sweat formed on Adam's brow as the attacks continued coming in ceaselessly. He ducked under a cutlass swung horizontally, stabbed out with his spear to impale the attacker, then yanked his spear back out and twirled the weapon around his body to [slash] at multiple targets. He was glad this skill had no cooldown time. His attacks hit several pirates and dealt them -990 damage, though he also missed several times.

More enemies were incoming. He had already adjusted his stance into a defensive form, feet planted firmly on the planks so he could knock back any attack that came his way. He was like a turtle hiding within its shell. The incoming swings from cutlasses glanced off his spear as though it was a shell instead of a weapon, but he knew he couldn't remain on the defensive forever.

As the battle continued, Adam realized he could feel the intent coming from his spear. It felt like it wanted him to attack. Then again, he could have just been imagining things.

Either way, he renewed his assault, attacking with an elegance and grace that caused the pirates around him to back off. They seemed wary of how intense his assault was. Thrust his spear. Danced again. Thrust his spear again. Had someone been looking at his dance from a bird's eye view, they would have seen how his movements formed the shape of petals on the ground.

-1,056; -1,056; -1,056; -1,056; -1,056!

Ding!

[Congratulations! Thanks to your comprehension of Spear Intent, you have learned a new skill: [Dance of the Sakura Blossoms]!]

Adam felt shock course through him like lightning when he saw the skill name, but he did not hesitate to activate it.

His dance continued the same as before, but this time, his attacks began dealing serious damage to the pirates. He shuffled along the ground and thrust his spear at lightning speed. None of his enemies could follow his movements either. They tried to attack him, tried to keep up, but he was constantly in motion.

-1,056; -2,112; -4,224; -8,448; MISS!

Adam had yet to see what the skill did, but the longer the dance continued with consecutive hits, the more damage he seemed to inflict on his enemies. Every time he missed, the amount of damage he could do was reset and his skill went into cooldown.

The unfortunate aspect of this skill was that it was limited to one person at a time, which meant he couldn't focus on multiple enemies. That said, the amount of damage he could deal with this new skill was enough to one-shot the pirates attacking him. As the amount of damage he inflicted increased, the pirates began falling in droves.

"What be going on here?!" a voice suddenly shouted.

The pirates all stopped attacking Adam and backed off as someone walked up to him. The dull *thunk, thunk* of a wooden leg echoed against the deck as a man dressed in a red overcoat with a lot of frills along the cuffs and collar appeared. He was a gnarled man with black hair and a thick beard. He was wielding two cutlasses. Titania cast [scan] to let Adam check his stats.

Name: Black Beard
Description: Black Beard is the king of the pirates in the Southern Sea. He is well-known for being vicious and never showing mercy even when the people he captures are women and children.
Class: 3-Star
Lvl: 25
Health: 60,000/60,000
MP: 5,000/5,000
Strength: 1,500
Constitution: 1,000
Dexterity: 100
Intelligence: 50
Speed: 200

Skills:
Slash: A slashing attack that does 200% damage and has a 100% chance of causing bleed
MP Cost: 50
Cooldown Time: 0 Seconds

Thrust: A thrust technique that causes critical damage
Damage = Strength * 3
MP Cost: 100
Cooldown time: 5 seconds

Dual Wielding: Black Beard can wield two weapons of the same type at the same time. This allows him to attack enemies twice as much!
MP Cost: 0
Cooldown Time: N/A

Ye Scurvy Cur: Black Beard has an incredible amount of charisma thanks to the fear he invokes in companions and enemies alike
All enemies have a 50% chance of gaining the fear status effect; Allies receive a boost that increases morale and lets them attack two times faster than normal
MP cost: 250
Cooldown Time: 60 seconds

This [Black Beard] had some incredible stats, and he was a 3-Star enemy at level 25 to boot. Adam almost groaned when he saw that. Was it fate or ill-fortune that had him constantly running into enemies he had no right defeating? When had he accrued such bad karma?

"Ya scallywag!" Black Beard shouted when he saw Adam standing in the center of his pirates. "What do ya think yer doing on my ship?!"

"The fuck kind of question is that?!" Adam snapped. "What do you think you're doing attacking *my* ship?!"

"Gya ha ha ha! A good question deserves a good answer. I be taking over that ship of yers. It is now me property, which means yer also me property. I bet ye'll fetch a lot of gold if I sell ya as a... slave..." Black Beard trailed off when he caught sight of Titania, but it was only for a moment. "A fairy?! Is that a fairy?! Why she be so short?!"

Titania bristled. "Stop! Calling! Me! Short!"

"Listen up, ye scallywags! The one who captures that tiny fairy will receive twice the profit as everyone else!"

"I'm not tiny!"

Those words caused the pirates to all yell and charge at Adam and Titania, who no longer found time to speak up. No witty comebacks for them. Adam activated [Blood Sacrifice] again as Titania sang [Song of Vigor] to increase his attack power. Then Adam once more began dancing, and this time, the damage he did was astronomical.

-1,056; -2,112; -4,224; -8,448; 16,896!

When Adam used [Dance of the Sakura Blossoms], the amount of damage he did at first was negligible, but it quickly stacked up as he continued attacking without missing. The following attacks became one-shot kill attacks. While he did sometimes miss, the cooldown time only reset when he wasn't using [Blood Sacrifice]. Even when it did reset, it didn't matter because he continued to dance, deflecting and countering numerous sword swings with his incredible spear work as he waited for the cooldown time to end. One. Two. Three. Six. Twelve pirates were cut down in less than half as many seconds.

"Arg! Ya blasted cur! I'm gonna rip ya to shreds!!!"

It wasn't until he'd killed what seemed like half the crew that Adam was attacked by [Black Beard] himself. The man wielded his two cutlasses with incredible skill. Each swing felt like a truck was slamming into Adam, but he was skilled enough to avoid blocking the attacks. Instead of blocking, he deflected them with his spear like he was parrying them, which caused Black Beard's swords to go wide and knocked the man off balance. This left him open to Adam's [Dance of the Sakura Blossoms].

-1,056; -2,112; -4,224; -8,448; 16,896!

Adam wore a fierce snarl as his first five attacks cut down more than half of [Black Beard's] health. He only needed to land one more successful [Dance of the Sakura Blossoms] on this man. If he could just keep up this level of intensity, he would be able to easily win!

Unfortunately, Adam's [Blood Sacrifice] chose that moment to run out of time, and then to make matters worse, Titania found herself unable to help him as a pirate managed to sneak up on her from behind and grab her. She screamed, which caught Adam's attention. This, however, distracted him long enough that Black Beard was able to land a blow.

-432!

The first attack hit Adam, but he managed to dodge the second attack. He was incredibly lucky. While [Black Beard] had a Strength of +1,500, Adam had a Defense of 560, and his newly acquired armor had a combined 55% resistance to slashing damage. Cutlasses did primarily slashing damage, so his armor was even more effective against it. Even with that level of defense, however, the searing pain of being attacked with a cutlass was burned into his mind.

This made him angry.

Adam felt a cold chill settle over his mind.

The first thing Adam did was take two [health potions], but then he spun around and sliced off the hand of the pirate... and he felt some surprise that he could actually cut the hand off. A large -5,000 floated over the screaming pirate's head. His attack also freed Titania, who began singing [Song of Vigor] again, which increased his attack power and allowed him to quickly dispatch the now one-handed pirate who had grabbed her.

[Black Beard] released an enraged cry and began swearing like a... well, like a pirate, Adam supposed. The man charged at him, wooden leg thunking against the deck, and Adam met his attacks head-on. The cooldown time for [Blood Sacrifice] ended, and so he activated the skill and used [Dance of the Sakura Blossoms] to finish the man off.

-1,056; -2,112; -4,224; -8,448; 16,896!

Adam took several deep breaths as [Black Beard] fell backward after Adam cut through his neck with his spear. The man twitched several times. There was no blood, but that somehow made the death twitches he released even creepier than if he had been bleeding.

Ding!

[You have defeated twenty-four 1-star [Black Beard Pirates]. Items dropped: x10 [Cutlass], x20 [Pirate Shirt], and 10,500 gold coins. +36,000 experience points earned! +5,000 ability points! +16,000 Reputation!]

Ding!

[You have defeated the 3-Star enemy [Black Beard]. Items dropped: [Black Beard's Twin Cutlasses], [Pirate Profession Scroll], [Black Beard's Hat], and 16,000 gold. +85,000 experience points! +6,000 ability points! +5,000 Reputation!]

Ding!

[Congratulations! You have leveled up. You are now at level 11! +300 HP! +10 MP! +5 SP!]

Ding!

[Congratulations! Titania has leveled up! She is now at level 10! +200 HP! +1,050 MP! +10 SP!]

Ding!

[Congratulations! Titania has leveled up! She is now at level 11! +200 HP! +1,050 MP! +10 SP]

ARRIVING ON THE
MAINLAND

Watershore was a small port town, but it was larger than the Village of Beginnings—about six or seven times bigger. All of the major roads seemed to converge upon the docks and spread out radially from there. There were six major roads, which meant the port town was divided into six sections. The buildings were all made from a combination of brick and wood. Roofs made with ceramic shingles appeared to be more commonplace here than in the Village of Beginnings, where most of the roofs had been made of straw and hay.

Adam walked through the town with Titania sitting on his shoulder. A combination of unusual scents filled his nose. There was the salty scent of the sea mixed with the smell of freshly baked bread and grilled fish. The grilled fish was the strongest smell, but that was because Adam had a stick of something that looked like a grilled sea bass in his hands. It had a very salty flavor. The primary seasonings for this grilled fish appeared to be simple salt and pepper.

"This is a pretty lively town," Adam said as he looked at several children who were running—only to watch as the kids stopped and began pointing at him.

He looked away.

"It is not *that* lively," Titania said as she also observed the town, her own gaze distant. "This tiny port town probably has less than ten thousand people living in it. Of course, that would be a huge number for us fairies, but for a human settlement, it is very small. Go to Sunestia, and you'll understand what I mean."

Several people hauling lumber walked on by. They were all large, burly men with arms thicker than his head and chests like barrels. When the guy in front saw Adam—or rather, the little fairy sitting on his shoulder—he dropped the lumber he was carrying, which caused the man behind to get smacked underneath the chin when one end of the lumber got stuck in the cobblestone and he walked right into the end he'd been carrying.

Adam walked passed the now bickering duo and continued to turn his head this way and that. This city was so different from cities like New York City, Los Angeles, and Dallas. It embodied the fantasy aesthetic from old movies. He remembered one movie about a fellowship and a ring that had cities built similar to this.

"And where and what is Sunestia?" asked Adam.

"Sunestia is the capital city of the Sun Continent," Titania answered. "I do not know where it is in relation to where we are now, however. This city must be new. I do not remember ever visiting it."

"Well, it has been three thousand years, right?"

"Indeed."

Since Adam had no idea where he was or where he needed to go, he decided to get himself a map. There were a number of shops in this town. Each store was identified by the sign hanging above the door. There was a store with a potion on the sign, one with a book, another with a sword and shield, and one with a scroll. He was certain the one with the scroll would sell maps, so that was the one he wandered into.

The store did indeed sell maps, and the woman who ran the shop even sold him a map after she finished freaking out upon seeing Titania. He and Titania soon left the store. Of course, his fairy companion was fuming.

"She called me short!"

"That's because you *are* short."

"That's only because my level is so pathetic! If I was at level 50, I would be the same size as a human! Just you wait! Once I reach level 50, my body will grow back to the size it is supposed to be, and then I will stun you with my incredible beauty! You'll be so stunned, you'll want to worship the ground I walk on!"

Adam didn't have it in him to argue with Titania, and he already thought she was a beauty. She was just... well, short. Really short. The mere fact that she could sit on his shoulder and he barely even felt her weight was all the proof he needed of her shortness.

"Why level 50?"

"Do you not know? Level 50 is when the people of this world are allowed to do a class upgrade. Currently speaking, my class is

Guardian of the Spear, which is the class I received after I became sealed away with that spear you are holding in your right hand. Once I reach level 50, I will be able to upgrade my class, which should let me regain my previous stature."

"Makes sense. So does that mean I will also be able to change my class when I reach level 50?"

"You can change your class before reaching level 50. A class upgrade is literally just that. An upgrade of your current class."

"So I can change my class from Warrior to something else? How do I do that?"

"I know of at least two methods of changing your class: you can find a master who can train you in a new class, or you can use a hidden class scroll." Titania looked up, tilted her head, and added, "Hidden classes offer incredible power far beyond a normal class upgrade. Good luck finding a hidden class scroll, though. Even before I was sealed, those were so rare I had only seen a few of them in my entire life."

"Hmm…"

Adam glanced at the sky and saw that dusk was quickly approaching. The sun was going down, the sky was painted with splashes of pink and streaks of orange, and he could see the beginning of the moon rising above a mountain range in the far distance. The moon had a ring around it like Saturn. He didn't know if this meant it was late in the real world. However, after fighting against those pirates, Adam realized he was honestly really tired.

"I think I'm going to log off… I mean, I am going to return to my world," Adam said at last.

"Very well." Titania agreed readily enough. "Let us find an inn first though. I would prefer you return to your world in someplace private."

"Sure." Adam didn't think much of her request and just agreed.

There were a number of inns at Watershore. Adam thought there were more inns than any other building. He wondered if that was because this was a port town. Historically speaking, port towns were always important because they were built along significant trade routes between other cities and nations. A lot of the people who stayed in port towns did not live there. They merely stayed temporarily until they set off for their next destination.

He didn't know if that was how things worked in *Age of Gods*, though.

The inn they ended up lodging at was smaller than some but bigger than others, at two-stories in height and wider than it was long. The shingles on the roof were red. It had several windows, though none of the windows had glass and were instead boarded up with wood. He wondered if that meant glass windows was a rarity in this world. Maybe the technique to make them was expensive? How was glass made back when technology had been this primitive anyway? The Village of Beginnings only had windows on the cathedral, now that he was thinking about it.

The owner of the inn was an old man who came close to fainting when he saw Adam's fairy companion. After once more dealing with Titania's outrage at being called short, they were able to secure a room with one bed. It didn't have much. The floor was made of wood, there was a small table next to the window, and the bed was made of simple straw and feathers. He sat on the bed. It wasn't very comfortable, but Adam did not intend to sleep on it, so that was okay.

"You are returning to your world now?" asked Titania, an odd look on her face. She floated a few feet above his head and was looking down at him with an inscrutable expression on her face.

"That's right," Adam said as he laid down and closed his eyes. "There are some people I need to speak with in the real world."

"Hmph."

Titania huffed and turned her head. Adam had no idea what she was upset about now, but he put it out of his mind as he logged out and found himself lying on his own bed. It was 6:45 pm, meaning he'd been playing the game for around five hours this time.

While he wasn't dirty, he did feel a little gross after lying in bed most of the day. He took a quick shower before getting changed into his normal black jeans and a white T-shirt.

Fayte was cooking dinner when he arrived in the living room. It was just simple pasta with marinara and meat sauce. He was certain she added some garlic into the mix because it had a bit of that garlicky kick. She had also baked some bread with melted mozzarella cheese on top. Adam helped her set the coffee table by getting them some drinks and taking their plates over. Fayte joined him after removing her apron.

"I still cannot believe you already reached level 10," Fayte mumbled in between mouthfuls of food. "Did you know the forums exploded after that announcement? I read some of the content posted before getting started on dinner. People are freaking out trying to figure out who you are."

"Was everyone shocked?" asked Adam.

"Of course they were," Fayte said, then giggled. She twirled some pasta around her fork, brought it to her mouth, and only continued speaking after she swallowed her food. "The first person people thought would reach level 10 was Lin Akamine. She is the current number one player on the Power Ranking Charts. However, not only was she not the first person to reach level 10, but she isn't expected to reach that level for at least another day or two. Meanwhile, the prominent guild leaders are stuck level 7 or 8. The only person at level 9 aside from Lin Akamine is the Spear God."

The level up system for *Age of Gods* really was quite ridiculous. Each time a person leveled up, the amount of experience points needed to reach the next level doubled. That was fine at the beginning of the game, but now that Adam was at level 11, he needed +153,600 experience points just to reach level 12. He didn't even want to think about how many experience points he would need to reach level 50.

Probably a couple trillion.

Dinner soon ended, and Adam put the plates and utensils in the dishwater and washed off the pots and pans that Fayte had used to cook. When he finished, he came back into the living room and saw his roommate putting on that ugly jacket of hers. Her veil was already being worn to hide her face.

"Heading out?" asked Adam.

"I noticed our food supply was low, so I'm making a run to the nearest grocery store." Fayte's eyes crinkled, making him think she was smiling at him. She hesitated a moment, then asked, "Would you like to come with me?"

Adam considered following her for a moment, but then shook his head. "I'd better not. There's a good chance someone might be watching you, considering who you are, and if they found out that you were living with a guy, it could cause problems, especially if Levon found out. They might decide to try and dig into my background. We also can't let them know that I'm helping you with your bet."

Surprise was the best element they had right now. Once people knew someone like him was helping Fayte, they would do everything they could to hinder her progress, but so long as they thought she only had Susan Forebear in her corner, Adam could continue working for her unhindered until it was the appropriate time to reveal himself.

"I guess… you're right. I'll be back soon."

"Be safe."

"Yeah. Thanks."

Watching Fayte's shoulders slump a little as she left the apartment made Adam sigh. He liked Fayte. He really did. However, he couldn't let himself get too close. The only reason he was living with her was because she had the only method that could cure Mortems Disease. What's more, for as much as he enjoyed spending time with Fayte, the person he loved was Aris.

Speaking of…

Adam wandered into the room with Aris's cryobed and sat down. He stared at the lovely girl's sleeping face, longing mixed with heartache filling his being, and told her about his battle against the pirates. He felt more animated than usual, but he believed the reason was mostly because he couldn't get Fayte's disappointed voice out of his head and was trying hard to forget about it. Adam believed he had done the right thing by telling her no. He needed to draw the line in their relationship somewhere.

That did not make him feel any less guilty.

Fayte came back about an hour later with some ice cream. It seemed she was having a sweet tooth craving. Adam joined her and discussed *Age of Gods* some more as she chowed down on ice cream. Fayte told him more about her mysterious new companion.

"Lilith is very quiet. I really don't know anything about her. She doesn't talk about herself much, or at all, really, but she's been very helpful. Susan and I are almost at level 9 thanks to her. If we keep up at the pace we've been going, I think we can reach level 9 some time tomorrow."

Adam couldn't quite keep the smile off his face. "That's good. Lilith should be able to help you reach level 10 quickly."

"I'm still really curious about her though." Fayte took a huge bite of her chocolate chip cookie dough ice cream. She had drawn her knees up to her chest. She wasn't wearing socks right now, so her tiny toes were visible as she wiggled them. "She told me that *Age of Gods* is the first video game she's ever played, but she's so good at it. I once asked her why she was so good, but all she said was that she has experience. I'm not sure what that means, but I guess maybe she has real life experience with combat. She certainly knows how to fight. And she's so stealthy too. It's enough to make me think she might be a real assassin!"

Fayte laughed at her own joke, not noticing the odd smile that stretched across Adam's face.

When the clock reached 9:00 pm, Adam and Fayte said good-night to each other and went to their respective rooms. Before Adam went to bed, he took out his phone, flipped through his caller ID, and pressed on the contact named Lilith.

"Master?"

"Hey. I hear you made contact with Fayte and Susan."

"I have. Just like you ordered, I joined their party."

"I know. Fayte has been extolling your virtues. She says you're so good, she thinks you might be a real assassin."

"..."

"How does the game feel? Have you noticed anything odd about it?"

"Odd? No. Not really. I do not have anything to compare it to since I have never played virtual reality games before. Games are Astaroth's forte, not mine. However, I have noticed that moving around in Age of Gods *feels a lot like moving around in my real body. That is probably why Fayte was able to tell I have experience with killing people."*

Adam nodded even though he knew she couldn't see it. Age of Gods was so realistic that Adam thought he might forget it wasn't a game if it didn't have all those game stats. Even the combat felt relatively realistic. It was, in fact, the realistic combat that allowed Adam to defeat enemies more than ten levels higher than himself.

"Please stay with Fayte. Once you, she, and her friend, Susan, have reached level 10 and left the Village of Beginnings, the three of you will hook up with me."

"Yes, Master."

Maybe it was just his imagination, but Lilith sounded pretty happy about joining up with him in the game world. Come to think of it, they had not seen each other for about five years now… not since Adam had met Aris.

"Also, tell Astaroth that he and the others are not to leave the Village of Beginnings until Aris is awake," Adam added.

"I am certain he already knows what you have planned, but I will be sure to inform him."

"Thank you… by the way, how are you?"

"Master?"

"Never mind. Anyway, please keep up the good work."

"Yes, Master."

Adam sighed as he hung up, placed his phone on the wireless charging stand, and ran a hand through his hair. How are you? Really? Why had he asked her that? He had not shown Lilith or anyone concern even once since they met, so why would he show it now?

"Maybe I have changed," Adam whispered as he laid down. With a tired sigh, he closed his eyes and pressed a forearm against his eyes. "I would have never felt this guilty five years ago."

***

Adam only slept for a few hours before logging back into the game. It was nighttime when he arrived inside of the inn. Adam was sure the clock would say 1:00 am if there were any clocks in this game. When he glanced out the window, he could see the dark sky and the stars glittering against the velvet canvas.

Titania was asleep as well. No longer floating in the air, she was lying on the pillow next to his head. When he shifted, Titania fell down the depression his head made and her big (for a one-foot tall woman) breasts came into contact with his face. It was an unusual sensation, having such squishy but small boobs along with an entire tiny body resting on his cheek.

Because he didn't want Titania to wake up with her body pressed against his face (he had no idea how she would respond), Adam sat up in bed and began stretching. His bones popped and his back cracked. He groaned.

Perhaps it was the sudden shift that woke Titania up. She sat up and stretched like him, then rubbed her eyes. It was a very cute gesture that didn't at all fit the woman he'd come to know these past few days.

"Oh. Adam. You are back," Titania said with a soft yawn. "What time is it?"

"It is around one o'clock in the morning," Adam answered.

"So early... I've noticed this, but you do not seem to sleep very much."

"I don't need much sleep to function."

"That may be so, but I do."

While Titania complained about needing sleep, she still fluttered off the bed and landed on Adam's shoulder as he stood up.
However, as though showing proof of how tired she was, her body
tilted to the side and she ended up leaning against his neck. She was
not asleep. Even so, it looked like she might fall asleep any moment.

Even though it was still early in the morning, before the sun
had even risen, Adam left the inn and traveled out of Watershore. He
didn't go too far. His plan was to return and see if there might be
some quests for him to do, but he also wanted to see what kind of
monsters were located within this area.

As he left the town, Adam looked at his stats. His level had increased and he had an extra +105 status points thanks to becoming
the first person to leave the Village of Beginnings. He didn't hesitate
to put all those points into his Strength stat.

Name: Adam
Class: Warriors
Lvl: 11
SP: 0
AP: 13,200
Experience: 423/153,600
Reputation: +50,500
Strength: +315
Constitution: +150
Dexterity: +5
MP: +5
Speed: +6
Physical Attack: +690
Health: 500/500
Hit-Rate: 6%

MP: 100/100
Movement: +6
Physical Defense: +435
Magical Defense: +150
Dodge-Rate: ???
Magic Attack: +5

Resistances:
Fire: 50%
Water: 50%
Earth:50%
Wind:50%
Lightning:50%
Darkness:50%
Slashing: 50%

Skills:
Slash: A basic skill where the player swings his or her sword and attacks the enemy!
Current Lvl: 5 MAXED
Ability:
Causes 150% damage to enemy if it hits
MP Cost: 1
Cooldown Time 0 seconds

Thrust: A basic skill where the player thrusts his or her weapon at the enemy!
Current lvl: 5 MAXED
Ability: Causes 160% damage with a 5% chance at getting a critical hit
MP Cost: 5
Cooldown Time: 1 second

Blood Sacrifice: By sacrificing half of your blood (HP), you have gained the ability to increase the damage you do

Current lvl: 5 MAXED
Ability: Causes 300% increase to attack power for 60-seconds
Disregards skill cooldown times
MP Cost: 20
Special Limit: Drops HP by half
Cooldown time: 30 seconds

Dance of the Sakura Blossoms: A skill only Adam can use. Attacks with numerous spear thrusts as the player dances around his enemy, eventually forming the shape of a sakura blossom
Current lvl: 1
AP needed to reach next lvl: 1,000
Ability: Unleashes five super-powered attacks, increases damage by 200% for every consecutive hit, and resets when Adam misses an attack. Hit-Rate has increased to 10%
MP Cost: 100
Cooldown time: 60 seconds

Item Pouch:
Item Name: Rusted Spear
Lvl: 6
Experience points needed to level up: 45,732/160,000
Item Type: Spear
Grade: ???
Use Requirements: Can only be equipped by Adam. Cannot be thrown away, cannot be given away, and cannot be unequipped.
Description: This unknown weapon was found by Adam. It has recognized him as its master and cannot be used by anyone else.
Abilities: Physical Attack+60; Strength+60
Special ability: Sentient Growth

Item Name: Dragon Bone Cuirass
Item Type: Armor
Use requirements: Can be equipped by Warriors level 10 and above.

Description: This chest plate was made from the bones of a powerful dragon. Not only does it look stylish, but it offers solid defensive abilities and some special stats.

Abilities: Defense+200; Constitution+100; 25% resistance to slashing, fire, earth, wind, lightning, and darkness damage

Item Name: Dragon Bone Gauntlets
Item Type: Armor
Grade: 1-star
Use requirements: Can be equipped by Warriors level 10 and above.

Description: These gauntlets are made from the bones of a powerful dragon. Not only are they stylish, but they offer solid defensive abilities and resistance to elemental damage.

Abilities: Defense+50; Constitution+10; 10% resistance to slashing, fire, earth, wind, lightning, and darkness damage

Item Name: Dragon Bone Greaves
Item Type: Armor
Grade: 1-star
Use requirements: Can be equipped by Warriors level 10 and above.

Description: Greaves made from the bones of a powerful dragon. They are not only stylish, they also offer solid defense and resistance against elemental damage.

Abilities: Defense+75; Constitution+25; 15% resistance to slashing, fire, earth, wind, lightning, and darkness damage

It looked like his [Rusted Spear] had also leveled up. It was at level 6 now, which meant his Strength and Physical Attack had gone from +50 to +60. That meant his spear was now several times more powerful than the weapon he had used during his fight against the [skeleton dragon].

The area outside of Watershore was mostly farmlands and open fields. Stalks of long grass swayed in a gentle breeze. The breeze carried an earthen scent that reminded him of the countryside. After walking for several hundred yards, Adam eventually discovered a monster wandering through the fields and had Titania [scan] it.

Name: Killer Bunny
Description: This rabid rabbit is vicious and violent. It is known for attacking both cattle and humans.
Class: None
Lvl: 15
Health: 5,000/5,000
MP: 500/500
Strength: +200
Constitution: +50
Dexterity: +50
Intelligence: +25
Speed: +200

Skills:
Rabid Kick: The Killer Bunny can jump really high in the air and use momentum and gravity to launch a powerful kick at its foe
Damage = Strength + Speed
MP Cost: 20
Cooldown Time: 0 Seconds

Bite: The Killer Bunny doesn't have the sharpest fangs, but it still hurts when it bites you!
Damage = Strength
MP Cost: 15
Cooldown time: 0 seconds

"You're kidding me," Adam muttered.

"What is the problem?" asked Titania.

"This is a monster? Really? A giant rabbit?"

Titania looked at the [killer bunny], which was indeed just a supersized rabbit. It was about the same height as a person. Other than its gigantic size, sharp fangs, and glowing red eyes, it looked like a normal rabbit with brown-gray fur.

"This is indeed a low-level monster," Titania confirmed. "I have run into them many times, though they used to avoid me when my level was higher." She placed her hands on her hips as she fluttered next to him. "I do not see what the problem is here."

"Well, whatever. Let's see how well this thing fights." Adam sighed. He just couldn't get motivated to fight a giant bunny.

Adam did not bother activating [Blood Sacrifice], though Titania did sing the [Song of Vigor], which already increased his physical strength by 220% anyway. With her song playing in his ears, Adam relied only on [slash] to dispose of the first [killer bunny].

-2,277; MISS; -MISS; MISS; MISS; -2,277!

While Adam missed quite a number of times, he continued using [slash] to strike the enemy, while dancing around its reckless attacks. The [killer bunny] shrieked at him in anger and continued to viciously attack with its dull fangs, but Adam wouldn't let it. He finished the enemy off with a few more attacks.

Ding!

[Congratulations! You have defeated the enemy [killer bunny]! Items dropped: [rabbit pelt] and 350 gold coins! +1,500 experience points!]

Adam looked at the announcement screen detailing what he had gained from this kill and sighed. The paltry amount of experience points was far too little for Adam, who needed a truly astronomical amount to level up. Even though it looked like the enemies in this vicinity did not give him much, he still went around to see what sort of monsters there were.

The enemies in the vicinity of Watershore were only at levels 11 through 15. Several different types of enemy appeared in this forested area just outside the port town; they were the level 11-15 [killer bunny], the level 15 [giant wild cat], the level 11 [killer ants], and the level 15 [black bear]. He did not run into any 1-star, 2-star, or 3-star enemies.

Adam killed several of each kind of monster, which earned him and Titania quite a few experience points. Sadly, the amount earned wasn't anywhere close to what he, Titania, or his spear needed to level up. Since it looked like leveling up here would take too long, Adam returned to Watershore when the sun came up and inquired with the first civilian he came across if there was any place he could go to take on quests.

"If you just want normal quests, you can always go to the tavern," the fisherman said. His name icon said he was Nelly Fishmonger, which was an odd name, but Adam didn't fault the man for what his creator named him. "However, if you're looking for something special, you should go and see the mayor. I hear he recently began requesting help from several travelers and even asked the mayor of Solum to send him soldiers."

Adam had never heard of Solum before, but he guessed it was a larger and more powerful city than Watershore.

"Why would the mayor ask for soldiers?" asked Adam.

Nelly Fishmonger looked around for a moment before leaning over and whispering into Adam's ear. "This isn't really a secret, but it also isn't something we're supposed to talk about. You see, the mayor's son went out exploring a while back, but he got poisoned. No one knows how it happened. One of the townsfolk found him collapsed halfway between here and the Forest of Gloom. The poison he was infected with is deadly and has been slowly killing him. We think he might have been attacked by a [basilisk] or something."

"I see. Thank you for the information," Adam said.

He let Nelly go and began traveling toward the mayor's house after getting directions. It was the largest house in town, though it was a little out of the way. The mayor's house was a large building situated on a bluff overlooking the town. Adam thought it was kind of ostentatious, but he knew this sort of setting was also common in fantasy games—the king overlooking his keep.

Whoever made this game must have been a nut for classic dungeons and dragons style storytelling.

The mayor's house was surrounded by a gate, and the entrance was guarded by two soldiers wearing leather armor. Their status screen stated they were both at level 40, which was more powerful than anyone else Adam had run into. He guessed the levels reflected not only the village's placement (since this was where players arrived after reaching level 10, he assumed the level of NPCs was weaker than other cities), but also had to be high enough that any player who wanted to cause trouble in town could not do so.

"Excuse me," Adam said. "I'm a play—I mean, I am an otherworlder who just arrived from the Village of Beginnings. I heard the mayor's son has been poisoned and wanted to ask if I could help."

The soldiers' eyes went wide.

"So you are an otherworlder? Huh. You don't look much different than us. However, your level is truly lacking. I do not know what makes you think you can help, but the mayor is pretty desperate right now. I am sure he'll accept all the help he can get," one of the soldiers said. He was a stiff-looking man with blond locks of hair sticking out of his steel helmet.

Adam bristled at being called weak, but he knew that compared to these people with their level 40 status, he was indeed much weaker than them.

Titania huffed. "Do not be deceived by this man's level. Even though he is technically weaker than either of you, his combat prowess far surpasses anyone of his level. You would do well not to underestimate him."

The two soldiers looked at Titania in shock.

"T-t-t-tiny fairy! Why is there such a tiny fairy?! Why is she so small?!"

"Have members of the Fairy Clan shrunk?! Is that why they disappeared thousands of years ago?! Did they all become pint-sized?!"

"There's no need to be rude!"

Titania's face turned bright red as she stomped on the air like she was stomping on the ground. Adam imagined she wished she could stomp on their faces.

The two soldiers let him and Titania through after that small interlude. They opened the gates for them. Titania went back to sitting on his shoulder as he walked up to the large double doors. Another guard at the entrance knocked once, then spoke with someone on the other side, who opened the door and allowed Adam inside.

An old butler by the name of Geeves asked Adam to follow him. Of course, this was only after panicking over the small fairy sitting on his shoulder. He led Adam and the vexed Titania to a small wooden door, which he knocked on once.

"Master, an otherworlder and his... companion have arrived," Geeves said. "They wish to discuss the matter regarding your son."

"Send them in," someone grunted from the other side.

Geeves held the door open and allowed Adam and Titania inside. The room on the other side was in no way opulent, but it was nice. Soft carpet covered the floor, bookshelves rested against the walls, and an older gentleman with graying sideburns sat behind a desk. He looked to be in the middle of his life, had a decent enough build, and sat with his back straight, but it was clear from his prominent gut that he wasn't in as good a shape as he used to be.

"You must be the otherworlder Geeves spoke of." The mayor, whose name was listed as Derek Waterton, pressed his hands on the desk and stood up. He looked at Adam, then at Titania. His eyes widened. "Is that a fairy?! Why is she so small?!"

Adam had to really resist face palming at the moment. He hoped this wouldn't happen every time they met a new person. It was funny enough the first time, but now it was getting annoying. He honestly, truly, fervently hoped people would stop freaking out every time they saw Titania, and he was certain she felt the same way.

"You people are incredibly rude," Titania denounced this man and everyone else who met them. "Must you all overreact like this? And why are you making fun of my height? Don't you know you are never supposed to make fun of a woman or even mention her height?"

"I think it's actually a woman's age that you're not supposed to mention," Adam corrected.

"Quiet, you."

"My apologies." The mayor wiped some sweat from his forehead with a handkerchief. "It has just been thousands of years since we humans have seen a fairy before. The only depictions we have of fairies these days are all in books. You match the book's description to a T, but every book we have on fairies say that members of the Fairy Clan are the same size as us humans."

"Well… I suppose I can forgive you," Titania groused. "You are not wrong about members of the Fairy Clan being the size of humans, but that is only for fairies over level 50."

"I will remember that in the future," the mayor said.

"Anyway, why don't you tell us about this problem." Adam smoothly shifted topics. "The person I spoke to said your son has been poisoned?"

Now that Adam had brought up the reason for their visit, the mayor's expression became distressed as he spoke. "That is correct. My son was out hunting with some of his friends, but they ended up traveling deep into the Forest of Gloom, which is about fifty klicks from here. We do not know what happened. The man who found my son said he only spoke a few fragmented sentences before collaps-ing. His friends were not with them. We assume they are dead, and my son has not woken up once since he was brought home."

"What did he say?" asked Adam.

"Forest. Temple. Spiders."

It sounded to Adam like there was some kind of spider monster in the Forest of Gloom, which poisoned the mayor's son and his friends.

"I assume you need someone to look for the antidote," Adam said.

The Mayor nodded. "That is correct. The doctor here in Water-shore is rather infamous as an eccentric but talented doctor. He said the only thing that can cure my son's poison is a flower called the [Panacea Flower], which grows in the deepest parts of the Forest of Gloom. If you can find this flower and bring it to me, I would be very grateful. However, you will have to be fast. The doctor said my son only has one month left to live."

Ding!

[You have been offered a new quest: [Cure Watershore Mayor's Son!] Please be aware that this quest has a time limit. If you cannot complete it within a month, you will fail the quest. Do you accept? Yes or no?]

An announcement screen appeared in front of Adam, but he did not even bother looking at it as he pressed the "yes" button. On the other hand, Titania kept her eyes locked on the screen. This didn't concern him. She seemed innately curious about these screens and announcements that came up every so often.

"Don't worry," Adam said. "I'll head to the Forest of Gloom and find the [Panacea Flower] for you."

"Thank you very much, otherworlder! If you can find the [Panacea Flower], I will be forever in your debt."

Ding!

[You have accepted the quest: [Cure Watershore Mayor's Son!]

FOREST OF GLOOM

The Forest of Gloom was fifty klicks west of Watershore, which meant it was about thirty-one miles away. If Adam were to walk there, it would have probably taken at least an entire day, and since he couldn't spend an entire day walking, that was a problem. Fortunately, the Watershore mayor had a means to resolve this issue.

"Take this letter of introduction to the stables near the main entrance," he said as he handed a slim scroll made of aged parchment to Adam. "This will let you use the village's fastest horse free of charge."

"Thank you," Adam said as he accepted the scroll.

Because there wasn't much need to remain with the mayor, Adam left after asking him a few more questions about the Forest of Gloom. No one really knew much about it, unfortunately. All the information the mayor had was mostly hearsay. The only thing they knew about the forest either came from stories passed down through the generations or from the few people who had traveled around the border.

None of it sounded very believable.

"I wonder if the information he gave us is even accurate?" Adam asked no one in particular as he strode down the street. "I mean, according to the mayor, it's been at least five hundred years since anyone saw the [Panacea Flower], right? What if it's not even there?"

"I imagine it is still there," Titania said from her place on his shoulder. She kicked her feet back and forth out of boredom. "The Forest of Gloom has been around since before I was sealed. There were [Panacea Flowers] back then, so they should still be there unless someone took them."

"Well, if you say so."

The warm sun shone down on Adam as he went to the stables, where he found an old man sitting on a stool out front. He wrinkled his nose slightly at the scent of hay and crap filling the air. However, that was the only sign of displeasure on his face as he walked up to the old man and handed him the letter.

Adam checked the old man's status screen, which said his name was Gumory Horseshoe. It was a terrible name. His parents must have hated him.

The old man read the letter and clicked his tongue. "Seems the mayor has given ya permission to ride our fastest steed. Let me tell ya something, boy; Midnight might be fast, but he has a right foul temper. Only the strongest of wills can tame a beast like that."

Adam shrugged. "I'm sure I'll be fine."

The old man snorted. "I've seen a lot of cocky lads like ya coming along. Well, let's see if ya can really tame that beast."

The old man went inside the stables and came back with a bucking and neighing horse with a shiny black coat and intelligent amber eyes. It was resisting the old man, struggling against the rope Gumory was using to pull it with. Adam was a little shocked the horse was so uncooperative. Of course, the man had said it was un-tameable, but he thought it was just in-game lore to make the horse seem more important than it really was.

Before Adam could try to get the horse to calm down, Titania floated over to it and began saying a few words as she pet its head, which caused a miracle to occur. The horse stopped bucking and be-came calm.

"Well, I'll be damned. Guess yer pint-sized fairy friend is good with animals," the old man said.

"Who are you calling pint-sized?!" Titania snapped.

The old man raised his hands in a gesture of surrender and backed off.

Now that they had their steed, Adam lifted himself onto the saddle and grabbed hold of the reins. Titania sat on Midnight's head. According to the status screen, Midnight was called an [untamed stallion] and was at level 20. What really impressed Adam was not its level, however, but its Speed stat. It had a Speed of +1,200 and a movement of +2,400.

Thanks to whatever Titania had said to the horse, Adam had an easy time getting Midnight to move. It was not long before they had traveled outside of Watershore and began heading toward the Forest of Gloom.

What would have taken twelve hours running at his fastest speed without rest only took one hour thanks to Midnight. The [untamed stallion] could travel at what Adam guessed was thirty to forty miles per hour.

Since he didn't know how long it would take for him to complete this quest, and he didn't want to enter the Forest of Gloom and have to leave, Adam logged off a little early, ate lunch with Fayte, and spent an hour talking to Aris. He logged back on immediately after and entered the Forest of Gloom alongside an angry Titania.

"I cannot believe you just left me here," Titania grumbled.

"Sorry," Adam said with a shrug.

"You don't sound sorry," she groused, to which Adam said nothing.

From the outside, the Forest of Gloom looked like a massive forest with trees that were so twisted their branches formed a tangled canopy overhead. The trees were so large and spaced so close together that there was very little room to maneuver. Of course, this also meant it would be hard to swing a weapon around. It could get caught on a branch, stuck in a trunk, and good luck finding it if it got knocked out of your hands. The scent of mildew and flowers was also quite thick. A poignant odor that assaulted his nose. It only grew thicker and more pungent after he climbed off Midnight, secured the steed to a tree, and entered.

"Hey, I've been wondering about something," Adam began as he stepped over a large tree root sticking out of the ground.

"What have you been wondering about?" asked Titania as she flew beside him for once. It looked like she was on guard in case monsters decided to attack.

"What happens to you when I log out?"

"What do you mean?"

"Like, do you just freeze, or does something happen when I log —no, when I return to my world?"

"I have no idea what you are blathering on about. Why would I freeze just because you 'logged out'?" When Adam merely rubbed the back of his head, she released a weary sigh. "Whenever you return to your world, it looks to me like you just disappear. Your body vanishes, and then I have to wait until you reappear again. I suppose I am fortunate you don't sleep much. I only have to wait several hours for you to return."

"So that's what happens…"

Adam had always been a little curious. This world was so realistic it was sometimes hard to think of it as a simple video game.

The further into the Forest of Gloom they went, the darker their surroundings became. Adam eventually needed to take out a torch from his storage so he could see. He had excellent night vision, but even he could not see if there was no light outside, and this place was practically pitch black.

Just as Adam was stepping around a large tree, a loud sound caused the hairs on his arms to prickle. It was not a sound he recognized. Halfway between a roar and a screech maybe. He didn't know what it was, or what had caused it, but Adam's instincts were warning him of danger.

And he always trusted his instincts.

Skipping backward, Adam traveled nearly two yards in less than a second. The second after he leapt away, a massive mouth suddenly slammed into the place where he had been standing. Adam gawked at the creature that appeared before him like something out of a nightmare. It didn't stand on legs but a dozen roots that wiggled and scrambled over the dirt. Its green body was large and bulbous like a glass vial. The "mouth" was attached to a large tentacle with sucker-like appendages, of which there were at least six.

"Titania!"

"I'm on it!"

Titania used [scan] on this thing the moment it appeared.

Name: Barbarian Plant
Description: A carnivorous plant that gained a form of sentience after consuming human flesh. These plants are vicious and will attack anything that moves.
Class: 1-star
Lvl: 20
Health: 20,500/20,500
MP: 1,000/1,000
Strength: +500
Constitution: +300
Dexterity: +100
Intelligence: +50
Speed: +200

Skills:
Vine Whip: The barbarian plant attacks creatures with its vines
Damage = Strength + Speed
MP Cost: 10
Cooldown Time: 0 Seconds

Poison Pollen: The Barbarian Plant releases a powerful poison

that causes the poison status effect
Any player infected with this poison will lose +5 HP every one
second for 120 seconds
MP Cost: 100
Cooldown time: 30 seconds

Flesh Consumption: The Barbarian Plant earned its nickname
because it has a habit of eating its victims
Many would-be adventurers have met their end at this plant
monster's power
Damage = Strength * 2.
MP Cost: 50
Cooldown Time: 30 seconds

Heal: The barbarian plant's poison pollen can be used to heal
the barbarian plant
It heals +2,000 HP every 5 seconds it remains within the pollen
MP Cost: None
Cooldown time: None

It looked like this thing had a pretty high level, and it was a 1-star monster, which meant it was stronger than a regular [barbarian plant].

Adam activated [Blood Sacrifice] and quickly went on the offensive. Titania floated back to give them some space and began singing [Song of Vigor]. Once both skills activated, Adam felt his body become stronger. It was like he'd taken those steroid shots that were sometimes given to soldiers when they needed an extra boost on the battlefield.

As he charged forward, the [barbarian plant] reacted by trying to attack him with its tentacles. There were six in total. That meant Adam was dealing with six attacks coming in from six different directions and angles.

Anyone else would have panicked at the sight, but Adam remained calm and his breathing steady as he shuffled along the
ground. He moved left, right, then left again. The constant zigzag-
ging motion allowed him to avoid being attacked by this giant plant
monster and its tentacles. Each tentacle struck the ground, gouging
out chunks of earth, sending dirt and grass into the sky. All of its attacks missed him, however. It did not take longer than a single second before he reached the [barbarian plant].

MISS; MISS; MISS; MISS; -4,554; -4,554!

Only two of his attacks hit, though that was almost enough to
take away half its health. Adam moved quickly, running around the
plant monster as it tried to attack him, dodging trees and leaping
over roots. A tentacle slammed into the ground on his left. Clods of
dirt kicked up everywhere. The scent of earth filled Adam's nose as
he maneuvered behind the [barbarian plant] and attacked it with lib-
eral use of [slash].

-4,554; MISS; MISS; MISS!

Adam was doing an excellent job if he did say so himself. The
[barbarian plant] kept attacking with its tentacle vines, but none of
them could touch him as he constantly wove around it, then attacked
with [slash] to whittle away at its health.

-4,554!

The plant monster's health was nearly gone. However, the moment after Adam dealt such significant damage, the [barbarian plant]
raised its vines, and the mouths on each vine opened up. He didn't
know what was going on at first, but then a green mist poured from
the mouths on its tentacles.

"Be careful!" Titania shouted a warning. "It's poison!"

"Thanks for telling me something I already knew!"

"There is no need for sarcasm!"

The green mist spread across the ground and covered nearly a dozen foot radius in all directions. This was the [Poison Pollen] skill that Adam saw on its status screen. It was an A.O.E. skill. Adam had no choice but to backpedal away from the [barbarian plant].

Adam frowned as he wondered how long it would take for this monster's mist to disperse, but then he saw the large +2,000 numbers appearing over the creature's head every five seconds and remembered the [barbarian plant's] last ability called [Heal], which let the [barbarian plant] replenish HP simply by sitting in its own pollen. Before Adam knew what was happening, the blasted thing's health was already back to +20,500.

"Oh, that is just great," Adam groaned.

"It's coming!" Titania warned before she began singing again

She was correct; the [barbarian plant] was indeed coming after him. It moved quite fast for a creature with no legs and only roots to propel it forward.

Adam gave a ferocious grin as the adrenaline in his body began pumping through him, heightening his perception and reflexes. His [Blood Sacrifice] skill had deactivated and was cooling down, but he neither noticed nor cared.

Most people would have probably tried to run away when confronted with such a terrifying sight, but Adam ran forward. He dodged left and right to avoid the incoming vine whips. One struck the ground on his left, and Adam used [slash] to hack into the vine.

Not only did he do -3,500 damage despite not having [Blood Sacrifice] active, but the vine was severed.

The [barbarian plant] released an odd squeal that made him think it was in pain. It stumbled backward on its roots, but then it unleashed another noise that sounded vaguely like a roar and attacked with the remaining five vines. Since it seemed these vines could be hacked off, Adam made sure to attack each one before attacking the main body.

-3,500; -3,500; -3,500; -3,500; MISS; MISS; MISS; -3,500!

All five remaining vines were severed seconds before the cooldown time for [Blood Sacrifice] ended. Adam didn't bother reactivating it, however, as there was no need to anymore. He flew forward with his spear tightly gripped in both hands. With the creature's vines gone, it no longer had anything to attack him with.

MISS; MISS; MISS; -2,277; -2,277!

Adam was relentless. He constantly activated [slash] over and over as he attacked the now helpless enemy. The [barbarian plant's] health was finally reduced to zero. Adam sighed as the plant monster flopped onto the ground and began spasming as its body turned dried and shriveled like a vegetable that had been left to rot in the sun. An unusually foul stench filled the air. It was like the smell of manure mixed with gasoline. Adam had no choice but to move back in order to avoid the stench.

Ding!

[You have defeated the 1-star enemy [barbarian plant]! Items dropped: x2 [fusion heart leaves] and 2,200 gold coins. +15,000 experience points! +1,500 ability points!]

While the experience points weren't enough for either him or his fairy companion to level up, Titania used the ability points she gained to level all of her currently available skills up to level 3. She also leveled [Song of Vigor] to level 4 because it was more useful than all her other songs. This increased the effect of her buff from 220% to 260%. That was a pretty massive increase. Adam hoped her skill would at least increase to 300% before maxing out.

They continued traveling deeper into the Forest of Gloom and encountered two more of those [barbarian plants]. Neither of them had been a 1-star enemy, but they were both at level 20, so while Adam and Titania gained more experience points, they did not gain any ability points.

Ding!

[Congratulations! Titania has leveled up. She is now at level 12! +200 HP! +2,200 MP! +10 SP!]

"How is it that you have reached level 12 before me," Adam grumbled.

"I am a fairy. It is only natural that I would level up faster than you," Titania stated as if her words were fact... though it wasn't like he could deny what she said. She had been at level 1 when they met, and he had been at level 9. Now she was at level 12, and he was still at level 11.

That seemed pretty unfair if you asked him.

Because it was so dark and there was no status screen that let him see what time it was, Adam did not know how long they had been inside of this forest. They kept walking, and walking, and walking, and Adam eventually discovered something that looked like a cave, but the cavern entrance was made out of vines. It looked like the mouth of another plant monster, but one that was at least twenty times bigger than a fully grown man.

"I guess we should head down?" asked Adam.

"I suppose so," Titania mumbled. "Though we will want to be cautious. There's no telling what lurks in those depths."

Adam didn't disagree with her, and so while Titania flew by his side, he took his first steps into this strange cavern.

Like the entrance, the inside seemed to be a tunnel made entirely of vines. Adam couldn't tell if this was underground because all he saw were green vines. He cast his torch along the walls and grimaced when the vines squirmed as though they were alive and disdained light. That did not leave him with a pleasant feeling and made him think more than ever that this was just a gigantic mouth and he was walking inside to be eaten.

Nothing seemed to happen, however, and so they traveled deeper into the cavern, until the vines became covered in thick webs.

Casting his torch across the passage, Adam saw hundreds of small spiders scurrying across the floor, walls, and ceiling. His lips became a thin line. He didn't hate spiders, but he certainly didn't like them either.

Titania curled her lips in distaste. "Disgusting creatures."

"Not fond of spiders?" asked Adam as he used the torch to burn the surrounding webs. The heat from the fire made him take several steps back.

"I loathe spiders," Titania stated firmly. "There is a clan of spider demons who once served a being known as the Demon Lord. The Spider Demon Clan is ruled by the Spider Queen, one of the thirteen Lords of Chaos. About five thousand years ago, the Demon Lord and the Lords of Chaos brought death and destruction to the land. If it was not for the four goddess working together, things could have ended very badly for this world. Of course," she added in a smaller voice, "even with the four goddesses combining their strength, the goddess's chosen hero was still forced to sacrifice his life to kill the Demon Lord."

So there was even more stuff that happened thousands of years ago? A Demon Lord? That was a pretty standard game concept as far as he was concerned. From what he understood, most fantasy games had something like a Demon Lord, which would be the final boss of the game. It sounded like this one had already been killed.

They continued traveling deeper into the cave. Adam burned every spider web they ran across. A few larger than usual spiders would leap out at him. They were called [baby man-eating spider] and were only at level 5. Adam was able to kill them with a single [slash] of his spear.

"Are the Lords of Chaos still alive? What can you tell me about them?" asked Adam.

"The thirteen Lords of Chaos were the generals of the Demon Lord's army," Titania said. "There is the Spider Queen, Balroth the Destroyer, the Frost Giant, the King of Serpents, the Black Dragon, the Primal Beast, the War Demon, the Sky Demon, the Manticore, the Undead King, the Headless Horseman, the King of Despair, and

Nightmare. Among the thirteen, Balroth, Nightmare, the Primal Beast, and the Manticore did not belong to any race and always fought alone. The others are all leaders of a demon clan. Nightmare is the most mysterious of the Lords of Chaos because no one actually knows what he looks like."

Adam listened attentively to Titania speak. He didn't think this information would be useful right now, but perhaps later, he would be forced to fight against these Lords of Chaos to complete a quest. Knowing this could help him later on down the line.

He didn't say anything else, and not just because he had nothing to say. Adam stopped walking as the sound of scuttling reached his ears. Titania had also stopped and was straining her ears to listen.

"Something is coming," she whispered.

He nodded and gripped his spear in one hand and the torch in his other. "Get ready."

Adam stilled his breathing and concentrated hard. The scuttling was getting louder, a *clacklackclackclack* sound like dozens of feet treading over a hard surface. The louder it got, the further Adam sank into a still calm. He could not afford to let himself panic no matter how creepy the situation seemed.

A large shadow burst into the passage, slamming into the wall as it charged toward him on eight spindly legs. Its dark body was covered in hair. It had no hands or arms, but it did have an ugly face with nearly a dozen compound eyes, large mandibles, and a bulbous body with a spinneret near the end. It was at least three times larger than Adam.

In other words, it was a giant spider.

Name: Man Eating Spider
Description: a member of the Spider Demon Clan, this monster hates the Races of Light. It follows the orders of the Spider Queen.
Class: 2-star
Lvl: 20
35,000/35,000
MP: 3,000/3,000
Strength: +1,000
Constitution: +500
Dexterity: +200
Intelligence: +50
Speed: +50

Skills:
Bite: The man eating spider uses its sharp mandibles to bite down on the flesh of its enemies
150% damage
25% chance of causing poisoned effect
MP Cost: 150
Cooldown Time: 0 Seconds

Poison Acid: The man eating spider shoots an acidic venom from its mouth
Damage = Strength + 25% acidic damage
25% chance of causing poison status effect
MP Cost: 250
Cooldown time: 30 seconds

Web Shot: Fires spider webs from its spinneret
If hit or stepped on after release, the web will entrap enemy for at least 30 seconds
MP Cost: 360
Cooldown Time: 20 seconds

Dark Entrapment: When an enemy has been trapped in its web, it casts an illusion over them that smothers their body in darkness and makes them lose all sensations in their extremities
50% chance of causing fear status effect.

MP Cost: 300
Cooldown time: 10 seconds

A 2-star enemy. And it looked like this one was quite powerful, according to Titania's [scan].

Adam leapt back as the [man eating spider] raced toward him, though he only did so to generate some kinetic force. He slammed his left foot against the ground and thrust his spear forward. He put his whole body into his attack. A loud roar of anguish erupted from the [man eating spider] as his double attack punched two holes through its body.

-1,104; -2,208!

Not only did both attacks land, but one of his attacks had been a critical hit to boot. Of course, it sucked that he hadn't activated [Blood Sacrifice] yet. This monster hadn't given him enough time.

Without further prompting, Adam activated [Blood Sacrifice] and Titania began singing her usual song. The [Song of Vigor] invigorated Adam and made him feel many times stronger. This further made him wonder how these skills worked. Not only did he do more damage, but he felt physically stronger than he was when she wasn't singing.

-5,382; MISS; -5,382; MISS; MISS!

When Adam's attacks dealt the [man eating spider] massive damage, the creature scuttled backward as though it had finally realized what kind of threat he was. Adam grinned and shot forward. There was no way he could let this creature go now that it had offered itself to him as a sacrifice. He needed more experience points.

-5,382; MISS; MISS; -5,382; MISS!

Adam had already shaved away nearly a third of its health. As the fight continued, they found themselves inside of what looked like a massive cylindrical room with several dozen floors beneath him. There were many catwalks in this room, all of them naturally formed by rocks that traveled down to reach the next level. Adam and the [man eating spider] were on the topmost catwalk.

-5,382; MISS!

Adam once again used [thrust] twice in rapid succession, though he wasn't quite sure how. Either way, his attacks nearly killed the creature. He only needed one more good hit.

The [man eating spider] released a loud squeal as it continued scuttling back, firing several webs at Adam, who used his insane reflexes to dodge each and every web. He danced across the catwalk like a rabbit hopping to and fro. After closing the distance from the retreating spider once more, he thrust his spar out one last time.

-5,382!

His spear penetrated the monster's skull, breaking through flesh and bone as he dealt the final bit of damage needed to kill it. The [man eating spider] slumped to the ground, its legs twitching sporadically several times before going still.

Ding!

[You defeated the 2-star enemy [man eating spider]! Items dropped: x5 [low-grade health potions], x5 [low-grade mana potions], and 4,000 gold coins! +20,000 experience points! +2,000 ability points!]

Adam released a weary sigh as the adrenaline left his system. It was a bit weird that he could feel the adrenaline pumping through this fake avatar body, but he did remember what the fairy, Lim, had said when he was making his character. This game sent his "spirit" into the virtual world in order to better simulate reality. Perhaps this incredible realism was the result of his spirit experiencing everything instead of just his mind.

It was something for the more philosophical to consider.

"Adam..." Titania said, a tremor in her voice. "Do not look now, but I believe we are surrounded."

The moment Adam heard her words, he looked up and noticed what she had noticed. Eyes. There were hundreds of eyes surrounding them on all sides. Disgusting compound eyes all staring at them. These eyes were attached to the bodies of giant spiders, some of which were smaller than the [man eating spider] he had just fought, and some of which were many times larger. Some spiders hung from webs. Others were on the catwalks. There were far too many for him to count, but he guessed there were at least a couple hundred.

Every spider was between level 20 and level 30.

Fuck.

THE FOX YOKAI

Spiders were everywhere. They had already covered the entrance, so he could no longer leave the way he had come. Looking around revealed no less than three hundred [man eating spiders].

"Titania," Adam said in a calm, collected voice.

"Yes?" Titania asked. She didn't sound as calm, but she was a fairy who had been alive for a couple thousand years. Something like being surrounded by a horde of [man eating spiders] more than 10 levels above her wouldn't be enough to make her panic.

"I need you to hold onto me as tightly as you can. Also, please cast [Song of Valor]."

"Okay."

Titania quickly landed on his head and grabbed a handful of his hair with her tiny hands. Once she was certain she had a good grip on him, she began singing [Song of Valor], which was a quick and upbeat tune.

Adam couldn't really explain how he felt as she sang. It was odd, like his body was suddenly thicker, more durable, like his skin had become harder, his muscles denser, and his body sturdier. This feeling was like a massive wellspring of energy was rushing through him, filling the gaps in his strength to increase his Physical and Magical Defense.

"All right." Adam took a deep breath. "Here we go."

The monsters this far down were called [man eating spider], and all of them were at level 20 or above, which meant they were not creatures that Adam could fight against. He could easily beat them if he was fighting one-on-one. However, he could not fight against a horde of them.

He almost cursed himself for taking this quest.

The first spider on the catwalk rushed up to him and lashed out with its front spider legs, but Adam leapt into the air and landed on its back. This [man eating spider] was bigger than the one he had killed. He ran across its back and leapt off after reaching its spinneret end. His knees jarred as he landed on the hard ground, but he bent them and rolled forward, which also allowed him to avoid being struck by the second spider that slammed mandibles first into the ground behind him. The two spiders tried to turn around and come after him, but their bodies were too big and they ended up crashing into each other.

Adam kept running. He didn't just run linearly, but raced across each catwalk in a zigzag pattern that allowed him to avoid the webs being shot at him from above. He leapt down to the catwalks below him when he could. Sometimes he would use the spiders as a springboard, while other times he would rely on the strength of Titania's song. With the [Song of Valor] boosting his Physical Defense stat to +957, even the +1,100 Strength of the attacking monsters could only deal -132 damage at most. His goal was to travel as far down this place as he could.

"What are we doing?!" shrieked Titania as he once more became airborne after leaping off another catwalk. "Why are we going down?!"

The wind rushed around Adam and buffeted his hair. He was only a few meters from the next catwalk, but a massive spider appeared where he was about to land. It raised its head, revealing ugly compound eyes, massive mandibles, and a hideous mouth. It looked like it was getting ready to spit acid at him.

"Outta my way!"

Adam roared as he spun the spear in his hand, slammed it over the top of the [man eating spider's] head, and used the resulting force to flip himself over the monster. The spider squealed in pain as he landed on its back and ran across it. It tried to buck him off, but Adam had already leapt and landed on the catwalk.

"We're going down because it will be easier to run than fight with enemies at our backs," Adam said, breathing in through his nose and out through his mouth. His breath came in ragged gasps. "If we go up, it will be slower. Those blasted spiders can surround us and attack whenever they want! Besides! Didn't you see? The spiders have already blocked off the exit!"

Titania couldn't deny the truth in his words, so she conceded his point and remained silent, clutching his hair so hard it hurt.

Adam's chest felt tight as he leapt off another catwalk and landed on the next catwalk with bone jarring force. It hurt. A -10 damage sign appeared over his head. However, he knew he couldn't stop now.

Two more [man eating spiders] appeared before him, one on either side of the catwalk. Meanwhile, a number of them were descending from the levels above on the webs they released from their spinnerets.

There were dozens of them.

Adam grimaced as he charged at the one below him. The [man eating spider] released a shrill cry and shot several globs of acid at him, but he avoided them with deft skips, moving left and right as he kept his eyes firmly locked onto the creature's mouth.

Once it saw its attacks being dodged, the spider became enraged and tried to impale him with its sharp legs. Adam lowered his body to the ground and slid across the gravel. Two spindly legs struck the stone catwalk but missed Adam as he slid underneath the [man eating spider], skipped back to his feet, and continued running.

This cavern had several side passages located on each level. Adam took several of them to try and avoid being surrounded, but he soon realized the problem with this idea when he found himself trapped on both sides. His shoulders heaved as he glared at the two spiders hemming him in. He felt like a rat trapped between two cats.

With a grimace, Adam activated [Blood Sacrifice], downed a [low-grade health potion], and charged one of the spiders. He spun the spear around his body, dodged the leg that nearly skewered him, and hacked at it with [slash].

-4,646!

While his attack barely dented this blasted thing's health, he must have hit one of its weak points because the leg came right off. The [man eating spider] let out an anguished screech and reared back. Adam grinned as he spun the spear around in his hands and used [slash] again to hack off another leg. This must have messed with its balance. The [man eating spider] fell down, and Adam leapt onto its back and attacked with [thrust] two times in quick succession.

-4,646; -4,646!

Because he couldn't afford to stick around and didn't have the strength to kill this creature in just a few blows, Adam did not bother doing any more damage. He raced forward and leapt off the [man eating spider], quickly exiting the side passage.

The moment he emerged, several other spiders attacked him, but Adam used his incredible reflexes to dodge them all. He ducked, spun, and danced around a series of long spider legs that attempted to impale him. Titania, tightly gripping his hair, finally screamed as one [man eating spider] came close to swallowing her whole when its mandibles snapped at her.

Once Adam was past the horde that tried to ambush him, he raced onto the next catwalk, leapt down to the one below that, then again, before he finally landed on the ground floor. There were several passages leading to other sections of this cave. He counted six in total. Several of them had at least one [man eating spider] coming out of it, so Adam chose the only one that didn't have anything coming out. It was a smaller passage that looked just big enough for an adult human to fit through.

Adam raced for it. The spiders were hot on his heels. His breathing became labored as he pushed his muscles to their limits. He didn't understand where this burning sensation in his chest came from, or why it felt like his limbs were going to tear off.

Wasn't this a just video game?

His foes were right behind him. One nearly clipped his foot. He grimaced and shook those distracting thoughts off. He ran, and ran, and ran, pushing his body to the limit, and he eventually made it through the small passage.

The spiders tried to follow him, but the one that had been close to taking off his heels slammed into the entrance and could not move any further. It screeched and fired several globs of acid at him. Fortunately, its aim was crap and Adam was great at dodging. He moved left, right, right again, and then left once more, avoiding each attack as he moved out of the monster's range.

"Haaah… haaah… haaah… I think… I think we're safe," Adam said, his breathing heavy. He felt like he'd just run twelve marathons in rapid succession without rest. Sweat poured from his forehead and neck, drenching his clothes, bringing a grimace to his face. "This game really is too realistic."

"I believe we are safe for now as well," Titania said as she finally released her hold on his hair and flew up. She checked the passage, which was so dark neither of them could see more than ten feet in front of them. "I do not want to travel back that way again. Shall we see what is over here?"

"Doesn't look like we have much choice. Let's go."

Adam and Titania traveled down the passageway. The ground, floor, and ceiling in this area was covered in a strange type of green moss, which gave off a very light glow. It allowed them to see a little of their surroundings. Oddly enough, this part of the cave seemed less like a cave and more like the derelict ruins of an ancient temple. The ground was mostly flat, though it was broken with cracks, indents, and pockmarks. The walls and ceiling were also surprisingly flat.

With a slight frown, Adam went over to a wall and brushed away the dirt and moss. He blinked when a mosaic motif appeared before his eyes. The motif depicted a woman of incredible beauty, with long hair, a figure that outdid anyone else Adam had ever seen save maybe Fayte and Lilith, and wielding incredible powers. It looked like fire was pouring from her hands, spreading across the land. Rather than death, however, this fire brought forth life.

"It looks like this is an ancient ruin," Titania said with a small frown. "A lot of temples used to have motifs etched into the walls like this. They depicted important moments in history."

"So what moment is this depicting?" asked Adam.

Titania bit her lip and frowned. "I am unsure. I do not even know who this woman is. I met the four goddesses when I became the Guardian of the Spear. This woman looks similar, but she is not one of the four goddesses. That said, this imagery makes it seem like her powers are comparable to theirs."

"Are there people with powers comparable to the goddesses?" asked Adam.

"Of course. There is Hades, ruler of the Underworld. He is a man who is so powerful even the goddesses have decided to leave him alone. Many believe he is the god of the dead. There's also Odin the Wanderer. I've never met him, but I hear he enjoys wandering the world, sampling local cuisine, and stirring up trouble with the locals. I believe there are a few more, but it has been many eons since I read about them."

"Interesting." Adam stared at the motif for a while longer before changing the subject. "I wonder why this place became infested with spiders."

"I do not know, but I recognize those spiders." Titania's eyes darkened. "They were definitely members of the Spider Clan. During the war against the Demon Lord, the second or third wielder of the spear you now hold fought against the Spider Queen. He was able to kill her but was gravely injured in the process and later felled by the War Beast. That is how the legends go, at least."

"So the Spider Queen is dead?" asked Adam.

"The original might be dead, but I am certain a new Spider Queen has been born. Unless the Demon Spider Clan is extinguished, there will always be a Spider Queen."

"Well, let's hope we don't run into her," Adam said after a moment's pause.

"Indeed. I do not wish to fight against a 4-star monster at this level."

"4-star?" Adam asked as they continued walking. "I'm gonna take a guess and say that's the next level up from 3-star."

"Monsters are divided by a classification system based on their strength, the type of monster they are, the purity of their blood, and so on. There are normal monsters that have no classification, but then there are the special classifications. Their strength is ranked in this order: 1-star, 2-star, 3-star, 4-star, 5-star."

"Which means 4-star monsters are the second strongest around," Adam said with a nod.

"Yes. If you're curious, the Demon Lord was a 5-star monster while his generals were all 4-star monsters."

"Good to know."

Adam and Titania finally emerged from the long passage and into what Adam first mistook for another cavern, but he soon discovered after spotting several giant statues that this place was, in fact, some kind of ruin or a temple. Each statue depicted a woman—the same woman. Each statue was covered in dirt and vines, but he could tell even through the grime that each woman was beautiful. He was sure the person these statues were based on was even more gorgeous in person.

"What do you suppose this place is?" asked Adam.

Titania was also looking around, her eyes alight with curiosity. "If I had to take a guess, I would say this is a place of worship. Perhaps this woman was an important figure before the time of recorded history. There are many such temples located throughout the four main continents. Some are still intact and humans continue to use them as places of worship, but many have also been destroyed. While I cannot figure out who this place is supposed to worship, it looks like this temple was built from before the Forest of

Gloom appeared. If I'm not mistaken, the Forest of Gloom is at least ten thousand years old, so this temple was abandoned before then, or perhaps this temple was abandoned as a result of this forest appearing."

So this place must have been built a really long time ago, perhaps even before the original continent was split into five. Adam nodded as he continued walking forward.

The room eventually ended in front of a dais where a large throne sat. The dais was massive, easily large enough to hold a couple dozen people, but that space was taken up by the throne. Sitting on the throne was a woman. It was the same woman he had seen from the other four statues, but this one appeared to be more detailed and intricate. The woman was wearing a one-shoulder toga and sat with a dignified and elegant posture. There was a gentle smile on her face that made her seem compassionate and understanding.

Adam was sure this statue used to look magnificent, but at the moment, it was dilapidated like the other statues. Cracks covered its body, part of its left foot was gone, and some of the chair was missing. It had definitely seen better days.

"Looks like there is a passageway behind the statue," Titania said.

Adam moved around the statue and found that, indeed, there was a passageway behind it. This passage was not large. He imagined it would only be enough to fit at most two people walking side by side.

He walked through the passage and into a long corridor. At the end of the corridor was a door, which Adam realized was unlocked when he grasped the handle and pulled. The door opened with a loud creak, but then it stopped. Adam grimaced and tugged harder, exerting his +295 Strength stat to open the door. When he finally got the door open, he noticed the thick cobwebs on the other side. Was this door stuck because of these spider webs?

That didn't bode well.

Despite the chill running down his spine, Adam entered the room.

The room he walked into was not large, but it was probably larger than what he perceived it to be. There were spider webs covering almost every nook and cranny of the room. As he walked further in, he stepped on something that crunched under his foot. He looked down. It was a skull. The skull was attached to a skeleton dressed in full plate mail.

Adam removed his foot and continued on.

"Hrm. Hrm."

"What was that?" asked Adam.

"Hrm. Hrm. Hrm."

"It sounds like a whimpering animal." Titania tilted her head. "A fox?"

After searching the room for a bit longer, Adam finally found what had created that noise. Just like Titania suspected, it was a tiny fox kit, a creature no bigger than his forearm. Its dark orange fur seemed soft and shiny, but it was currently covered in spiderwebs. It had two cute little ears with white tufts of fur inside of the inner part. Perhaps the most unusual thing about this creature were the two tails wavering behind it.

"It's a fox yokai!" Titania exclaimed.

"Fox yokai?" asked Adam. "What is that?"

Titania continued to stare at the helpless fox. "Fox yokai are creatures from a small island nation just off the coast of the Moon Continent. They're considered part of the beastmen race, but they are actually powerful divine beasts that serve the Moon Goddess as servants and representatives. I have had the pleasure of meeting one a long time ago. She was wandering the world in search of something, though I never asked what. You can tell a fox yokai's age and power based on the number of tails it has. Nine tails is the highest one can go. This little fox yokai only has two tails, so it is obviously just a child."

As Titania spoke, the little fox yokai finally seemed to notice their presence. It lifted its head and looked at them with pitifully big eyes. Adam was not the type to let himself be affected by cute creatures. This thing was adorable, but his Aris was much cuter.

"What should we do?" asked Adam.

"We should definitely save it," Titania said. "Fox yokai are very rare. There can't be more than maybe a hundred in the entire world. If you save this little fox yokai, it might remember this debt. It might even choose to follow you. I don't think I need to tell you this, but while this little fox only has two tails right now, it will eventually possess a lot of power and could become a stalwart companion if it joins our party. Fox yokai wield incredible magic."

Hearing that he could have a fox yokai as a companion sealed the deal for Adam, who believed he would need some extra fire-power to escape from this blasted forest.

Adam swung his spear, which cut through the spider webs with ease. There seemed to be some kind of energy covering the webs, though it didn't matter in the face of his spear. He wondered about that. However, he didn't care enough to question why his spear could cut through these webs so easily.

Once the little fox was free, it landed on the ground and yipped happily. Titania smiled as the tiny creature began jumping around as though enjoying its newfound freedom. After it had its fill of simply stretching its legs, the little fox yokai trotted up to him and nuzzled its face against his pant leg.

Adam leaned down and began petting the creature. He might not be the kind of guy who would go crazy over a cute animal, but that didn't mean he felt nothing. Having such an adorable critter act affectionately toward him brought out his natural desire to pet it.

Ding!

[The [young fox yokai] would like to join your party. Do you accept? Yes or no?]

Adam looked at the status screen that appeared before him. He reached out and pressed "yes."

Ding!

[Congratulations! The [young fox yokai] has joined your party. The [young fox yokai] called Kureha has now become your pet.]

Adam was confused when he saw that Kureha had become his
pet instead of a party member, but he wasn't given time to question
it because a status screen for Kureha suddenly appeared before him.

Name: Kureha
Class: Fox Yokai
Lvl: 1
SP: 0
AP: 0
Experience: 0/100
Strength: +10
Contitution: +20
Dexterity: +100
Intelligence: +50
Speed: +100
Physical Attack: +10
Health: 200/200
Hit-Rate: 100%
MP: 800/800
Movement: +200
physical Defense: +100
Magical Defense: +100
Dodge-Rate: +100%
Magic Attack: +200

Skills:
Skill Name: Fireball
Description: Kureha has incredible control over fire thanks to
her first tail. She can create fire through the power in her tails
and launch a fireball at opponents.
Current lvl: 1
AP needed to reach next lvl: 100
Ability: Deals 200% damage to a single enemy
Has a 20% chance of causing burn damage
MP Cost: 100
Cooldown time: 10 seconds

Skill Name: Firestorm

Description: Kureha has incredible control over fire thanks for her first tail. She can create fire through the power in her tails to unleash a powerful storm of fire.
Current lvl: 1
AP needed to reach next lvl: 100
Ability: Deals 160% damage to all enemies within a 5 yard radius
Has a 20% chance of causing burn
MP Cost: 100
Cooldown time: 10 second

Skill Name: Thunder Bolt
Description: Kureha's second tail has the power to control lightning. She can launch a powerful lightning bolt at her enemies.
Current lvl: 1
AP needed to reach next lvl: 100
Ability: Deals 250% damage to one enemy
MP Cost: 100
Cooldown time: 10 seconds

Skill Name: Thunder Storm
Description: Kureha's second tail has the power to control lighting. By gathering magical power into her tails, she can create a massive thunder storm that rains down on enemies from above.
Current level: 1
AP needed to reach next lvl: 100
Ability: Deals 150% damage of Magical Attack Power to multiple enemies within a ten yard radius.
MP Cost: 100
Cooldown time: 10 seconds

Adam was admittedly impressed by the status and abilities of this little fox yokai. It only had four skills right now, but all those skills were incredible ranged attacks that could deal exponential amounts of damage. There were even two A.O.E. attacks. If this little fox yokai leveled up, he could only imagine how terrifying it would be in the future.

However, he did have one question,

"Why is Kureha listed as a pet?" he asked Titania.

"Because even though fox yokai are technically considered a member of the Races of Light, they are still beasts at heart. Unlike beastmen, fox yokai are divine beasts created to serve the Moon Goddess. Since they are subservient creatures, they become pets instead of companions," Titania answered.

Adam didn't think that was much of an answer, but he realized this was probably the only answer Titania could give him. He didn't know what differences there were between beastmen and divine beasts. He guessed this was just one of those parts of the in-game lore that he needed to accept without thinking too deeply.

"Well..." Adam stood up. "Now that we have a new companion, I believe it is time we left this place."

"Oh, no. I do not think you should go anywhere," a voice said that sounded like it came from all around them. The voice was female and oozed with a scintillating sensuality that he could only describe as deadly.

Adam spun around, eyes darting to and fro as he tried to find the source of that voice. A chill ran down his spine. He could not see anything, but even so, Adam thought he heard scuttling somewhere to his left. When he turned to look in that direction, there was nothing.

"In fact, I think you should all remain here. It has been so long... so long since I had any guests to entertain," the voice continued. Where the heck was this voice coming from?!

"Adam! Look up!" Titania shouted.

Adam tilted his head, lifted the torch in his hand, and found himself stunned as he finally spotted what had been talking.

The first thing he noticed was this creature had the body of a woman... a very large-breasted woman that didn't believe in clothes, apparently. Her massive tits were jiggling for all to see. They complimented her thin waist. She had a very curvaceous figure, one that could make men everywhere submit to her.

Adam had to wonder about her nudity. He had assumed this game would be rated for all ages, but this woman blew that idea right out of the water.

Her face was just as beautiful as her body. Mature and well defined, surrounded by glossy white hair, her face made him think of a queen. She had ice cold features, but her smile was seductive and reminded him of a viper. Her red lips contrasted starkly against her light blue skin, and she also had glowing red eyes... six glowing red eyes.

While that made him pause, there was something else about this woman that made him think twice.

Her lower half.

While the upper half of her body was that of a beautiful woman, the lower half was all spider. The bulbous carapace was shaped like an oval. A spinneret stuck out from her back end. She walked on eight spider legs with segmented joints. Unlike the [man eating spiders] that had attacked him in the cavern, this woman's spider body was pure black, sleek, and glossy. The only part of color he could see on this woman's carapace as she hung upside down was the red hourglass imprinted on her back.

The symbol of a black widow.

While he was staring at the woman… spider… spider woman in shock, Kureha leapt in front of Adam and began snarling at her. An amused chuckle escaped the spider woman as she lowered herself to the floor. Adam realized only now that she'd been hanging on a thread being projected out of her spinneret.

Now that she was on the ground, Adam realized she wasn't much bigger than him. Her spider body gave her maybe a couple of feet over him, but her human half looked around the same size as his torso. He'd say she was maybe nine or ten feet tall thanks to that carapace.

"A human, a very tiny fairy, and a young fox yokai. My, but I do have some interesting company this time," the woman said with a smile as she walked over to them with slow, meticulous steps. The *clack, clack, clack* of her spear-shaped legs created an ominous echo in the still room. "You do not know how boring it is here. Not only are my loyal Demon Spider Clan subordinates a complete bore, but I have not had anything good to eat in centuries. So how about it? Think you three can help a woman out? I promise it won't hurt. You might even enjoy how it feels when I gobble you up."

Those words did not instill Adam with confidence. He shivered from head to toe as Kureha, perhaps sensing how dangerous this woman was, whimpered and moved back a little, though she still remained in front of Adam as though to protect him from harm. That made him a little touched. If for no other reason than this, he planned to make sure the fox made it out of this alive.

While no one said anything, Titania did cast [scan] on this ter-rifyingly strange woman.

Name: Spider Queen
The queen of the Demon Spider Clan. She was born several hun-
dred years after the first Spider Queen was killed by the Hero
chosen by the Four Goddess.
Class: 4-star
Lvl: 90
Health: 3,000,000,000/3,000,000,000

MP: 1,000,000/1,000,000
Physical Attack: +9,000
Constitution: +10,000
Dexterity: +5,000
Intelligence: +5,000
Speed: +2,000

Skills:
Deadly Venom: The Spider Queen releases a venomous mist
from her mouth that causes incredible damage
Damage = Intelligence + Physical Attack
MP cost: 1,500
Cooldown time: 30 seconds.

Death by Embracing: When the Spider Queen gets a hold of her
enemies, she never lets go and squeezes the life out of them
Causes -9,000 damage for every one second she has you in her
grasp
MP cost: 2,500
Cooldown time: 60 seconds

Web Entrapment: The Spider Queen can shoot many webs from
her spinneret
They will always form an intricate pattern after striking a solid
surface
The web is incredibly strong and sticky
Nothing can escape it
MP cost: 10,000

Cooldown time: 30 seconds

Eight-Legged Slash: The Spider Queen uses all eight of her legs to hack her enemies to pieces
Causes 9,000 damage for every leg you are struck with
MP cost: 1,500
Cooldown time: 10 seconds

Seductive Delusions: The Spider Queen is a master of illusions and can trap every enemy within a ten yard radius
Causes enemy to become trapped in an illusion depicting their wildest fantasies for 120 seconds
MP cost: 30,000
Cooldown time: 360 seconds

Slash: The Spider Queen slashes at the enemy with one of her legs
Damage = Physical Attack
MP Cost: 50
Cooldown Time: 0 seconds

Call: The Spider Queen can secrete pheromones that calls her brethren to aid her
Summons all spider clansmen within a 200 meter radius
MP Cost: 10,000
Cooldown Time: 120-seconds
Special Limit: Can only be used when the Spider Queen's health is less than 25%

When Adam saw the stats this woman was boasting, her level, her class, and her title, he knew there was absolutely no way they could defeat her.

Unless they could escape, they were absolutely fucked.

FRANTIC ESCAPE

Adam was not the kind of person who panicked when the situation became hopeless. He'd been in plenty hopeless situations before. Back when Lucifer first began sending him on missions to kill important and powerful individuals, he had been pinned down by overwhelming opposition, injured to the point of being nearly crippled, and nearly lost his life so many times that the thought of death no longer phased him. He hadn't panicked back then. He wouldn't panic now.

Still, the situation was not looking good.

"So you're the Spider Queen?" Adam asked, taking a long, slow look at her human body and making sure to keep his eyes away from her spider body. "Not exactly what I was expecting."

The Spider Queen smiled and placed a hand against her cheek. It was a very human gesture, but the hand, which was segmented with black obsidian armor and fingers shaped like claws, gave even that simple gesture an inhuman feeling.

"Now aren't you an interesting human." She hummed and studied him just as he did her. The look in her vibrant pupils was like a spider looking at the butterfly trapped in its web. "Your breathing hasn't changed since laying eyes on me, your heart rate is the same as before, and your expression remains unchanged as well. You are masking your fear very well. I'm impressed. A weak little critter with a level of only 11 has somehow managed to make his way down here, slipped past my children, and found this lair of mine. Most intriguing."

"So this is your home?" Adam made a big show of looking around as he scooped Kureha into his arms. "I can't say I like what you've done with the place. Have you ever thought about redecorating?"

"Ah ha ha ha! You're quite the joker! Is that your way of disguising the terror you feel? I once heard humans possessed such coping mechanisms, but this is my first time seeing it."

The Spider Queen's laugh probably would have been pleasant, but it was laced with a deadly coldness that sent chills down Adam's spine and froze his veins. As he took a step back, she took several steps forward. Her smile widened with every passing second, until it was a full blown grin that peeled her lips back, revealing her ridiculously sharp teeth. Those things looked like they could tear the flesh and muscles right off a human's bones.

"Kureha," Adam whispered. "Can you use [Firestorm] to burn all these cobwebs?"

The little fox in his arms softly yipped. He didn't know if that was an affirmative, but, well, he decided to take it as such. They were short on time.

"Then on my signal, use [Firestorm] to burn everything here," he continued as Titania landed on his head and grabbed his hair. She seemed to understand what he was up to. Perhaps the past few days of journeying with him had given her some sense of his tactics and personality, or maybe she just understood that there was realistically no way for them to defeat this monstrosity right now. Even Adam wasn't reckless enough to go against a level 90 4-star monster.

"What are you whispering about?" asked the Spider Queen. "You know that secrets do not make friends."

"You want to eat us, so it doesn't really matter if we keep a few secrets from you," Adam said in a sharp tone. "We aren't friends to you. We're just food."

"Oh, well, you do have a point." The Spider Queen tapped an index finger against her cheek as she moved ever closer. "I guess I should come up with a new saying. I once heard that what I just said was a human saying, but maybe it only works among humans? Oh, well. I've never really cared for such human eccentricities. Anyway, I've grown bored of this, so I suppose it's time for you to die now."

"Sorry, but not today. Now, Kureha!" Adam raised his voice in a shout.

Kureha released a loud yip that sounded somewhat like a howl, then one of her two tails pointed straight into the air. A tiny ball of fire lit up above the tip. It was barely the size of his thumbnail, but then it quickly expanded, growing until it was nearly the size of an adult human.

Adam began sweating as the heat from the flames seared his skin. He couldn't feel any pain, like there was a program or something that prevented friendly fire, but he could feel the incredible heat washing over him. He could even see the air around him distorting with heat waves.

"Gyaaa!" the Spider Queen shrieked and backed off. It seemed she didn't like fire.

Kureha launched the fireball into the sky, where it exploded and shot dozens of projectiles in every direction. Each projectile crashed into a spiderweb, igniting it and causing the fire to spread. A raging heat filled the room as the conflagration grew to cover almost the entire interior. It wasn't long before smoke and flames filled Adam's lungs, making him cough.

"Damn you!!! Blasted human!" the Spider Queen screeched. It was a shrill sound filled with hatred and rage, a noise akin to needles being driven into his flesh.

Adam did not pay anymore attention to the Spider Queen as he turned on his heels and ran. Sweat poured down his back as he covered his face with his shirt. The smoke was clogging his lungs, making him cough, burning his eyes, and causing his vision to distort. He could barely see where he was going. Also…

-10; -10; -10; -10!

It looked like he was suffering from the burn status effect. His health was dropping -10 points every second, which he guessed he should have expected, but he had really been hoping this wouldn't happen. It seemed that even if Kureha's attack didn't damage him, the lingering effects as everything around them caught fire did.

Because Adam didn't want to go back up the way he came and deal with the Spider Queen's children, he ran in the opposite direction and found another hallway. There were spider webs down this way as well. All of them were already burning. Many of the Spider Queen's tiny offspring were scuttling around as they also caught fire and turned into living torches.

-10; -10; -10; -10!

Adam downed a [low-grade health potion]. He was about to give Titania one, but then she began singing a gentle song called [Song of Refreshing Rain]. This melody seemed more like a lullaby than a song. Soothing and sweet, soft and gentle, it made Adam feel like he was being embraced by a loving spouse. It made him feel like... yes, like Lexi and Aris were with him again.

Magic like raindrops poured down from above. If it was real rain, it would have dispersed into steam upon coming into contact with the fire, but this was not real rain. It healed +30 of his, Titania's, and Kureha's HP every one second, which completely negated the effects from the burn damage.

Adam had no idea how long he ran for, but he took several flights of stairs that led up, passed through numerous corridors, and eventually realized that the area they were in contained no spiderwebs. Did that mean the Spider Queen had yet to make this part of the temple her home? He didn't know if that was the reason, or if there was another reason, but he decided not to think about it.

"Haaah... haaah... haaah... okay... I think we're safe for now," Adam said as he pressed his back against a wall and slid down until he was sitting on his bottom. Sweat poured from his forehead, neck, and back in thick rivulets. It was so disgustingly real that he decided to take a shower the moment he exited the game.

"That was some pretty impressive thinking back there," Titania said. "Very reckless and completely stupid, but it also managed to get us out of a dangerous situation. Who could have possibly imagined we would run into one of the Lords of Chaos here of all places?"

Adam shook his head, but he didn't answer Titania as he closed his eyes and tried to relax. He was so tired.

Kureha climbed out of his embrace and hopped onto the floor. She sniffed the air a little bit, looked back the way they had come, and then looked at the other end. There didn't seem to be anything down that way except for more corridors. After another moment, she yipped and turned to him.

"What's up, Kureha?" asked Adam. "Is something down there?"

Kureha yipped some more and nodded. She then gestured with her paw as though pointing deeper into the hallway.

"Fox yokai are highly intelligent creatures," Titania explained. "Not only can they understand the human tongue and learn how to speak it when they gain a human form, but they have very keen senses. Their sense of smell is particularly good, though they also have amazing hearing."

"That so?" Adam stood to his feet. "So she can sense some-thing up ahead?"

"Probably," Titania said.

"Guess we've got no choice," he mumbled as he picked up his spear. "We can't stay here anyway, so we just gotta keep moving forward."

The sound of Adam's footsteps resounded off the stone walls as they pressed on. A slight chill caused him to shiver. There was no wind or anything blowing through this corridor, but he'd been sweating so much that without the heat from the searing flames to keep him warm, it felt like the temperature had dropped several dozen degrees.

Adam soon came to realize that the lair where the Spider Queen was staying only consisted of a small portion of this dun-geon. Not only did this place contain numerous rooms, but many of them appeared to be several times larger than the one belonging to the Spider Queen. One particular room he ended up in looked a lot like a temple of worship. It contained more statues of the goddess from before. Each statue sat against the wall, probably a dozen times taller than him. There were also several other statues present that were not of the goddess.

Stopping in front of one statue in particular, Adam could not help but be reminded of those creepy suits of armor he sometimes saw in horror movies, the ones that moved and attacked people when you least expected them too. Aris hated those movies. It was enough to make him wonder why she kept watching them, but then he imagined she'd done so as an excuse to cling onto him.

Not that either of them really needed an excuse.

"I feel like this thing is going to come to life and attack us," Adam said.

"It probably will," Titania agreed. "After all, this is a [guardian statue]."

"What is that?"

"Rather than tell you, it would be better if I showed you."

With that, Titania cast [scan] to display this statue's stats.

Name: Guardian Statue
Description: This statue is a golem that was created in ancient times to guard temples from enemies. Once activated, it will attack anyone it deems an enemy.
Class: None
Lvl: 20
Health: 25,000/25,000
MP: 2,000/2,000
Physical Attack: +900
Constitution: +1,000
Dexterity: +50
Intelligence: +10
Speed: +30

Skills:
Swing: The guardian statue swings its massive limbs to swat its enemies away
Damage = 900 * 2
MP cost: 100
Cooldown time: 0 seconds

Crush: The guardian statue raises its hands above its head and uses its incredible power to crush its enemies

Damage = 900 * 3
50% chance of Instant Death
MP cost: 150
Cooldown time: 0 seconds

"Oh, that looks much more manageable than those [man eating spiders] and the [Spider Queen]," Adam said. "I can actually beat this."

Titania gave him a dry look. "The mere fact that you can defeat an enemy that is nine levels higher than you is ridiculous."

"Must be my plot armor."

"Your what?"

"Never mind. Anyway, let's keep going. It looks like Kureha can sense something up ahead."

Indeed, Kureha was staring deeper into the room, so they began moving again. As they walked, the area up ahead came into view. It looked like there was a large door guarded by two statues that were even bigger than the one he had just been looking at. While the [guardian statues] were maybe a head taller than him, these ones stood at twice his height. They wore what looked like heavy armor and wielded halberds that were at least six meters tall. A single blue crystal could be seen in the center of each stone statue.

"So… another [guardian statue]?" asked Adam.

"These ones are [knight golems]," Titania corrected him. "They are far more formidable than the [guardian statues]."

Because she knew what Adam would want, Titania cast [scan] on the [knight golem].

Name: Knight Golem
Description: Created by a powerful mage from ancient times,
the knight golem is the final line of defense for most temples. It
is very sturdy and has high attack and defense stats.
Class: 2-star
Lvl: 25
Health: 250,000/250,000
MP: 5,000/5,000
Strength: +1,500
Constitution: +3,000
Dexterity: +100
Intelligence: +10
Speed: +20

Skills:
Swat: knight golems can swing their halberds around with ease,
knocking any opponent struck away
Damage = 200% Strength
100% chance of casting stun.
MP cost: 100
Cooldown time: 0 seconds.

Impalement: The knight golem thrusts its halberd at speeds the
human eye cannot track, dealing critical damage to its enemy
Damage = 1,500 * 3
MP cost: 150
Cooldown time: 0 seconds

Kick: When Swat and Impalement do not work, the knight
golem will kick its enemies away
Damage = Strength + Constitution
100% chance of throwing enemy
MP cost: 200
Cooldown time: 5 seconds

Quake: When the knight golem's HP reaches 10%, it will stomp on the ground and cause a terrifying earthquake that is guaranteed to stun any enemy within a ten yard radius for 60 seconds
MP cost: 1,500
Cooldown time: 30 seconds.

egeneration: Whenever one of the knight golems reaches 50% HP, the other knight golem will cast heal to automatically restore HP to 100%
MP Cost: 1,000
Cooldown Time: N/A
Limitations: Can only be used when the other knight golem is at 50% HP

"I'm guessing we have to defeat all the [guardian statues] and these two [knight golems] in order to proceed, right?" Adam asked.

"I believe that is most likely to be the case," Titania agreed.

At that moment, a soft rumbling filled the air. Adam turned around when the sound of footsteps echoed around him. A [guardian statue] had come to life and was now walking toward him with ponderous steps that caused the ground to shake.

Kureha charged in front of Adam and growled at the moving statue, but Adam didn't think growling would help here, so he stepped in front instead.

"Kureha, attack this thing with [Fireball] and [Thunder Bolt]. I want to see how much damage they do," he said.

With a yip, Kureha raised one of her tails and pointed it at the [guardian statue]. A bright ball of blue lightning crackled to life along the tip of her tail. It was only there for a split second before the sphere turned into a bolt that shot forward and struck the [guardian statue] in the chest.

-825!

It didn't do much damage, but Adam didn't expect it to since Kureha was only at level 1. Shaving off -825 of its health was already shocking enough. He could not even do -100 damage when he was at her level.

The statue lumbered on. It was still moving slowly, so Adam didn't actually feel a sense of danger. He just stood there as heat flared to life around Kureha's other tail. A fireball soon appeared above the tip, but it was soon launched at the [guardian statue], slamming into the statue's head and exploding.

-600!

"It looks like [Thunder Bolt] does more damage," Adam observed. "Kureha, use [Thunder Bolt] whenever you have the opportunity to do so. Titania, you know what to do."

"I shall back you up," Titania confirmed as she flew above his head and began to sing [Song of Vigor].

Adam activated [Blood Sacrifice], dropping the health he had by half in exchange for 300% damage for 60 seconds. He quickly charged forward and attacked the [guardian statue] with a continuous stream of seemingly never ending stabs and slashes.

-7,488; MISS!

-7,488; MISS!

Adam realized only after trying to use it twice that [Dance of the Sakura Blossoms] was a lot harder to activate than he initially gave credit for. His attacks kept missing, which forced him to back off, wait for the cooldown times on both this skill and [Blood Sacrifice] to end, then start them again. He ended up taking a [low-grade health potion] because his health dropped more than he was comfortable with.

Because the skill reset and activated the cooldown time whenever he missed, he only managed to do -17,000 damage. Of course, this thing didn't have more than +25,000 health. One more attack would finish it, but [Blood Sacrifice] had worn off while he was waiting for [Dance of the Sakura Blossoms's] second cooldown time to end, meaning the amount of damage he did was lessened.

-2,475!

Kureha yipped and released another [Thunder Bolt], which slammed into the [guardian statue] with unparalleled ferocity. The statue stumbled back several steps. Adam took advantage of its sudden stumble to rush in and swing his spear around in a simple [slash].

-4,320!

That was all the damage Adam needed to inflict to kill this thing. The [guardian statue] stopped moving after its HP dropped to zero, cracks appeared along its body, and then it crumbled away, turning into a pile of rubble.

Ding!

[You have defeated a [guardian statue]! Items dropped: 5,000 gold coins. +11,000 experience points! +5,000 ability points! +3,000 Reputation!]

Ding!

[Congratulations! Kureha has leveled up! She is now at level 2! +40 HP! +500 MP! +10 SP!]

Ding!

[Congratulations! Kureha has leveled up! She is now at level 3! +40 HP! +500 MP! +10 SP!]

Ding!

[Congratulations! Kureha has leveled up! She is now at level 4! +40 HP! +500 MP! +10 SP!]

Ding!

[Congratulations! Kureha has leveled up! She is now at level 5! +40 HP! +500 MP! +10 SP!]

Ding!

[Congratulations! Kureha has leveled up! She is now at level 6! +40 HP! +500 MP! +10 SP!]

Adam could only blink as Kureha's level shot up. Of course, he had expected this since she was at level 1 and the [guardian statue] gave +11,000 experience points. She ended up gaining a whole 5 levels, going from level 1 all the way to level 6. Like Titania, she also gained +10 status points per level gained. Unlike with Titania, Kureha seemed incapable of allocating her own status points because she was classified as a pet. That being the case, Adam allocated her status points accordingly.

He put +30 of her SP in Intelligence, +10 in Constitution, and another +10 in speed. Once done, he looked at her status screen.

Name: Kureha
Class: Fox Yokai

Lvl: 6
SP: 0
AP: 5,000
Experience: 900/6,400
Strength: +10
Constitution: +30
Dexterity: +100
Intelligence: +80
Speed: +110
hysical Attack: +10
Health: 280/280
Hit-rate: 100%
Hit-rate: 100%
MP: 2,300/2,300
Movement: +220
Physical Defense: +30
Magical Defense:+120
Dodge-Rate: 100%
Magic Attack: +360

Skills:
Skill Name: Fireball
Description: Kureha has incredible control over fire thanks to
her first tail. She can create fire through the power in her tails
and launch a fireball at opponents.
Current lvl: 1
AP needed to reach next lvl: 100
Ability: Deals 200% damage of Magical Attack
Has a 20% chance of causing burn damage
MP Cost: 100
Cooldown Time: 10-seconds

Skill Name: Firestorm
Description: Kureha has incredible control over fire thanks for
her first tail. She can create fire through the power in her tails to

unleash a powerful storm of fire.
Current lvl: 1
AP needed to reach next lvl: 100
Ability: Deals 160% damage of Magical Attack to all enemies
within a 5 yard radius
Has a 20% of causing burn
MP cost: 100
Cooldown Time: 10-seconds

Skill Name: Thunder Bolt
Description: Kureha's second tail has the power to control light-
ning. She can launch a powerful thunder bolt at her enemies.
Current lvl: 1
AP Needed to reach next lvl: 100
Ability: Deals 250% damage of Magical Attack to one enemy
MO Cost: 100
Cooldown Time: 10-seconds

Skill Name: Thunder Storm
Description: Kureha's second tail has the power to control light-
ing. By gathering magical power into her tails, she can create a
massive thunder storm that rains down on enemies from above.
Current level: 1
AP needed to reach next lvl: 100
Ability: Deals 150% damage of Magical Attack to multiple ene-
mies within a ten yard radius
MP Cost: 100
Cooldown time: 10 seconds

Just as Adam finished allocating Kureha's status points, another rumbling sound echoed around them. Adam looked toward his
left and saw another [guardian statue] come to life. It walked off the
small stand, moving with lumbering steps that caused the ground to
shake, and turned to face him, Kureha, and Titania.

"It looks every time we defeat a [guardian statue], another one activates," Adam said as he spun the spear around in his hands. "I guess I should have expected as much. Well, it's not like killing these things are very hard."

The moment those words left his lips, a second [guardian statue] suddenly rumbled to life and stepped off its stand, coming to stand beside the other statue as they both moved toward them. Adam blankly stared at the two statues with a frown. He was certain the vein he felt bulging on his forehead wasn't his imagination.

"I do believe you jinxed us," Titania said in a calm yet mocking voice.

"Shut up," Adam muttered as heat sprang to his cheeks.

Because there were two [guardian statues] now, Adam did not hesitate to let Kureha bombard one of them with [Thunder Bolt], while he activated [Blood Sacrifice] and had Titania sing [Song of Vigor] to increase his attack power. He rushed forward and began [Dance of the Sakura Blossoms] to try and quickly dispose of the first [guardian statue].

-7,488; -14,976; MISS!

Adam snarled as he missed, thereby resetting [Dance of the Sakura Blossoms] and forcing it to enter a cooldown time. Since he couldn't use his newest skill, Adam spun the spear around his body and used [slash] to finish off the [guardian statue], then turned around and raced toward the second one.

This [guardian statue] had been moving toward Kureha because she had pulled all of its agro with her magical attacks. [Thunder Bolt] normally did -825 damage, but thanks to Titania's [Song of

Vigor], she did 300% more. She'd only attacked twice, but that had
dropped the [guardian statue's] health by about -5,000 points.

Adam very quickly reached the ponderous enemy and attacked
with [slash], which did an astonishing -7,488 points of damage, followed by [slash] two more times. The three simultaneous attacks
drew a trio of lines across the [guardian statue's] body as they dealt
a combined total of -22,464 damage. With Kureha already dealing -
5,000 damage to it, this was enough to defeat the [guardian statue].

Ding!

*[You have defeated two [guardian statues]! Items dropped: x2
[Guardian Heart] and 10,500 gold coins! +20,000 experience
points! +12,000 ability points. +6,000 Reputation!]*

Ding!

*[Congratulations! Kureha has leveled up! She is now at level
7! +60 HP! +800 MP! +10 SP!]*

Ding!

*[Congratulations! Kureha has leveled up! She is now at level
8! +60 HP! +800 MP! +10 SP!]*

Kureha once more leveled up twice, and Adam decided to put
all of her status points into her Intelligence stat, bringing it up to
+100.

Adam never got the chance to look at how this changed her
stats, however, because four of the [guardian statues] began moving
next. They were the last four fortunately. However, the fact that
Adam had to face four of these giant things before fighting against
the two [knight golems] was a little daunting. At the same time, he
could not help but grin. His adrenaline was pumping at the thought

of combat against these things. They were so slow and ponderous. It was like this game was simply giving him experience points.

***

-31,680!

Ding!

[Congratulations! You have defeated four [guardian statues]! Items dropped: x3 [Guardian Heart] and 46,000 gold coins! +34,000 experience points! +20,000 ability points! +12,000 Reputation!]

Ding!

[Congratulations! Kureha has leveled up! She is now at level 10! +60 HP! +1,000 MP! +10 SP!]

Adam released a weary sigh as he wiped the sweat from his forehead. Standing over the last of the four [guardian statues] remains, he could only wonder if there might be some kind of bug in this game.

He'd been thinking about this for awhile now, but his stats were kind of broken. His spear still didn't have very good stats, but he had his two abilities: [Blood Sacrifice] and [Dance of the Sakura Blossoms]. [Blood Sacrifice] halved his HP in exchange for tripling the damage he did for 60 seconds, while [Dance of the Sakura Blossoms] did twice the damage for every consecutive hit, and the damage itself stacked. Granted, he missed a lot when using this attack and the cooldown time was awful, but if he attacked something even four times with [Blood Sacrifice] and Titania's [Song of Vigor] activated, he could deal over -200,000 points of damage.

That was surely a broken ability if he had ever heard of one.

Speaking of broken abilities, Adam only now realized he had +53,700 ability points and hadn't once upgraded [Dance of the Sakura Blossoms]. It only took +1,000 ability points to raise his ability to level 2, another +2,000 to raise it to level 3, +4,000 to raise it to level 4, and +8,000 to raise it to level 5. He assumed that was the level cap for [Dance of the Sakura Blossoms] like all his other skills, but then he noticed the status screen did not say his level was maxed out. He added another +16,000 ability points to raise its level to 6. He now had +22,700 ability points, but [Dance of the Sakura Blossoms] sadly required +32,000 ability points to reach the next level.

Skills:
Skill Name: Slash
Description: A basic skill where the player swings his or her sword and attacks the enemy!
Current lvl: 5 MAXED
Ability: Causes 150% damage to enemy if it hits
MP Cost: 1
Cooldown time: 0 seconds

Skill Name: Thrust
Description: A basic skill where the player thrusts his or her sword at the enemy!
Current lvl: 5 MAXED
Ability: Causes 160% damage with a 5% chance at getting a critical hit

MP Cost: 5
Cooldown Time: 1-second

Skill Name: Blood Sacrifice
Description: By sacrificing 50% of your blood (HP), you have
gained the ability to increase the damage you do
Current lvl: 5 MAXED
Ability: causes 300% attack power for 60 seconds. Disregards
skill cooldown times, allowing the user to attack with every skill
MP Cost: 20
Special limit: Drops HP by half.
Cooldown time: 30 seconds

Skill Name: Dance of the Sakura Blossoms
Description: A skill only Adam can use. Attacks with numerous
spear thrusts as the player dances around his enemy, eventually
forming the shape of a sakura blossom
Current lvl: 6
AP needed to reach next lvl: 32,000
Ability: Unleashes five super-powered attacks, increases damage
by 300% for every consecutive hit and resets when Adam misses
an attack
Hit-Rate has increased to 60%
MP Cost: 100
Cooldown Time: 15-seconds

Everything was maxed out except for [Dance of the Sakura
Blossoms], and it looked like his current upgrade had increased the
stacking damage it did by 300% and decreased the cooldown time to
15 seconds. He also noticed that his Hit-Rate for this attack had increased to 60%, which was probably the most useful part of this
skill since it meant he was likely to score hits more frequently.

Since he was already looking at his stats, he proceeded to add the extra +10 status points that Kureha received from her level up into her Intelligence stat. He figured the higher her Intelligence was, the better she would be in battle.

"That was oddly boring," Titania mumbled as she fluttered over to him.

"What are you talking about?" asked Adam, stretching his arms above his head as he turned around and began walking toward the [knight golems]. He took a [low-grade health potion] to recover the HP he had lost. Funnily enough, all of his lost HP came from him constantly halving his own health by using [Blood Sacrifice]. Those [guardian statues] had not hit him even once.

"Do not give me that." Titania sounded cross as she placed her hands on her hips and stared down at him. "Those [guardian statues] were all at level 20, yet you were able to easily dispose of them despite only being at level 11."

"Well, yeah. What's the problem?" asked Adam.

Titania rolled her eyes. "The problem is that what you are doing should be impossible. Even adding my own unique enhancement abilities, being able to slay monsters nine levels above you is not something a normal person can do. Just what in the heck are you?"

"I'm not really sure how to answer that," Adam admitted.

Adam was certain the reason he could do these things was because the virtual world simulated the real world so closely that his real life abilities were applicable in this game world. He had noticed it before, but his Dodge-Rate was listed as "???." It was something he had been curious about but didn't think much of at first. Now, however, he was beginning to realize the reason his Dodge-Rate was listed as "???" was simply because his ability to dodge attacks in real life had crossed over into the virtual world.

On the other hand, the reason he couldn't always hit his enemies was not because he lacked the ability to hit them, but because of his enemy's own Dodge-Rate. They probably had some hidden stats that determined how many times a player's attack could hit or miss based on each player's Hit-Rate.

As he was thinking about his stats, Adam remembered that he still hadn't looked at the new items he had acquired. He opened his inventory and checked out the [Guardian Heart] items.

Item Pouch:
Name: Guardian Heart x5
Item Type: Magic Core
Grade: 1-star
Use Requirements: Only people with the Crafter and Blacksmith secondary class can use this.
Description: Guardian Hearts are the energy source of guardian statues. They can be used to enhance the abilities of armor, weapons, and certain magical items.
Abilities: Can increase stats and attributes of items and armor.

"Secondary class," Adam muttered to himself.

"Did you say something?" asked Titania.

Adam shook his head. "No. I was just talking to myself."

After he finished talking, Adam sped up and then stopped in front of the door once again. He didn't have to wait long before the two [knight golems] came to life. The crystals on their chest began releasing a stream of particles that he guessed was magical energy.

The stream merged with their bodies, which transformed the once gray stone into a steel blue color. A pair of gleaming red eyes appeared on either golem. They seemed to flash with malevolence.

As both [knight golems] stepped down from their stands, Adam twirled his spear around and adopted the traditional spearman stance taught to him by Lexi.

All he had to do now was defeat these things, and then he could move on.

Simple enough.

KNIGHT GOLEM
TIMES TWO

A dam started off this battle by casting [Blood Sacrifice]. It wouldn't matter if he lost 50% of his health since a single attack from either [knight golem] could kill him. Titania also seemed to realize that healing and defense wouldn't help and began singing. As the vigorous and uplifting melody for the [Song of Vigor] raised his strength, he rushed toward the enemy on his left and attacked with [Dance of the Sakura Blossoms].

-8,640; -25,920; MISS!

Adam spun the spear in his hands, attacking with a ferocious grace that was expected from someone who had spent at least three years of his young life killing. He wondered what Lexi would think if she learned he'd turned their most beautiful skill into an artifice of death. She probably wouldn't be happy, but it wasn't like Adam could undo the damage that had already been wrought.

Besides, Lexi was dead.

Unfortunately, while Adam was backing off after initiating his attack, the other [knight golem] arrived and attacked him from behind. He sensed the movement and leapt aside just as the spear in its grasp came down. The earth rumbled as the spear impaled the ground, cracks spreading out from the point of impact. The [knight golem] had missed its companion by barely a foot. It pulled the spear back and turned to face him, red eyes flashing with an ominous light.

-4,400!

A lightning bolt slammed into the [knight golem] that had attacked Adam from behind. The attack was so powerful the giant stumbled backward several steps and was only able to right itself by slamming the back end of its spear into the ground, using the weapon as a crutch. The floor cracked beneath its weight, but it pushed itself up and turned to glare at Kureha—the one who had launched the attack.

"Not on my watch!"

Adam raced forward and attacked the [knight golem] who turned its aggression on his companion. Kureha had a 100% Dodge-Rate, which he assumed meant she could probably avoid any attacks sent her way, but it was better to be safe than sorry.

-7,488; 7,488; MISS; MISS; MISS; MISS; MISS; -7,488!

He tried to use [Dance of the Sakura Blossoms] but missed, and then [Blood Sacrificer] ended. With both skills now in cooldown, he was forced to use [slash] and [thrust] to attack. He swung the spear with incredible speed. It was nothing more than a blur, a flash of rusted silver, as he attacked the [knight golem] several times. Sadly, much like last time, the other [knight golem] came in with its own spear swinging.

Adam growled as he leapt back to avoid the attack. The powerful force when the spear met the ground sent him tumbling. He landed on his back, grunting as the hard surface jammed his tailbone. He only received -1 damage because he wasn't hit with an attack, but just like stubbing your toe or stepping on a lego, it hurt a lot more than people gave it credit for. Meanwhile, the [knight golem] he had been attacking stalked up to him and raised its spear.

-4,400; -3,520!

Kureha sent another [Thunder Bolt] straight into the [knight golem], striking its chest just above the crystal, once more sending it stumbling backward. Before it could recover, Kureha launched a second attack. It was [Fireball] this time, a brilliant red flame that flew from her first tail. The fireball flew through the air, slammed into its face, and exploded. A wave of heat washed over Adam as the [knight golem] stumbled even more. It crashed into the [knight golem] behind it, which sent them both to the ground.

Adam was not one to miss such a great opportunity. He raced toward his fallen foe and began attacking. [Blood Sacrifice] and [Dance of the Sakura Blossoms] had finished their cooldown time, so he activated both to create a constant stream of attacks, his spear spinning and flashing like glints of silver.

-7,488; -22,464; MISS!

Gritting his teeth as he missed and the cooldown time for his skill activated, Adam leapt back several times to gain distance. Both [knight golems] stood to their feet. He knew thanks to Titania that each [knight golem] had +250,000 health, but he hadn't even come close to halving that. The one he just finished attacking, according to his calculations, should have around +190,000 health, while the other one should have somewhere around +213,000. He still had a long way to go before either of these monsters were killed.

Titania was still singing [Song of Vigor], but Adam's [Blood Sacrifice] chose that moment to run out of time. It entered the cooldown phase. Adam cursed, but he didn't let himself worry about this as he avoided a spear thrust toward his chest.

-4,400; -3,520!

Kureha once again struck the [knight golem] with fire and lightning. It turned to her, but Adam came in quicker than a flash and attacked with [thrust] and [slash].

-4,608; -4,320; -4,320; MISS; MISS; -4,320!

Adam soon worked out a rhythm that allowed him to maximize his efficiency. He attacked one of the two [knight golems] until the other one tried to hit him, then backed off and allowed Kureha to blast one of them with fire and lightning. This usually resulted in both golems crashing to the ground, unable to get up for several seconds as though they were stunned, which he used to his advantage, hacking away at both of them.

It took what Adam estimated was one hour, but he eventually pulled one [knight golem's] health down to +100,500, while the other one had +175,000. He was really proud of his accomplishment. However, just as he was about to thrust his fist into the air like a victory cheer, the [knight golem] with more health pointed its spear at the other one.

Adam wondered what was going on. He soon remembered the unique abilities these monsters possessed, however, when he saw the spear begin glowing a soft green. The green light emitted from the spear and soon encompassed the other [knight golem]. Adam then watched in horror as the [knight golem's] [Regeneration] skill kicked in, completely healing the [knight golem] that had less than 50% of its health.

"You have got to be kidding me," Adam muttered in a bitter voice. "All that hard work… right down the drain."

"Adam," Titania stopped singing and floated down to him. "I think this calls for a tactical withdrawal."

"I'm surprised you know what a tactical withdrawal is." Adam took a deep breath. Titania puffed out her cheeks in a pout. "But you're right. We're not going to beat these two if we just keep doing what we've been doing. Let's retreat for now. Kureha! We're heading back toward the hallway we came in from!"

Kureha yipped to let him know she heard him, then all three of them began retreating together. The [knight golems] stalked after them, of course, but neither of them moved very fast, so they were able to reach the hall and slip inside safely. Since the hallway was not very large, neither [knight golem] could fit inside. After a few seconds of trying to stab him, Titania, and Kureha with their spears, the enemies rumbled back over to the large double doors.

Adam sighed as he slid down the wall and landed on his butt. Now that he had stopped fighting, he realized how tired he was. It was like when people got an adrenaline high. All those chemicals were pumping through their bodies, keeping them going even though they should have exhausted themselves long ago. They only realize how tired they were after they stopped moving and the effects of being pumped full of hormones vanished.

"I'm so exhausted," Titania muttered as she landed on Adam's left knee and sat down with her legs crossed.

Kureha seemed tired as well, for she placed her head on his other knee and whimpered in what sounded like agreement. Adam sighed as he reached over and scratched Kureha behind the ears. He wasn't quite sure if this was instinct since he had never owned a pet, but he wouldn't deny that stroking the fox yokai's soft fur helped calm him down.

"We need to figure out a plan to deal with those two," Adam said at last. "If we don't have a solid plan, we're not going to be able to beat them."

"Do you really think people with our levels are capable of beating those two?" asked Titania. "Maybe if they had less health, but with 250,000 health... forget planning. It doesn't really matter what you do. You can't kill a [knight golem] with a single attack, but unless you manage to kill those things in a single hit after its health reaches 125,000, I'm afraid there's nothing any of us can do."

Adam grimaced as he realized this woman was right. Unless he could somehow miraculously deal at least +125,000 points of damage in a single attack, he was pretty much screwed. They would just use [Regeneration] to bring their health back to 100%.

[Dance of the Sakura Blossoms] theoretically had the potential to deal enough damage to one-shot these monsters, but his luck with that skill wasn't good so far. He hadn't been able to strike all five times.

"What about weaknesses?" asked Adam. "Surely something like a [knight golem] must have some kind of weakness, right?"

"I don't think—no, wait." Titania paused and cupped her chin, her brow furrowing in thought as she looked at something beyond his line of sight. "I think I do remember [knight golems] having at least one major weakness."

"What is it?" Adam asked.

"It's the crystal on their chests," Titania exclaimed. "That crystal is basically the source of all their power. It's what gives them life and allows them to attack. Destroy the crystal, destroy the golem."

"So the crystal, huh? We should test that theory out. Kureha!" As he called out her name, Kureha lifted her head and looked at him with a curious expression. "Think you can knock those two down like you did last time?"

Kureha tilted her head. If he didn't know any better, he would have said she was thinking. After what must have been one or two seconds, she nodded and yipped in what Adam decided to take as an affirmative.

"Okay. Then let's test that theory out," Adam said at last.

After resting for several more minutes, Adam stood up, spun the spear around in his hands, downed a [low-grade health potion], and rushed out of the hallway. Kureha and Titania followed right behind him.

Both [knight golems] had gone back to standing on either side of the door, though they began moving the moment he got within a certain distance. Adam noticed their health had completely regenerated, even the one that had been at +175,000 HP. That did suck a little, but it ultimately shouldn't matter too much.

Titania once more began singing [Song of Vigor]. However, Adam did not activate [Blood Sacrifice] right away like he normally did. He raced forward and attacked the [knight golem] on the left side of the door.

MISS; MISS; -4,608; -4,320; -4,320; MISS!

Adam retreated after attacking the [knight golem] several times to pull in its agro. As it chased after him, he kept a careful eye on the other [knight golem], making sure to maneuver himself so the two enemies were eventually following him in a single file line. When he saw them do just that, he shouted.

"Now, Kureha!"

"Yip!"

-4,400; -3,520!

Like last time, Kureha fired off one [Thunder Bolt] followed quickly by [Fireball]. The lightning attack slammed into the [knight golem] in front and knocked it backward, and then the fire attack struck it once more and sent it stumbling into its partner. A loud crash preceded the pair of giant moving statues falling to the ground. Once they were down, Adam activated [Blood Sacrifice] and charged forward.

The first golem he attacked was the one that he and Kureha had been attacking since they restarted this battle. Adam reached it and began flowing into a series of rapid thrust and slash attacks that caused [Dance of the Sakura Blossoms] to activate.

14,967; -44,928; -134,784; MISS!

Adam bit his lip as the two [knight golems] stood back onto their feet. His last attack had brought the first one's health down to +55,321, but the moment they stood back up, he knew his turn this time was over. The [knight golem] with 100% percent of its health used [Regeneration] to restore the other [knight golem] back to full health as well.

He nearly groaned in frustration. Adam wanted to tear his hair out because now he was back at square one.

"At least now we know the core on its chest is its weakness. My attacks did twice the damage they usually do. Let's try this again! Ready, Kureha?!"

"Yip!"

Kureha yipped an affirmative and Adam once more charged in. He began slowly whittling away at the first [knight golem]'s health, though he did a lot less damage since the duration time for [Blood Sacrifice] once more ran out. Even though his attacks only did -4,320 damage, he still managed to knock out -34,560 health points by the time the cooldown period for [Blood Sacrifice] ended.

"Hit them now, Kureha!"

Adam once more lined the two [knight golems] together and let Kureha do her thing. The lightning bolt struck the first [knight golem] in the chest, smashing into the crystal sitting right in the center and dealing an amazing -8,800 damage. The fireball attack dealt -7,040 damage. By the time the [knight golems] crashed into each other and went down, the health for the first one had dropped to +199,600.

-14,967; -44,928; -134,784; 404,352; MISS!

With [Blood Sacrifice] active once again, Adam used [Dance of the Sakura Blossoms] to continuously deal extensive damage. He spun the spear in his hands as though it was an extension of his own body and used his real world talent with a spear to attack. It was impossible for him to feel the difference between his real body and this avatar made up of pixels and polygons. He really felt like he was using his own limbs to slash and stab into this thing.

This time, he dealt more than enough damage to the [knight golem]. Its health was reduced to zero. The crystal on its chest cracked, going dim, and the glowing red eyes went out like candles being snuffed by the wind. Even the hand holding the spear went limp. The heavy object rolled across the ground with a loud clang. Adam took several gasping breaths as the last remaining [knight golem] clambered to its feet.

Perhaps the other monster knew its partner was gone. Maybe it had some form of sentience. The [knight golem] raised and shook the spear in its hand as though it was bellowing in rage, and then it picked up the spear its partner had dropped.

Adam's eyes went wide as the thing attacked him with twice the ferocity and three times the speed as before. It swung the spear in its left hand so fast it left afterimages. Adam managed to duck and avoid being cut in half, but then it thrust out the spear in its right hand. He rolled across the ground and avoided it. The poor ground was not so fortunate. A loud cracking sound echoed around the chamber as the ground cratered, as cracks spread across the floor and several stone tiles were upended.

"What the hell is going on?! Does this thing have a berserker mode?!" Adam demanded.

No one answered him. Titania was busy singing the [Song of Vigor] and Kureha could not speak human.

With nothing left to do but dodge, Adam found himself scrambling to get away from this monstrosity. His breathing had already grown heavy. A sharp pain stabbed his chest whenever he breathed in. His raspy breathing and the rapid pumping of his own blood echoed in his ear. He ducked, dodged, spun, and ran to get away from this psychotic enemy. He even tried hiding behind a column, but that plan fell through when the column was destroyed by a single swing of his enemy's spears.

"Damn it! Guess I've got no choice!"

Adam waited for the cooldown time on [Blood Sacrifice] to run out, then activated it once again and closed the distance between himself and the [knight golem]. He ferociously attacked the enemy, a vicious grin on his face as he spun, slashed, stabbed, and danced around the monster. He could feel the blood pumping through his veins. The sound of his heartbeat struck his ear in staccato bursts.

MISS; MISS; -7,488; MISS; -7,488; MISS; MISS; MISS!

Adrenaline was pumping through his body, causing his perception of everything to slow down. It felt like his entire body had become a live wire. Energy flowed through him as he attacked the [knight golem] over and over again.

-7,488 ; -7,488; -7,488; MISS; 7,488; MISS; MISS; -7,488; -7,488; MISS; MISS; MISS; -7,489; -7,488; -7,488!

Even with all of the attacks he launched, he only did about - 60,000 points worth of damage, which was nowhere near enough to beat the [knight golem]. He did not give up, however, and continued to attack.

-7,488; MISS; MISS; MISS; -7,488; MISS; MISS; MISS!

[Blood Sacrifice] soon ended. Adam spun to the left as a spear slammed into the ground. The attack had enough force that he pitched forward, but he shoulder rolled across the ground, came back up, and downed a [low-grade health potion] as he ran away from the [knight golem].

While waiting for the cooldown time on [Blood Sacrifice] to end, Adam kept on eye on Kureha, who was waiting in the rear to be of some use. Titania was next to her, but he wasn't worried about her since she could fly. He continued to move across the chamber, until his skill's cooldown time ended and the [knight golem] was standing in front of a column, and then called out to his fox yokai companion.

"Hit it with magic, Kureha!"

Kureha once more unleashed two attacks. [Thunder Bolt] and [Fireball] slammed into the [knight golem] in quick succession, knocking off just short of -10,000 points of damage. More importantly, the [knight golem] fell into the column, which cracked apart underneath the incredible force and sent the giant creature sprawling onto the stone floor

Adam once more ran up and activated [Blood Sacrifice] and [Dance of the Sakura Blossoms] to attack. Just like last time, he attacked the core.

-14,967; -44,928; -134,784; MISS!

"Haaah… haaaaaah… haah…"

Adam stepped back as the crystal cracked and the eyes of his enemy went dim. The two massive hands slackened and the spears rolled onto the ground with the dull sound of stone grinding against stone. His shoulders heaved as he stared warily at this monster as though expecting it to return from the dead, even though its health had reached zero.

Ding!

[You have defeated two [knight golems]! Items dropped: x2 [Golem's Sacred Stone], x2 [Golem Spear], [Golem Gauntlets], and 30,400 gold coins. +200,000 experience points! +20,000 ability points! +10,000 Reputation!]

Ding!

[Congratulations! You have leveled up! You are now at level 12! +300 HP! +10 MP! +5 SP!]

Ding!

[Congratulations! Titania has leveled up! She is now at level 14! +200 HP! +2,400 MP! +10 SP!]

Ding!

[Congratulations! Kureha has leveled up! She is now at level 11! +60 HP! +440 MP! +10 SP!]

Several screens flashed across the air, making several announcements about how he, Titania, and Kureha had leveled up. While Titania was used to this, Kureha was not and stared at the screens with curiosity.

Once he was sure the announcements were finished, Adam accessed both his and Kureha's status screens. He added his status points to his Strength, then added Kureha's status points to her Constitution. He wanted to shore up her defense and give her more health in case they ran into an enemy that could get past him and attack her.

Adam also decided to upgrade all of her current skills to level 5. This was the max level these skills could have. Even after maxing out each skill, Kureha still had plenty of AP leftover.

Not only was he able to upgrade all of Kureha's attacks, but Adam was also able to upgrade [Dance of the Sakura Blossoms]. Once Adam was done allocating status points and ability points, he took a look at his and Kureha's stats.

It looked like their stats were growing a bit more, but it was still far from what Adam wanted. He could probably one-shot any enemy with health below +12,000 now, but he wanted to have even greater strength. At the same time, he wanted Kureha to be so powerful that her A.O.E. skills could one-shot multiple enemies with health at least around +10,000. Right now, the best she could do was -1,700 damage when [Song of Vigor] wasn't activated. That wasn't enough to fight mobs, though he believed there wasn't a player alive that could withstand her magic at present.

Out of curiosity, Adam also decided to look at Titania's stats since he couldn't control those.

Name: Titania
Class: Guardian of the Spear

Lvl: 14
SP: 0
AP: 28,620
Experience: 39,650/409,600
Strength: +10
Constitution: +100
Dexterity: +10
Intelligence: +230
Speed: +50
Physical Attack: +10
Health: 800/800
Hit-rate: 20%
MP: 15,400/15,400
Movement: +250
Comprehension: +10
Physical Defense: +200
Magical Defense: +300
Dodge-Rate: 20%
Magic Attack: +380
Luck: +1

Skills:
Skill Name: Song of Refreshing Rain
Description: A song that Titania can sing. When sung, this song
will constantly replenish +10 HP of all party members for as
long as it is being sung.
Current lvl: 5 MAXED
Ability: Indefinitely heals +30 HP every one second for as long
as Titania is singing.
MP Cost: 50 MP per second
Cooldown time: 0 seconds

Skill Name: Song of Vigor
Description: A song that Titania sings to increase the strength of
her companions. When sung, this song will increase the Physical

Attack and Magic Attack of every companion.
Current lvl: 5 MAXED
Ability: Raise the Strength of all allies 300%.
MP Cost: 50 per second
Cooldown Time: 0 seconds

Skill Name: Song of Valor
Description: A song that Titania sings to increase the defensive abilities of allies. Defense and Magical Defense doubles for as long as this song is being sung.
Current lvl: 5 MAXED
Ability: Doubles Defense and Magical Defense stat of all Titania's party members by 300%
MP Cost: 50 per second
Cooldown Time: 0 seconds

Skill Name: Scan
Description: Titania can scan any enemy regardless of level and send that information to all members of her party.
Current lvl: MAXED
Ability: Reveals an enemy's stats. Can only be used on one enemy at a time.
MP Cost: 100
Cooldown Time: 0 seconds

"You maxed out all your songs," Adam said.

"Of course," Titania muttered as she fluttered her wings and landed on his shoulder. "I maxed out [Song of Vigor] first since that is the skill you prefer I use. It's also one of the biggest reasons you've been able to defeat opponents you have no right beating." She eyed him like he was some kind of monster. "Of course, that ridiculous ability to dodge enemies and your broken skills are two more reasons."

Adam shrugged and decided not to let himself be bothered by her accusing tone or gaze. Instead, he looked at the new items he had acquired. There were three of them.

Item Pouch:
Item Name: Golem Gauntlets
Item Type: Armor
Grade: 2-star
Use requirements: Can be equipped by any combat class level 20 and above.
Description: These gauntlets are made from the remains of a knight golem. They have been imbued with incredible magic powers that raise defense, constitution, resistance to physical damage, and the elements.
Abilities: Defense+200; Constitution+250; -10 speed; 20% resistance to slashing damage; 30% resistance to fire, earth, wind, and darkness damage.

Item Name: Golem's Sacred Stone
Item Type: Enhancement
Grade: 2-star
Use requirements: Must have magic staff with crystal slots.
Description: This is the magic stone used to power the knight golem. It can be added to staffs for the Priest and Mage classes to increase Intelligence, MP, and Magic Attack Power.
Abilities: Intelligence+150; MP+500; Magic Attack Power+250; -10 Speed

Item Name: Golem Spear
Item Type: Spear
Grade: 2-star
Use requirements: Can be equipped by any spear-wielding combat classes above level 20.
Description: This golem spear was born from the dying magic of

the knight golem. It has incredibly destructive powers, but it is also very heavy.
trength+200; Physical Attack+500; Piercing Damage+10; Speed-10

Adam sighed when he saw that none of the new items he received were what he would have called useful. The two items he would be interested in equipping required a level of at least 20. He was currently at level 12, meaning they weren't useful to him now. What's more, both of them decreased his Speed by -10. Even if he *could* equip them, doing so would put his Speed at -14. He didn't know what that would do. Was it even possible to have a negative stat?

Since all of the equipment he got was useless, Adam turned toward the large double doors and walked over to it. As if the doors could sense his arrival, or perhaps sense the defeat of the two [knight golems], they opened with a dull creak all on its own.

LEGENDARY HIDDEN
CLASS!

" Giant moving statues, doors that open on their own, evil spider women... whoever made this game really went all out," Adam said as he walked past the door.

Kureha yipped at him like she didn't understand and Titania tossed him one of those looks, the kind that said she wanted to say something but wasn't sure it was worth the effort, from where she sat on his shoulder.

Adam ignored their looks and observed his new surroundings.

On the other side of the door was not a corridor but a large room. Adam looked at the columns that were set up in a circle around a small garden. This garden featured a lot of grass that possessed an odd glow, like it contained magical power or was perhaps bioluminiscent, and was releasing softly glowing motes of light that danced through the air. A variety of colorful flowers also swayed like they had a life of their own. There were pink ones, blue ones, yellow and orange ones. It was no surprise to Adam that he did not recognize any of them.

He wasn't well-versed in plant biology.

Knowing what kind of flowers existed and their meanings wouldn't help him kill people, after all.

And even if it did, he wasn't sure any of these flowers existed in real life.

"Look, Adam! That's the [Panacea Flower]!" Titania pointed at the largest flower sitting in the very center of the garden.

It was bigger than all the others. It looked like an inverted bell. The bulb of the flower was about the size of his head, making it easily one of the biggest he'd ever seen. Only a few plants located deep within tropical rain forests like the ones found in Africa and South America ever became this large.

As he walked up to it, a gentle fragrance drifted into his nose, making him take a deep breath, causing his shoulders to unconsciously relax. It was like the scent of the flower had a calming effect on his mind. He hadn't felt this relaxed in a long time.

Adam walked up to the flower, careful not to ruin the other flowers, and stopped. He furrowed his brow and looked at Titania.

"Sooo, how do we remove this? Is it safe to just pluck it by the stem?"

Titania crossed her arms and likewise furrowed her brow. She slowly nodded after another moment.

"I believe it is safe to just pluck it. That storage pouch of yours should be capable of keeping it frozen in time."

Adam sighed in relief and reached out to pluck the [Panacea Flower], but just before he could touch it, a soft and withered voice, like the rustling bark of an ancient tree, came from behind him.

"Young wielder of the Spear, I have been waiting for your arrival."

Blood boiling, adrenaline pumping, Adam spun around and adopted a combat stance, dominant foot forward, spear pointed at a forty-five degree angle toward the ground. He narrowed his eyes and readied himself for combat, but he paused upon seeing who… or maybe the better word would be "what"… was standing behind him.

"What the… heck?"

Adam couldn't decide if the figure behind him was a person or an apparition. They were decked in full plate mail, a vile obsidian color with gleaming runes painted a startling crimson. The runes pulsed like veins being pumped full of ichor. They felt evil. A repulsive energy emitted from the chest plate, gauntlets, and greaves adorning this figure's body. The vicious helmet covering the person's head similarly held repulsive runes glowing the color of blood. Sickly yellow eyes flashed within the slitted black visor.

What really got Adam was not the person, however, but the fact that they were floating about a foot off the ground.

"What exactly are you? A ghost?" asked Adam.

"That is not a ghost," Titania corrected. "He's a soul remnant."

Adam made a face. "There's a difference?"

"Of course there is!"

A raspy chuckle like the soft growling of a rabid dog emitted from beneath the helmet. Perhaps it was because of the helmet, but this man's laugh had a metallic quality.

"The young fairy is correct," he said, then went on to explain himself. "Ghosts and apparitions are the souls of those who have departed their fleshly coil, but they cannot die because of their unfinished business. This undying regret keeps them alive and eventually turns them into foul creatures that attack the living."

"And that is different from you?" asked Adam. "Are you not here because you have lingering regrets?"

The dark knight shook his head. "I do not have any lingering regrets, but I do have a duty that I must fulfill. Also, I am not the soul of someone who died with lingering attachments to this world. I am merely a fragment of the original soul. I split this fragment of myself off before dying in the hopes that it would eventually meet the next wielder of the Spear. Ten thousand years have passed, several wielders have come and gone, and now I have finally met you."

"Ten thousand years…" Titania muttered as her eyes suddenly widened. "You are the original wielder of this spear! You're the one who split the continent into five!"

"Ah. So there are still some who remember my deeds," the knight said, though it didn't sound like he cared one way or the other.

"Hardly," Titania snorted. "I only know because I became the Guardian of the Spear. I doubt there are many who remember you. Even my Fairy Clan has long forgotten who you are. We only know of the vile man who challenged the goddesses and split the world."

"Challenged the goddesses?" The dark knight tilted his helmeted head. It was a curious gesture, like something an innocent boy would do when he was confused, but it looked... wrong coming from a man decked in repugnant black armor. "Is that what people believe happened? I see the people of this world truly have forgotten about what happened ten thousand years ago."

"And what happened ten thousand years ago?" asked Adam.

He glanced at Kureha by his side, but the little fox yokai didn't seem bothered by this man's presence. She was just looking at him curiously, like he was an oddity but not dangerous. Since animals often had a stronger danger sense than humans, he was inclined to believe this knight was not dangerous, despite his unsightly appearance.

"That is part of the reason I have remained here for so long," the knight said. "It is to explain the circumstances that gave rise to my birth, or rather, to explain the birth of that weapon you now clasp firmly in your hand."

As the knight paused, Titania crossed her arms and glared at the man like he was the most suspicious person she'd ever met. Well, Adam couldn't necessarily blame her. He *did* look awfully suspicious.

"I was born to a simple family," the knight began. "We lived on the outskirts of a small village. We were poor but happy. I had a wife and a child, and we worked on a small wine vineyard that had been in my family for many generations. One day... all that changed."

"Let me guess..." Adam crossed his own arms. "War came to your village?"

"Yes." The knight chuckled mirthlessly. "I am not surprised you understand where this is going. I smelled the blood on you the moment you entered through that door. You are correct. War came to my village, but it wasn't just my village. The entire world had become embroiled in war as conflicts happened all across the continent." He paused again and changed subjects. "Tell me, do you know how this world and its many races were created?"

Adam was startled by the sudden change, but Titania snorted and answered the man. "The world was created by the four goddesses. Gaia, Goddess of Earth, created the world. Aqua, Goddess of Water, created life. Stella, Goddess of the Sun, created the sun and light under which all life lives. She created justice and law. And finally, Luna, the Goddess of the Moon, created the night so the people of this world knew of rest and would learn to appreciate the light. She was also responsible for the leveling system that governs our world."

The knight nodded. "That is indeed what the people of this world are taught these days... but what if I told you everything you just said is a lie, a complete and utter fabrication? And what if I said holding that spear in your hands has made you the number one enemy of the goddesses?"

"I would say you have lost your hold on sanity," Titania said with scorn, her nose wrinkling as she turned to Adam. "The goddesses would never harm the wielder of the spear. This is their weapon!"

"Ha!" The man barked with laughter. "*Their* weapon? No, dear fairy. This spear was never theirs. The four goddesses were unable to destroy this weapon after I died, and because it was so powerful, they decided to use it for their own purposes. They would seal the weapon away until there was a need for it, and then they would have some unwitting buffoon come along, become its wielder, and send them off on an impossible quest. They might use this spear and its wielders, but it is not theirs and it never has been."

"What a load of garbage. I've never heard anyone who can spew so much shit." Titania's scowl was fierce to behold and would have looked terrifying... had she not been barely a foot tall. "We need not listen to this fool, Adam. Let us grab the [Panacea Flower] and be off."

The dark knight shrugged. "You can leave if you wish, but you should know that once the goddesses learn you possess the Spear, you will both be hunted to the ends of the earth by the goddesses and those under their control. Don't you at least want to know why they will hunt you?"

While Titania looked ready to bolt, Adam was not so ready to just leave. Perhaps it was because he was a player, but he did not have the same feelings that Titania had toward the goddesses or this man. He didn't think there was anything wrong with hearing what he had to say.

"Let's stay a moment," Adam said. "Even if what he says is a complete lie, there is nothing wrong with hearing him out."

"Hmph!" Titania floated off his shoulder and fluttered away. "You can listen if you want, but I'll not hear one word of the drivel that spews from this man's mouth."

Adam watched as the small fairy fluttered over to the garden and sat down amongst the leaves. It looked like she was taking comfort among the plants. He turned back to the dark knight.

"So… what's your story?" Adam tapped his spear against the ground. "Will the goddesses really try to kill me?"

"Thank you for giving me a chance to explain. I will get to the part about how and why they will attempt to kill you in a moment," the dark knight said before continuing his tale. "When the world became embroiled in war, it was not a war against the forces of darkness. It was a war amongst the goddesses themselves. The goddesses of the earth, sun, moon, and water challenged the Goddess of Creation. It was, in fact, the Goddess of Creation who created this world and all who exist within it. The other goddesses were but her younger sisters. They ruled over specific laws created by the Goddess of Creation. However, jealous of their eldest sister's power and the love she inspired in her people, the four goddesses took control of her creations, poisoned their minds, and set them loose upon each other."

This was something Adam had not heard yet. He tried to imagine siblings fighting against each other out of jealousy. It was surprisingly easy, but he had an example of a terrible sibling already. Lexi had always complained to him about how awful Levon was, how he always treated her like she was a second-class citizen, and how he was constantly expressing his hatred toward her whenever she won their spars.

She won all of their spars, so he pretty much hated on her all the time.

"The Goddess of Creation, upon learning of the wars that were happening across the world, came down and tried to stop her creations from fighting. But the minds of her people had already been thoroughly poisoned. They could not recognize their goddess anymore. She spent all her energy and power to try and dispel the corruption invading their souls, but she exhausted herself in doing so, and her four younger sisters chose that moment to strike. They sealed her away, never to see the light of day again."

Adam listened to this story, but however fascinating he found it, there was something he just didn't understand. "What does this story have to do with you? And why will the goddesses come after me? Didn't you say they were using this spear for their own purposes?"

"This part of the story has nothing to do with me, but it is necessary for you to understand what I have just told you, so that you will understand my part in all this." Adam could not see the man's face, but he thought he sensed a wry smile hiding behind that dark helmet. "You see, just before the Goddess of Creation was sealed away, she used the last remainder of her power to forge a spear and a set of armor."

"Ah." Adam breathed out. He looked down at the spear in his hand, then back at the soul remnant floating before him. "It was this spear, the same spear you wielded ten thousand years ago when you split the continent into five."

"Correct," the knight said, his armored joints clicking together with a grating sound of steel on steel. "At the time, I had been lost and destitute. My wife and child had been killed by the war, which raged on even after the Goddess of Creation was sealed. In my anguish, I attempted to end my own life, and that is when I came across the spear... or perhaps I should say when the spear came across me."

Once more, the knight paused as if reminiscing about the past. Adam didn't interrupt him. Finally, a breathy sigh escaped from that visored helm.

"When the spear appeared before me, I was tempted to ignore it and simply commit suicide so I could reunite with my wife and child, but something stopped me. Perhaps it was the final will of the Goddess of Creation, perhaps it was my own rage at the unfairness of this world. Whatever it was, I took the spear in hand, donned the armor, and when I did, I became filled not only with power, but with all the sorrow, rage, and resentment the Goddess of Creation felt when her four sisters betrayed her. It mixed with my own sorrow, rage, and resentment, and it made me understand what happened, made me focused and gave me a purpose. After that, I waged a one-man war against the four goddesses. The result of that war was my defeat and the continent being split into five."

Adam felt like he could somewhat understand how this man felt. Thinking about it, this man's past somewhat mirrored his own. His life had not been simple even from the beginning. He had lived on the streets, but he met a girl who loved him and whom he loved in return, but then her jealous brother and uncaring family had taken all of that from Adam. It was, in many ways, Levon's fault that Adam had ended up in the hands of Lucifer and Lexi had disappeared.

"I see. That is certainly a very interesting story if true," Adam allowed. "But that doesn't explain why they would come after me. Didn't you say they have been making use of this spear by letting other people find it?"

"It is because you are not the goddesses' chosen wielder," the knight explained. "The goddesses always choose who wields the spear. I can tell you are not someone chosen by the goddesses because the spear has taken its own initiative to choose you as its master. That would not happen if they chose you because, to the spear, the goddesses are its enemies. From the moment that spear accepted you as its master, you were destined to battle against the four goddesses."

"Hmm…"

Adam honestly didn't care much about this particular in-game plot. He didn't want to fight the goddesses unless doing so would grant him more prestige and money. After all, the reason he was playing this game was to help Fayte win the bet she made with Levon.

"Well, perhaps you do not particularly care about what happened in the past," the knight said at last, as if he could sense Adam's disinterest. "I can also sense that the spear has lost all of its resentment, so I doubt the goddesses will be able to recognize it now. You also do not have the armor."

"Tell me more about this armor," Adam said.

"It is known as the Goddess of Creation Armor. It is a helmet, a chestplate, gauntlets, greaves, and leggings. This armor was likewise forged from the Goddess of Creation's resentment and grants an abnormal boost in power. Like the spear, I imagine the resentment festering in the armor is long gone. You should search for the armor. While it is unlikely the goddesses will find you right away, they will eventually realize their favorite toy has gone missing before they can choose its next wielder. I imagine they will begin looking for the spear once that happens. Having the Goddess of Creation's armor will give you a huge boost to all your stats. It might not be enough to defeat them, but it should help."

"I can't promise anything, but if I do find this armor and it turns out to be as amazing as you say, then I wouldn't mind wearing it," Adam said.

"Good. This remnant fragment will disappear soon, now that its purpose has been fulfilled. But before I disappear entirely, I would like to give you some help."

Adam raised an eyebrow. "Help how?"

"I see that your current class is Warrior," the knight said. "This is a beginner's class. All people who follow the path of battle and glory will start off with this class before eventually switching over to more advanced classes. You can wait until level 50 to receive a class upgrade, change your class with the aid of a trainer, or use a hidden class scroll and change your class. As you are the wielder of the Goddess of Creation's Spear, you are able to gain your own unique class right now. I can unlock that class for you."

"And what are the benefits of this unique class?" asked Adam.

"The benefits are many and myriad." The knight shrugged, shoulder joints clicking together. "Your stats will receive a significant boost every time you level up, you will have more skills available to you, and you will unlock extra skills more frequently."

"I see." Adam nodded. "I can see how useful that would be. In that case, please help me unlock this class."

"Very well. I am beginning now."

The knight raised his gauntlet-covered hands. Adam noticed they were covered in blood, but since this guy was just a soul fragment, it probably wasn't real. Maybe it was like the last remnant of what happened in his life before he died. As this thought passed through Adam's head, a small orb of light appeared between the knight's outstretched hands. It didn't remain there, but shot forward and entered Adam's body.

Adam did not feel anything at first, but as the seconds ticked by, his body felt like it was suddenly being engulfed in warmth, like energy was suffusing every corner of his body as it entered his pores and rushed through his veins. He closed his eyes and bit his lips as this warmth turned into a fiery heat. It still didn't hurt, but it gave him a strange kind of pleasure.

Ding!

[Congratulations! You have unlocked a hidden class. Hidden classes are located all throughout the world and can only be unlocked under certain circumstances like completing a difficult quest,

finding a hidden class scroll, or gaining the approval of someone who has already mastered a hidden class. Your current hidden class is more unique than most. It does not have a name, and so you can name it yourself. What name would you like to give this class?]

As the announcement screen appeared before him, Titania looked up from where she was sitting among the flowers and Kureha also glanced at Adam. He did not pay them more than a cursory glance.

A name, huh? What name would fit a unique class meant for a spearman? He frowned.

"Adam! Adam! I've got a huge surprise for you! I just began learning my family's spear techniques! Do you want me to teach you? It's called..."

"Seven Forms Spearman," Adam whispered.

Ding!

[Congratulations! Your new class has been named [Seven Forms Spearman]! Your old class of [Warrior] has now been replaced with [Seven Forms Spearman]. This new class has several extra skills. The [Seven Forms Spearman] is currently listed as Age of God's *strongest class. You are also the first person to achieve a new class. An international announcement will be made regarding your new class. Is that okay? Yes or no?]*

Adam pressed "yes."

Ding!

[We have an international announcement to make! As of 1:29pm Eastern Standard Time, the player known as Adam has acquired the first hidden class in the game. He will be rewarded +100,000 experience points, +10,000 reputation, +1,000 abilities points, and +100 status points. We hope that everyone else will work hard to acquire a hidden skill for themselves. We also hope that these rewards will motivate other players to try their hardest to win fame, fortune, and glory as they enjoy the wonders and mysteries of the Forgotten Realm.]

Ding!

[Because you listened to the knight's story, you have gained [Comprehension]! Your [Comprehension] is now at +1. [Comprehension] is a unique stat that makes it easier for you to acquire new skills and upgrade existing skills. This stat cannot be altered with status points. The only way to gain a higher [Comprehension] is to learn more skills and acquire more knowledge about the Forgotten Realm.]

Adam remained still as the announcements kept coming. He didn't speak, but these announcements were honestly annoying. He knew it was necessary, that this was a game and these were needed to inform him of certain important in-game aspects and accomplishments, but he thought it really killed immersion.

"Maybe I should complain to the creator?" Adam wondered out loud before dismissing the idea. Annoying as these announcements were, he didn't care enough to complain… and he was sure whoever created this game wouldn't listen to the complaints of a single player. Come to think of it, he didn't even know the creator's name. No one did, in fact.

He found that odd, but dismissed it.

"I have done what I was meant to do," the knight said. "Now it is time for me to depart."

"Yeah. See you."

"See you?" The knight once more tilted his head. "There is no 'see you.' You and I shall not meet again."

"It was a figure of speech," Adam muttered, though the knight did not hear him because he had already vanished into particles of light.

Since Adam was a little curious about his newly acquired hidden class, he opened his status screen and looked at the new class.

Class Name: Seven Forms Spearman
Description: A unique class that only the wielder of the Goddess of Creation's spear can have. Because this class has no name, it was named by the player, Adam.

Leveling System:
Strength+1 = +5 Physical Attack
Constitution+1 = +5 Health; +10 Physical Defense; +5 Magical Defense
Dexterity+1 = 10% Hit-Rate; 10% Dodge-Rate
Intelligence+1 = +4 MP; +5 Magical Attack
Speed+1 = +5 Movement

Skills:
Energy Sweep
Description: The wielder of the Seven Forms Spearman class infuses his MP into a sweeping attack that releases a powerful energy blade that extends past his natural range
Current lvl: 1

AP needed to reach next lvl: 2,000
Ability: Attacks every enemy within five yards of the user. Does
100% damage
MP Cost: 50
Cooldown Time: 15 seconds

Energy Thrust
Description: The wielder of the Seven Forms Spearman class in-
fuses his energy into a thrust that ignores all defenses and armor
Current lvl: 1
AP needed to reach next lvl: 2,000
Ability: Ignores enemy's defense and armor to deal 150% dam-
age
MP Cost: 50
Cooldown Time: 15 seconds

Adam rubbed his eyes several times to make sure he wasn't seeing things. He was shocked by how stupidly powerful this hidden class was. This was surely some kind of broken ability, wasn't it? There was no way a game developer would create such a stupidly powerful hidden class. In all the games he had played, there was never a class like this, which he believed would utterly demolish the in-game mechanics.

In his shock, Adam decided to check his stats next.

Name: Adam
Class: Seven Forms Spearman
Lvl: 12
SP: 100
AP: 10,700
Experience: 295,180/307,200
Reputation: 72,000
Strength: +325
Constitution: +150

Dexterity: +5
MP: +5
Speed: +5
Physical Attack: +1,695
Health: 1,100/1,100
Hit-Rate: 50%
MP: 120/120
Movement: +51
Comprehension: +1
Physical Defense: +1,500
Magical Defense: +750
Dodge-Rate: ???
Magic Attack: +5

After staring at his new class in astonishment for several seconds, Adam put every status point he had into Strength and watched as his Physical Attack went from +1,695 to +2,195. That number was stupid ridiculous. With this kind of Physical Attack stat, he wouldn't even need to use [Blood Sacrifice] to kill the players who were currently at level ten. Heck, he could one-shot himself right now!

He looked at his available ability points. 10,700. That was just barely enough to upgrade [Dance of the Sakura Blossoms], but he could also upgrade [Energy Thrust] and [Energy Sweep] if he wanted to. After thinking about it for a moment, Adam put +6,000 into [Energy Sweep] and +2,000 [Energy Thrust], bringing [Energy Sweep] up to level 3 and [Energy Thrust] to level 2. This left him with 2,700 ability points left.

Now that Adam had leveled up, he added enough status points to Kureha's Constitution to bring it up to +100 and added the remaining points to her Intelligence. Kureha's skills were already maxed out, so he couldn't use her ability points. He would save those and use them whenever she gained a new skill. Maybe he could max out whatever skill she gained immediately after she acquired it.

It looked like there was nothing more he could do in this place, so Adam grabbed the [Panacea Flower], stored it in his item pouch, and left the empty room with its myriad of colorful flora.

He needed to deliver this to the mayor of Watershore.

And he needed to log out. He had spent way too much time in the game.

A SHORT BREAK

Becuase Fayte felt like she had been playing *Age of Gods* a little too much, she decided to meet up with Susan today. She woke up early that morning and prepared breakfast, but Adam hadn't come out of his room to eat. She had checked on him. He was still playing the game when she left, which made her shake her head in both admiration and some resignation. It would have been nice if they could have eaten breakfast together. At around noon, Fayte left the apartment, hopped into her car, and traveled to New York City Town Square Mall.

Every nation had been ravaged by World War III. That was true of the American Federation as well. Originally known separately as Canada, Mexico, and the United States, the American Federation had formed out of necessity after the war. With nearly every country in the grips of poverty and having depleted their manpower during both the war and the wave of Mortems Disease, countries either banded together or perished.

Signs of the war were visible in all parts of the world, includ-
ing New York City. While most of the city remained intact, there
was plenty of visible damage. She passed one of those areas while
driving, and she could only turn away at the sight of destroyed
buildings that made her think of the skeletal remains of fantasy
monsters.

Currently the largest shopping center in New York City, the
mall was built up instead of out. Since New York was so crowded,
there was no room to build a mall that took up space, so this had
been done to conserve the already limited space the city possessed.

The mall was sixty floors high and had just about everything a
person could ever think of. There were places to eat, places to shop,
places to club, places to play games, hair salons, even dating services and travel agencies. When people talked about traveling out
for the evening in New York City, this was where they usually ended
up.

Of course, this mall had been built before World War III. It was
designed with the idea that hundreds of thousands of people would
travel there on the weekends and after work.

While New York City had not been hit by any nuclear missiles
because it lacked strategic value, it was one of the hardest hit cities
when Mortems Disease spread. An estimated 16.6 million people
had died within the first year Mortems Disease swept over the city,
literally killing more than half of New York City's population. Even
more died in the following years. With such a sharp decline in the
population, the New York City Town Square Mall was, while still

heavily populated, nowhere near as busy as the builders had expected.

After parking her car and paying the parking fee, Fayte waited just outside the mall for her friend. Dozens of people walked past her. All of them were bundled up similarly to her, but none of their clothes were quite so ugly nor did anyone else wear a veil. This resulted in many people looking at her as they walked by. She, however, didn't spare a single one of them so much as a glance.

She was only waiting for about five minutes before a limousine pulled up. It stopped in front of her and the door automatically opened. The inside looked quite spacious, but Fayte didn't get to see much of it before a tiny figure hopped out.

Susan Forebear looked just as adorable in real life as she did in the game world. She was very tiny, a slip of a woman sanding at about five foot five inches or so. This made her doe-like brown eyes and young face appear even more childish and innocent. At the moment, she was wearing simple jean pants, a name brand t-shirt, a red jacket, and soft brown boots with white fur lining the tops.

"Susan, it's good to see you outside of the game," Fayte said with a smile.

"Y-you too, Fayte. I'm glad to see you are doing well… er, relatively speaking, of course," Susan said, shyly averting her eyes to look at the ground.

Fayte's smile and gaze became gentle behind her veil as she stepped up and hugged the young girl. Susan had been Fayte's friend for a few years now, even before Levon declared his intent to marry her, and they had always gotten along well. The shy Susan would often find herself being dragged out to the mall for shopping by the more outgoing Fayte.

Fayte sometimes worried that she was taking advantage of her shy friend, but Susan always assured her that wasn't the case.

"Miss Susan, I will be sure to pick you up by at least five this evening," the driver of her limousine said. His name was Sebas. He was Susan's personal butler and someone that was trusted by Susan's father. "Be sure to make your way outside a little before then."

"I understand. Thank you, Sebas," Susan said.

The driver nodded to her, then again to Fayte, before he entered the limousine and drove off.

"Well, what should we do first?" asked Fayte as she and her friend walked into the mall.

"Er, why don't we check out that new store that opened up?" asked Susan.

"You mean the store opened by Auspicious Inc.?"

"Yes."

"Hmm… let's do that then. I'm curious to see if Euphemia Chrysos has come up with a new clothing line."

There were already a couple thousand people inside even though it was technically a weekday. The signing of the WWIII Armistice and the creation of the virtual world had changed the face of everyday life. Many people no longer had full-time jobs. They'd dedicate maybe half their time to a job in the real world, while the remainder of their time was spent in the virtual world. Since people could earn money in the virtual world, there was no need to waste all that time working. Some people had even fully dedicated themselves to the virtual world and were now making a living as mercenaries or as part of large guilds run by powerful families. Because of their newfound free time, it wasn't unusual for the mall to be just as crowded on the weekdays as it was the weekend.

A pair of young twenty-something-year-old men walked past them. They glanced appreciatively at Susan who, although not a knock-out, was simply too cute for words. Then they looked at her. Fayte almost snorted when the first one slammed his own foot into the back of his ankle and stumbled forward. He probably would have smacked face-first into the floor if his friend hadn't caught him.

"Even when you're covered in baggy clothes and a veil, you still attract attention," Susan mumbled.

"It's only because they never imagined someone would wear such a hideous outfit," Fayte said with a slight huff. "Now, come on. Let's check out that store."

The store in question was called Auspicious Imported. Auspicious Inc. was a British clothing company that had been opened by the Chrysos Family. As one of the largest clothing brands in the world, Auspicious Imported was located in the most bustling part of the mall, and the store interior, while not one of the largest present, was large enough that about five thousand people could enter at any given time.

Of course, brands like Auspicious Imported didn't rely on the number of customers for their income but the type of customer. While Auspicious Inc. did have several brands that catered specifically to the masses, everything located within this shop catered to the wealthy.

In other words, people like the Dairing and Forebear Families.

"Ugh. G-good afternoon." The beautiful lady who greeted them only slipped a little when she saw what Fayte was wearing. However, Fayte clearly noticed how her smile became fixed. "Please let me know if there is anything I can do to help you. Also, if you would like to check out Auspicious Inc's more *affordable* brands, this mall has our Austerity store on the first floor in the east wing."

"Thank you." Fayte ignored the subtle jab. "I believe we are fine for the moment, but we will be sure to call you if we need assistance."

"Oh. Great," the woman said like she wasn't sure what else to say. With a shake of her head, she walked off and went back to the other side of the store, though she occasionally glanced back at Fayte.

"All right. Time to dress you up," Fayte said as she turned to Susan.

"Huh?! Again?!" asked the startled Susan.

Though she couldn't see Fayte's mischievous smile, the young woman still shuddered at the glint in her friend's eyes.

Fashion was constantly changing with the times, and in this day and age of virtual reality, Cyberpunk fashion had become a major player within the industry. As one of the top ranking and most fashionable brands in history, Auspicious Inc. was constantly keeping up to date on all fashion trends. Shirts with angel wing cutouts. Ombre-shirts with blood red dye that gradiated to black. Industrial pants with neon biohazard symbols imprinted on the hips. Fayte was particularly enamored with the avant-garde kimono jackets.

"F-Fayte… I don't think this looks very good on me…"

"What are you talking about? You look adorable."

"D-do you really think so? I don't know…"

"Of course I think so. Would I ever lie to you?"

"W-well… I guess not…"

"Haaaah. You are just too cute, Sue."

After searching the store for a little under five minutes, Fayte selected an article for Susan to wear. It was a crop hoodie with removable bonrage straps. It was black but possessed hot pink straps that crossed around the back. Fayte also chose a black shirt that showed off some of Susan's chest. The young woman's chest wasn't very big, so there wasn't much there to show, but it worked well with the hoodie. The shirt also revealed some of her flat stomach, which was nice and toned from her yoga classes. She finished off the outfit with small shorts and fluffy leg warmers with a similar hot pink color scheme.

"I don't think… Daddy will approve of this outfit," Susan muttered as she looked at herself.

"Maybe not, but I don't think he will say no either. We both know how much he dotes on you." Fayte studied the girl for a moment and nodded several times. "I was right. You look great in this."

Susan pouted, but that just made her look like an adorable chipmunk to Fayte.

Fayte also tried on several outfits. Even though she was unlikely to ever wear them in public, she still had an interest in fashion and wanted to see how she looked in them. The astonished look on the store clerk's face when she removed her veil and ugly jacket had also been priceless.

She briefly wondered if Adam would enjoy seeing her in these outfits, but she shook that thought off. Adam had Aris. While Fayte was confident in her own appearance, she knew her looks would not sway him away from such a cute lover—and she didn't think she wanted to break those two up. Ever. She saw from their interactions how much Adam loved Aris. Trying to interfere in their relationship was a sin she would never commit.

"Fayte, are you okay?" Susan asked.

"Huh?"

Startled, Fayte looked at Susan and realized she was still standing outside the changing room. She was wearing a cyborg loincloth with straps, a cleavage revealing black shirt with a diamond cutout in the center, and a pointed hood made of leather. The shirt stretched across her chest, which was large even though she wore a sports bra. The fishnet tights also covered her long legs, which ended in a pair of leather boots with a lot of buckles.

"I asked if you were okay?" Susan looked concerned as she peered into Fayte's eyes. "You started talking about something and then spaced out. You had… a really sad look on your face."

Realizing she'd been lost in thought, Fayte shook her head and smiled. "I'm fine. Thank you for being concerned."

"O-of course. We're friends, after all." Susan offered her a shy smile that she returned.

Because it was considered poor taste to window-shop at Auspicious Inc., Susan ended up buying the outfit Fayte had dressed her in. Fayte was certain she'd hide it in her closet and never let her parents find out, but then Susan would secretly wear it when no one else was home. Her friend's closet had several such outfits stuffed inside a hidden compartment.

After shopping, Susan and Fayte went down to the food court and got something to eat. They could have gone to an expensive restaurant like the Phoenix Roast, but neither of them was the type to appreciate extravagant food. It reminded them too much of the parties they were often forced to attend by their parents.

That was why they got simple hamburgers from Mack & Jack.

Because Fayte wore a veil and had no intention of removing it, eating was a little difficult. She moved the veil to one side so her mouth was visible and took small bites, then chewed thoughtfully after the veil fluttered around her face, and then repeated the process all over again. Several patrons sitting at other tables gave her weird looks, but those were nothing compared to the looks she received when she went without the veil.

"By the way, did you hear about what Adam did?" asked Susan, for once speaking very animatedly. "He just acquired *Age of God's* first hidden class! It was announced a little before I arrived at the mall."

"I did not hear about that." Fayte blinked. "I haven't gone onto *Age of Gods* today or looked at any of the forums. Wait. Were you playing?"

"J-just a little," Susan admitted sheepishly.

Fayte sighed and scratched the back of her head. "I should have guessed. You feel a lot more at ease in the virtual world than you do in the real one, huh?"

"Th-that isn't true," Susan muttered, though she looked away when Fayte continued to stare at her.

"It's okay," Fayte said softly. She reached out and patted her friend's hand. "I understand how you feel. I feel much more power-ful in the virtual world than I do in the real one."

Susan didn't respond at first, but then her eyes grew a bit dis-tant as she said, "It is a lot easier to live in the virtual world. I some-times wish... I could live there instead of here."

"Agreed."

As they were eating lunch, several nearby tables stopped talk-ing. Fayte frowned when she noticed this, but she didn't pay much attention... not until Susan released a soft squeak and looked at something behind her.

"Is that you, Fayte? You're dressed... differently," a voice said.

Fayte was glad she wore a veil. It meant no one could see the way she was gritting her teeth. The baggy clothing also hid the way her entire body had stiffened. It was only because her face was hid-den that she turned in her seat and looked at the young man standing before her.

Even Fayte would admit that Levon Pleonexia was an attrac-tive man. His tall stature and well-developed physique were the kind people could only enjoy if they had good breeding. It was the result of countless generations of beautiful people producing children with other beautiful people. His light brown eyes were dark and smoldering, carrying a sharp intellect. He wore a faint smirk, which appeared arrogant, but was something he wore quite well. Soft peach skin. Thin lips. A perfectly straight nose and a strong jawline. A titanium white mohawk that was styled just so.

Like the last time she had seen him, Levon wore a black suit with leather straps and a duster that traveled down just past his knees. It was obviously an expensive outfit. She could see the fine quality of the leather, the articulate designs stitched into each article. If she had to give the outfit a name, she would called it a cyberpunk business suit.

"Levon... we had an agreement," Fayte said, her tone flat.

Levon raised his hands in an "I surrender" gesture. "Don't be like that. I haven't forgotten our agreement. Until one of us wins the bet, we will not see each other. I honestly didn't know you would be here, so I was just a little shocked when I saw you and noticed your... unique choice in clothes. As you can see, I've been out shopping."

At this, Levon gestured to the woman standing between two men. The woman was beautiful, with dark skin, bright eyes, and long straight hair. In her hands was a small package with the logo to a well-known American clothier brand.

"I see." Fayte's voice was still flat. "Well, it looks to me like you still have some shopping to do. Please do not let me stop you."

Fayte did not narrow her eyes, or give any indication that she had seen it, but how could she not notice the simmer in Levon's gaze at her blunt dismissal? Of course, she also noticed the way the woman's nostrils flared in anger. The two men did not react, but they were just hired hands designed to look intimidating. That woman was the real danger.

"Very well. I apologize for disturbing your meal with your friend."

While Levon's voice was polite, there was an undercurrent of anger, but no one else would have noticed it. The polite smile on his face had not changed. He nodded once to her, then again to Susan. Then he turned around and left. Fayte waited until he was gone before turning back to Susan.

"I'm sorry, Fayte," Susan said in a morose voice. "I should have checked to make sure he wasn't here. I would have chosen another mall if I'd known."

"This isn't your fault, Su." Fayte reached out and placed her hand over her friend's hand. She squeezed it once reassuringly. "You can't keep track of someone's location all the time. That would exhaust you. What happened just now as merely an unfortunate accident."

She did not believe for one second that Levon was just "out shopping." He never went out shopping for himself since he had dozens of servants who could do it for him. He had probably found out she was here because someone had seen her shopping at Auspicious Imported, called him, and he did some shopping to make this whole incident seem coincidental. That was the only explanation that made sense.

Susan bit her lower lip before eventually nodding. Fayte couldn't stop the pained smile that appeared on her face. It made her glad for the veil. She knew her friend would take what happened personally, but she wished the girl would accept that no one was perfect.

They eventually finished their late lunch, spent some more time walking around the mall, and then went their separate ways.

***

"Oh, thank you! Thank you so much for delivering this to me! Now my son can be saved!"

"You're welcome, Mr. Mayor. Can you let go of my hand now?"

Adam couldn't stop a stiff smile from forming on his face as the mayor of Watershore profusely shook his hand and shed tears of joy. He didn't believe there was anything wrong with a man shedding tears, but there was just something disturbing about a man dripping water and snot all over the place. Worse still, this man had been shaking his hand for the last five minutes.

Titania wore something of a smirk as she watched this interaction, while Kureha sounded like she was yipping with laughter. He tossed them both a mild glare. This was not funny.

"Ah. My apologies, young hero." The mayor finally stopped shaking his hand and took a step back. At least he had the decency to look embarrassed. "I was so overcome with joy that I couldn't contain myself."

Adam sighed. "It's fine. Anyway, about that reward…"

"Yes, yes. Do not worry. I have your reward right here." After saying this, the man produced several items that were stashed in a small vault behind his desk. "These items are the reward. The first is a letter to the mayor of Solum. Solum is one of the five major cities found on the Sun Continent and the one closest to Watershore. This letter is to let the mayor know about what you did for me. If you show it to him, I am certain he will extend his trust to you. Who knows? He might even give you a quest of his own."

Adam accepted the letter and placed it within his pouch. He expected to hear the traditional "Ding!" that came whenever he got a new item or completed a quest, but it didn't come, much to his surprise.

"The next items are these." The mayor turned back to the vault, grabbed something, and presented them to Adam. "These boots are an artifact that has been passed down in my family for many generations. We do not know who made them, where they come from, or even why my family has them. The story passed down says they washed up on shore one day and became a good luck charm, but who knows if that is true."

The boots in question were remarkably well-crafted and beautiful for something that washed up on shore. They were made of leather, had laces going up the front, and straps near the top and bottom. Several metal fittings that protected the feet and shins gleamed in the light. Strange runes were etched into the surface. They looked oddly familiar...

As he stared at them, a status display appeared in his field of view.

Item Name: Goddess of Creation Greaves

Item Type: Armor
Use requirements: Can only be equipped by the wielder of the
Goddess of Creation's Spear.
Description: These greaves are made from an unknown mate-
rial. They were created by the Goddess of Creation and can only
be worn by the chosen wielder of her spear.
Abilities: Constitution+150%; Physical Defense+200%; Magical
Defense:+200%; Speed+200%
Special abilities: 60 seconds of Flight; Double Jump

Adam and even Titania seemed shocked to discover what kind
of boots these were. The Goddess of Creation Greaves? This was
part of the armor the soul remnant of the knight had spoken of!
Adam understood very well that if he wore these, it was like paint-
ing a target on his back for the goddesses. That said, it seemed only
the goddesses would recognize these boots, so he should be safe so
long as he didn't meet a goddess.

And those stats were way too tempting for him to pass up.

"Thank you very much."

Adam did not let the mayor of Watershore know how astonished he was as he accepted these greaves.

"You are welcome. The last reward is small, but please accept
these ten thousand gold coins as compensation for saving my son.
Once again, I am truly grateful for all you have done for me and my
family."

At that moment, the familiar "Ding!" that Adam had been expecting echoed around the room, though only he, Titania, and
Kureha seemed to hear it. The mayor reacted like nothing happened
even after the announcement screen appeared before them.

[Congratulations! You have completed the quest: [Cure Watershore Mayor's Son!] Rewards include [Goddess of Creation Greaves], [Letter of Recognition], and 10,000 gold coins! +150,000 experience points! +25,000 reputation points! +15,000 ability points!]

Ding!

[Congratulations! You have leveled up! You are now at level 13! +1,125 HP! +20 MP! +5 SP!]

Ding!

[Congratulations! Kureha has leveled up! She is now at level 12! +200 HP! +1,600 MP! +10 SP!]

Once the announcements ended, Adam equipped the [Goddess of Creation Greaves]. The boost he received after putting them on was quite phenomenal, though it was a purely defensive power instead of an offensive one.

If his stats hadn't been broken before, they most certainly were now. Not only did his Constitution, Physical and Magical Defense, and Speed receive an exponential increase, but he saw that his Physical Attack and Strength stats had also increased by +10. When he looked at his spear's stats, he noticed that it had reached level 8 without him knowing, meaning the spear's Strength and Physical Attack had gone up to +80.

Kureha's stats had also increased with her level up.

After completing the quest, Adam left the mayor's residence and traveled down the hill toward Watershore.

"Now that we've completed this quest, I think it's about time for me to log off," Adam said. "I've been playing for way too long and need to see some people in the real world."

"Hmph. Do whatever you want. It's not like you'll listen to me," Titania muttered.

Adam grimaced. "Are you still mad at me for listening to the soul remnant?"

"I'm not mad. Why would I be mad? I am merely concerned that you don't take anything I say into consideration. I am also beginning to wonder whether or not I should even bother giving you a warning when you're about to do something dangerous. It seems you do not really care for my opinion."

As Titania turned her head, Adam recalled how she had not spoken to him once since they left the Forest of Gloom. She had helped him escape and aided him with her songs, but she refused to say a single word. Every time he tried to converse with her, she would pretend she hadn't heard him. She hadn't even sat on his shoulder.

He knew she was mad. From what he understood, the four goddesses who ruled over this world were very important figures both religiously and from a political standpoint. They ruled over all, governed the four continents with fairness and grace, and were respected by everyone—including Titania herself. She did not like that he had listened to the spearman talk about how the goddesses only came to power because they were jealous of their older sister and decided to usurp her position.

"Fine then. I'll see you two later."

After giving Kureha a scratch behind the ears, Adam logged off of *Age of Gods*.

***

Kureha released a startled yip when Adam suddenly vanished. The little fox ran around for a moment as though expecting Adam to reappear. When it became clear that Adam was gone, she whimpered and laid on the ground.

Titania didn't blame Kureha. Even now, after seeing it several times, she still hadn't gotten used to how Adam could just vanish. She stared at the spot where her companion had been for several long seconds, then closed her eyes.

"Yip? Yip yip!"

Titania opened her eyes and looked at Kureha, who stared at her with a questioning gaze. Fox yokai were extremely perceptive and very smart. Even though Kureha did not yet possess a human form, she retained a human level of intelligence.

"I do not know where he goes when he 'logs off' either, I'm afraid. I just know that he returns to his original world." Titania floated down and pat Kureha on the head with her small hands. The tiny fox yipped once more as her two tails waved behind her. "You think I was being too harsh on him? Perhaps I was. It is not his fault that he doesn't understand why what that soul remnant said is dangerous. Maybe I will apologize to him when he returns and explain things properly."

Titania glanced at the spot where Adam had vanished once more and sighed. There was nothing for either of them to do now except wait.

***

The first thing Adam did after logging off was take a shower. It was 3:45pm, and even though he'd been doing nothing but lying in bed all day, he still felt gross.

After his shower, Adam wandered into the living room. Fayte wasn't present, but she had left a sandwich and some vegetables like carrots and celery in the fridge. He assumed she made this for him before going out.

He took the food with him into Aris' room. The gentle thrum of machinery echoed all around him. A soft buzzing from the vents blew cool air into the room, which was always kept at a temperature of sixty-two degrees. Everything in this room was completely sterilized. This place looked a lot like a laboratory or medical facility. In the center of it all was the large cryobed, within which Aris slept.

He always felt a chill whenever he entered this room. There was a part of him—an admittedly small part—that felt regret over putting his Aris into something created by that madman.

But if it could heal her... if she could really be cured, then he would put up with it.

"Hey, Aris. Sorry it took me so long to get off today." Adam sat down on the chair in front of Aris's cryobed, placed the plate on his lap, and immediately began talking. "I played *Age of Gods* a lot longer than I intended to, but some really interesting stuff happened. You remember how I told you about my new companion in *Age of Gods* last time? Well, I just got another one. She's a little fox yokai named Kureha. Do you remember when we used to watch those old Japanese cartoons? They sometimes had a fox that could shapeshift into a human. That's what she is. Titania told me she doesn't have a human form yet because her level is too low, but she'll apparently get one after reaching a certain level. Oh! I also got a hidden class! It's really powerful!"

Adam kept up a constant stream of upbeat chatter as he slowly consumed his late lunch. He tried not to think about how much he missed hearing Aris's voice, the warmth of her body, or the scent of her hair. The bed he slept on was incredibly lonely right now, but he believed he could bear it as long as Aris got better.

"That's quite the story," a voice said from the doorway as he finally finished telling Aris about how he'd faced off against the Spider Queen. "Just what the heck have you been doing in *Age of Gods* anyway?"

"Fayte." Adam smiled as he turned to face the young woman leaning against the door with her arms crossed. "Had a good time with your friend?"

"And how do you know I was with my friend?" asked Fayte as she walked into the room. She was wearing a simple pair of pajama bottoms and a button-up shirt. She was not wearing shoes or socks, so her small, beautiful, jade-like feet were about the only thing besides her forearms, neck, and face that was visible.

Fayte was a gorgeous woman with shimmering blonde hair and intelligence blue eyes. Her skin was soft, unblemished, and fair. As expected of an aristocrat who'd been born from several generations worth of selective breeding, she had beautiful features. Her small nose, pouty lips, and soft cheekbones were framed by several bangs that trailed down either side of her face. Adam absently found himself following the elegant curve of her neck before shifting his attention back to her eyes.

"Our fridge is full," Adam explained. "I figured if you were out and didn't need to pick up anything, you'd be with that friend you told me about."

"Susan," Fayte supplied as she pulled up a second chair and sat next to him. She looked at the girl still sleeping in the cryobed, then turned to him. "I see you're eating the lunch I made for you... though it's a little late for lunch."

Adam shrugged. "I only woke up a little over an hour ago."

"What time did you start playing?"

"About... two or three this morning."

"You've been playing for that long?" Fayte's eyes went wide. "Isn't that dangerous? I know entering the virtual world doesn't leave any long-term mental effects like a lot of people used to believe, but it's still not good to remain in bed all day. Your body needs nutrition, after all."

"Don't worry. You know my body has that regeneration ability, right?" When Fayte nodded, Adam continued. "Thanks to that power, my muscles are always at their peak physical condition. They will never atrophy from disuse. I can even survive long periods of time without food."

"So… what you are saying is that you'll always be…"

"A stud?"

Fayte's worried expression changed into an amused smile. "Yes, I suppose that word does fit you."

Adam shrugged. "I will be like this for the rest of my natural life."

"And how long is that?"

"Don't know. I'll probably live longer than most humans, but I'm not sure how much longer," he admitted.

"That's still very impressive. I wish I could remain eternally youthful."

"Don't we all?"

Because he didn't have to worry about his muscles atrophying from disuse, Adam could have gone back into the game after talking to Aris… but he decided not to when Fayte asked if he wanted to play some old-school video games with her. That night, he spent most of his time kicking Fayte's butt at multiplayer fighting games.

It was a lot of fun.

THE FIRST PLAYERS
TO REACH LEVEL 10

They were called [cockatrice], and they looked like a two-legged dragon or a serpentine creature with a rooster's head. Wings sprouted from their torso, but they weren't the kind of wings that Adam would have expected to see on a chicken. Covered in thick green leather, these pinions possessed a reptilian quality that went well with their dragon-esque body. Three taloned feet scraped against the ground as one of them snorted, fire shooting from the nostrils in its beak.

These [cockatrice] were all at level 15. There were sixteen of them.

They were also surrounding him and his party.

"Kureha!" Adam shouted. "Light 'em up!"

Kureha released a loud yip as her first tail pointed straight into the air, flames igniting from the tip and turning into a scorching ball of fire, an inferno that shot upward for several feet before exploding.

The explosion created a series of flaming bullets that fell from the sky like rain. This was her skill [Firestorm].

-3,876;-3,876; -3,876; -3,876; -3,876; -3,876; -3,876; -3,876; -3,876; -3,876; -3,876; -3,876; -3,876; -3,876; -3,876!

[Firestorm] was an AOE skill that attacked all enemies within a twenty yard radius of the user. That might not sound like the attack covered a very wide area, but when all of your enemies were bunched close together and surrounding you, it could be used to devastating effect.

The [cockatrice] were all struck, their bodies igniting, leathery skin turning a scorching black. Adam wrinkled his nose as the scent of burnt leather filled the atmosphere. While the game avoided blood and gore, it was still way too realistic. Fortunately, he was fairly used to the smell of burning flesh.

High in the sky above the battle, Titania was singing [Song of Vigor]. Thanks to her vigorous and upbeat song, Kureha's attack power increased from what would have been around -680 points of damage to over -3,876. Such a substantial rise was only possible because Titania's song increased their Physical and Magical Attack by 300%.

These [cockatrice] only had around +13,000 health, so the moment Kureha released her attack was the moment the battle had been decided. Adam finished them off with [Energy Sweep], swinging his spear in a full circle and unleashing a wave of energy that washed over these creatures.

-11,347; -11,347; -11,347; -11,347; -11,347; -11,347; -11,347; -11,347; -11,347; -11,347; -11,347; -11,347; -11,347; -11,347; -11,347; -11,347!

Even Adam became surprised when he saw the massive damage sign over all of the surrounding [cockatrice]. It was only after thinking about it that he realized this was natural. Even though he had not activated [Blood Sacrifice], his attack still did -2,225 damage naturally. Multiply that by the 170% increase his skill did and then multiply it further by 300% and this was what you got. Still…

"This feels like overkill," he muttered to no one in particular.

Ding!

[You have defeated sixteen [cockatrice]! Items dropped: x10 [Cockatrice Feathers] and 40,000 gold coins. +40,200 experience points!]

"Good girl," Adam said with a smile as he affectionately rubbed Kureha's head. The fox yokai really seemed to like having her head pet. She rubbed herself affectionately against his hand and released a strange mrrring noise, which he guessed was like a fox's version of purring.

Titania fluttered down on her ephemeral wings, arms crossed and a displeased look on her face. "You realize, of course, that Kureha was not the only one who aided you, yes? Without my songs, neither of your attacks would have done nearly enough damage to defeat these monsters so quickly."

"You are right," Adam said with a nod. "Does that mean you want me to pet your head too?"

"D-do not be daft! I am not some simpleton who enjoys having her head pet!" Titania snapped, cheeks lighting up like a bonfire at night. She turned her head and huffed. "However, you cannot just praise Kureha. A compliment or two would be nice. You should learn to show more appreciation toward me and everything I do for you."

"Mmm. You bring up a good point." Adam stood back up, much to Kureha's displeasure. He ignored the fox as she rubbed herself on his leg and smiled at Titania. "Thank you. Ever since you joined my party, fighting monsters has been much easier."

"You are very welcome," Titania said with a slight smile.

"I also rely on you a lot for your knowledge. Thank you for knowing so much."

"Ah. Well, you are welcome, of course. I'm glad I could be of help."

"And I'm really glad to have someone I can talk to. Thanks for being around to converse with me."

"I-I do not think you need to go that far."

"Also, I appreciate your beauty. Thanks for being such great eye candy."

"I don't know that means! But I know you are making fun of me!"

It had been two days since their journey into the Forest of Gloom. Adam had spent an entire day logged off *Age of Gods*. He believed he deserved a break after what he had been through. That day had been spent either sitting by Aris's side or playing console games with Fayte, which he had won more often than not.

After logging in the previous day, he had begun his journey with Kureha and Titania to Solum, which was the first major city he could travel to within the game. According to the map he had, the journey would take about a day on foot—of course, he didn't mean walking, but running. If he walked, it would probably take several days. A one day trip was only about five hours with his +50 Movement stat. He'd already calculated how fast he could travel, and it seemed like he could go thirty miles per hour if he ran at full speed.

Of course, that was on the off chance they didn't run into any trouble.

Which they did.

While it was rare for monsters to appear on the road, Adam made it a point to fight some on their journey. He needed to constantly grind his level so he'd have a leg up on all the other players when they arrived from the Village of Beginnings. So far, his level had increased to 13, Kureha was at level 12, and Titania was at level 14. He felt they were doing a pretty good job of leveling up, but now his ability to level up was progressing slowly because he required more than a million experience points to reach the next level.

"I feel like it's going to take forever to reach level 14." Adam sighed as he began running again. The wind whistled through his hair. While the world around him blurred because he was moving so fast, he didn't feel like he was exerting himself very much. His breathing remained even and steady as he breathed in through his nose and out through his mouth.

Titania was sitting on his shoulder, her small hands gripping his shirt as she swung her legs back and forth, and Kureha was riding on his head. He thought she could have run alongside him. Her Speed and Movement stats were better than his, but she chose not to, and he didn't really feel like there was a problem, which was why he let it be.

"Were you expecting it to be easy?" asked Titania, snorting. "Listen, it is extremely difficult to level up. It normally requires joining with a party and taking on high level quests or raiding dungeons to level up quickly. When I was leading the Fairy—erm, when I was with my friends before becoming the Guardian of the Spear, we would join up with a lot of human adventurers and act as their healers to gain experience and level up. Back then, we would raid dungeons and help defeat dungeon bosses. That was how I reached level 90."

"Level 90, huh? Reaching that level seems like a pipe dream to me," Adam muttered.

Titania shrugged as if to say, *"That's just how it goes."*

The *Age of Gods* world featured an extreme degree of realism. Not only were NPCs like Titania and Kureha fully capable of holding a conversation, but the environment felt more realistic than any game he had ever played. The gravel road beneath his feet was uneven and bumpy. He could smell the scent of grass, dirt, and trees. A soft breeze blew across the road, ruffling his hair and clothing, while the clicking of his metal Goddess of Creation Greaves echoed in his ear, mixing with the crunch of gravel under foot.

They didn't run into anymore enemies on their way to Solum. Adam had considered doing some more grinding, but it was clear that simply killing enemies wouldn't avail him anything. Titania had said it best. If he wanted to gain more levels, he needed to take on quests or raid dungeons.

On that note, he wondered if defeating the Spider Queen would count as beating a dungeon boss…

"Adam?" Titania suddenly called his name, sounding uncertain.

"Yes?"

"I wanted to… apologize."

"Hm?" Adam glanced at the woman sitting on his shoulder. "You mean for the other day?"

Titania slowly nodded, her face growing into a frown. "I was rude to you and said some things I am not proud of. But I also want you to understand why I was upset."

"Isn't it because you worship the Four Goddesses?" Adam asked.

"That is indeed part of the reason," Titania admitted. "But the bigger reason is because the ideas that soul remnant spoke of are dangerous. The Four Goddesses are the foundation of our society. Slander against them will not only make you reviled by everyone, but you will be branded a heretic, which will cause a lot of problems later on down the road. If anyone heard you speak of the Four Goddesses like that man did…"

"I understand." Adam nodded once. "I promise to never repeat what that man said or speak ill of the goddesses."

It wasn't like Adam had any problem with the Four Goddesses. Everything he had learned from that knightly soul remnant was just an interesting bit of in-game lore to him. Whether the Four Goddesses were truly benevolent maidens or secretly backstabbing bitches who would betray their own sister was not something he ultimately cared about. His only concern was whether he would have to fight them or not.

"That is good. Oh, look! I can see Solum," Titania said, pointing at something ahead of them.

Adam looked up to find that, indeed, a large city had come into view. The most prominent object in view were the city gates. It looked like a rampart surrounded most of, if not all of, the city. He could only see a few buildings peeking above the city gates, which stood at about thirty yards high and had crenelations at the top for archers and mages to fire down at enemies from safety.

This was his first time seeing crenelations in real life. While they had been used at some point before the creation of guns, missiles, and other forms of technological warfare, they had not been used in a very long time. There only remained a few historical sites in the European Federation with battlements and ramparts like this.

Several guards stood in front of the gates. There were a number of people coming in and going out. Most had carts being pulled by horses. All the caravans were having their goods checked, while the individuals walking in simply paid a fee. When he reached the gate, one of the guards held up a hand.

"Hold on a moment, son. We need to check your identification before you can pass through," said the middle-aged man in basic leather armor. It reminded him of the armor he'd seen in pictures of people from ancient Europe.

"Adam," Titania whispered into his ear. "Show him the [letter of recognition] you got from the Mayor of Watershore."

"Hm. Right."

Adam reached into his item pouch and pulled out the [letter of recognition], which he gave to the guard. The man flipped the letter over, saw the wax seal on the back, and handed it back to Adam.

"It seems you're an otherworlder," the man said. "Only an otherworlder would be given a [letter of recognition] from Watershore's Mayor."

"That's right. I'm surprised you know what an otherworlder is," Adam said curiously.

"Are you kidding?" The middle-aged man laughed. "Everyone knows about otherworlders, though I will admit this is my first time seeing one myself."

This must have been part of the in-game lore, or maybe NPCs were programmed to recognize players through some unknown means. Adam wondered how the coding for that worked.

"Anyway, since you're an otherworlder, you should probably head over to the training center. Judging by your equipment, your class should be Warrior right now. There are several trainers who can help you acquire new skills or even change your class—for a fee, of course. Keep walking straight and you'll find a large, cathedral-like building. That's the training center."

"Thank you," Adam said. "By the way, can you direct me to the mayor's residence? I was told by the Mayor of Watershore to deliver this letter to him."

Adam waved the letter in his hand for emphasis.

"Ah. After reaching the training center, take a left and keep going straight. You can't miss the Mayor's residence. It's the biggest building in the vicinity and surrounded by a gate. Show that letter to the guards near the front and tell them you were tasked with delivering it to the Mayor. They should let you in."

"Thank you," Adam said.

He began walking away, but just before he could get too far, one of the other guards began speaking to the one he'd just finished his conversation with.

"Hey, you don't think that thing on his shoulder was a fairy, do you?"

"Couldn't be. Too short."

Adam glanced at Titania out of the corner of his eye and almost snorted when he found the woman fuming. She had her arms crossed, cheeks puffed out like an angry squirrel, and her face was redder than a strawberry. He almost expected steam to start rising from her head.

"So this is Solum," Adam muttered as he glanced around. "It's very renaissance."

"What? Renaissance?" asked Titania.

"It's an era from my world. The renaissance era was a period my world's history known for its cultural, artistic, political, and economic regrowth from what many people call the dark age."

"Interesting."

The bustling city was filled with all kinds of people. An old lady was milling down the street. Some kids a few yards off looked like they were playing a game of tag. A young couple walked arm-in-arm like they were out on a date. There were people on horses, riding in carriages, and others who chose to walk. Not only were there a lot of people, but it was easy to tell someone's social status by the extravagance of their clothing and mode of transportation.

Adam sniffed the air as the scent of grilled meat wafted through it. He looked over and found a man kneeling behind a stand, grilling a giant boar on a rotisserie, fat dripping off the meat and into a tin bucket, which he scooped back up and used to baste the meat again. Even though he knew this was a game, his stomach still gurgled.

"Let's find the Mayor and deliver that letter," Adam said, shaking his head to dispel his hunger.

"Sniff… sniff sniff…"

"Titania?"

"Oh. Er… Yes, let us speak with the mayor," she said.

"Are you hungry?" asked Adam.

"What? N-no. Of course not. Why would I be—"

Titania's words were interrupted by a loud gurgling sound, which came from her stomach. Adam stared at Titania. She looked away. Her cheeks were glow in the dark red.

"Yip, yip!"

Titania wasn't the only one who was hungry. Kureha was drooling on his head.

Since it looked like all of them were hungry, Adam went up to the guy selling roasted meat and ordered a couple of meat skewers. It cost one gold coin per skewer, and he ended up buying three.

Since Titania was currently too small to hold a skewer, Adam placed a slice of meat on a toothpick and gave it to her. She didn't eat much, being so tiny and all. On the other hand, Kureha got a whole skewer to herself, though she couldn't hold it because her paws did not have opposable thumbs. He had to hold the skewer up to his head for her to chow down. Meanwhile, he ate two skewers himself.

Just like the guard had said, the mayor's house was large and far more intricate than the rest of the buildings near it. Surrounded by a gate was a mansion that resembled classical Roman architecture. It had a square, symmetrical appearance in which the proportions of the building was based on a module. The primary features were facades, columns, and a pilaster. Sitting atop the structure was a dome. Adam had once read that domes like this were an indispensable element of architecture during the Renaissance era in Europe. It seemed like this building was a strong mixture of various elements from historical time periods in the real world.

There were two guards at the gate. Adam was about to wander over and ask to see the mayor, but a soft ringing alerted him to someone on his friend's list calling.

"Fayte?" Adam asked after accepting the call.

"Adam. Me, Susan, and Lilith just reached level 10. We left the Village of Beginnings several hours ago. Currently, we're in a port town called Watershore," Fayte said, getting right to the point.

"That's great," Adam said. "Are you three the first to arrive?"

"No. Several players arrived ahead of us. They were all the top players for big guilds. I hear Levon Pleonexia was actually the third person to leave after Lin Akamine and the Spear God."

Adam bit his lip for a moment as he realized he'd finally run out of time. It looked like the other players would be arriving soon.

"In that case, the first things you should do is get a map and then talk to the mayor of Watershore. He should give you a quest to do. After you complete the quest, he will give you a [letter of recognition], which you can use to enter Solum."

"And Solum is…?"

"It's the first major city in a player's journey. That's where I am right now."

"Got it. We'll buy a map and talk to the mayor."

Adam finished his conversation, gave the curious Titania an apologetic smile, and scratched Kureha behind the ear as he walked up to the gate guards.

After giving the guards his envelope and stating that he'd been tasked with delivering it to the mayor, the guards opened the gate and escorted him inside. He was asked to wait in the entrance hall while one of the guards went with an old butler to speak with the mayor.

The entrance hall featured many Corinthian columns and a ribbed ceiling. The hallways leading out of the entrance hall featured high arches. He tapped his foot against the tiled floor, listening as the *clang, clang* of his steel tipped boots echoing through the large interior.

Adam did not need to wait long before the butler and guard reappeared with an older gentleman in tow. Gray hair. A dignified face lined with age. The man was dressed in an elegant doublet crafted from fine cotton, with a body of rich silver and a black cotton brocade. His pants and long-sleeved shirt were made of glimmering silk. Attached to a belt at his side was a basic but finely crafted fencing sword.

"I take it you are the otherworlder my butler informed me of? I did not expect to see an otherworlder so soon. Welcome to Solum. I am Bromley Paxton, the Mayor of Solum," the man introduced himself.

"Adam Lancer. I'm an otherworlder," Adam introduced. "This right here is Kureha." He pointed at the fox yokai on his head. "And this is Titania, a fairy." He pointed at Titania. "Also, please do not mention her height. She is very sensitive about it."

"I am not sensitive," Titania muttered bitterly. "I just do not like people commenting on my height. It is not my fault my level is so low. We fairies are always born above level 50, which means we often have the same height as a regular human. It is absolutely ridiculous that my level has fallen so low my height has decreased."

As the woman rambled about the terrible fate that had befallen her and her height, the mayor wiped some sweat from his forehead with a handkerchief. He seemed a bit nervous about being in the presence of a fairy.

"An otherworlder who has managed to gain a fairy companion," he breathed as though in awe. "You must be an extraordinary man. You may not know this, but we have not seen a fairy in this world for over five thousand years. They disappeared during a time of great strife. Some people believe they died off, but many think they simply grew tired of the constant fighting and chose to isolate themselves from the outside world."

Adam glanced at Titania after Bromley had finished speaking. She had been sealed about five thousand years ago after becoming the Guardian of the Spear. He wondered if her being sealed had something to do with the Fairy Clan's disappearance, but it didn't look like she would be telling him anytime soon.

"I have a letter from the Mayor of Watershore," Adam said.

He handed the envelope to Bromley, who undid the wax seal, removed the letter, and began reading. While he was busy reading, Adam took a quick look at his status.

Name: Bromley Paxton
Title: Mayor of Solum
Lvl: 30
Health: 12,000/12,000

His basic stats didn't tell Adam much. He could probably get more information if he asked Titania to use [scan], but he didn't think knowing this man's stats would matter. It was unlikely the mayor of a city would ever become his enemy. That would be impractical.

Bromley finished reading the letter and handed it back to Adam, who placed it inside of his storage pouch.

"It seems you did a great deed for the Mayor of Watershore," Bromley mused. "I can see why he would personally write a letter for you to deliver to me. He also says that you are quite capable and would be perfectly suited to quests I cannot ask my own soldiers to perform."

"I will certainly welcome any quests you have for me," Adam stated.

Bromley nodded as a pleased smile stretched across his old face. "Good. Very good. I do have a number of quests for you, if you feel up to the challenge. I will warn you, however, that all of them are quite hard. These are all quests I originally ordered my soldiers to complete, but every person I have sent off has not returned. I believe they have perished."

"What are the quests?" asked Adam, now curious.

"The first quest is to journey to the Deadlands and find out why the dead keep rising there," Bromley said. "I have sent over a hundred people to discover what is happening, but none of them have returned. There is apparently a strange type of fog that permeates the entire place and makes it impossible for anyone to see through it. This fog has also been rumored to steal your soul… but because no one has returned, none of us know if that is true or not."

Ding!

[You have been offered a new quest: [Journey to the Deadlands!] Do you accept? Yes or no?]

"Can you tell me a little more about the Deadlands?" asked Adam, ignoring the screen that appeared before him.

"The Deadlands is a large section of land that died thousands of years ago. Legends state it was the site of the last battle between the Demon Lord, the Lords of Chaos, the four goddesses, and their chosen hero… but no one knows whether that is true or not. What we do know is that it's a land controlled by the dead. While we cannot see beyond the fog, many undead monsters have been emerging from there for centuries. Most of them are weak, but sometimes a more powerful monster will emerge that wreaks havoc on the surrounding villages."

Adam crossed his arms and absorbed the information. It was all pretty standard stuff. Even someone like him, who had only played a few virtual reality games in the past, could recognize this type of quest.

"I have a few companions who are on their way to Solum. Do you think they can join me?" asked Adam.

"If you think they can help," Bromley said with a frown. "Though I will warn you that if their levels are not very high enough, they will only be a liability. The weakest undead monster to emerge from the Deadlands is the [wraith], and they are all at level 15."

A level 15 monster shouldn't be a problem for him, though he did wonder if weapons would have an effect on undead monsters like a [wraith]. There were some games where [wraiths] and other spirit type monsters could only be killed with magic. Well, even if that was the case, he could just rely on Kureha.

"I will definitely keep that in mind," Adam said as he pressed the "yes" button. "Okay. I'll accept this quest."

Ding!

[The quest: [Journey to the Deadlands!] has been accepted!]

"Good luck. If you manage to complete this quest, I will not only give you a suitable reward, but I will also give you a more challenging quest... should that be something you want," Bromley said.

After meeting with Bromley, Adam left the mayor's residence and decided to explore Solum. The city was a lively place. There were a lot of people traveling through it, though all of them appeared to be NPCs. No players had appeared in the city besides him yet.

Something that really hit Adam was how different all the NPCs looked. No two people looked the same. That might have sounded odd if he'd told someone who wasn't knowledgeable about virtual reality games, but an experienced player would understand.

A lot of VR games, to cut on the cost of producing the game, had a habit of reusing NPCs over and over again. It wasn't unusual to see several of the same models being reused hundreds of times. He'd once played a game where an entire village was made with just three models that simply changed hairstyles and skin tone to make them look like different people.

Yet as Adam looked at the NPCs in this game, he could not see one model being used more than once. Every person looked completely different. He didn't know if the creator had simply demanded his employees create countless NPCs, or if he used some kind of random NPC generator to build them, but it was rather astounding either way.

From what he could see, the city was built like a castle town from medieval Europe, but the architecture was closer to that of the

Renaissance period. Three-fourths of the city was walled off, while the remaining third was blocked off by a large river that ran past it. The river also featured several watermills, each of which seemed to have a different function.

On top of the watermills, Solum had several key features. The first was the arena. It was a multistory building located south of the mayor's residence in its own district. There was also the market district, the bazaar, the residential district where people could buy houses, and several large plots of empty land that seemed to serve no purpose.

Adam planned to ask the mayor about those plots of land later.

The cathedral was another place of interest since that was where players who died would appear after being revived. In order to revive there, he had to pay a total of one hundred gold coins and place his hand on a large stone tablet inside of the cathedral. The stone tablet glowed brightly and his name was added to it. This apparently meant he would be revived at this cathedral every time he died, and if he wanted to be revived somewhere else, he would have to do the same thing at another cathedral.

"That should do it," said a young nun. She smiled at him. "Now you will revive here every time you are killed. I feel like I should mention this, but just because you revive doesn't mean you should be reckless. You will lose a level and all of your experience points, ability points, and status points every time you die."

"Got it," Adam said.

"Also, if you die, your two companions will not get revived with you. They will be stuck wherever you died, which means it is highly possible they will die in the process. Should that happen, they will not revived. Only otherworlders have the ability to revive after death."

"Understood."

Adam felt a shiver crawl down his spine. He hadn't thought about that before, but it was a grim reminder that this game was different from other games. If an NPC died in this game, it was permanent.

Just after Adam finished making this cathedral his reincarnation point, he received a call from Fayte.

"Hey. I'm guessing you finished your quest for the mayor?" asked Adam.

"Yes. The Mayor asked us to kill a powerful monster that was in a forest close to the town. It was a level 20 1-star [chimera]. Honestly, Su and I would have died if it wasn't for Lilith's help. She managed to keep it distracted and pulled all its agro while we peppered it with magic and arrows from a distance."

"Sounds like Lilith has been earning her keep," Adam said.

"She has! Even though she's really quiet, I don't know what we would do without her."

"Since you received the [letter of recognition] from the mayor, does that mean you are heading to Solum?"

"Yes. We were told it will take at least a day of travel by foot though..."

"It should only cost five hundred gold coins to rent out horses. I think the lowest level horse has a Speed of +200. If you three rent horses, you should be able to make it within a couple of hours."

"Oh! That is a good idea. We'll do that then."

"In that case, give me a call when you've reached Solum. I'll come out to the front gate and greet you."

"Will do. You can also introduce us to your companions."

"Sounds good."

Adam canceled his call with Fayte. During this time, Titania had been quietly observing him with a perplexed frown on her face.

"I know you have told me this before, but are you sure this Fayte is not your lover?"

Not it was his turn to frown. "Of course not. Why would you ask me that?"

"Because the smile you wear whenever you are talking to her is something I would expect from a man speaking with his lover," Titania answered without shame. "You have a very gentle and tender smile. It's like just hearing her voice is enough to make you happy."

Adam glared at the woman, annoyance suddenly surging inside of him.

"You don't know what you're talking about," he said coldly. "I already have a lover, and it is not Fayte. Now let's stop talking about this."

Without waiting for the woman to respond, Adam turned around and decided to check out the bazaar. He was hoping there would be a place to sell all the items he had in his item pouch.

"There is no need to be defensive," Titania muttered as she fluttered her wings and chased after him.

MEETING IN-GAME

Fayte's call came about four hours after she informed him of their successful completion of the quest given to them by the Mayor of Watershore. Adam traveled to the gate, plain white mask still in place, and discovered that Fayte's party was not the only player party entering Solum. Numerous players were traveling inside—and many more were already inside. There were so many that the poor gate guards looked completely harried as they asked everyone to form a line so they could check to make sure each player had a [letter of recognition].

"It looks like you're good to go. Please enter. Welcome to Solum!"

"You guys have a [letter of recognition]. Very good! You are free to enter Solum."

"It seems you otherworlders don't have a [letter of recognition]. In that case, I am afraid you can't enter. Please go back to Watershore and speak with the mayor there."

While most of the players had a [letter of recognition], there were a few who did not, and these players were turned away at the gate. Some of them accepted this. A few looked unresigned but could only sigh and leave. However, there was at least one group that didn't look pleased and refused to accept it.

"Do you really think you can hold my Black Beard Alliance at the gate like this?! You fools! We are not some simpering weaklings who can be controlled by a group of NPCs! Make way!"

The man who had spoken was somewhere in his sixties, though he didn't have a spot of gray hair. His face was lined with a few wrinkles to denote his age. He also stood with a slight stoop. Even so, his black hair was long and thick, and he was sporting a full bush of hair on his face. His beard made Adam think of a really prickly shrub.

Adam didn't know who this man was or what kind of guild the Black Beard Alliance was, but his outfit resembled an old-school pirate costume. He guessed these people were pirate role players or something to that effect.

"Do not contest us guards, otherworlder," the gate guard who had spoken was the same one who'd talked to Adam when he first arrived. "If you try to force your way into the city, I can promise you won't like the results."

While some of the players present realized what was going to happen and backed away from the guards, the members of the Black Beard Alliance became belligerent.

"You think we're afraid of you?!"

"Don't make us laugh!"

"Bring it on!"

"I'll make mincemeat outta ya!"

Adam had no idea who these people were, but they were clearly stupid. Stupider than stupid. They were as dumb as a box of rocks. Did they not look at the guard's level? Every guard was at least level 40, and the man they were currently shouting at was a level 50 guard captain. While he couldn't see the levels of these players, he doubted any of them had a higher level than he did.

Which meant all of them were, at most, at level 10 or 11.

"I cannot see this ending well," Titania said with a frown.

"Me neither," Adam admitted.

"Yip, yip!" Kureha added her own two gold coins.

While their conversation was softly spoken, it seemed several people near them still heard their words. Several eyes turned to them. The moment they noticed the masked person standing beside them with a fairy on one shoulder and a two-tailed fox on his head, they freaked.

"Who is that?! How does he already have two pets?!"

"I don't know... but isn't that thing on his shoulder a fairy?"

"She definitely looks like a fairy. Oh, my gosh! Can you make a fairy your pet?!"

"She's very pretty. Too bad she's so tiny."

"Wait a moment! I've heard of this guy! Isn't that Adam?! He's the player who all those international announcements have been about!"

"For real?!"

"For real, man. We'd better not mess with this dude. I heard he killed the Rising Phoenix Alliance's guild master just for looking at him wrong."

The conversations cropping up around them didn't bother Adam, but Titania gained several throbbing veins on her forehead. She looked like she wanted to murder everyone present. Her face was also red with humiliation and shame.

"These people… think I'm a pet… and they called me short. Damn it."

"They don't know any better," Adam soothed. "Don't let it bother you."

She sent him a sharp glare. "How can I not let it bother me?"

Adam didn't say anything, partly because he couldn't think of anything constructive to say, but also because the argument between the guard captain and the Black Beard Alliance had reached a peak. He was looking forward to whatever happened next.

"That does it! We're forcing our way through!" the old man in charge shouted.

With a loud "arrrg!" that made them sound like cliched pirates, the group charged at the guard captain and the gate. The one in front wielded a cutlass. Adam wondered where he got it. The rest were just using normal swords.

None of them realized the danger they were in.

It happened in the blink of an eye. The guard captain drew his sword and swung it several times in a flash. It was so fast that even Adam needed to blink twice because he realized he had actually missed what happened.

-20,000; -20,000; -20,000; -20,000; -20,000; -20,000; -20,000; -20,000!

The large numbers that appeared above the Black Beard Alliance was enough to shock and frighten everyone in the crowd. Even Adam was a little surprised by the high damage number, but he also expected it. That level 50 wasn't just for show.

Right now there was not a single player who had more than +3,000 HP. Even Adam only had +2,225 HP. Never mind -20,000 damage. Even if the guard captain had only done -2,000 damage, he would have still insta-killed these idiots.

The members of the Black Beard Alliance dropped to the ground, their bodies unmoving. Adam had learned that player bodies would remain for an entire hour before dissolving and reappearing in whatever town or cathedral they were registered to. While he was sure this wouldn't normally bother anyone who played a lot of VR-MMOs, right now it served as a grim reminder of what happened to people who disobeyed the rules of the game.

The guard captain scoffed as he sheathed his sword and glared at everyone present. "Henceforth, the otherworlders who just died and anyone calling themselves a member of the Black Beard Alliance are banned from entering Solum, regardless of whether they have a [letter of recognition] or not. Let this be a reminder to anyone who wants to try entering Solum without a [letter of recognition]."

Ding!

[This is a national announcement. As of 9:30am Eastern Standard Time, Black Beard, Maverik Blade, Blood Red, Darth Vicious, Burning Fighting Fighter, Bold Flavor, Bloodletter, Howler, Captain

D, and That Scurvy Cur have been banned from entering Solum.
Anyone who associates with them will similarly be banned from en-
tering Solum. We hope everyone who plays Age of Gods *will follow*
the rules from now on.]

A nationwide announcement was only announced to players of
a specific nation, unlike the international announcements involving
Adam. This meant only people from the American Federation heard
this announcement, though he was sure word would soon spread
across the entire world. People loved to spread news in online forums and chat groups.

"Those announcements are very odd," Titania muttered. "Just
why do they keep happening?"

Adam did not know how to explain announcements to an NPC,
so he didn't say anything. He'd caught sight of several distinct individuals out of the corner of his eye as well. They forced his attention
away from Titania.

A group of three had appeared within the crowd, drawing the
attention of everyone present, men and women alike. Everybody
gave the group a second glance, if not because of the veiled beauty
standing in the middle, then because of the cute girl and the gorgeous masked woman by her side.

The veiled woman was wearing a mage's robe. It wasn't anything special, but the color was light blue and had silver lining the
hem, sleeves, and collar.

Her outfit wasn't what attracted everyone's attention though. It
was what she was hiding underneath that outfit. Her chest was so
large that it strained against the robes, practically bulging out of her

clothes. Adam guessed clothes in *Age of Gods* didn't come with built-in bras. On top of having a large chest, the woman possessed a wasp-thin waist and curvaceous hips, the kind that could turn any hot-blooded male into a vicious beast. And while she had a veil covering her face, nothing could be done to hide her stunning blue eyes.

Standing on the veiled woman's left was a girl in light armor: a leather jerkin, brown boots, white pants, and carrying a bow and quiver of arrows on her back.

She couldn't have been more than fifteen or sixteen years old. Seventeen at the most. At about two heads shorter than the veiled woman, the girl was rather petite, with a small body that was more adorable than beautiful. Adam was vaguely reminded of a cute, little mouse. He was sure there would be many men who'd love to act like a starving cat in front of her, but there would probably be just as many who desired to protect her from harm. She had that kind of harmless aura that brought out a virtuous person's protective instincts and a vicious person's merciless ones.

Last but not least was the woman on the right, who looked sinful even when compared to the buxom woman in the middle.

Decked out in all black clothes, with a mask covering the lower half of her face, the woman looked very much like an assassin. What little could be seen of her skin was pale but unblemished. Her eyes were dark and cold, causing the woman to give off an untouchable feeling, like she was a queen none could lay their hands on. She, like the veiled woman, had a rather impressive figure. Large breasts. A small waist. Wide hips. However, it wasn't as pronounced as her companion's. Even so, the sinful curves of her body were the kind that could undoubtedly send nations into ruin.

He was reminded of a Greek story about a woman whose beauty was so renowned that two men actually started a war over her.

Adam walked toward the group, who were also staring at the corpses of the Black Beard Alliance. No one else stood near them. Perhaps the men and women present felt a sense of shame or reverence toward this trio.

The women's attention shifted when he stepped in front of them. No one said anything for a moment, but then Adam finally spoke.

"I see you made it," he said.

"Adam?" Fayte stepped forward.

"It's me." Adam raised a hand in greeting.

Fayte placed a hand against her chest and heaved a deep breath as though to calm her racing heart. He wondered if perhaps she'd been worried he was someone else, but he discarded the thought when she focused on him. While he could not see her face, Adam knew her well enough to understand that she was smiling.

"It looks like we've finally met in the game world," she said.

"Seems so," he agreed.

"Allow me to introduce you to my two companions." She gestured toward the two on either side of her. "The one on my left is Susan. She's the person I kept telling you about. And this person here is Lilith. She's been a big help since she joined us."

"U-um… hello," Susan said in a very shy voice. "It's very nice to meeth—ack! I-I bit my tongue!"

Adam's lips trembled for a moment as he watched the girl press a hand to her mouth, tears in her eyes. He'd never met some-one who got so nervous they bit their tongue during their own intro-duction. A part of him was tempted to pat this girl on the head and gently reassure her.

"It's nice to meet you too, Susan," Adam said. Even he was surprised by the softness in his voice, but he couldn't deny that he didn't want to frighten her. This girl reminded him of a rabbit. She might die of a heart attack if he acted too forward. "I hope we can get along together."

Susan froze at his words, her eyes growing wide, but then she blushed and manage to give him a trembling smile. There were still tears in her eyes.

"M-me too," she said.

Lilith did not speak, but she did nod in his direction. To anyone else looking, Adam was certain they would just assume she was a quiet beauty who refused to talk, but he knew better. She was indeed quiet. However, the reason she wasn't talking to him was merely be-cause she didn't want to accidentally blow her cover.

"Since you've introduced your companions to me, I guess I should do the same." Adam gestured to Titania, who fluttered her wings and flew off his shoulder.

"My name is Titania," she introduced herself in an imperious fashion, hands on her hips, large chest thrust out. "It is a pleasure to meet you three."

"So you're the famous Titania I've heard so much about," Fayte murmured, her voice tinged with awe. "You're extraordinarily beautiful. Adam neglected to mention that."

Adam coughed and looked away. On the other hand, the compliment caused Titania no end of pleasure, causing her to preen like a peacock who'd just had their feathers primped as a wide smile appeared on her face. It almost made him snort. No matter how elegant this woman tried to act, it was clear that she also had a childish side.

"You were thinking something rude just now," Titania accused.

"Was not," Adam said out of reflex.

"And this is Kureha." Adam grabbed the fox yokai from his head and held her in his arms. Kureha merely shifted at her new elevation, lifting her head to gaze at the three women with her intelligence amber eyes. "She's a fox yokai I met when I was traveling through the Forest of Gloom. While Titania is a member of my party, Kureha is classified as my pet."

"She's so cute," Susan muttered.

Fayte also seemed to find herself enamored with the adorable little fox. If this was a cartoon, Adam was certain hearts would have appeared in the eyes of these women.

"May we pet her?" asked Fayte.

"That would be up to Kureha," Adam admitted.

The two girls looked at Kureha, who yipped once and nodded, which they both took as an affirmative. Fayte and Susan began petting the tiny fox yokai. Kureha seemed to enjoy the attention she was getting. Titania did not. She huffed and crossed her arms, jealous to see Adam's pet stealing her thunder. While two of the three women began petting the fox, Adam noticed one of them who was not.

"Did you also want to pet Kureha, Lilith?" asked Adam.

For once, Lilith's cold demeanor broke as her eyes widened. She glanced from him to the fox, then back to him.

"Oh, no. I… that wouldn't be proper," she said, the coldness in her voice thawing as she spoke to him.

"What wouldn't be proper? Go ahead. Kureha has given you her permission," Adam said.

Lilith hesitated for a moment longer before walking up to them and extending her hand. She drew her hand back several times as though afraid of something, but then Kureha licked her fingers once, and that seemed to break the woman's reluctance. She began petting Kureha in earnest. Both Fayte and Susan smiled. Only Adam noticed how the tips of Lilith's ears had turned red.

Lilith eventually realized the others were staring at her and quickly retracted her hand. However, the cold and aloof persona she had possessed until now was irrevocably shattered. She sent Adam a look of helplessness, like she was begging him to give her a hand, but all he could do was shrug.

Since they had finally met in the game, the group waited together in line. Adam stayed with them and spoke of what he'd discovered about Solum so far. Susan and Fayte listened attentively, but Lilith did not appear to be paying attention, though he knew otherwise. Titania also chimed in occasionally. This caused Fayte and Susan to look at her in awe several times. He assumed they were shocked that an NPC could have such a realistic personality.

They were eventually let inside of Solum. Adam did not need to show his letter again, but he did need to pay a tax for entering. It seemed players were only allowed free entrance on their first visit.

After entering Solum, Adam took them on a brief tour of the city, showing them the river with its watermills, the mayor's house, the arena, and also having them register the Solum Cathedral as their revival point. It took him nearly three hours to show them around the city. When they were finished, it was probably somewhere around noon.

"We'll have to log off soon," Fayte said. "It's about time for lunch."

"I'll make us lunch today," Adam told her, which caused some weird looks from Susan. Fayte shook her head back and forth as though to say "don't tell them anything." Seeing that, Adam decided to change topics. "However, I think we should form a party before logging off. I also believe it would be a good idea if we knew about each other's strengths and weaknesses."

"That's a good idea," Fayte agreed with a nod. "I'm already fairly familiar with Susan's and Lilith's abilities, but I don't know anything about yours, Kureha's, or Titania's. You also don't know anything about ours."

"It won't take long to form a party, but it will take a while to learn about everyone's levels and abilities," Titania added. "We should adjourn to the food court."

The food court was where Adam, Titania, and Kureha had been before traveling to the gate to meet Fayte, Susan, and Lilith. It was an expansive space, an outdoor courtyard filled with wooden benches and tables. There were several food vendors cooking all kinds of meals. Each one smelled delectable and caused the stomachs of everyone present to gurgle. While the players would still need to eat in real life, they decided there was no harm in getting something to eat in the game.

The food sold at the stall vendors were primarily grilled meat dishes, though there were also a few stalls that sold stew and baked bread. Adam had already eaten once during his time in the game, so he was not surprised by the bold and complex flavors of the food, but Fayte, Susan, and Lilith seemed startled when they realized their food not only had a flavorful scent but also tasted great. Food in the game not only had flavor, but Adam noticed it acted similarly to [health potions] and [mana potions]. What they healed depended on the type of food. Meat seemed to heal HP. Drinks restored MP.

Forming a party was a simple affair. Fayte disbanded her current party, then Adam followed Titania's instructions and invited Fayte, Susan, and Lilith to join his party. They accepted.

Ding!

[Congratulations! Changing_Fayte, Little_Su, and Lilith have now joined your party!]

"We should be able to see each other's levels now," Adam said.

"I can't deny I'm a little excited," Fayte said as she accessed his stat window. "I've wanted to see what your level looks like for a while now, especially after finding out you gained a hidden class."

"M-me too," Susan added.

"Hmph. Adam's level is certainly impressive, but you can't judge his strength based on levels and stats alone," Titania announced. "This man is a freak of nature."

"I rather resent that," Adam murmured. His response was fairly mild since he didn't mind being called a freak, but Lilith sent Titania a fierce glare like she'd been personally insulted.

While the expressions of Susan and Fayte slowly transformed from eager to gawking as they opened a status screen with his stats on display, Adam opened his status screen with a thought and accessed their stats one by one.

Since he had known her the longest, he accessed Lilith's level first.

Name: Lilith
Class: Assassin
Lvl: 11
SP: 0
AP: 20
Experience: 2,650/153,600
Strength: +50
Constitution: +10
Dexterity: +125
Intelligence: +5
Speed: +100
Physical Attack: +150
Health: 200/200
Hit-Rate: ???
MP: 65/65
Movement: +200
hysical Defense: +60
Magical Defense: +10

Dodge-Rate: 625%
Magic Attack: +25

Skills:
Skill Name: Hide
Description: A skill that allows Assassins to hide their presence
Current lvl: 5 MAXED
Ability: Makes Assassin invisible to everyone 10 levels above their own
Ability lasts indefinitely or until the assassin moves
MP Cost: 20
Cooldown time: 10 seconds

Skill Name: Throat Slit
Description: Coming up behind an enemy, the Assassin slits their opponent's throats
Current lvl: 5 MAXED
Ability: Causes 400% damage
Has a 25% chance of causing instant death
X4 critical damage dealt if enemy is unaware of your presence
MP Cost: 30
Cooldown time: 10 second

Skill Name: Slash
Description: A basic skill where the player swings his or her sword and attacks the enemy
Current lvl: 5 MAXED
Ability: Causes 150% damage to enemy if it hits
MP Cost: 1
Cooldown time: 0 seconds

Equipment:
Item Name: Plain Dagger
Item Type: Dagger
Grade: 1-star

Use requirements: Can only be equipped by Assassins
Description: A nondescript dagger
Abilities: Strength+25

Item Name: Assassin Cowl
Item Type: Armor
Grade: 2-star
Use requirements: Can only be equipped by Assassins level 10
and above
Description: A cowl worn by assassins who wish to remain
anonymous
Abilities: Defense+10; 5% chance of remaining unseen when
moving slowly

Item Name: Assassin Boots
Item Type: Armor
Grade: 2-star
Use requirements: Can only be equipped by Assassins level 10
and above
Description: Soft boots made from leather. They are designed to
increase stealth
Abilities: Defense+5; Speed+90; 10% chance of remaining un-
seen when moving slowly

Item Name: Assassin Pants
Item Type: Armor
Grade: 2-star
Use requirements: Can only be equipped by Assassins level 10
and above
Description: Black pants worn by Assassins. They increase de-
fense and stealth
Abilities: Defense+5; 20% chance of remaining unseen when
moving slowly

Item Name: Assassin Shirt

Item Type: Armor
Grade: 2-star
Use requirements: Can only be equipped by Assassins level 10
and above
Description: An Assassins long-sleeved shirt. Increases Defense
and stealth
Abilities: Defense+30; 25% chance of remaining unseen when
moving slowly

Like Adam expected, all of Lilith's stats and equipment were geared toward helping her increase her stealth and attack power. She had basically neglected Intelligence and Constitution. While this sounded illogical, the reason was because an Assassin's primary ability lay in their high attack power and stealth. If an Assassin was spotted and attacked, it meant they had already failed as an Assassin.

Next he checked Fayte's stats.

Name: Changing_Fayte
Class: Mage
Lvl: 11
SP: 0
AP: 200
Experience: 1,050/153,600
Strength: +5
Constitution: +25
Dexterity: +10
Intelligence: +30
Speed: +5
Physical Attack: +5
Health: 250/250
Hit-Rate: 10%
MP: 180/180

Movement: +5
Physical Defense: +46
Magical Defense: +90
Dodge-Rate: 10%
Magic Attack: +100

Skills:
Skill Name: Energy Bolt
Description: A mage aims their staff and calls the name [Energy Bolt] to release a bolt of magical energy at enemies.
Current lvl: 5 MAXED
Ability: Deals 200% non-elemental damage to enemies.
MP Cost: 20
Cooldown time: 2 seconds

Skill Name: Energy Blast
Description: An area of effect attack that targets multiple enemies and fires a beam that sweeps across the battlefield.
Current lvl: 5 MAXED
Ability: Causes 150% non-elemental damage to multiple targets
MP Cost: 25
Cooldown time: 5 second

Equipment:
Item Name: Magic Staff
Item Type: Weapon
Grade: 1-star
Use requirements: Can only be equipped by Mages
Description: A basic staff given to a beginner Mage
Abilities: Magic Attack+10

Item Name: Mage Robes
Item Type: Clothes
Grade: 1-star
Use requirements: Can only be equipped by Mages level 5 and

above
Description: A robe worn by the Mage class
Abilities: Defense+10; Magical Defense+10

Item Name: Hermes Boots
Item Type: Clothes
Grade: 2-star
Use requirements: Can be equipped by any class level 10 and above
Description: Boots made from the wool of a flying unicorn. They are kind of old
Abilities: Defense+10; Magical Defense+10 Speed+30

Skills: 60 seconds of flight.

Item Name: Peasant Pants
Item Type: Clothes
Grade: 1-star
Use requirements: Starter equipment. Can be equipped by anyone
Description: Pants worn by a peasant
Abilities: Defense+1

Item Name: Mage Shirt
Item Type: Clothes
Grade: 1-star
Use requirements: Can only be equipped by Mages level 5 and above
Description: A shirt worn by Mages. Provides basic defense against magic attacks
Abilities: Magical Defense+20

Like how Lilith chose to specialize in stealth and attack power, Fayte had chosen a specialization in magic, so all of her stats were geared primarily toward increasing her magic power. She did put a few status points into her Constitution to increase her health and defense, and there were some put into her Dexterity to increase her Hit-Rate and Dodge-Rate. But even those had been selected merely to help her survive. He wondered if Lilith had been giving her advice on how to allocate status points.

Finally, he looked at Susan's stats.

Name: Little_Su
Class: Archer
Lvl: 11
SP: 0
AP: 150
Experience: 560/153,600
Strength: +25
Constitution: +20
Dexterity: +20
Intelligence: +5
Speed: +5
Physical Attack: +70
Health: 280/280
Hit-Rate: 100%
MP: 55/55
Movement: +55
Luck: +1
fense: +90
Magical Defense: +20
Dodge-Rate: 80%
Magic Attack: +5

Skills:
Skill Name: Deadeye
Description: Archers can increase their hit-rate and critical hit-

rate by increasing their perceptions through the Deadeye skill.
Current lvl: 5 MAXED
Increases Hit-rate to 110%
Deals x2 critical damage
MP Cost: 5
Cooldown time: 5 seconds

Skill Name: Rain of Arrows
Description: Archers who learn this skill can fire a hailstorm of
arrows that deals damage to multiple enemies.
Current lvl: 5 MAXED
Ability: Causes 150% damage to all enemies within 15 yards of
targeted enemy
MP Cost: 5
Cooldown time: 10 second

Equipment:
Item Name: Beginner's Bow
Item Type: Bow
Grade: 1-star
Use requirements: Can only be equipped by Archers
Description: A bow given to beginner Archers
Abilities: Physical Attack+20

Item Name: Leather Jerkin
Item Type: Armor
Grade: 1-star
Use requirements: Can be equipped by any class above level 5
Description: A leather jerkin that offers minimal protection
Abilities: Physical Defense+20

Item Name: Ranger Boots
Item Type: Footwear
Use requirements: Can only be equipped by Archers level 10
and above

Description: These boots are worn by Rangers, people who wander the wilderness and protect others from monsters
Abilities: Physical Defense+20; Speed+25

CREATING A PLAN

A dam stared at the stats on his screen for a long, long, *long* time. He felt like his brain was unable to compute what he was seeing. That probably explained why the first thing out of his mouth was…

"These stats suck."

"Well, excuse me. Not everyone has your insane luck." Fayte rolled her eyes while Lilith trembled in place and Susan teared up a bit. "I'm not sure what you did to get such ridiculously high stats, but I can promise you that *our* stats are fairly normal. Most players of the same level only have slight variations depending on where they allocated their status points."

"I know." Adam sighed and ran a hand through his hair. He was sorely tempted to take this mask off since it was getting in the way. "I still think your stats are awful."

"I-I'm sorry," Susan apologized.

She looked down at the table in dejection, which made Adam wince as he realized he had done a pretty terrible job of explaining himself. He didn't think he was normally this bad at socializing. Then again, this was his first time he had spoken to people other than Aris, Fayte, and his small group of elite assassins.

Elite assassins didn't make the best conversationalists.

"No, don't worry. I know this isn't your fault," Adam assured her. "But I do think we need to figure out a way to raise your current stats. Titania, can you think of how to help them?"

Everyone turned their attention to the tiny fairy, who was not sitting at the table because she was too small. She was instead sitting on top of the table with her legs crossed as she slowly munched on a small piece of bread. Upon hearing the question, she swallowed what she was eating and looked at everyone present.

"There are several ways to raise your stats," she explained, coughing into her hand before continuing. "The first and most obvious way is to simply raise your level. Every time you level up, you gain status points, which you can allocate into your various stats for a permanent increase. However, you only get a limited amount of status points each time you level up, so this method is incredibly slow and something you need to work on over time."

"The other method is finding good equipment that can boost your stats, right?" Adam said.

Titania nodded at him. "That is certainly one method, yes. Powerful equipment can boost your stats. I know that right now, Adam is wearing several powerful pieces of equipment, which gives him an incredible boost to almost every stat, except Dexterity and Intelligence. Some equipment will boost your primary stats like Strength, Speed, Constitution, Dexterity, and Intelligence, but others might boost your secondary stats like Physical Attack, Health, Hit-Rate, Magic Points, Movement, and so on. The most powerful pieces of equipment are usually the ones that boost your primary stats since those also affect your secondary stats."

Fayte shifted in her seat. Adam wished he could see beyond her veil to know what kind of expression she was making. Taking a deep breath, she placed a hand on the table and began tapping her finger against it. The steady *thump, thump* echoed around them briefly as the woman considered Titania's words.

"I understand what you are saying, but finding good equipment isn't that easy. We've only been able to find the equipment we have now thanks to the quests we took in the Village of Beginnings, and none of it is what I would call great."

"You three are actually in luck," Adam admitted. "While I don't have equipment for everyone, I did stumble upon some equipment for the Mage class during my time in the Village of Beginnings."

After saying this, Adam removed the [Staff of Darkness] and [Cloak of Despair] from his item pouch. He handed both items to Fayte, who looked shocked to receive something from him so soon after their first in-game meeting. She became even more surprised after she checked out the stats on both items.

"This... this equipment has the highest star rating I've seen!" she shouted in surprise.

"You remember that [Necromancer] I told you about?" Adam gestured toward the equipment. "When I defeated it, this is what it dropped." He shrugged. "I'm not a Mage, and while I could have sold it, I kept it in case it turned out to be better than what you currently have equipped."

"Thank you," Fayte murmured before pressing the equipment to herself.

There was a brief flash of light before the equipment appeared on her. The cloak was a pure black item that emanated a dark aura. Adam would even go so far as to say it felt evil, but this equipment was still better than anything else she possessed. Similarly, the [Staff of Darkness] was another evil item, but again, it granted her numerous boosts to some of her stats and even gave her a skill to raise the dead.

"It looks like my stats, particularly my Intelligence and Magic Attack, have all received a huge increase," Fayte announced.

"That's not the only benefit to wearing equipment like this," Titania added. "While your primary stats are being boosted by that equipment, you will gain more benefits every time you level up. The next time your level increases, you should receive a lot more magic points than you normally would since your Intelligence stat is much higher"

"I guess having good equipment is definitely a must," Fayte sighed.

"B-but how can we find good equipment?" asked Susan.

"I'm sure there are item shops, weapon shops, and blacksmiths here in Solum that sell better equipment than what you currently have, but I don't think they will grant you a huge boost to your primary stats, which is what we want," Adam said.

Titania agreed with him. "The best way to find excellent equipment is to either take on a quest, explore new locations, or go dungeon crawling." She paused. "Of course, there is another method of increasing your stats that I haven't mentioned yet."

"What method?" asked Fayte.

Everyone else was focused intently on the little fairy as she stood there with her hands on her hips. She didn't seem bothered by how everyone else towered over her.

"You're talking about hidden classes, right?" asked Adam.

Titania nodded. "That's right. Hidden classes are the greatest way to permanently increase your stats. A hidden class is better than any class you can gain naturally. Of course, you could go to a trainer and change your current class to something better, or wait until you reach level 50 and upgrade your class, but doing either of those tings won't be as good as getting a hidden class, which will always and without fail provide a massive boost to all your stats."

While there was no disputing her words, what Titania failed to mention was how difficult it was to find a hidden class. There was a reason they had the word "hidden" in their name. Adam was lucky to have discovered his hidden class by sheer coincidence. How many other people could be as lucky as him?

"Let's shelve the idea of hidden classes for now," Adam said. "It sounds like dungeon raids are the best way to get equipment, but the only dungeon we know of is located in the Forest of Gloom, and we're not strong enough to defeat the [Spider Queen] right now, so that's out." Adam crossed his arms. "I also don't think our levels are high enough to explore too many areas at the moment. However, I did receive a quest from the Mayor of Solum, asking me to explore a place called the Deadlands and find out why the dead are rising in that area."

"And you think this is what we should do right now?" asked Fayte.

"Yes." As Adam gave her a nod, Kureha pranced over to his plate, which still had some leftover kabobs. The little fox didn't hesitate to eat the remainder of his food. He reached over and plucked the tiny thing from the table before setting her on his head. "I think that would be our best bet for gathering new equipment."

"A quest like this will always provide better equipment than simply wandering aimlessly. Of course, finding good equipment is a matter of luck more often than not." Titania paused before adding. "Fortunately, we have a girl who has the [Luck] stat, so we should be able to receive some decent item drops. [Luck] plays a key role in the items dropped by monsters."

Everyone quickly agreed to the proposal of completing the quest Adam had received from the Mayor of Solum, but that was for their next session. They had already spent several hours within the game. It was time for everyone to log off.

"Oh! I'd like to speak with you before you log off, Lilith," Adam said.

While Fayte and Susan gave him an odd look, Lilith only nodded at him and remained behind. After the two other women logged off, the beauty in black immediately knelt before him in deference like a knight kneeling before their liege.

"Master, do you have a task for me?"

Adam scratched his cheek… until he realized his mask was in the way. He briefly considered taking it off before deciding against it. There weren't many people present, no one that he knew at least, but it was better to be safe than sorry.

"Sit down, please. I wanted to ask what your impressions are of Fayte and Susan."

Adam gestured to the table, an obvious invitation. Lilith hesitated for a moment before, with the grace only an assassin could possess, she stood up from her kneeling position and sat down beside him.

"Excuse me," she muttered in a soft voice. After straightening her back, she stared at Adam with her seemingly cold eyes and answered in an icy voice. "From my observations, Fayte is a very determined and intelligent woman. It's rare for someone who is only nineteen-years-old to have such a strong will." She hesitated again, but Adam gestured for her to continue. "She reminds me of you in that regard. It left a very good impression on me."

That coincided with what Adam thought of the woman as well. It was good to know his impression of Fayte was accurate. He hadn't been worried, per se, but he understood that Fayte could have been putting on an act for him. However, he didn't think she'd put on an act around Susan since they were friends.

"Susan is… very meek," Lilith said at last. She hesitated like she was choosing her words with care. "I don't have a very strong impression of her, but she seems like the kind of person who can't tell others 'no' and will do something she dislikes just to make the people close to her happy."

Because he didn't know Susan very well and couldn't judge her from their first meeting, he needed to know Lilith's opinion. What she said was pretty close to what Fayte had once told him. A young woman who couldn't say "no" to others. Of course, Fayte had also added that Susan was highly intelligent and an amazing hacker to boot.

While he was speaking to Lilith, Titania and Kureha watched the conversation in silence. Neither of them seemed to really understand why he was asking Lilith about their other two companions. Furthermore, Titania seemed greatly confused as to why Lilith was referring to him as "Master." She even mouthed the word several times, her expression odd, like she'd been given a puzzle she couldn't solve.

"Thank you for letting me know your thoughts," Adam said. "I feel reassured now. Get some rest. I plan on having us go on this quest later in the afternoon."

"Yes, Master," Lilith said before logging off.

"Adam," Titania said in a soft voice before he could log off. "Why was that girl calling you 'Master'?"

"It's a complicated story," Adam said. "And not one I'm comfortable sharing right now. Maybe I'll tell you later once we know each other a bit better."

Titania did not look at all pleased that he was not willing to tell her about his relationship with Lilith, but she didn't have any choice other than to accept it. If she was willing to force the issue, then wouldn't that mean she would also have to expose her own secrets?

Everyone had something they weren't willing to share with others. Everyone had some skeletons hidden in their closet.

Lilith was probably his greatest skeleton.

After setting Kureha onto the ground, Adam logged off and made his way into the living room. Fayte had already gotten started on making lunch. Adam glanced at the clock. It was 1:36pm, a little past noon. Since he didn't want Fayte doing all the work herself, he joined her in the kitchen and set about making drinks and slicing up some fruits for them to eat along with the sandwiches his roommate was making. They ate together. Then Adam spent an hour sitting beside Aris before heading back into the game.

He reappeared in the food court. Titania and Kureha were in pretty much the same place he left them. Titania had moved across the table and was sitting with her legs dangling over the edge, while Kureha was sleeping. There were two men next to her.

"Hey there. You're a fairy, right? Why don't you join our party?"

"You're cute. I'd love it if you teamed up with us. I promise we'll treat you well."

The men did not appear to mean any harm, but it did seem like they had been bothering Titania for some time. She had a large vein throbbing on her forehead.

"Titania," he called out as he walked over.

"Ah. Adam. I'm glad you finally made it back." Titania stood up and dusted herself off. "I hope your time back in your world was pleasant?"

"It was. Thanks."

His casual conversation with Titania was enough to make the two men back off. They clicked their tongues and left.

"I'm glad you came when you did. Had you arrived even a second later, I might have said something I'd come to regret," Titania confessed.

"Good thing I arrived in the nick of time then," Adam joked.

It only took a few minutes before the others appeared, first Fayte, then Lilith, and finally Susan. Once everyone was there, they headed toward the stables.

Because Fayte, Lilith, and Susan did not have much money, Adam bought everyone a horse. They could have bought a wagon for all of them to fit in, but horses on their own were faster. Wagons slowed a horse down because it added a negative effect to their Speed stat. What he wanted right now was for them to hurry up and reach the town nearest to the Deadlands.

The Deadlands were located one thousand miles west of Solum and about six hundred miles from Watershore. Traveling by foot would have taken a long time. The horses had a +300 Movement stat, meaning it would only take about ten hours to reach their destination... which was still a long time to be traveling by horse, but it was better than walking.

During the journey, Adam discovered a new side to Fayte as she teased Susan over things that were happening to them in the real world. She reminded him of an older sister during these moments. Susan also responded just like an easily embarrassed younger sibling. At least, that was what he believed. It wasn't like he had ever had a younger sister, and Aris had acted nothing like Susan when she was younger.

His lover had been rather shameless even when she was a pre-teen.

Lilith remained mostly quiet during the journey. However, when Adam decided to have Kureha ride on her horse, the woman nearly had a heart attack. It had been very amusing to watch her struggle against her desire to remain cool and her wish to hug the little fox yokai in her arms. Adam was certain he felt more amused watching her than he should have.

Because it was a ten hour journey, they did not make it before the day ended. All of them logged off at around 5:00pm, Adam had dinner with Fayte, then spent a few hours playing video games with her.

At around 8:00pm, he went into the game and did some grinding to increase his level. Of course, he did not increase his level at all, but his spear was less than +100,000 experience points away from reaching level 9.

Since Adam only needed two hours of sleep to be at peak efficiency, he went to bed at around 3:00am and woke up at 5:00am. He spent another hour within the game, though this time he merely talked to Titania as Kureha nuzzled into his lap and slept while he stroked her fur. At around 8:00am, he ate breakfast with Fayte in the real world, and then all four of them logged onto *Age of Gods* and continued their journey.

They reached Hope Village around mid-morning.

***

Hope Village wasn't as small as the Village of Beginnings, but it wasn't as large as Watershore. Most of the houses were made of logs and possessed simple thatched roofs. If Adam had to guess, he would have said the roofs were made of straw and water reeds. The village had an earthy scent mixed with the smell of fresh water, which was likely because of the lake located in the center of the village. Trees intermixed with buildings to create the aesthetic of a village in harmony with nature.

Adam noticed there were only a few people staying outdoors as he, Fayte, Lilith, Susan, Titania, and Kureha wandered through the streets. Most of the houses were also boarded up. While the sun was bright and the sky was blue, a sense of desolation hung over the small village.

"What should we do now?" asked Fayte.

"We need information," Adam said. "Let's check in with the mayor and ask if he knows anything about the Deadlands."

Everyone agreed that this was the best course of action, and so they asked one of the few people outside for directions to the Mayor's house. The young woman they asked pointed at the largest building located right next to the lake. It was two stories but still modest. It looked nothing like the mansion that belonged to the mayors of Watershore and Solum. The mayor of Hope Village also didn't have any guards outside to greet them.

Adam and his companions climbed off their horses and knocked on the door. They didn't have to wait long before a pretty woman with brown hair tied into a braid, brown eyes, and simple clothing made of earth-tone fabrics answered it.

"Hello? Can I help you?" asked the woman, glancing at them all curiously. Her eyes lingered on Titania and Kureha, but she also looked oddly at Adam's mask, Lilith's mask, and Fayte's veil.

"Is the Mayor in?" asked Adam. "We wanted to ask about the Deadlands. You see, the Mayor of Solum asked us to discover why the dead have been returning from the grave."

The woman's face paled when he mentioned the Deadlands, but she calmed down after he told her it was a request from Solum's Mayor.

"I understand. I am the Mayor of Hope Village. My name is Abigail Hope. Please, come in."

While Adam was a little surprised to learn that this seemingly modest woman was the mayor of Hope Village, he got over his shock quickly and entered the house with everyone else. The front door was attached to a living space. Adam and his companions were directed to a pair of couches, which were just large enough to comfortably fit four people. It was a good thing Kureha and Titania were so little. They might not have all been able to fit if those two had been bigger.

Abigail brought them all some fresh tea. Adam couldn't tell what kind it was, but it had a slightly bitter scent. When he looked at it, a screen popped up to display what kind of tea it was and its effects.

Item Name: Bitter Tea

Item Type: Drink
Grade: 2-star
Equipment Requirements: None
Description: A bitter tea made from tea leaves found near Hope
Village. They calm the mind.
Abilities: Cures Confusion

"You said you wanted to know about the Deadlands?" Abigail asked.

"Yes, please. We were hoping you could tell us whatever you know," Fayte said as Adam took another sip of tea. It was becoming more agreeable with his palette the more he drank it.

"I'm afraid I don't know much." Abigail frowned as she pulled her long braid to her front and began playing with it. "The Deadlands have always been a place where the dead wander. Legends say that a battle took place there many thousands of years ago, but we don't know if that's true since there are no written records of that time. That said, the dead have become a lot more active lately. Several villagers who have wandered too close were attacked and one was even killed."

"That sounds like trouble," Adam muttered, then asked in a louder voice. "Is it true that there is a fog surrounding the Deadlands that drains people of their health?"

"It is true." Abigai's pale face gained a dark appearance as she tilted her head forward. "The Deadlands have always been like that, which is why we villagers have always been told to stay away."

"Is there a way to counteract the effects?" asked Titania. "What? Why are you looking at me like that?"

Abigail was gazing at Titania with an uncertain expression…
but it was a look she and Adam were intimately familiar with by this
point.

"She is a fairy, if that is what you're curious about," Adam
supplied for the woman who looked like she was barely holding her
tongue. "The reason she's not taller is because she's only at level 14
right now."

"S-so I see." Abigail flushed pink at being caught staring and
tried to get back on topic. "Anyway, you asked if there was a way to
counteract the fog? There is not. At least, not completely. We do
have a medicine that the local doctor created, which can lessen the
effects, but the medicine only lasts for two hours and it only lessons
the effects by 50%. You will still lose health, so you'll want to be
careful if you plan on traveling through the Deadlands."

After she finished speaking, Abigail gave each person in their
party a single dose of medicine, which was called [Death Antidote].
It had the effect of cutting the [Death Curse], which Adam presumed
was the fog surrounding the Deadlands, by 50%. She also told them
that if they wanted more, they needed to travel to the doctor's home
and buy some from him.

Because Adam didn't know how long they were going to stay
in the Deadlands, he bought twenty [Death Antidotes] for 10,000
gold coins from the doctor. That price seemed kind of steep to him.
However, he wasn't able to haggle the price down. Once they had
enough antidotes, Adam and his companions journeyed to the Deadlands, which was only half an hour away from Hope Village.

Just like he'd been told, the Deadlands really was covered in a thick fog. Not even he could see through it. The fog was black and seemed to roil back and forth, never traveling beyond a certain point. It was like there was an invisible barrier that kept the fog from spreading further.

Adam and Lilith tethered everyone's horses to a tree so they wouldn't run off. He didn't know if horses in this game could run off, but he figured it was better to be safe than sorry.

"Titania, once we enter the Deadlands, I think you should sing the [Song of Refreshing Rain]. That might help counteract the effects of the fog," Adam said.

"That is a good idea," Titania agreed.

"Is everyone ready?"

Adam looked at his companions. Fayte was standing beside him with a determined gaze, Susan looked frightened but unwilling to back off, and Lilith appeared as emotionless as always. Kureha hopped down from his head and gave an enthusiastic yip. It was like she was telling him without words that she was ready.

"All right. Let's decide on our formation, and then we can head in."

Because it looked like he'd been silently nominated as the party leader, Adam decided on their formation. He was at the front, while Lilith had the rear. Fayte would be next to him and Kureha would travel alongside Lilith. This was because his and Kureha's stats were higher than Lilith's and Fayte's. Having her at the front with him would have unbalanced their party formation. Titania and

Susan were in the center of the formation since one of them was a long-range attacker and the other was a healer/support type.

They took the antidotes and Titania began to sing [Song of Refreshing Rain] as they journeyed into the Deadlands.

-3-; -3; -3; -3; -3!

From the moment they entered, Adam and the others experienced the health draining effects of the Deadlands. Their health was brought down by -3 every second, which was -15 every five seconds.

More than the drop in their health, however, what really made Adam surprised was the feeling standing in this fog gave him. It felt like his soul was being drained. His mind and body felt sluggish. He was able to shake it off, of course, but the fact that he could feel it was proof of how powerful this cursed fog was.

+30; +30; +30; +30; +30!

Fortunately, Titania's [Song of Refreshing Rain] recovered +30 health every one second, which meant they were recovering more health than they lost. His only concern was whether she could keep it up. Fortunately, she had a crap ton of magic points.

"Let me know if you are running low on magic," Adam said. "I have [low-grade mana potions] ready."

Titania said nothing, but she did nod at him.

The ground was thick and wet like a marshland. Their feet made squelching noises as they walked through what Adam believed was mud. He realized after checking his stats that the terrain affected their Speed and Movement. Adam had a -5 negative status effect applied to his Speed, which meant he was reduced to +5 for

Speed and +25 for Movement. The others were similarly affected, except for Titania who was flying.

They didn't run into any enemies for several minutes, but then a figure appeared within the fog. It floated through the air, its entire body covered in a tattered black cloak. White bones peeked out from beneath its long sleeves. Red eyes flashed within a skull from underneath the hood covering its head. It didn't carry any weapons, but Adam didn't think this creature needed them.

Titania cast [scan] before quickly switching back to singing.

Name: Wraith
Description: A lost soul born from intense despair and hatred.
Wraiths wander the earth, resurrecting the dead and attacking
the living.
Class: None
Lvl: 15
Health: 3,000/3,000
MP: 10,000/10,000
Physical Attack: +40
Constitution: +50
Dexterity: +25
Intelligence: +120
Speed: +25

Skills:
wraith releases a monstrous and bone-chilling howl that causes
100% damage and has a 10% chance of casting Stun
MP cost: 150
Cooldown time: 5 seconds

Rend: The wraith can use the sharp bones of its hands like claws
to tear the flesh off a human

250% damage
MP cost: 50
Cooldown time: 0 seconds

Summon Undead: wraiths have the ability to summon undead
Limits: Only one undead can be summoned at any given time
MP cost: 1,200
Cooldown time: 15 seconds

"It looks like our first enemy has arrived," Adam said, turning to Fayte, Lilith, and Susan. "I would like to see what you three can do before we travel too far into this fog. Would you mind fighting this [wraith]? If it becomes too much of a problem, I'll step in and take care of it."

"It would be good for you to see how we fight." Fayte turned her gaze to him before looking at Susan and Lilith. He was sure she was smiling behind her veil. "Let's show Adam how we deal with monsters."

"I will provide cover fire," Susan said. For once, she sounded confident and sure of herself. It was very unlike the girl he'd been getting to know. Adam wondered if perhaps she was one of those people who could only feel confident when she was role playing as someone else.

"As will I," Fayte added. "Lilith?"

Lilith didn't respond with words and instead readied her dagger and rushed across the ground. She was a little slower than normal because of the mud, but she still reached the [wraith] within a few seconds and attacked with [slash].

-150!

The moment she struck the [wraith], it turned to her and released a fierce [howl] that caused -50 damage, though it didn't stun Lilith, and Titania's [Song of Refreshing Rain] ensured most of the damage was healed two seconds after she was injured. During that time, Fayte launched an [Energy Bolt] at the [wraith]. The colorless energy ball slammed into the [wraith] and knocked it back.

-170!

Susan also knocked back an arrow and used [Deadeye] to fire at it. The attack struck the [wraith] right in the face, penetrating its left eye and dealing -140 damage, which meant she'd struck a critical hit.

Of course, the [wraith] still had over +2,500 health. Those three attacks were practically negligible, but the three women did not give up and continued with the strategy of having Lilith pull its agro and dodge its attacks, while Susan and Fayte peppered the monster with long-range attacks.

At some point, the wraith used [Summon Undead] to summon a skeletal creature with +1,000 health. This added to the level of difficulty they were faced with. However, Adam decided to take care of it himself. He used [slash] once to reduce its health to zero, allowing the women to continue attacking the [wraith] until, at last, its health reached zero.

Ding!

[Congratulations! You have defeated a [wraith]! Items dropped: [Wraith's Cloak], [Ghastly Ring], and 1,000 gold coins! +200 experience points!]

Adam noticed right away that the amount of experience he gained was far less than what he normally gained from defeating enemies of the same level. He knew this was because the experience gained was being shared by everyone. Likewise, he did not get the item drops, which ended up going to Susan, who struck the killing blow. Of course, she couldn't use the cloak and the ring didn't have any useful abilities for her since all it did was boost someone's resistance to darkness and increase their Magic Attack by +10. She gave them both to Fayte.

"You three work well together," Adam said after the spoils had been sorted.

"Thank you," Fayte said. "We've been working together for several days now, so I think we've become intimate with each other's attack patterns and fighting styles."

"That [Luck] stat of yours is also pretty useful." Adam looked at Susan. "It seems your [Luck] stat is part of what gave you the chance to land the killing blow."

"You think so?" asked Susan.

"Well, maybe. It's hard to say for sure, but I think [Luck] affects every aspect of a player's gameplay." Adam still didn't know exactly what [Luck] did. This was honestly just guesswork right now. "Anyway, let's continue on. We need to figure out what is causing the dead to rise."

Everyone gave him a firm nod, and so the group of six got back in their original formation with Adam in the lead and journeyed deeper into the Deadlands.

BROKEN SILENCE
WITHIN THE CRYPT

Ding!

[You have defeated a [wraith]! Items dropped: [Ring of Darkness], [Cloak of Darkness], [Dark Heart], and 2,000 gold coins! +200 experience points!]

Adam watched as another enemy fell before his spear. He had long since lost count of how many enemies they came across. Sometimes they came in groups of two or three, but other times they came alone. In either case, he had wanted to show the girls—Fayte, Susan, and Lilith—what kind of skills he had but...

"They're dying too quickly," Adam said with a sigh. "I can't show them my skills if they die in a single hit."

The problem, Adam concluded, was that his skill [Blood Sacrifice] was simply too powerful. Whenever Adam activated the skill, his damage increased from -2,465 to -7,395. These [wraith] monsters only had +3,000 health, which meant he dealt more than double what they actually had. Even his attacks like [thrust] was enough to one-shot these things without relying on [Blood Sacrifice].

-3-; -3; -3; -3; -3!

+30; +30; +30; +30; +30!

The effects of the [Death Curse] continued to drain their health, but Titania's [Song of Refreshing Rain] restored the damage before it could become a problem. Since the [Death Antidote] they had taken before entering reduced the damage they received by half, Adam concluded they could have not taken the antidote and would still have been fine thanks to Titania.

"I feel like you're way too powerful," Fayte muttered as Adam walked back over to her.

"If you think this is bad, you should see what happens when Titania uses [Song of Vigor]," Adam said.

-3-; -3; -3; -3; -3!

+30; +30; +30; +30; +30!

"You're really strong," Susan agreed, though unlike Fayte, who seemed displeased somehow, she had stars in her eyes.

"Ahahaha, thank you, Su," Adam said with a grin, even though he knew she couldn't see it behind his mask.

Lilith said nothing, but how could Adam not see the pride shining in her eyes whenever she looked at him? It was enough to make him uncomfortable.

They had been journeying through the Deadlands for about half an hour now. While the quest was to discover why the dead were rising, they hadn't found anything that would indicate how or why that was happening. So far, all they had discovered was a disgusting marshland.

The marshlands seemed to stretch on for miles, though that might have been Adam's perception of the place. He couldn't see more than ten feet in any direction thanks to the fog surrounding them.

"Doesn't this fog vaguely remind you of the 'fog of war' found in old-school RTS games?" asked Fayte.

"You know… it kind of does." Adam smiled as some good memories appeared within his mind—not that anyone could see it with his mask on. "Aris and I used to play RTS games all the time. She was an avid fan of *War of Worlds*."

"I played that one!" Susan suddenly announced. "Isn't it a great game? I love how they combined realistic military equipment with a futuristic twist. I also appreciated how it didn't rely on a turn-based system. It made everything seem so much more exciting, and the way the terrain affected soldiers and vehicles was such a great touch that I—oh! I-I'm sorry! I completely forgot myself and spoke out of turch—ouch! My tongue!"

-3-; -3; -3; -3; -3!

+30; +30; +30; +30; +30!

Adam could not stop himself from wincing as the embarrassed and nerve-wracked Susan suddenly bit her tongue... again. He was really worried about this girl. He hoped she didn't bite her tongue like that in real life.

"I don't think you were speaking out of turn at all," Fayte said as she reached over and rubbed the younger girl's head, her actions soft and gentle. "Feel free to speak up whenever you have some-thing to add."

"Fayte is right," Adam added. "Don't hold back on my ac-count."

Adam didn't know what it was about Susan, but ever since they began this journey, he'd felt an odd desire to protect her. It was different from the feelings he had toward Aris. He wanted to protect Aris, and he gave his all for her, but Susan brought out a desire that felt like half-primitive male instinct and half-older brother. He won-dered if Fayte maybe felt something similar.

Well, the female equivalent of whatever he felt.

"I wish I knew what you people were talking about," Titania said with a huff. She did not like it when they started talking about things from the real world.

Fayte and Adam shared a look. Like him, Fayte and Susan had been stunned by Titania's realism, by how "human" she felt. This was, of course, disregarding the fact that she was only one foot tall and had wings on her back.

"Don't forget to keep singing," Adam said.

"I know," Titania muttered as she began singing [Song of Re-freshing Rain] again.

-3-; -3; -3; -3; -3!

+30; +30; +30; +30; +30!

"There is something up ahead," Lilith announced.

"It's a castle!" Susan gasped.

Indeed, as they walked closer to the shadow that had suddenly appeared in front of them, the group found themselves standing next to the large wall of a very old rampart. The stones were aged and worn. Moss and vines grew all over the stones and stuck out between the cracks. Adam placed his hand against the wall. He couldn't feel the texture thanks to his [Dragon Bone Gauntlets], but the vines felt squishy and pliant.

They traveled along the rampart wall and soon came upon the derelict remains of an archway. Judging from the remains lying on the ground, the twisted metal strewn about, this place had once housed a portcullis, but it had long since been destroyed. Adam couldn't say by what. The metal was warped so bad he could figure out nothing from this simple observation.

With Susan sticking close to Fayte, Adam taking point, and Lilith and Kureha in the rear, they walked into the castle courtyard. Titania fluttered down and landed on Adam's shoulder. Perhaps she was getting nervous because she grabbed a fistful of his hair. She fortunately did not stop singing [Song of Refreshing Rain] to replenish the health they continuously lost.

-3-; -3; -3; -3; -3!

+30; +30; +30; +30; +30!

Perhaps it was because of the fog, but Adam could not see anything, not even the remains of the castle that should have been around there somewhere. The only thing present seemed to be his companions. However…

"Do you hear that?" asked Adam.

"Did you hear something?" Fayte asked.

"It is the sound of footsteps," Lilith, whose hearing was nearly as good as his, said. She narrowed her dark eyes and held her dagger in a reverse grip.

Susan huddled closer to Fayte, who stood protectively in front of the girl. Adam closed his eyes and tilted his head, steadying his breathing as he stretched out with his senses, trying to determine where the source of those footsteps was coming from. The footsteps themselves were uneven. However, they were moving much faster than the [undead skeleton] he fought back in the Village of Beginnings.

His eyes snapped open as he suddenly turned around.

"Lilith! It's coming from behind you!"

Lilith spun around just in time to see what looked like a woman dressed in ragged clothes leap out of the fog and attack her. She jumped back. This allowed her to dodge the initial attack, but the ground was wet and affected her Movement. She wasn't just slower. Her movements were awkward. The ground sucked her foot in deep and made her stumble.

With a curse, Adam rushed forward and thrust his spear into the chest of the woman.

-1, -3,944!

He didn't activate [thrust] during his initial attack, but he quickly did so for his second attack. The woman to stumble backward, away from Lilith, whom Adam quickly hauled to her feet.

Now that he was closer, Adam was able to see what kind of enemy had attacked them. To call this thing a woman was most definitely an insult to women everywhere. It certainly looked like a woman, but only in that it had the body proportions expected of one. It wore a ragged black dress, had sagging breasts, and its skin looked ancient and decayed. Frizzy white hair trailed down its decrepit head in drab strings. Sunken red eyes. Disgusting yellow teeth. Adam did not know what kind of monster this was, but Susan seemed to recognize it.

"That's a [banshee]!"

Titania briefly stopped singing [Song of Refreshing Rain] in order to cast [Scan] on the [banshee].

Name: Banshee
Description: Banshees are women who died with great resentment for wrongs committed against them in life. They will violently attack anyone living, but they harbor an especially intense hatred for other women. The more attractive the woman, the greater their hatred.
Class: 1-star
Lvl: 30
Health: 81,055/85,000
MP: 15,850/16,000
Physical Attack: +600
Constitution: +1,120
Dexterity: +200
Intelligence: +130
Speed: +300

Skills:
Banshee's Shriek: When the Banshee unleashes her fierce shriek, anyone within a ten yard radius has a 50% chance of getting hit with the fear status effect
MP cost: 300
Cooldown time: 10 seconds.

**Nail Cutter: The banshee's nails are very sharp, capable of cut-
ting through even steel
310% damage
MP cost: 150
Cooldown time: 0 seconds**

**Iron Maiden: The Banshee unleashes a unique cry that sum-
mons an iron maiden to capture an enemy
Anyone captured by the Iron Maiden dies instantly
MP cost: 6,000
Cooldown time: None
Limited to one use per battle
Can only be summoned once the Banshee reaches 10% health**

"A 1-star [banshee]," Adam said. "This thing might be trouble."

"What should we do?" asked Fayte.

Adam thought quickly for a moment before issuing orders.
"Fayte, Kureha, and Susan, move to the rear and provide cover fire!
Titania, keep singing! Lilith, you're with me! Let's go!"

"Yes, Mas—yes!"

While the others moved to the front, Lilith quickly leapt to
Adam's side. She was so enthusiastic that she almost called him
master. That would have been bad. Very bad. Fortunately, she
seemed to catch herself at the last second, though he hoped neither
Fayte or Susan heard her slip up.

With Lilith forming up slightly behind him, Adam did not activate [Blood Sacrifice] since he didn't want to finish this monster off

too quickly. This was a great chance for their party to work as a team.

As he charged forward, he could hear the loud squelching of Lilith's footsteps mixing with his own as they raced across the ground. Behind them both, Fayte called out the name of her attack and Kureha yipped as she launched a powerful bolt of lightning from her second tail.

"[Energy Bolt]!"

-190!

"Yip!"

-2,970!

Fayte's [Energy Bolt] was launched first and struck the [banshee] in the chest. It looked like an invisible ripple traveling across the space between her and the [banshee], slamming into it and forcing the wailing creature back. Not even a second after the [Energy Bolt] struck it, Kureha's even more powerful [Thunder Bolt] slammed into it.

The amount of damage Kureha did was a lot more significant than what Fayte had done, but it was still a drop in the bucket for this creature. The [banshee] had +85,000 health. They still had a long way to go.

It was at this time that Adam arrived in front of the [banshee] and used [Dance of the Sakura Blossoms] without hesitation. He swung the spear in his hands with an incredible amount of grace, dancing around his enemy, forming what, if looked at from a bird's eye view, would have been the shape of a sakura blossom. The five points where petal met stem were his attack points.

-2,465; -7,395; -22,185; MISS!

-170; -170; -170; -170; -170; -170!

Lilith quickly replaced Adam and activated [slash] multiple times. While her attacks didn't do much damage, she made up for it by attacking numerous times and not missing even once. The [banshee] wailed and shrieked as it tried to knock her back, but Adam interposed himself between them, intercepted the attack with his spear, and redirected it.

-3,944!

"[Energy Bolt]!"

-190!

"Yip!"

-2,367!

-170; -170; -170; -170; -170; -170!

-2,465; -7,395; MISS!

They kept up their assault. Adam tried to use [Dance of the Sakura Blossoma] once the cooldown time wore off but missed, which caused his skill to deactivate and enter the cooldown time again. He growled and leapt back as the [banshee] swelled around the chest. It opened its mouth like it was going to shriek at them. This was different from its first shriek. Adam could tell without having seen it before that it was about to activate its [Iron Maiden] skill.

"[Deadeye]!"

-140!

After calling out the name of her technique, Susan released an arrow from her bow. It flew forward and pierced the [banshee] through the throat. This stopped the enemy from using its [Iron

Maiden] skill. With the arrow still stuck in its mouth, the [banshee] reached up, grasped the shaft, and tried to pull it out.

-3; -3; -3; -3; -3!

+30; +30; +30; +30!

It was at this moment that Lilith attacked again, appearing behind the [banshee] like a shadow, reaching around its neck with her dagger, and slitting the creature's throat. This was [Throat Slit]. It was a skill unique to Assassin class players and one that dealt 400% damage with a chance of instant death and another chance at dealing x4 critical damage if the enemy was unaware of the assassin's presence.

-2,400!

The amount of damage Lilith's attack did was negligible despite doing 400% times more and getting the x4 critical damage. Her stats were just too low. Adam really needed to find her and the others some good equipment and a hidden class—if he could—that would bring their stats up.

"[Energy Bolt]!"

-190!

"Yip!"

-3,944!

Kureha and Fayte attacked once more to distract the [banshee]. During that time, the cooldown period for [Dance of the Sakura Blossoms] ended and Adam dashed forward again.

MISS!

-3; -3; -3; -3; -3!

+30; +30; +30; +30; +30!

Unfortunately, he missed and the skill deactivated, meaning he did absolutely no damage this time. With a grimace, he leapt back as Lilith took his place and attacked with [slash] several times. She held her dagger in a reverse grip and maneuvered around the [banshee] to attack from different angles.

-170; -170; -170; -170; -170; -170!

Once the [banshee] had turned on Lilith, Adam rushed up and attacked the enemy from behind. Since the cooldown time for [Dance of the Sakura Blossoms] was still going, he opened with [thrust] and followed through with [slash] several times. Each attack sliced into the flesh of his foe, though the only sign of damage being done was the strange slash marks that appeared on the body of the [banshee] every time one of his attacks hit.

-3,944; -3,697; -3,697; -3,697!

Since Adam did the most damage out of everyone, he was also the one who pulled the most agro. When he attacked, the [banshee] focused entirely on him, forcing him to back off by using [rend] several times, its arms swinging at him in wide, violent arcs. Moving in this marsh was difficult, however. If it wasn't for Adam's innate grace, born from years of grueling training, dangerous missions, and genetic modifications, he would have no doubt been killed already.

-3; -3; -3; -3; -3!

+30; +30; +30; +30; +30!

It was a good thing Lilith was there to take the heat off him. She moved in and attacked from behind, dealing critical damage to the [banshee] and forcing its agro on her. Once she pulled the agro off him, she would move back, allowing him to recover, and then

Kureha, Fayte, and Susan would pepper the [banshee] with long-range fire.

Adam's cooldown time ended, and so he finally activated [Dance of the Sakura Blossoms].

-2,465; -7,395; -22,185; MISS!

"Haaah… haah… haah…"

Adam took several deep breaths as the [banshee] released a loud wail. Smoke rose from its body. Adam and Lilith backed away from the creature as it thrashed, its body growing thinner and thinner before it disappeared entirely, leaving nothing behind but the ragged cloak it had been wearing.

Ding!

[Congratulations! You have killed the 1-star enemy [banshee]! Items dropped: [Evil Staff], [Evil Ring], [Cloak of Evil], and 20,300 gold coins! +60,000 experience points! +20,000 ability points!]

Ding!

[Congratulations! Kureha has leveled up! She is now at level 13! +200 HP! +1,800 MP! +10 SP]

Ding!

[Congratulations! Changing_Fayte has leveled up! She is now at level 12! +50 HP! +75 MP! +5 SP!]

Ding!

[Congratulations! Lilith has leveled up! She is now at level 12! +10 HP! +5 MP! +5 SP!]

Adam received an announcement that Kureha, Fayte, and Lilith had leveled up. He looked over to find them opening the windows for their levels. It looked like they were allocating status points to their stats. He decided to place all of Kureha's SP into her Intelligence once more.

He checked his own stats and discovered that while he hadn't leveled up, his spear had. It was now at level 9. Nothing about it had changed yet, but his Strength and Physical Attack were both at +90, increasing his Strength to +485 and his Physical Attack to +2,505.

"Is everyone okay?" asked Adam.

"I am okay," Fayte called.

"M-me too!" Susan added.

"I'm fine," Lilith said.

"Yip!"

"We are also all right," said Titania for herself and Kureha.

"Then let's keep going," Adam said.

After ensuring everyone was uninjured, the group moved off and eventually reached what the walls had been protecting. It was not a castle—not really. It was just a single building with an archway containing a rusted metal door embedded into it. Adam walked over and touched the doorknob. It was rusted over and wouldn't turn, but the door was actually opened, as it moved inward when he pushed.

Susan and Titania covered their ears at the loud squealing that echoed from the door while Kureha whimpered, placed her head on the ground, and covered her head with her paws. Adam and Lilith narrowed their eyes as they stared into the darkness beyond the door. Fayte stepped forward with a frown.

"It looks like we're going to need a light," she said before producing a torch from her item pouch. "It's a good thing I came prepared."

The torch ignited and Fayte took the lead, descending into the darkness beyond. This archway led into a staircase. Their footsteps produced an ominous echo as they walked down the steps, through an ancient and decrepit hallway, and reached another door. Adam went first and opened the door, leading the way through.

What appeared on the other side was a massive space with numerous columns that disappeared into a ribbed ceiling. Cracks ran along the walls and floors. Several sections of the walls were carved into alcoves and had large coffins sitting inside of them. The moment she saw those coffins, Susan shook as she realized what this place was.

"I-it's a crypt!" she squeaked.

"Seems like it," Adam agreed.

"I have a bad feeling about this." Fayte frowned and looked at Adam. "Do you think we should keep going?"

Adam debated with himself. To be honest, he had a bad feeling about this too. His instincts were telling him not to keep going, to turn back, but they had already accepted this quest and could ill afford to turn back now. He closed his eyes for a moment, then made his decision.

"Let's keep going," he said. "If the situation becomes untenable, we can always retreat, but I would at least like to complete this quest sometime today, if at all possible."

Fayte looked like she wanted to disagree with him, convince him to travel back, but Lilith backed up Adam, and Susan said she would follow them no matter what they decided. Titania also said it would be better to press on since they were already here. Outnumbered, Fayte had no choice but to accept the majority vote. Thus they began traveling into the crypt.

While the space was confined to simple hallways, it was clear from how long they had been exploring that this place was gigantic. Each hallway led to numerous other hallways. The hallways all looked the same too, with alcoves carved into the walls and coffins inside of each alcove. Adam almost expected the coffin lids to slide off and undead to rise out of them and attack, but none did.

That made him even more nervous.

-5; -5; -5; -5; -5!

+30; +30; +30; +30!

One thing Adam noticed was that his health was dropping more rapidly than before, decreasing by -5 every second. It still wasn't enough to concern them, but he hoped the amount of damage they took didn't increase too much. Titania's [Song of Refreshing Rain] could heal +30 HP every second, so as long as it didn't go above that, they should be good.

This crypt had several staircases leading further down. They decided to take one. When they did, the amount of damage they took increased.

-10; -10; -10; -10; -10!

+30; +30; +30; +30; +30!

"We're still doing good, but I hope this [Death Curse] doesn't become any more powerful than it is now," Fayte said as she watched the health on her status screen drop, rise, and then drop again.

"I'm running low on magic points," Titania said.

"I know what you mean," Adam said as he removed a [low-grade mana potion] so Titania could replenish her magic points. "It looks like we might really have to go back. Everyone, I've stocked up on potions. If we begin accumulating more damage, be sure to take one once your health drops past a certain point. Let's press on for now, but if the amount of damage we receive increases past what Titania's song can replenish, we'll leave."

They pressed on, moving deeper into the crypt. It didn't look like there was another staircase, but there were many rooms. In this second basement level were also several undead enemies that had risen from their coffins and attacked when their group appeared. They were just level 20 [zombies] and easy enough to deal with. Their health was +6,000, which meant Adam could one-shot them after activating [Blood Sacrifice]. Even when there were multiple enemies, so long as they were close by, he could use [Energy Sweep] to half their health and let Fayte, Kureha, and Susan bombard them with long-range attacks. Lilith would normally finish them off with [Throat Slit].

Thanks to all the killing they did, their group gained a collective total of +60,000 experience points. Susan's level also increased, and she put her SP into Constitution instead of Strength like Adam expected. Her reasoning was that she could always increase her

Physical Attack and Strength stats with weapons, but there might not be equipment that would increase her Constitution and therefore her health. It was sound logic that Adam couldn't disagree with. It also told him she, like Fayte, was an experienced gamer.

It was during this time that the medicine they had taken before entering the Deadlands wore off, increasing the damage they received from -10 to -20. They quickly downed another vial of [Death Antidote] to keep the effects of the [Death Curse] at bay. Fortunately, they still didn't need a [health potion].

Finally, after what felt like another hour of tension, they arrived inside of a gigantic room shaped like a cylinder. Several eerily glowing candles rested in candelabras on the wall to offer sparse amounts of light. They revealed several other halls that led deeper into the crypt—not that any of them had the desire to travel deeper. There was no telling what horrors awaited them should they proceed further.

By this point, the amount of damage being done to them had increased from -10 to -30, which meant Titania could not afford to stop singing. The [Song of Refreshing Rain] was now the only thing keeping them alive. That was also a point against proceeding further. They would not be able to survive if the damage they received was any greater.

-30; -30; -30; -30; -30!

+30; +30; +30; +30; +30!

"There's nothing here," Fayte said, turning about to look at everything this room had to offer.

"Yeah, and I don't think we can proceed any further than this," Adam said. "Let's go back. We might have to scrub this mission, or at least wait until we're able to completely counteract the effects of the [Death Curse]."

No one disagreed with him. Their health was not dropping yet, but that was because they had taken a [Death Antidote] and Titania's [Song of Refreshing Rain] canceled out what they lost. That would change once the effects of the [Death Antidote] ran out. And once they ran out of the antidote, the [Death Curse] would begin reducing their health by -60 every second, meaning not even Titania's song would be able to heal them. They would die in seconds.

It was time to leave.

However, just as they were about to leave, a loud rumbling like distant thunder echoed all around them, shaking the room they were in and causing Susan to scream out loud. Because he was the closest to her, Adam placed a hand against her back to steady her. Perhaps she assumed he was Fayte because she buried herself against him.

"Ha... ha... ha... ha..."

The rumbling sound echoed around them again, and accompanying it this time was dark, ominous laughter that sounded like a bass rumble. It was a deep sound that made their blood run cold. Adam grimaced as he pulled Susan behind him to protect her and warily observed their surroundings.

"Let's leave now," Adam said to everyone.

"Ha ha ha ha." The laughter became even more distinct. The sound was followed by a voice. **"Look at this. Look at this. It looks like some tasty humans have made their way into my lair.**

Do not be in such a hurry to leave, humans. It has been so long
since I've had anything to eat."

"Run!" Adam shouted to everyone as he pushed Susan off him
and began prodding her and the others toward the hallway they had
entered.

At that moment, something massive appeared within another
hallway several dozen yards to their left. They could see nothing of
it at first, but then a massive foot emerged from the darkness. It was
nearly two times bigger than they were tall. There was no flesh or
muscle on this foot. The pure black bones looked like something
Adam would expect to see from a charred corpse. The foot was followed by a leg and another foot. Then, appearing before them in all
its glory was a massive skeleton clad in rusted chainmail, black armor, and wielding two claymores that were at least two times bigger
than Adam.

"Good evening, humans," the skeleton said, though its mouth
did not move. It was like this creature was speaking directly into
their minds. Adam was reminded of espers who had telepathic abilities, but they did not chill his blood like this thing did.

"Don't stop and stare at the giant skeleton! Move!" Adam
commanded.

**"Do you really think I would let you run away?! All of you
are staying here! Now, let yourselves be devoured!"**

When Adam and the others began running, the giant skeleton
bounded after them. The floor shook each time its foot struck the
ground. Susan was knocked off her feet from the shaking, but Adam

scooped the girl into his arms, carrying her like a princess as he ran full speed ahead.

"It's a good thing you're so light," he muttered.

Susan just blushed.

They ran past the archway that led into the hall they first emerged from. The giant skeleton slammed into the wall and extended its arm to try and grab them, but Kureha launched a [Fireball] from her place on Adam's head.

-2,250!

"Grrraaaaaa!!!"

While the attack didn't do much damage, the skeleton jerked its hand back as if it had been stung. This presented them with an opportunity to escape.

"Damn fox! Wait until I get my hands on you! I will make you suffer for this!!!"

They raced up the stairs. The damage went from -30 to -10, then to -5 before finally going back to -3 as they traveled through the crypt. They didn't bother fighting any of the undead inside and instead ran until they emerged from the crypt, gasping and panting for breath.

Adam was still holding Susan as he looked at everyone else. Fayte was hunched over on her hands and knees, shoulders heaving. He couldn't see her face, but her eyes were wide. Lilith appeared much more calm than she was. However, the skin around her eyes was a tad paler than usual.

Now that they were no longer in the crypt, Titania's [Song of Refreshing Rain] was able to quickly recover the damage being done to them by the [Death Curse]. However, none of them wanted to remain here any longer.

"Let's head back to Hope Village," Adam said. "I'm sure several hours have passed, so we should log off and get some rest. We can log back on later tonight or tomorrow and continue on to Solum."

Everyone nodded their heads. They were all exhausted from this latest ordeal. It was time to get some well-deserved sleep.

ANOTHER HIDDEN
CLASS

A fter logging out, Adam took a quick shower and made lunch for himself and Fayte. It wasn't anything special. He whipped up a quick salad by chopping up some vegetables, added chickpeas and other annul legume with a good blend of protein and fiber, then made his own sriracha style dressing to give the food some kick. He made sure the sriracha was milder than normal so it wouldn't be hard on Fayte's pallet.

Fayte had thanked him for the meal before saying she was going out to stretch her legs. Adam had learned there was a gym in this complex. He had never been there. Fayte told him the equipment was all very old, but it at least contained a treadmill so she could get her cardio in without having to leave the complex.

While Fayte did her own thing, Adam went to Aris's room and talked to her, telling her about everything he had done while playing

Age of Gods. He had a bit more to say this time since his party had just come back from a dangerous quest.

As Adam talked to Aris, he wondered if she could hear him. She was basically frozen in time right now. The cryobed was also sturdily built and airtight, with heavily reinforced glass that could withstand bullets, meaning it was probably sound proof as well. He didn't think she could hear him. That, however, did not stop him from wishing she could.

Adam logged back onto *Age of Gods* at 3:00pm, the designated time for their group to meet back up in the game. Lilith was already there. Titania and Kureha were, of course, also present since they could not leave the game like he and the others did. When he appeared before them, Titania was merely fluttering through the air while Lilith was playing with Kureha.

"Aren't you just the cutest thing ever! Who is super cute? Is it you? Is it you?"

Lilith was sitting on her haunches and rubbing Kureha's belly. The cute little fox yokai was making mrrring noises that were like a fox's version of purring. Lilith was so into pampering the fox that she didn't seem to have realized he had logged on.

It was very rare for Adam to see Lilith act like this, and while he knew he should have let her know he was present, some part of him felt like standing back to watch.

"Adam," Titania suddenly greeted him when she noticed his arrival. "You have returned."

The moment his name was spoken, Lilith squeaked and leapt to her feet like she'd stuck her finger into an electric socket. She turned her frightened eyes on Adam. He could not see her face thanks to her mask, but it wasn't like he needed to. Even with everything covered, he could tell she was blushing.

Adam wondered what Fayte and Susan would think if they saw this.

"M-Master," Lilith stuttered as Kureha, not sure why the nice woman clad in black had stopped pampering her, nuzzled against Lilith's pants like a cat seeking affection. "This... this is just..."

"It's been a long time since I've seen you go crazy over something cute." Adam scratched the back of his head and tried to smile, but he thought it felt awkward. He was glad for his mask. "Wasn't it... five years ago?"

"Y-yes..." Even if she wanted to, Lilith could not lie to him. He doubted the idea of lying had even occurred to her. "It was... just after we escaped from Eden. You said we were... going our separate ways. I didn't want that, but..."

"But I was going to see Lexi and wouldn't let you come with me," Adam said with a sigh.

Back then, after they had escaped from Eden, Adam had been determined to see Lexi again. He had tried to cut ties with everyone who escaped with him. He told them they were free and no longer needed to follow him, but all of his fellow escapees had refused.

And the most adamant among them had been Lilith.

"That was why you bought me that fox plushie. You said... even though we'll be apart, I could think of you whenever I hold it..."

Adam rubbed the back of his neck, unsure of what to say. He wasn't bad with words, could talk just fine, but he preferred not to, especially when the topic of their conversation was something he often tried to forget about.

"I still have it, you know," Lilith confessed. "The fox plushie, I mean. It's in my bedroom."

"Ah. Well… I'm glad you like it," Adam said, though he was cursing on the inside.

Lilith was not a normal woman. Older than him by several years, she was one of the more experienced members of Lucifer's assassination unit. Cold and calculating, a terrifying beauty who could chill your blood just as quickly as she could make it boil, Lilith almost never showed any emotion. The only times she did was around him or when she saw something cute.

Like Kureha.

"I really wish you two would not talk about things I am unaware of when I'm right here," Titania suddenly said.

While Lilith quickly looked away and tried to pretend this conversation never happened, Adam merely ran a hand through his hair and sighed. He'd completely forgotten about Titania.

"My bad," he said.

Titania merely huffed.

Fayte and Susan arrived not long after that embarrassing interlude. He greeted the pair as Lilith remained silent.

They were still in Hope Village, so they mounted their horses and journeyed back to Solum (it took two days), where they paid the entrance fee and traveled to the Mayor's house. Unlike last time when he was asked to wait in the entrance hall, this time they were led by the butler to the mayor's office.

"You have returned," Bromley Paxton said once they all entered. "And you brought friends, I see. I assume you three are otherworlders like Adam. Please allow me to welcome all of you to Solum."

Bromley Paxton stood up and moved around his large desk, which had several stacks of papers on top. He smiled at the group, looking for all the world like an affable uncle.

"Thank you for your warm welcome."

Fayte elegantly curtsied Bromley Paxton. Despite her face being covered by a veil, in spite of not wearing a sophisticated dress or something even remotely fashionable, the action was so smooth, so refined that even the old Mayor of Solum could not stop his cheeks from turning red.

"Yes… well… ahem… you are welcome," he said, coughing into his hands several times. "N-now, I believe we should get to the point. I am assuming the reason you are here is because you had some success in the quest I gave you? Did you find out the reason for the dead rising in the Deadlands?"

"I think we did. I'm… not sure." Adam stepped forward, placed his hands behind his back, and stood straight like a soldier giving his commanding officer a debriefing. "We journeyed into the Deadlands. While there, we encountered a… a monster."

"A monster? What kind?" asked Bromley Paxton.

"I believe it was the Undead King," Titania said, flying forward.

"The Undead King?! Truly?!" asked a now shocked Bromley Paxton, whose eyes had become the size of dinner plates.

"Indeed." Titania nodded. "At the very least, the monster we ran into matches a description of the Undead King I read about in a book. It is said that the Undead King has absolute power over death. During the Great War, he raised an army of the dead and used it to destroy many cities. I suspect he is in hiding. The goddesses would not allow him to live if they knew he was there. The excess power his body constantly leaks is the most likely cause for why the dead have been rising. The [Death Curse] is also a result of his power."

"Yes… that makes a lot of sense," Bromley Paxton murmured, eyes going unfocused. Then he sighed. "If only we could contact the goddesses, but neither they nor their representatives have been seen for thousands of years. It is unfortunate, but it seems the only thing I can do is make the [Deadlands] off limits to everyone—at least until someone strong enough comes along who can take care of him."

Ding!

[You have been offered a new quest: [Slay the Undead King!] This is a long-standing quest that does not have a time-limit. It can be completed whenever you wish. However, be warned that this quest may be offered to other players as well. If another person completes this quest, then it will no longer be available and will be listed as a failed quest. Failed quests result in a reduction of Reputation, so be careful when accepting quests. Do you accept the quest? Yes or no?]

Adam and the others stared briefly at the new window that appeared, but it was only for a moment before he reached out and pressed the "yes" button.

"Don't worry," Adam said to the mayor. "We aren't strong enough to defeat him yet, but I'm confident we can beat the [Undead King] in quick order once we're stronger."

"Truly? This will be a tall order, but... hm... yes, I believe if you are the ones accepting the quest, you may just be able to succeed," Bromley Paxton said. "In either event, you have done what I asked of you. I believe we can consider this quest a success."

"Certainly," Adam agreed.

Ding!

[The quest: [Slay the Undead King!] has been accepted!]

Ding!

[Congratulations! You have completed the quest: [Journey into the Deadlands]! +100,000 experience points! +20,000 Reputation! +10,000 AP!]

"Now!" Bromley Paxton clapped his hands while Adam and his party were distracted by the announcement. "For the reward. Because the quest was accepted by you, Adam, I can only give you the reward. However, I do have several items for you to choose from. Come with me. I will take you to my treasure vault, and you can select one item from inside. This might not sound like much, but I assure you that all the items in my vault are priceless artifacts you cannot find anywhere else."

Since Adam was the only one allowed inside the vault, the others were asked to wait outside of the mayor's house. They were led away by the butler, Geeves. In the meantime, Adam followed Bromley Paxton through a series of hallways, down two flights of stairs, and up to a large door that reminded him of a high-security vault in a bank—except without the lasers and security cameras.

The vault was guarded by two guards who were both at level 60, signifying even more than words how much value the mayor put on whatever was inside. Opening it required the guards to insert a pair of keys at the same time, which unlocked the mechanisms keeping the vault shut. They opened the door and allowed Adam and Bromley Paxton inside.

Having never actually seen a vault in a fantasy-style VRM-MORPG, Adam was not sure what to expect, but whatever he had been expecting, the neat and orderly room with rows of shelves containing various kinds of equipment was most definitely not it. Maybe he really had been expecting something more fantasy-esque. Where were the piles of gold? The massive amounts of treasure chests? This looked more like a blue blood's museum of unusual artifacts.

"Feel free to choose any one item you see here," Bromley Paxton said with a sweep of his hand. "Please remember to limit yourself to just a single item."

Adam nodded as he walked into the room and began perusing the shelves. There were a lot of items. He found swords, shields, spears, bows, magic staffs, and scrolls. Adam walked up to one shelf and looked at one of the items titled [Bow of Prosperity].

Name: Bow of Prosperity

Item Type: Bow
Grade: 3-star
Use requirements: Can be equipped by Archers level 40 and above
Description: The Bow of Prosperity was given to the Bromley Family by the Fairy Clan before they disappeared. It is one of the highest class of bow in existence
Abilities: Physical Attack+400%; Hit-Rate+200%; Luck+40

Special skills:
Arrow Storm: Fires a hailstorm of arrows
Damages all enemies within 150 feet of targeted enemy

Bewildering shot: Fires an arrow with deadly accuracy to hit an enemy's funny bone
100% chance of causing Confusion

Critical Shot: Fires an arrow with 100% chance of being a critical hit
Does x4 critical damage

The bow itself was pretty amazing and had some of the most impressive abilities and stats he had seen thus far in the game… but it was too bad the bow was useless right now. It would be perfect for Susan once she reached level 40. However, that was so far off there wasn't any point in thinking about it right now. It would probably take at least a year of heavy grinding and dungeon raids to bring her to that level.

He moved on.

Like the [Bow of Prosperity], there were a multitude of powerful items that were all 3-star, possessed incredible stats, and offered a wide range of skills, but the levels required to use them caused him to turn away. What good was a magic staff that offered a 500% Magic Attack increase if it required someone to be at level 50 to use it?

Just as Adam was beginning to wonder if he would find anything that would be immediately useful, he came across a small shelf filled with scrolls. Most of them were spell scrolls. There was a [teleport scroll] that would allow him a one-time opportunity to teleport to any location he had already been to. He also saw a [Fire Blaze scroll], which activated a [Fire Blaze] spell that caused -100,000 damage to every enemy within a twenty yard radius. Among all the scrolls, the one that interested him the most was the [Fairy Archer Scroll].

Name: Fairy Archer Scroll
Item Type: Hidden Class Scroll
Grade: 4-star
Use requirements: Can be used by players with an Archer class profession.
Description: The Fairy Clan was once very close to the humans. To honor their friendship with humanity, the Fairy Clan created scrolls that would allow humans who have done them a great service to change their class into a fairy class.
Abilities: Changes Archer class to Fairy Archer class.
Leveling System:
Strength+1 = +3 Physical Attack
Constitution+1 = +5 Health; +5 Physical Defense; +5 Magical Defense
Dexterity+1 = 20% Hit-Rate; 15% Dodge-Rate
Intelligence+1 = +2 MP; +4 Magical Attack
Speed+1 = +4 Movement

Skills:
Fairy Shot: increases accuracy by 50%
If enemy is hit, critical damage is dealt
X2 critical damage.

Light Arrow: Infuses the power of light into arrow
Deals 400% damage to undead and enemies with an affinity for
the darkness element

Nature Arrow: Infuses the power of nature into an arrow
When an enemy is struck, vines will sprout from the arrow and
entrap the enemy for 60 seconds

The Fairy Archer Class wasn't as good as his Seven Forms Spearman class, but it was still a lot better than Susan's current Archer class. After thinking about it for a moment, he grabbed the scroll and returned to Bromley Paxton.

"You found what you want?" The mayor looked at the scroll in Adam's hand and furrowed his brow. "A class change scroll, huh? Those are quite rare. This is the only one I have ever seen. However, none of us can change into this class, though a few have tried. Are you sure that's what you want?"

"I'm sure," Adam said.

"Then you should now return to your companions," Bromley Paxton said.

They left the vault and Adam parted ways with Solum's mayor. His companions were waiting by the gate outside. Susan was playing with Kureha, while Fayte watched on, her eyes gentle and tender like she was watching over her younger sister. Lilith stared enviously at Susan like she wanted to be in the girl's place. Titania was just fluttering around. She was also the first to notice him.

"Did you find something beneficial in the mayor's vault?" she asked.

"I did." Adam nodded. "However, let's not talk about it here. I think we should find an inn or some place where no one can potentially overhear us."

Everyone except Lilith seemed a little confused about why he'd be worried about people overhearing them, but no one argued and they eventually found an inn. It was a simple inn called the Blooming Peony.

In keeping with the fantasy setting, the three-story building had a tavern when people first entered. It was already pretty rowdy by the time they arrived. Adam immediately picked up the smell of alcohol just after entering. Susan covered her nose when she also caught the scent, and while it was impossible to know what sort of expression Fayte was making behind that veil, it could not have been pleasant. She was staring daggers at some of the men and women laughing as booze sloshed around in their mugs.

"I feel like the creator went a little overboard when they were trying to mimic the classic settings of a fantasy world," Adam said.

"You're telling me," Fayte muttered.

Titania crossed her arms and glared at them. "Just what do you mean by 'fantasy world?'"

Neither of them knew how to answer the woman. How could they tell an NPC that all of this—her, this tavern, and everything else—was just a game?

It wasn't just NPCs who were sitting down to enjoy a drink. Adam caught several other players who were sharing a round of drinks with each other. It was easy to tell players from non-players because a basic screen didn't pop up over the players. Only using a skill like [scan] allowed people to see a player's stats.

He had once heard that VRMMOs were used by some people as a form of escape from the daily struggles of real life. Some people didn't come into the virtual world for money, but to live out a fantasy life, the kind they could never find in their ordinary, average, everyday lives. However, this was his first time seeing examples of that type of player.

Perhaps it was because of the company he was keeping, but a lot of people were looking his way and talking. They were quite loud.

"Hey, check it out. Don't you think that group looks like one of those harem parties?"

"I've heard of those! It's a party that consists of nearly all women and just one guy, right?"

"Yeah. I heard they're rare, but some players who play VR games will bring their harems into the game."

"Lucky sonofabitch. I wish I had my own harem to play with."

Adam sighed and did his best to ignore the gossiping people as he walked to the counter near the back of the bar. Fayte, Susan, and Lilith followed close behind him. Kureha was in Susan's arms right now instead of on his head, while Titania had once more perched herself on his shoulder.

"I'd like to rent a room for the night," Adam said to the barman.

The old barman set the mug he'd been cleaning on the counter and turned to him, pressing his hands flat against the counter. His face reminded Adam of a road map. It was covered in crisscrossing scars that lent him a frightening appearance.

"A single room for one night is 50 gold coins."

Adam didn't bother trying to barter with the man, handing him 50 gold coins in exchange for a key and gesturing for his party to follow him.

The room he rented was surprisingly nice. It contained four beds, though all of them were relatively small. There was also a table and a nightstand. An oil lamp sat off to the side, providing a gentle illumination that complimented the evening sunset.

Adam sat down on one of the beds while Fayte, Susan, and Lilith took the other three. Kureha and Titania climbed onto his bed. While Kureha curled up on his lap, Titania sat with her legs dangling over the edge, kicking them back and forth like a bored child.

"Do you mind if I ask what you retrieved from the mayor's vault now?" asked Fayte, finally unable to contain her curiosity.

"I got this." Adam pulled out a scroll from his item pouch. "Su, catch."

"What—ah!"

Startled when Adam tossed the scroll, Susan fumbled for several seconds before reaching out her hand to catch it. The others remained silent as they looked curiously at the scroll in her hands. None of them could read it since the item was currently being held by someone. Only Susan could read it right now, and her eyes went wide.

"This is…!"

"Do you remember when we talked about hidden classes?" Adam asked. "It's one of the few ways to gain higher stats per level. When I saw this, I knew it was something I needed to get for you."

The words "hidden class" rang out like a gunshot. Fayte, Lilith, and even Titania looked like they had been struck dumb.

"You got this… for me?" Susan looked up from the scroll to him. Her eyes were wide. "Why?"

"What do you mean? We're companions, aren't we? You needed one, so I got one for you." Adam shrugged as if that was answer enough.

Susan's lips trembled. She looked ten seconds away from crying. Adam almost had a panic attack when he saw the tears in her eyes, but then Susan wiped her eyes before the tears could fall and smiled at him.

"Thank you very much," she said, voice overcome with emotion.

"You're welcome." Adam found himself smiling as well. What a cute girl. She really did bring out a man's protective instincts. "Anyway, you should activate that scroll to gain your new class. All you have to do is unfurl it."

Susan nodded once before doing just as he instructed. The scroll released a flash of light when she unfurled it. Susan gasped as the light emitting from the scroll engulfed her body, covering it from head to toe in light particles that completely blocked her from view.

When the light died down, everyone looked at Susan, but they didn't see anything different. There were no changes—physically, at least.

"Well?" asked Fayte. "How do you feel? Any different?"

"Um... I do feel a little different," Susan admitted after a moment. "I'm not really sure how to explain it, but... it's like I suddenly feel more energetic? Lighter? Something like that, I guess."

"That is the effects of your class change," Titania informed her. "You don't realize how much strength you are gaining when you level up because the increase happens in small increments, but a class change generally has some big changes. The Fairy Archer Class you just changed into is a great example. Fairy classes bring about some of the most significant status changes as well, so you feel the difference more readily."

"So that's how it is," Susan muttered.

Everyone was amazed by this new information. Even Adam was a little shocked. He had of course experienced the unusual phenomena that was the increase in energy and power after gaining the Seven Forms Spearman Class. However, he had brushed it off as just an in-game effect. Now it seemed like there might be even more to these classes than he realized.

Just because he was curious, Adam decided to check out Susan's new stats.

Name: Little_Su
Class: Fairy Archer
Lvl: 12
SP: 0
AP: 30,150

Experience: 199,460/307,200
Reputation: +20,000
Strength: +25
Constitution: +25
Dexterity: +20
Intelligence: +5
Speed: +50
Physical Attack: +145
Health: 320/320
Hit-Rate: 400%
MP: 60/60
Movement: +200

Skills:
kill Name: Deadeye
escription: Archers can increase their hit-rate and critical hit-rate by increasing their perceptions through the Deadeye skill.
Current lvl: 5 MAXED
Ability: Increases Hit-rate to 110%
Deals x2 critical damage
MP Cost: 5
Cooldown time: 5 seconds

Skill Name: Rain of Arrows
Description: Archers who learn this skill can fire a hailstorm of arrows that deals damage to multiple enemies.
Current lvl: 5 MAXED
Ability: Causes 150% damage to all enemies within 15 yards of targeted enemy
MP Cost: 5
Cooldown time: 10 second

Skill Name: Fairy Shot
Description: A skill that can only be used by someone of the Fairy Archer Class. Increases accuracy and damage dealt by ar-

rows.
Current lvl: 1
AP needed to reach next lvl: 2,000
**Ability: Increases accuracy by 50%. If enemy is hit, x2 critical
damage is dealt**
MP Cost: 10
Cooldown time: 10 seconds

Skill Name: Light Arrow
**Description: A skill used by the Fairy Archer Class. Infuses ar-
row with the power of light.**
Current lvl: 1
AP needed to reach next lvl: 2,000
**Ability: Deals 400% damage to undead and enemies of the dark-
ness element**
MP Cost: 20
Cooldown time: 10 seconds

Skill Name: Nature Arrow
**Description: A skill used by someone with the Fairy Archer
Class. Infuses the power of nature into the arrow.**
Current lvl: 1
AP needed to reach next lvl: 2,000
**Ability: When an enemy is struck by a Nature Arrow, they be-
come entrapped in vines for 60 seconds**
MP Cost: 30
Cooldown time: 10 seconds

While her abilities were not the most impressive he had seen,
they were a lot better than they had been, and now that she had a
better class, her stats would only increase from here.

It was evening now. The sky was growing dark in the Forgotten Realm, which was synchronized to match the time in the real

world. Everyone agreed to log off and meet back up tomorrow morning at 8am.

When Adam logged off and wandered into the living room, he found Fayte coming out of the other hallway that led to her bedroom at about the same time. She smiled at him and gestured toward the video game console sitting by the television.

"Loser makes dinner?" she asked.

He grinned. "You're on."

Adam turned on the television and console as Fayte sat on the couch. He handed her a controller, then sat down beside her as the startup screen for Street King VII appeared before them. Both of them selected the characters they wanted to battle with, then selected the random battlefield setting so neither of them had an advantage over the other.

"Thank you for getting that hidden class for Su," Fayte said as the game began.

"Why are you thanking me?" asked Adam. "I didn't really do anything that amazing, and having someone with a better class will benefit us in the long run. I'm just doing what's expected of me."

"That may be so, but I appreciate what you did, and I know Su does too. You don't know this, but she was very nervous about meeting you for the first time."

"Is that so?"

"It is so."

"Hmmm…"

Adam tapped several buttons on his controller, manipulating his character into attacking Fayte's with a powerful combination that

knocked down nearly a third of her health. Fayte wore a grim yet determined expression as she countered him with a combination of her
own. Her character shot forward and spun like a drill, slamming into
Adam's character and removing about a fourth of his health.

"Well, I guess I kind of expected that," he said at last. "She's
such a meek girl."

"She is at that," Fayte agreed. "I have tried for a long time to
help her become more outspoken, but nothing I've done has ever
worked. I'm honestly getting worried. If she keeps going on like
this, she'll wind up—"

Adam glanced at Fayte out of the corner of his eye. The
woman was not looking at him and focusing instead on the game,
but her lips were now drawn into a thin line. She looked like she
was berating herself over something.

"I'm guessing you just said something you shouldn't have,"
Adam guessed.

Fayte sighed. "Something like that. Please forget I said anything."

"If that is what you want."

"Thank you."

The game continued and Adam won the first round. He also
started off strong in the second round, but at the very end, Fayte
pulled off a startling victory by trapping him within a combination
attack that he couldn't guard against. In their last round, he and
Fayte did not speak at all but instead focused entirely on their characters.

Adam thought about Susan during his small competition with Fayte, wondering what her circumstances were. Should he ask Astaroth to look into it? He considered the idea before deciding not to. It would not be appropriate to butt into someone else's business. He and Susan weren't very close either, so he was sure she would not appreciate him sticking his nose in where it didn't belong.

"Ah... I won," Fayte murmured as her character struck a victory pose on the screen. She seemed shocked, but it only lasted for a moment before her eyes began sparkling. "I won! I finally won!"

"Looks like it," Adam agreed calmly.

She sent him a suspicious glance. "You didn't let me win, did you?"

Adam had learned through constant exposure to her that Fayte was a sore loser. A *very* sore loser. Every time she lost made her that much more determined to win the next time. At the same time, she hated it when someone gave her a victory because she felt like they were being condescending to her. What Fayte enjoyed the most about competitions was winning on her own merit and skills.

"Do I seem like the kind of guy who would go easy on someone?" asked Adam.

"I guess not." Fayte furrowed her brow, then relaxed her expression, the wrinkles on her skin disappearing as a beautiful smile like the blooming of a rose appeared on her face. "Sorry. I guess I'm just shocked. I never expected to beat you."

"Well, you have, which means it is my turn to make dinner tonight."

"I can't wait to eat your cooking."

Adam smiled wryly as he stood up and made his way into the kitchen. He checked the fridge and pantry to see what kind of ingre-dients he had to work with.

He ended up making buffalo chicken quesadillas.

JOURNEY TO SUN-CREST MOUNTAIN

"GRAAAAAA!!"

The howl of the [chimera] was bone-chilling—or that was how Adam imagined it was supposed to sound. It was low and deep, a vicious growl laced with blood lust.

Unfortunately, its terrifyingness was lost on Adam.

[Chimeras] were horrific abominations. They walked around on four multi-jointed limbs, were covered in bright yellow and red fur, and possessed the head of a lion, the body of a goat, and the horns of an ox. It looked like an amalgamation of various creatures combined together with little thought or reasoning. In all his years, he had never seen anything quite like it.

Even Lucifer wouldn't make something that hideous.

Because its limbs had multiple joints, it had an awkward way of moving that made it look lopsided, but it was still incredibly fast and even more agile. According to Titania's [scan], the [chimera] had a level of 20, with a Speed stat of +200 and +150 Strength. Adam's Speed right now was only +50. That went to show him how much faster this enemy was than him.

Of course, for as powerful and fast as this enemy was, its movements were far too predictable for it to hit him.

"Kureha!" Adam called out as he leapt backward.

With a yip, the little fox yokai standing several yards behind him raised her second tail. Blue arcs of lightning erupted from the tail, agglomerated into a sphere, and flashed forward in a powerful bolt that rent the air. The [Thunder Bolt] slammed into the chest of the [chimera], which howled in pain as a large damage sign appeared above it.

-7,524!

The [chimera] had +30,000 health, and Kureha's attack had just taken away almost a third of that. Adam had already whittled away most of its health using [Dance of the Sakura Blossoms]. He only managed to hit it once, but thanks to [Blood Sacrifice] and [Song of Vigor], the amount of damage he did per attack was pretty ridiculous. Honestly, if he hadn't missed with his second attack, he would have one-shot killed this ugly creature.

With the last of its health sapped away, the [chimera] let out a pitiful howl before falling onto its stomach and going still.

Ding!

[Congratulations! You have killed 6 [chimera]! Items dropped: x4 [Chimera Core], [Jade Ring], and 6,600 gold coins! +15,000 experience points!]

Ding!

[Congratulations! Kureha has leveled up! She is now at level 14! +200 HP! +1,800 MP! +10 SP!]

Adam couldn't stop the smile from rising to his face as he finally saw the familiar announcement. He had been grinding levels for several hours now, killing [chimera] and [diamond serpents] in the forests just outside of Solum. It had taken a lot of effort, far more than he would have liked, but one of his companions had finally leveled up.

Of course, now Kureha needed over one million experience points to reach level 15, but that was something he would deal with later.

Like when he was trying to level Kureha up again.

With a swipe of his hand, he opened Kureha's status screen, put her 10 SP into her Intelligence.

"Congratulations, Kureha," Titania said to the little fox. "It looks like you have finally reached the level where leveling up becomes difficult."

Kureha yipped in what Adam thought was a happy voice. It was hard to tell. He leaned down as the little fox yokai ran up to him and began pawing at his leg. The happy mrrring noises she made as he scratched behind her ear were oddly soothing.

"Nice job, Kureha. I knew you had it in you."

"Yip!"

"So what now?" asked Titania as she fluttered over to Adam and sat down on his shoulder.

"Now we return to Solum," Adam said. "I would like to speak with the mayor before Fayte, Lilith, and Susan arrive."

It had only been one day since they completed their first quest together. Everyone had agreed to log in today at 8:00am. Adam, as someone who only needed two hours of sleep to remain at his peak physical and mental condition, had woken up at 12:30am this morning, logged into Age of Gods, and began grinding his, Kureha's, and Titania's levels ever since.

Because Adam wanted to maintain a higher level than all the other players in Age of Gods, he was working a lot harder to maintain a strong lead. He was worried, however. It took so many experience points to level up. The only way to do so would be to take on quests or raid dungeons, but he didn't know where any dungeons might be. He planned on taking another quest with his party again at some point, but there were several other things he wanted to do first.

One of them was talking to the mayor. Thanks to the quest he did for the man, Bromley Paxton was more than willing to see him.

"Adam. I did not expect to see you again so soon. Are you here for another quest?" the man asked.

They were back in Bromley Paxton's office. Adam was standing at attention, but the mayor was sitting behind his desk this time. It looked like he was working on papers… which surprised Adam. Was this also part of Age of God's setting? He'd never seen an NPC do actual work. Their only real purpose in games was to offer insight, lore, and quests.

"I do plan on taking another quest, but not right now. I actually had a question," Adam said.

"A question? Well, feel free to ask. I will answer if I am able to." Bromley Paxton wore an amicable smile. It was very diplomatic and made Adam think of some of the aristocrats and dignitaries he had killed during his time as Lucifer's assassin.

"I wanted to ask about hidden classes," Adam said. "Specifically, do you know if there's any place I could go to find either a [hidden class scroll] or a master who can train someone in a hidden class?"

"Hmmm…" Bromley Paxton stopped working when he heard Adam's question. A frown grew on his face as he leaned back in his seat and crossed his arms. "That is quite the question. You understand that hidden classes are very hard to find, yes?"

"I am aware," Adam said with a nod. "But I was hoping you might know something. Even a rumor would be fine."

The mayor hummed once more and scrunched his face up in thought, which made him look like a pug.

"I do know of a rumor regarding a place where you might be able to find a hidden class," Bromley Paxton admitted. "Legends say there is a cave several hundred klicks north of here, in a place filled with enemies that are all over level 40 called the Sunset Mountain Range. This cave is located on the tallest mountain on the Sun Continent, the Suncrest Mountain, and it's said to have been the last hiding place for the sole survivor of the now extinct Demon Knight Clan."

"Demon Knight Clan?" Adam asked.

It was Titania, still sitting on his shoulder, who answered him. "The Demon Knight Clan is a group of powerful demons who came here from the Forgotten Continent. Unlike the many other warlike demons who reveled in death and mayhem, the Demon Knight Clan cared more about money and sold their services to anyone who was willing to pay the right price." She snorted. "Because they have pointed ears, some people used to think they were related to my Fairy Clan."

"Are they not?" asked Adam.

"Of course not!"

"It was just a question. No need to get upset," Adam muttered.

"The Demon Knight Clan went extinct over a thousand years ago," Bromley Paxton said. "However, this legend about the cave only began around five hundred years ago. I am not sure if the cave really was the hideout of the last surviving Demon Knight Clansmen, or if it is just a rumor since no one has even found the cave. However, rumors have persisted that the last survivor of the Demon Knight Clan left behind a trial, and that those who complete the trial will gain a hidden class called Demon Knight Assassin."

"Thank you for the information," Adam said with a slight bow.

"Of course. Come to me if you need anything else."

Adam left the mayor's residence after getting the information he wanted. He traveled to the food court and bought Kureha several kebabs. She seemed to enjoy eating those the most. He also bought a loaf of honeyed bread and sliced it up for Titania.

"You are awfully considerate," Titania said as she grabbed one of the slices. It was just large enough to fit in her hands without looking obscene.

"What do you mean?" asked Adam.

"I mean you are always looking out for us," Titania said before nibbling on the bread. Her pointed ears wiggled in what Adam could only assume was joy. "I have noticed it ever since we met, but you seem to observe everyone in your party and anticipate our needs. I've never met such a considerate human before."

"Ah. Well, I guess you could say I've become used to looking after people," Adam admitted, not sure what else he could say.

"Hmm… is that so? So you look after people back in your world?"

"Yes. My lover."

After mentioning his lover, an image of Aris flashed in his mind, of her eyes closed, her lips ice blue, and her body frozen in stasis. His heart ached. Every day she was not with him was another day where the hole in his chest expanded. He did his best to ignore the pain, but Aris had been an inextricable part of his life for five whole years. How could he ignore something like that?

Titania must have seen the pain in his eyes. After studying him for another moment, she turned her head and focused on eating. Adam was grateful.

Fayte arrived several minutes after his conversation with Titania. She walked up to their table, her face hidden behind her veil as always, and sat down next to Adam.

"Good morning," she said in a soft voice. "You weren't at breakfast today. Have you been playing since early this morning?"

"More or less." Adam shrugged, then smiled sheepishly. "Sorry about missing breakfast. It's hard to tell the time when I'm playing."

"It does not help that they do not have a clock in any of the popup windows," Fayte added with a twinkle in her eyes.

Kureha finished eating while they spoke. The little fox yokai hopped off the table, onto the bench, and curled up on Adam's lap, where she promptly fell asleep. Adam began stroking the yokai's fur. His fox companion emitted soft noises in her sleep that reminded him of snoring.

"Lilith would flip if she saw this," Fayte said in a voice that seeped amusement.

"Probably," Adam agreed.

Lilith was the next person to arrive. The moment she saw Kureha sleeping on Adam's lap, her hands began twitching. It looked to him like she was just barely restraining herself from squealing like a love struck fool, or maybe she was resisting the desire to pluck Kureha from his lap and stroke her fur. Only the cool and mysterious persona she had cultivated for over a decade allowed her to maintain her composure as she sat down on Adam's other side.

"I-I'm sorry for being late!" Susan said as she rushed over to their table, the last one to appear.

"It is okay," Fayte said, though her eyes held an unknown glimmer in them as she looked at the heavily breathing young girl. "Are you okay, Su?"

"O-of course," Susan said, turning her head and looking away.

Adam frowned for a moment as he noticed this and realized something had happened with Susan, though the girl seemed unwilling to share. He didn't want to pry into her personal life too much. At the same time, it was clear that Fayte was concerned by whatever had happened to their youngest companion.

"Sit down, Su. I think we should discuss what to do now that everyone is here," Adam said.

Susan sent him a grateful look before sitting down on the opposite side of Adam, Lilith, and Fayte. These benches could seat six, but the other two women had already claimed the spots next to him.

Now that everyone was present, Adam informed the group about the legend he had learned from Bromley Paxton, the one that said a Demon Knight Clansman had left a trial that would allow someone to change their class into Demon Knight Assassin. The three women listened to him with attentive expressions. They had already learned the benefits of having a hidden class after Adam got the [Fairy Archer Scroll] from Bromley Paxton's vault.

"So you think we should head there?" asked Fayte.

Adam nodded. "At the moment, there are only a few thousand players who have left the Village of Beginnings, but more will come soon. Before that happens, I believe we should make sure all of us have a hidden class. That will help give us an edge over everyone else when the elite members of society begin forming guilds."

"Speaking of, how does one form a guild in this game?" Fayte inquired.

"People can form guilds once their Reputation is high enough. Guilds can be formed by using a [Guild Creation Token] and registering your guild with the Guild Association," Titania said. Having finished her meal, she once more fluttered up and sat on Adam's shoulder. "The Guild Association is a long-standing group that's been around since before I became the Guardian of the Spear. It's their responsibility to manage guild registration. They keep track of things like guild rankings, each guild's net worth, and how many quests they have completed."

Adam had not known this. He blamed himself for not asking her. The information about guilds would definitely be useful later, but they would not have to concern themselves with that until some-one found a [Guild Creation Token].

"And how does one find a [Guild Creation Token]?" asked Fayte.

Titania's beautiful red hair wavered like rippling waves as she shook her head. "No one knows. Sometimes they are dropped from powerful monsters and raid bosses that people defeat. Other times they might appear inside of a treasure chest deep within a dungeon. Not much is known about [Guild Creation Tokens]. It has always been assumed that the Four Goddesses created them and scattered the tokens throughout the world."

Talking about [Guild Creation Tokens] wouldn't do them much good right now. This was something they wouldn't need to worry about for a while. That being the case, Adam and his party decided it was time to head off. They had a hidden class to find.

After renting out four horses, Adam, Fayte, Lilith, Susan, Tita-nia, and Kureha left Solum and traveled north. Each of the players got their own horse. Titania was too small to ride a horse and Kureha was a fox. What did she need a horse for? Both Titania and

Kureha hitched a ride with Adam, same as usual. Titania rode on his shoulder and Kureha turned his hair into a bed.

He hoped he wouldn't smell like fox when this was done.

Lilith had looked jealous, though whether she was jealous of the fox or Adam was not something he could figure out.

North of Solum was a large expanse of mountains and valleys that seemed to stretch on for hundreds of miles. The valleys were vast and deep. Sometimes there would be a large lake at the bottom. Other times there would be a massive forest. Adam could not judge how large each valley was, but he estimated that most of them were about the size of a large city like Phoenix or Houston.

According to Bromley Paxton, the cave was located within the surrounding mountain range. It was known as the Sunset Mountain Range and it was the largest mountain range on the Sun Continent, stretching from one side to the other as it divided the continent in half. Among the mountains, the biggest was located smack in the center, a snow-capped mountain surrounded by clouds.

Suncrest Mountain.

Bromley Paxton said that if there really was a cave where a Demon Knight Clansman had hidden themselves, it would definitely be there.

However, to get there, they had to contend with the monsters.

A fierce roar shook the ground as Adam and Lilith danced around a pair of massive feet, each of which were about two times bigger than they were. These feet were attached to trunk-like legs that reminded Adam of the massive trees in the Redwood Forest.

Whenever these feet landed on the ground, they shook the earth, threatening to knock him and Lilith off their feet.

These creatures were called [validodon]. They were colossal dinosaurian-like creatures that closely resembled a triceratops. Three large horns sprouted from its forehead, while six more, three on either side, emerged from near its cheeks. Its body was covered in hard scales like armor and possessed multiple spiky outcroppings. Its brilliant brown eyes were covered by thick brow ridges that acted like a helmet to protect its one vulnerable point.

"Watch out for its tail!" Fayte shouted.

While Lilith lowered herself onto her stomach, Adam leapt into the air as the [validodon] swept its tail at them. Attached to the tail was a very large spiked ball. He would have assumed it was a weapon someone had attached to this creature, but it was actually growing out of its tail. A natural weapon.

After dodging its tail swipe, Adam and Lilith charged forward and attacked its underbelly. Lilith could only use [slash], but Adam activated [Dance of the Sakura Blossoms] to deal maximum damage.

-742; -742; -742; -742!

-22,545; -67,635; MISS!

While Adam and Lilith attacked from up close, Kureha, Fayte, and Susan fired their spells and arrows from a distance. Kureha used [Thunder Bolt] and [Fireball]. She switched at regular intervals to deal with the cooldown time between spells. Fayte only had [Energy Bolt] for single person attack spells, but her skill was maxed out and didn't have a cooldown time, so she could fire constantly until she ran out of MP.

It was a good thing they had bought a lot of [low-grade mana potions].

-600; -600; -600; -600!

-6,000; -7,920; -6,000; -7,920!

While Kureha and Fayte fired off their spells, Susan took aim with her bow and shot arrows at the [validodon]. She primarily used her [deadshot] skill, but whenever the cooldown time for [Fairy Shot] ended, she would charge up her attack and fire it. The [Fairy Shot] flew from her bow like a streak of light and slammed into the monster's hide like a cannonball.

-870; -870; -870; -1,740!

The [validodon] was a tank-type enemy. It possessed +545,000 health and dealt -6,000 to -12,000 points of damage depending on the skill it used, meaning it could easily one-shot any of them if its attacks actually hit. This meant Adam and Lilith, who were darting between the creature's legs, needed to be careful not to get hit even once.

While Adam and Lilith attacked at close range and Fayte, Susan, and Kureha attacked from a distance, Titania sang the upbeat [Song of Vigor] to increase everyone's Physical and Magical Attack. Thanks to her, the damage they did was three times greater than it would have been otherwise. It was largely because of her power that they were able to demolish the enemy's HP so quickly.

Adam was confident that even if Fayte, Lilith, and Susan weren't with him, he could have still defeated the [validodon], but it

would have been much harder. Altogether, the three women did a total of around -10,000 damage every time they attacked. That meant
he was still the heaviest hitter, but their presence definitely helped.

After fighting for nearly half an hour, they defeated the [vali-
dodon]. The one who struck the killing blow was Adam after he activated [Dance of the Sakura Blossoms] for the third time.

Ding!

*[Congratulations! You have defeated the [validodon]. Items
dropped: [Heavy Plate Mail], [Validodon Horn], [Monster Core],
[Ring of Vitality], and 100,000 gold coins! +150,000 experience
points!]*

Ding!

*[Congratulations! You have leveled up! You are now at level
14! +1,125 HP! +20 MP! +5 SP!]*

Ding!

*[Congratulations! Changing_Fayte has leveled up! She is now
at level 13! +50 HP! +90 MP! +5 SP!]*

Ding!

*[Congratulations! Lilith has leveled up! She is now at level 13!
+10 HP! +5 MP! +5 SP!]*

Ding!

*[Congratulations! Little_Su has leveled up! She is now at level
13! +125 HP! +10 MP! +5 SP!]*

Adam shook his head when several announcements about him
and his party members leveling up appeared in a window before
him. The disparity between Susan's and Titania's gains over Fayte's
and Lilith's was astronomical. It once more let Adam know he was

making the right choice by trying to get them a hidden class instead of taking on quests.

Since he had also leveled up, Adam added his SP into his Strength, bringing it up to +490. He also glanced at his spear, which was currently at level 8 still. He needed over +460,000 experience points to level it up.

"Nice work, everyone!" Fayte said as he and Lilith regrouped with the others.

Fayte, Susan, Titania, and Kureha had stayed far away from the battlefield. The [validodon] had a skill called [Earthquake], which was an AOE skill that did more than just -12,000 damage. It also had a 100% chance of causing stun. Of course, since it caused -12,000 damage, the stun effect was a moot point, but it was just another reason to remain outside of its range. Adam and Lilith could avoid being damaged by leaping into the air at the exact moment when [Earthquake] was cast. The others were not so skilled.

"Congratulations, Su," Adam said. "How does your first time leveling up with your new class feel?"

"I-it feels good," Susan mumbled, looking down at the grass and blushing bright red. "I feel a lot stronger now than when I leveled up before. It's hard to describe."

Titania nodded. "This does not surprise me. The strength you gain from a beginner's class is nothing compared to a hidden class, never mind an excellent class like Fairy Archer. It's only natural you would feel the difference."

While Titania treated her words as if they were gospel, Adam and the others who lived in the real world understood what Susan meant. The feeling of strength they had in the game felt a lot different than real life. Each increase in level gave them more energy, more strength, and made them feel more invigorated. Of course, these levels only affected them in the game. In real life, they felt the same as always.

Because they still had a long way to go before reaching the cave—if the cave really did exist—Adam and the others mounted their horses again and began racing across the valley toward Suncrest Mountain.

While they were traveling, Adam checked out the new items they had acquired.

Item Pouch:
Name: Heavy Plate Mail
Item Type: Armor
Grade: 2-Star
Use requirements: Can only be equipped by Warriors level 20 and above.
Description: This heavy plate mail is designed to maximize protection at the cost of mobility. It is great for people who rely on Defense over Movement.
Abilities: Defense+500; Speed-50

Item Name: Ring of Vitality
Item Type: Ring
Grade: 2-Star
Use requirements: Can be used by any class level 10 and above.
Description: This ring was crafted and enchanted by a Dwarf apprentice. It grants a boost to Constitution and restores health!
Abilities: Constitution+50; Restores +5 HP every one second.

Item Name: Monster Core
Item Type: Core
Grade: 2-Star
Use requirements: Can only be used by players with the Black-smith, Craftsmen, or Enchanter secondary classes.
Description: Monster Cores can be used by Blackmiths, Crafts-men, and Enchanters to enhance armor, clothing, or create skill scrolls. They can also be used in the construction of magical de-vices.
Abilities: +50% MP; +50% Magic Attack; Can be used in the creation of a defensive skill

While the [validodon horn] and [monster core] were not items he could use right now because they were for players who had a sec-ondary class, the other two pieces of equipment seemed pretty good... though the [Heavy Plate Mail] was not something he could equip, nor would he want to. He looked at the [Ring of Vitality] for a moment. It was a simple ring made of gold and adorned with a carnelian gemstone.

"Lilith!" Adam called as he pulled on the reigns of his horse and made it move so he was trodding alongside the woman in ques-tion. Once he was sure he had Lilith's attention, he held out his hand with the ring resting on his palm. "Here. Put this on. It isn't much, but it should help increase your stats."

Lilith took the [Ring of Vitality] from his outstretched hand, gazed at it for a little bit, then looked away.

"Thanks," she mumbled, slipping the ring onto her finger.

Adam nodded and moved his horse once more so they weren't so close. He didn't know if you could collide with each other while riding in this game, but he wouldn't put it past the creator to make such a thing possible. He'd always said it, but this game was so realistic it was sometimes hard to believe he wasn't in the real world right now.

Out of the corner of his eyes, Adam caught someone staring at him. It was Fayte. The moment she realized he had noticed her, she smiled at him and looked away, resuming a conversation with Susan. He frowned for a moment. Why had she been looking at him? After thinking about it, he couldn't figure out the reason and decided to put it out of his mind.

They eventually reached Suncrest Mountain after passing through a valley. The landscape changed from grassy plains and forests to dirt and rocks. It had taken four days to reach this place. They had logged out several times to eat and sleep, much to Titania's displeasure. There was only a small path up the mountain side, and it was steep and winding, making Adam worry about whether their horses would be able to climb up it.

To be safe, they left their horses tied to a tree at the entrance of the mountain trail and began walking up it on their own. The mountain pass was fairly treacherous. Not only was it steep, but there were several places where the gravel was unstable. Fayte and Susan relied on Adam and Lilith to find the safe paths for them. Even then, there were several missteps.

"Aaaahh!"

Susan screamed when her foot stepped on an unstable rock that came loose. Her body teetered over the edge, more gravel coming loose, and she soon pitched backward. She tried to regain her balance by pinwheeling her arms, but she was already falling by that point.

Because she didn't want to see what would happen to her when she fell, Susan closed her eyes, which was why she missed Adam grabbing her hand and pulling her into his chest. It wasn't until her face bumped against his chest that she opened her eyes again. After realizing she wasn't dead, she looked up at his relieved face.

"You okay?" he asked.

"Ah…" Susan's voice became caught in her throat. She could say nothing, only nod her head once.

"I'm glad. Here. Hold my hand until we move past this point. I don't want you falling again."

Susan did not say anything, which made Adam frown a little, but she did nod as she tentatively grasped his hand. She really was one of the shyest people he had ever met. It made him wonder when she'd get used to his presence, or if maybe she would never get used to him.

Since Adam was helping Susan, he let Lilith take the lead while he took the rear. Lilith was just as talented as him at finding the correct path to continue traveling up. They continued climbing up the mountain, and eventually reached a small cliff face.

And situated just several feet away from the path they had climbed was the entrance to a cave.

THE DEMON KNIGHT CLANSMAN'S TRIAL

The cave entrance was not very wide nor very tall. Susan could probably fit through it without any trouble, but Adam would have to stoop down while walking to pass through. It didn't have any sense of foreboding like the cavern Adam had gone into during his time in the Village of Beginnings. However, he knew better than to just assume nothing dangerous was lurking inside based on that.

"Is this… the cave the Demon Knight Clansman hid himself in?" asked Fayte, sounding uncertain.

"I don't know." Adam shook his head. "But it is the first cave we've discovered. We should at least check it out. I'll take the front. Susan and Fayte, I want you two in the middle. Lilith will take the rear. Kureha and Titania? I'd like it if you two could head in right after Fayte and Su."

"We shall do as you say," Titania said, then crossed her arms. "Though you should know I'd prefer staying close to you. You are the spear's master."

Adam shrugged. "I understand your desires, but this time, I think it would be best if you all stayed a little further back, just in case there are traps. I'm pretty good at disarming traps, but the same can't be said for the rest of you."

Lilith was also good at spotting and disarming traps, but Adam couldn't tell anyone that since he wanted to keep their relationship a secret.

Titania frowned like she wanted to deny his words. When she found herself unable to, she huffed and formed up behind Fayte and Susan alongside Kureha. Fortunately, Adam's little fox yokai companion didn't have the same issues Titania did.

With Adam in the lead, they journeyed into the cave. Just as he first suspected, he was forced to bend his knees and stoop to fit through. Not only was the cave small, it also wasn't very wide, meaning he had to scrunch his shoulders in. It was a good thing he wasn't claustrophobic, or Adam was certain he would have been panicking.

The cavern fortunately widened after they walked for several yards. What he saw upon exiting from the small tunnel was a much larger interior chamber that looked unnatural, like someone had built it instead of being formed naturally through erosion over the course of several centuries. Shaped like a cylinder, the chamber walls were relatively smooth and the floor was also flat. A ceiling sat high over their heads. At the far side of this chamber was a door, and in the center of this chamber was a monolith.

"What is that?" asked Susan, staring curiously at the monolith.

Titania fluttered over to it with a flap of her wings, Adam and the others following close behind her. Glowing symbols appeared when they neared it. Neither Adam nor anyone else from the real world could understand what those glyphs said. It looked like they were written in a form of runic alphabet, but he didn't recognize which language, so they must have been a made up language for the game. It was a good thing they had Titania with them.

"I journeyed here after our clan was betrayed by Beleques. Injured and dying, I will turn this cave into my final resting place. Here, I will leave my most treasured possessions deep within this mountain. Should any brave soul find this place, you may take everything that lies beyond the door, but only if you have the skills to do so. Be warned. My trial is one that only someone with the heart of an assassin can survive."

Titania read the glyphs out loud, and everyone else listened with uncertain expressions. Fayte glanced at Adam, but then she looked at Lilith, who stood silently behind the rest of them. It was impossible to tell what Lilith was thinking.

"There's no name here," Titania said with a sigh. "I'm not sure who this place belonged to, but it looks like we must pass the trial to get whatever is on the other side of that door. Since this is a trial left by a member of the Demon Knight Clan, and it specifically states only someone who has the 'heart of an assassin' can survive, I believe only someone with the Assassin class may take the trial."

Everyone turned to look at Lilith, who remained collected and cold even under the intense scrutiny of four different people and one fox. She looked at them all. Her eyes stopped on Adam, a question in her gaze. He nodded once.

"I'll go," she said at last.

"I do not know what sort of trial you will face, but I should warn you there is a good chance you will die," Titania stated. "The Demon Knight Clan was a cold and deadly clan of demons from the Forgotten Continent who specialized in assassination. While they were known for not hating the Races of Light, their infamy for cold-blooded murder is something all races of this world are well-aware of even to this day. Be careful."

Lilith only nodded at the fairy before she walked over to the door. Nothing happened when she stepped in front of it, but then she placed her hand on the door, causing several glyphs to light up. A loud rumble shook the cave. The door opened with a ponderous and glacial slowness. When Lilith stepped through the door, it closed behind her, trapping her on the other side.

"Do you think Lilith will be okay?" asked Susan, casting a worried glance at the door.

Fayte rubbed the girl's head. "I'm sure Lilith will be fine. Don't forget about how skilled she is. We would have never leveled up as fast as we did without her."

"Yes. You're right." Susan placed a hand against her chest and took a deep breath, as though trying to calm herself down. She smiled, but everyone could tell from the way her lips trembled that she was still worried. "I'm certain you're right."

Adam did not express any concern for Lilith. He knew her talent better than anyone else, and he was certain she would succeed no matter the trials she faced. Of course, even if she didn't, she wouldn't die permanently. She'd just lose a level and be sent back to the cathedral in Solum.

He turned to Titania. "I've heard you mention the Races of Light before. Can you explain them in more detail?"

"The races of light are what we call the races who were created by the four goddesses. Humans, fairies, beastmen, and dwarves are members of the races of light. The Demon Knight Clan, the Spider Clan, the Black Dragons, the War Beasts... all of them are demons and not members of the races of light. They came from the Forgotten Continent, which continues to churn out powerful monsters that even the strongest members of the Races of Light have trouble defeating."

Fayte, Susan, and Kureha wandered over to them as Titania continued talking. While it was clear that Kureha wasn't paying any attention, the two humans girls seemed interested in what Titania was saying.

"So there are four Races of Light. How many demon races are there?" asked Fayte.

"Twelve," Titania answered immediately. "Aside from the four I just mentioned, there are also the Sky Demons, the Hell Clan, the Frost Giants, the Serpent Clan, the Dullahans, the Manticores, the Clan of Despair, and the Prime Clan, which is said to be the strongest of the twelve demon clans."

"It sounds like there are a lot of demons," Adam muttered. "I'm surprised the races of light haven't been overwhelmed."

"Aside from the Spider Clan, demons have very low birth rates," Titania explained. "That's why there aren't as many demons as there are humans. However, demons are also much stronger than humans. A level 40 demon will be four to five times stronger than a level 40 human, regardless of what class they have."

Hearing Titania speak of the demons who hailed form the Forgotten Continent, Adam remembered his time inside the Forest of Gloom, where the Spider Clan had taken up residence, and could not help but grimace. If he was at least level 20, he'd go back there and try to shove his spear up that blasted spider woman's ass. He hated how he'd been forced to flee from that wretched [Spider Queen].

Adam had always been a sore loser.

Lilith knew the moment the door shut behind her that she would not be able to leave unless she completed this trial or died in the attempt. The door was sealed shut with some kind of magic. There was also no doorknob. It would not budge no matter how many times she pushed on it and even using attacks did not work.

Since she could not go back, she could only move forward.

Unlike the previous tunnel, the area she walked through now was a proper hallway. She judged it to be about five feet wide and maybe seven tall. The walls, floor, and ceiling were smooth. That Demon Knight Clansman had probably spent the last bit of his strength creating this trial before quietly dying. She wondered if he had been content when he died or if he'd been filled with bitter regret.

There was a door at the other end of this hallway. It was large, made from stone, and did not have a knob. There weren't any identifying marks either. Lilith could not see any way to open it.

She walked up to the door, eyes on her surroundings, and watched as several glowing glyphs appeared, not on the door, but on the floor. Lilith's sense of danger flared up. She only had a moment to act.

Leaping backward, she avoided certain death when the floor disappeared. She walked over and looked down. At the bottom of the trap door was a pit full of spikes. This sort of trap was something that had been used long before the creation of modern security in the real world. She had never dealt with traps like this before, but she had made a few to catch animals when she was hunting for food in the wilderness during some of the missions that took her to very remote locations.

After the floor vanished, glyphs appeared on the door seconds before it slid open. The trap door was only about two feet across. Lilith easily leapt over the gap, landed with a crouch, then jumped forward once more when the floor beneath her wobbled. She looked back and narrowed her eyes upon seeing the floor she'd been standing on had vanished into darkness.

Beyond the door was a large interior space that was several hundred times bigger than the room where Adam, Fayte, Susan, Titania, and Kureha were waiting for her. Even she could not judge how high the ceiling was or how big the space was. She estimated it to be the size of at least two football fields, so at least two hundred yards long and maybe three hundred and twenty feet wide, but that was only a guess.

Judging the size of this place was hard because of the gigantic object in the very center of this cavernous space.

What stood in the center of this space was a structure, but it did not have the medieval European aesthetic of everything else she'd seen from this game. This place looked like a Chinese palace. It was an elaborate structure of considerable size, possessing four compounds that ranged from the size of a three-story house to single-story buildings. It was made from black stone and possessed a dark, foreboding aura.

Imposing was a good word to describe this place.

Lilith kept a careful eye on her surroundings as she walked up the stone steps leading to the first building. She could see the other buildings as she crested the stairs. Many of them were walled off and surrounded by gardens, but these were not the zen gardens so often found in Chinese architecture. Filled with dead plants and black sand, these gardens looked like they had been cultivated by Yanluo himself. Even the motes surrounding some of the buildings were filled with murky, black water.

The first building did not contain anything inside. It was just a large, empty space. However, the moment she walked through the doors, they slid shut behind her.

With reflexes honed from years of brutal life and death battles, Lilith flipped through the air, landed on the ground, and performed several back handsprings. As she did, the floor beneath her feet disappeared. Each tile vanished into thin air, revealing a dark pit that seemed to go on forever.

As she landed in the center of the room, the floor beneath her sank but didn't vanished. It was like she had stepped on a button. A loud sound like cranking chains echoed around her. She looked up just in time to see a spiked section of the ceiling swiftly descend. She rolled across the floor. The spiked ceiling slammed into the floor, punctured the tiles, and was reeled back up. Numerous holes were left in the floor.

What followed appeared to be a game of cat and mouse as Lilith did everything she possibly could to avoid being killed. Sometimes the floor beneath her would vanish. Other times the ceiling would come down. Poison gas sprayed from vents in the ground. Projectiles shot from the walls. This entire room had become a death trap.

Lilith's breathing grew heavy as she avoided certain death by the skin of her teeth. Her reflexes were a tad slower than Adam's, but she made up for that by having several years of experience over him. She'd been training in Eden for at least four years longer than he had. Even now she still remembered the small child who had joined their ranks when she was sixteen years old.

As she dodged death by the narrowest of margins, Lilith cast her gaze around the room. The door she had entered through was gone. There was just a large wall in front of where it had once been, and there was no door on the other side of the room either, meaning she had no way out. If this was reality, there would probably be no way to escape from this room except blowing apart a wall. This was a video game, however, which meant there was always a way out.

It took her nearly two whole minutes, but after dodging another spiked ceiling that came down, Lilith found a switch located on the ceiling about sixteen yards to her left. She looked around some more and noticed that most of the floor was gone, which meant she couldn't reach it the normal way.

She bunched her legs underneath her and used her powerful muscles to leap onto the spiked ceiling before it could retract. As she stood on the ascending platform, Lilith noticed the mechanical network of chains and pulleys that activated the falling ceilings. Once her ceiling stopped moving, she leapt forward onto the next one, then the next one, and the next open before finally reaching the switch. She flipped it.

In that moment, a change occurred inside of the room. The tiled floors reappeared as if by magic, the spikes on the falling ceilings retracted, and the walls that blocked off the entrance and exit slid into the floor.

Lilith dropped to the floor. Her knees felt a jolt, but she crouched low to absorb the shock of impact, stood back up, and walked toward the exit. It was a paper door, the kind she had seen before on her trips to Asia. The door was painted to depict a group of gray-skinned men and women dressed in black armor slaying all kinds of humans, demons, and various other mythical creatures.

She slid the door open and stepped outside.

Past the door was a complex of buildings, gardens, motes, and bridges. The gardens were all filled with dead plants and black soil.

She didn't know if it had always been like this, or if they died because no one was there to take care of them. In the center of the garden was an island with a single tree at its center—a dead sakura tree whose petals had long since withered. In front of the tree was another stone tablet.

Lilith did not have Asteroth's gaming experience. She had never joined the virtual world until this game. However, experience or not, even she understood that the tablet likely contained the information she would need to successfully complete these trials.

There did not seem to be a method of crossing over the water, but she did not believe swimming was the proper method. The lake surrounding the island was at least fifty feet across. That meant it was deep. Since this was a world of monsters and fantasy, she would not be surprised if some monster burst from the water and attacked her.

She walked around the circumference of the lake. As she did, Lilith eventually discovered a small stone panel that caused several stone pillars to rise from the lake when stepped on. Each stone pillar was about four yards high and maybe one foot in diameter. That wasn't a lot of room to work with, but she would make do.

Lilith took a running leap and landed on the first pillar, then smoothly leapt once more and landed on the second pillar. She hadn't lost her momentum. However, the pillar she stood on suddenly shook and began descending. Narrowing her eyes, she hopped across the third, fourth, fifth, sixth, up to the fifteenth pillar before finally landing on the island. Each pillar sank below the lake the moment she landed. She did not look back and instead walked up to the stone tablet and peered at it. There were three hexagonal slots near the bottom and glyphs above them.

Her eyes narrowed at the glyphs.

She couldn't read this.

Kneeling before the tablet, Lilith reached out and brushed her fingers across it. The moment she did, a beam of light shot out and struck her in the forehead. She didn't feel any pain. However, a voice soon echoed inside of her mind.

"In order to receive my inheritance, you must complete three trials: The trials of the heart, the body, and the mind. When you have completed each trial, return here with the emblems of your victory to receive my inheritance."

The voice sounded old—ancient even. It reminded her of crinkled parchment.

It said she needed to complete three trials before coming back here. Lilith turned around and glanced at the three buildings inside of this complex. Those must be where each trial was held, though she did not know which building contained what trial.

There was another stone tablet on this small island. She stepped on it to make the pillars rise once more. Hopping back across the pillars, Lilith first traveled inside of the building on her left. The door slid shut and locked the moment she entered. However, she was not paying attention to the door.

The room before her was familiar.

Her heart could not help but shudder as she walked across what was obviously a training ground. This stadium-like training field was something she had seen thousands of times before. It was hard not to recognize the training ground where she, the other members of Lucifer's assassination unit, and Adam had nearly died over and over again to increase their strength.

The desolate field was covered in scorch marks, scarring, and blood. No one had ever cleaned up the blood. Lucifer once said it was because he wanted it to be a constant reminder, a lesson on what happened to those who showed weakness.

A man stood in the center of the field. No, not a man. A boy. He could not have been more than eleven-years-old. His blond hair and chubby cheeks made him seem cute, but his eyes were dead, filled with a complete willingness to kill that caused Lilith to shiver.

"M-Master?" she gasped in surprise.

The one she called "Master" spun a spear around in his hand. She had no idea when or where he had gotten it, but that hardly mattered now. Without even a moment of hesitation, his entire figure blurred.

Lilith only had a split second to raise her dagger and block.

The loud clang of metal on metal rang in her ears as Lilith stumbled back. The young boy surged forward and struck at her knees, hoping to lop them off. She back flipped out of the way.

"Master, what are you doing?! It's me! It's Lilith!"

Even though she screamed and called for him, he did not answer her. His dead eyes stared into hers, sending a chill down her spine, freezing her blood, and making tears sting her eyes.

This was Adam from seven years ago. Back then, Adam had just been a child, but he had also been Lucifer's greatest creation. His strength, speed, reflexes, intelligence, and ability to regenerate even after having his arms and legs cut off had made him the deadli-est weapon ever conceived. Adam had dominated the training field ever since joining their group. Even Lilith, the strongest at the time, began losing to him after a year of constant battle. His ability to learn and adapt only made him more deadly. However, there was one difference between the Adam she had known back then and the one standing before her now.

The eyes.

Adam had always possessed intense eyes. Eyes that burned like molten lava. There had been a determination in his eyes, a will to live and escape, and there had also been a kindness. It was his eyes that had swallowed Lilith whole and made her willingly pledge her undying loyalty to him.

These eyes were dead. They contained nothing. All she saw was an intent to kill.

"M-Master! Snap out of it! I don't know what's happening, but you mustn't let yourself be controlled like this!"

Adam did not listen to her and charged again. Lilith gritted her teeth as she blocked his attack, but his blow was far stronger than hers. He was using one of the Seven Forms. It was not a style taught to him by Lucifer, but one he had learned from a girl named Alexis before he even arrived in Eden. His movements were staggered and erratic like he was walking on eight legs instead of two. Lilith be-lieved this form was called…

"Dance of the Spider," she whispered to herself.

Adam's attack broke her guard and slammed into her, slicing apart her flesh and spilling blood all over the floor.

Or that would have happened if this was real life.

Instead, all she felt was a brief flaring of pain followed by a -65 floating over her head.

That was when she realized this wasn't real, she was not back in Eden, and this person wasn't her master.

This was a game.

Once she realized this, her shock wore off and she thought about the situation analytically. This was a trial. Since she had been brought to a place that called forth painful memories, she believed it was the Trial of the Heart, though she didn't understand how a game was able to pull up her memories. Could all games do this?

As Adam charged at her again, she dodged and redirected his attacks accordingly, tilting her weapon at an angle so she could avoid having to face the full brunt of his spear. He was using the Dance of the Dragon now. It was a dance that relied on pure power, just like the raging of a violent and powerful dragon. Sparks flew as her dagger clashed with the blurring streak of silver in his hands. Even though her arms still shook with each strike, she wasn't as bad off now as she had been at the start.

She backed up and tried to figure out what this trial was about. It was testing her heart, but how? What was she expected to do?

Lilith wondered if maybe this was a trial to overcome her master. Maybe it wanted her to prove that she had the heart of an assassin by killing Adam. She bit her lower lip as her nose wrinkled in a grimace. She had indeed been trained to kill her heart like an assassin should, but she could not under any circumstances raise her sword against the man she had pledged herself to, not even an illusion of him.

Once this thought occurred to her, Lilith dropped to her knees, bowed her head, and offered her neck. Even if this was not the real Adam, she could not raise her blade to him.

"Master," she whispered in a soft voice. "You are my lord. If not for your kindness back then, I would have been lost. I pledged myself to you. I pledged my heart, my body, and my soul. All of these are yours to take. If you wish to claim my life, you can."

Lilith waited for Adam's spear to impale her, but when it didn't, she lifted her head. She had to blink upon seeing that Adam was no longer there. In fact, the entire training ground had vanished. All that was left was a small room that looked like a typical Chinese room that was mostly empty, save a single pedestal upon which a small emblem sat.

Standing up, she walked cautiously over to the pedestal and looked at the small emblem sitting on it. The emblem was shaped like a hexagon, about one inch thick, and just large enough to fit on her palm. It was the same shape and size as the three slots on the stone tablet. In the very center of the hexagonal shaped emblem was the symbol of a heart.

She picked up the stone and stared at it. Had she succeeded with the trial? But how? Assassins were people who killed their heart in order to accomplish their mission. For an assassin, nothing was more important than completing the mission at any cost... or was that not right? She had been taught by Lucifer that an assassin completed their task no matter what, but were they not also loyal to the one who assigned them these tasks? Perhaps this Trial of the Heart was not one in which she killed her heart to complete her mission, but one where she proved her loyalty to her master.

After all, what was a master if not the one who controlled her heart?

While she was still a little confused, Lilith realized she had completed this trial, and so she left the room with the stone tablet in hand, journeyed across the garden, and entered the building on the opposite side.

This room was much larger than the previous one. Several wooden pillars jutted from the stone floor and disappeared into the ceiling. A number of candles situated on ornate candelabras about a yard tall flickered to provide a dim illumination. There was a pedestal against the far wall opposite the door, but it was guarded by a pair of golden statues with six arms, three faces pointing in opposite directions, and a dadao—a Chinese sword with a broad blade that was between two and three feet long—grasped firmly in each hand.

Lilith walked forward as the door sealed shut behind her, and when she reached the center of the room, the two statues shuddered. They raised their legs at the same time and took a single step forward. Then they raised their other leg and took another step. The two statues, now brought back to life, turned to face her before charging forward.

DEMON KNIGHT AS-
SASSIN

L ilith could not use the [scan] skill since her class was Assassin, but even though she didn't know what sort of stats this enemy had, she was able to glean some basic information on these two statues that had suddenly charged toward her from the window display that appeared above them.

Name: Asura
Description: A statue created from powerful dark magic. These statues embody chaos and attack anything within range, includ-ing their creator.
Class: 1-star
Level: 13

Known as [Asura], both 1-star enemies were at level 13, the same level as her. From this, she judged that the trial was made to be difficult but not impossible to complete. She strongly suspected that these [Asura] would have been at level 15 if she was at level 15 and level 30 if she was at level 30.

In other words, it was meant to test her current abilities.

Lilith leapt backward as the [Asura] on her left swung two of its six swords in a vertical slash. The twin blades slammed into the ground and, much to her astonishment, cut right through the floor. This floor was made of stone. It was obviously extremely durable. For this creature to cut through the floor with such ease meant its strength stat must have been ridiculously high.

With a grimace, Lilith realized she could not let herself get hit even once.

Spinning on the balls of her feet, Lilith dashed away from the two [Asura], charging toward a wall. She didn't pause. Upon reaching the wall, she ran up it, pushed off the surface, and stretched out her hand, latching onto a wooden beam that traveled the expanse of the ceiling. The muscles in her arm flexed. With a grunt, she swung herself up and landed on the beam in a crouch.

She activated the [hide] skill and looked down.

Before launching any kind of attack, it was always important to learn more about the enemy. This went doubly so when the enemy was more powerful than you. While these [Asura] had the same level as her, Lilith understood that enemies and monsters always had more health and higher stats than players. The game would be too easy if that wasn't the case.

On a side note, Lilith realized that Adam was a paradox within the game, being a player who could defeat enemies many levels higher than himself. There probably weren't many people like him.

Aside from enemies just being stronger than players of the same level, these two [Asura] were 1-star enemies. Their stats would be even more impressive than a regular enemy.

The two [Asura] walked aimlessly on the floor below, sometimes twirling the swords in their hands as if they were real people. Since virtual reality games ran on logic and programming, there was probably a pattern to their movements, which was what she wanted to look for. It would be easier to attack these two if she could discover their pattern.

However, she wasn't going to figure out their attack pattern by just crouching there.

Lilith took a deep breath, held it in, and then stood up. Her [hide] skill deactivated because she moved. This meant she was now visible and would probably draw the agro from both [Asura], but she moved before either enemy could notice her.

She tipped over the side of the beam and kicked off the surface. Her speed accelerated as she fell. Curling herself into a ball while still in midair, Lilith struck the floor and rolled across it before skipping back to her feet. There was some discomfort in her back from the heavy landing. Even so, she ignored the slight twinge as she came up behind the first [Asura] and struck it with [throat slit].

-1!

Lilith's eyes went wide when she saw that her attack barely did any damage. Assassins were supposed to deal the heaviest amount of damage out of all the beginner fighting classes. Warriors were all-rounders. Their stats were normally evenly balanced between attack, defense, and speed. On the other hand, Assassins specialized in attack and had no defense to speak of.

Of course, compared to the damage she had seen Adam inflict on the opponents they had run across, the damage she could deal was insignificant. She did not judge herself by his standards, however. Asteroth had always called Adam a freak of nature. While she would never call her master that, even she acknowledged that the things he did were not things a normal human could do.

Either way, seeing her most powerful attack only doing -1 damage was shocking.

-1; -1; -1; -1; -1!

Lilith attacked several more times with [slash], swinging her dagger up, down, and across her enemy's chest. Each attack caused sparks to erupt from the stone statue. A loud squealing sound grated on her ears. Her attack arm was beginning to feel numb every time she hit her enemy, and yet, no matter how many times she attacked, the amount of damage she inflicted didn't change.

The [Asura] turned around and swung at her with three of its six swords. Lilith leapt back to avoid the attack, but then the second [Asura] came up on her left and attacked as well. Unlike the first one, this one swung all six swords at differently timed intervals. Each attack was well-coordinated and designed to leave opponents with little room to counter.

Lilith found herself being forced into a corner. She wove left, right, ducked, and jumped to keep herself from being sliced apart. A diagonal slash was narrowly avoided when she tilted her body. A horizontal swing from two of the [Asura's] swords were dodged when she skipped backward. Lilith soon found herself pressed against the corner of the room, but rather than allow herself to remain pinned, she leapt up and pressed her hands and feet against each wall. There she remained as the [Asura] closed in on her. When the two [Asura] were within swinging distance, she pushed off the wall, leapt over their heads, landed on the ground, and spun around to attack the nearest enemy.

-1; -1; -1!

Backing off after the [Asura] turned to attack her, Lilith found herself frowning. She did not know how much health these things had. In other words, there was no way for her to tell how long it would take to defeat them. Times like this made her wish she had a [scan scroll]. It would be even better if this game was more like the real world.

In the real world, when you slit someone's throat, they died.

Before Lilith could contemplate this issue more, the [Asura] on the left raised its top left arm. She was confused at first. It was several yards away from her, way too far for its attacks to reach, but then she became shocked when the [Asura] threw its sword at her!

Even though she was surprised, Lilith was still a trained assassin. She shifted out of the way. However, the other [Asura] used the moment she was distracted to close the distance. It swung at her with three of the six swords on its grasp, and Lilith realized she did not have enough time to dodge every attack.

The world around her seemed to slow. Her breathing grew heavy. Out of desperation, she raised her blade and tilted it at an angle, allowing the first attack to glance off her weapon. Sparks flew and the force from its swing nearly sent her stumbling backward, but she used the resulting force to spin around and counter the next attack. More sparks flew. Lilith went with the blow once more. This time, she swung her dagger upward, striking the [Asura] on the wrist.

-2,700!

She became surprised when her attack finally did damage. It didn't just do the typical -270 of [slash], but ten times more than what she normally did. She was even more surprised when the arm up to the [Asura's] elbow was severed, falling to the floor with a heavy thud.

Ding!

[Congratulations! You have learned the unique skill: [counter]! This skill is one people can only learn when their reflexes in the real world have completely synchronized with their bodies in the Age of Gods *world.]*

Lilith didn't have the time to be shocked when the announcement appeared in front of her. The [Asura] had not stopped attacking her just because she removed one of its arms. However, now that she had the [counter] skill, Lilith discovered that it was much easier to deal with this enemy's attacks.

-2,700; -2,700!

She did not necessarily understand the mechanics behind the [counter] skill, but as the [Asura] attacked her, she found that it was much easier to counterattack than it was to attack. One of her skills as an assassin had been countering her opponents to begin with. Not only was it easier, but countering her enemy's attack dealt more damage than simply attacking. This was especially true when she aimed for the [Asura's] arms. She dealt ten times the damage each time she removed one of its arms.

-2,700; -2,700; -2,700!

Lilith finally removed each of the [Asura's] six arms. With her enemy now unable to attack her, she mercilessly slashed her dagger across its throat, drawing a thin line that bit into the statue.

-10,000!

The amount of damage she did was staggering. Even she could not contain her surprise at the number that floated above the [Asura's] head. Immediately after her attack landed, the enemy's three-faced head fell off the body, and then the statue crumbled to the ground, leaving only one enemy left.

Now that Lilith understood how to defeat these [Asura], the situation became much easier. This Trial of the Body was testing her reflexes. It was necessary for assassins to hone their reflexes until they were finer than a razor's edge. As the enemy closed in and attacked, she relied purely on the [counter] skill she had acquired to withstand its attacks and return them with attacks of her own.

-2,700; -2,700; -2,700; -2,700; -2,700; -2,700; -10,000!

At last, she finally killed the only remaining [Asura]. As it crumbled into dust, she walked toward the pedestal, unafraid of potential traps. This trial was obviously the Trial of the Body, which meant it was one that tested her combat abilities.

Ding!

[Congratulations! You have killed two 1-star [Asura]. +300,000 experience points! +30,000 ability points! +3,000 Reputation!]

Ding!

[Congratulations! You have leveled up! You are now at level 14! +10 HP! +5 MP! +5 SP!]

Lilith was surprised when the announcement that she had leveled up appeared, but she quickly placed her status points into her Strength, then opened the window to look at her new skill.

Skill Name: Counter
Description: a skill that Lilith learned because she was already naturally predisposed to using it. Allows user to counter enemy attacks.
Current lvl: 1
AP required to reach next lvl: 3,000
Ability: Redirects attack and strikes with counterattack
Does 200% damage
Requirements: Users must have precise timing when countering. If your timing is off, the one who suffers from the critical damage will be
MP Cost: 5
Cooldown time: 20

Countering an opponent's attack was something that all skilled assassins could do, though some were better at it than others. Lilith's two greatest assets were her stealth and her reflexes. The only person who had better hand to eye coordination and reflexes than her was Adam.

Since Lilith had +60,020 ability points to spend, she spent almost everything on upgrading this skill, leaving her with only +15,020 ability points left. That brought her skill up to level 5. She would need +48,000 ability points to upgrade it again.

The hexagonal emblem resting on the pedestal had the depiction of a human torso with flexing arms carved into the flat surface. She picked the object up and stored it in her item pouch. After making sure there was nothing more for her inside the room, she left the building and traveled toward the last building within this courtyard.

While the previous two rooms weren't very large, this last one seemed unusually big, or at least oddly long. She found herself standing in a long corridor that seemingly stretched on forever. So long was it that she couldn't even see the end. However, with no way out after the door locked behind her, she could only press forward.

She began walking.

And walking.

And walking.

Lilith stopped when she realized that walking was getting her nowhere. The end of this corridor was still nowhere in sight. To make matters more unusual, when she turned around, the door was still only a few feet away. It was like she hadn't moved at all.

Was this an illusion?

The last trial had been of the body, and the one before that was of the heart, which meant this was the Trial of the Mind. That meant this trial was something that would in some way test her mind, but just what that meant was still something she wasn't clear on. Was it testing her ability to think? Was it testing to see if she could cut through this illusion to reach the last emblem? She didn't know.

Since she couldn't figure out what this test wanted from her, Lilith studied her surroundings. She pressed a hand against the wall. This wall was made of rice paper, though it was not actually made from rice. That was a name the west gave it because it sounded Asian. It was called shoji paper. From what she understood, shoji paper were wooden sliding doors with translucent paper on them. The doors slid on wood tracks and worked as room dividers or window coverings.

Walking forward several steps, Lilith found that this shoji paper had a door. She reached out, slid the door open, and stepped into the room.

The room was mostly empty save the wall on her left. A large figure dressed in armor stood inside an alcove. The armor was made of iron laced into horizontal rows. It was called lamellar armor because it consisted of small platelets known as "lamellae" or "lames," which were punched and laced together. This sort of armor had been used across many countries, including European countries, but the style for this particular suit of armor was definitely Chinese.

The suit of armor was grasping a zhanmadao—a type of Chinese sword called a horse chopping saber that originated during the Han Dynasty. It possessed a long, broad blade with a long handle that was suitable for two-handed use. It was great for slicing at the legs of horses to stop cavalry charges, but it was generally impractical to use in single combat against a normal opponent.

Hanging from the wall on the right of the armor suit was a scroll. The same glyphs from the stone tablet was written on the scroll, but oddly enough, Lilith realized she could actually read what had been written. She didn't understand how, exactly, but she knew it must have happened when the light from that tablet entered her head.

"Alive as you but without breath,"

"As cold in my life as in my death;"

"Never a thirst though I always drink,"

"Dressed in mail but never a clink."

"What am I?"

Lilith read the riddle out loud and puzzled over the answer. She looked at the suit of armor. It would no doubt attack if she answered wrong. After thinking over the riddle for a moment, she nodded and answered confidently.

"A fish."

The sound of something sliding caused Lilith to spin around. On the other side of the room, a door had slid open. She walked through it without hesitation.

This time she found herself in a room that had two alcoves with two suits of armor. Both suits of armor were in the same Chinese style, but one was red and the other black. They each had a scroll hanging on the wall next to them.

Lilith went over to the red suit of armor and read the next riddle.

"It brings back the lost as though never gone, shines laughter and tears with light long since shone; a moment to make, a lifetime to shed; valued then but lost when you're dead. What is it?"

Something that brought back the lost? Was that talking about finding something that was missing? No, this wasn't lost as in missing but lost as in gone. It brought back something that was gone, and it only took a moment to make that something. What could people make that brought back something that was lost? An item? A camera? A picture? That could bring back the item in a sense, but she didn't think that was what it meant since this world did not have cameras. If that wasn't what it meant, then it could only be one thing.

"A memory."

There was no sliding door opening this time, but a soft click did echo around the room. Lilith frowned. However, when nothing else happened, she traveled to the next riddle.

"The man who invented it,"

"Doesn't want it for himself."

"The man who bought it,"

"Doesn't need it for himself."

"The man who needs it,"

"Doesn't know it when he needs it."

"What is it?"

"A coffin," Lilith answered.

Another click. Another door opened.

Lilith was beginning to understand this Trial of the Mind a bit more. It was testing her ability to think and reason by giving her riddles. Since this was a trial set by a member of the Demon Knight Clan, and they were an extinct race known for their assassination skills, most of the riddles focused either on death, transient concepts, or misleading answers like the first riddle she had solved.

She ended up having to answer six more riddles, then entered a room where a small pedestal with a hexagon shaped emblem sat atop it. This one had the silhouette of a head on it. Upon stowing the item in her item pouch, she left the building and came back to the stone tablet located on the island in the center of the lake.

Lilith took out each stone emblem and placed them into the depressions one by one. She placed each one inside of the depression that she believed corresponded to the buildings where she took the trials. The one with the heart was on the left, the one with the head was in the middle, and the one with the body was on the right.

As soon as she set the last emblem into place, a loud rumbling shook the earth. Lilith bent her knees and readied her dagger. She soon found, however, that she didn't need to fight. No enemy appeared before her. Instead, what happened was the stone tablet rose up from the ground, revealing an archway and a staircase beyond it.

The stairs were dark. She could not see anything down below. But since she had already come this far, how could she back out now? Lilith took a single step forward, then another and another, until she was walking down the nearly pitch black staircase.

As she reached the bottom, several flames burst into existence, one after the other, until they revealed a circular room. This room had a stone floor, a stone ceiling, and torches at even intervals along the stone wall. In the very middle was a long coffin, ornate carvings of a humanoid demon silhouetted against the moon etched onto the lid. Next to the coffin was a pedestal with a scroll on it.

While still feeling a little cautious, Lilith warily walked up to the pedestal and looked at the scroll.

Item Name: Demon Knight Assassin Scroll
Item Type: Hidden Class Scroll
Grade: 4-Star
Use requirements: Can only be used by Assassin class players
Description: The Demon Knight Clan had once been known as the rulers of shadows due to their unparalleled ability to kill while remaining unseen. This talent eventually led to their extinction. To prevent the skills they had acquired from being lost, the last surviving member poured his life and soul into creating this scroll.
Abilities: Changes Assassin class to Demon Knight Assassin

Leveling System:
Strength+1 = +8 Physical Attack
Constitution+1 = +3 Health; +3 Physical Defense; +3 Magical Defense
Dexterity+1 = 40% Hit-Rate; 40% Dodge-Rate
Intelligence+1 = +2 MP; +2 Magic Attack
Speed+1 = +5 Movement

Skills:
Shadow Masking: Uses the shadows to remain unseen even while moving
Offers complete invisibility at the cost of 10 MP per every 10 seconds

Pinpoint Strike: Everybody has a weak point
Targeting the enemy's weak point deals 400% damage

**Dual-wielding: This passive skill allows users to wield two
weapons at the same time for twice the damage
Demon Knight Assassin's can only use weapons of the dagger
class**

While Lilith rarely displayed emotion unless something cute
came along, that did not mean she didn't have them. Her face was
still blank. Yet even though she didn't reveal her innermost thoughts
on her face, she could not help but marvel at the hidden class's potential. This class was so much better than the Assassin class that it
wasn't even funny. She now understood why Adam had been so
adamant on helping them attain one.

Lilith unrolled the scroll just like she'd seen Susan do. The
scroll began glowing. Then the glow encompassed her. An unusual
but not uncomfortable warmth spread through her chest, though it
was accompanied by an odd sense of her vision, hearing, and sense
of smell vanishing. Everything came back soon enough, and when it
did, Lilith felt like her senses had increased somehow. The light
from the torches seemed brighter. She could make out the flickering
flames more easily. The ancient and musty scent of this room was
sharper. She could even hear the *drip, drop* of water falling somewhere in the distance.

It felt very odd.

Before she could ponder these new sensations for too long, the
coffin slid open. Lilith was surprised to find there was no corpse inside. There wasn't even a skeleton. However, resting inside the cof-

fin was a set of black armor and a weapon. There was a mask, chest plate, gloves, leggings, boots, and a glimmering obsidian dagger.

Item Name: Demon Knight Mask
Item Type: Armor
Grade: 1-star
Use requirements: Can only be equipped by Demon Knight Assassins
Description: The face mask of a Demon Knight is used to ensure no one can discover or steal their identity
Abilities: Physical Defense+50; Magical Defense+50; 20% chance of remaining hidden when using skills like [hide] and [shadow masking]; makes it impossible for players 10 levels higher than the wearer to [scan] your level

Item Name: Demon Knight Chest Plate
Item Type: Armor
Grade: 1-star
Use requirements: Can only be equipped by Demon Knight Assassins
Description: This black chest plate offers protection against attacks and still increases your aptitude for stealth
Abilities: Physical Defense+100; Magical Defense+100; 10% chance of avoiding a critical hit; 20% chance of remaining hidden when using skills like [hide] and [shadow masking]

Item Name: Demon Knight Gloves
Item Type: Armor
Grade: 1-star
Use requirements: Can only be equipped by Demon Knight Assassins
Description: The gloves of a Demon Knight offers protection and increases your skills at stealth
hysical Defense+25; Magical Defense+25; 20% chance of re-

maining hidden when using skills like [hide] and [shadow masking]

Item Name: Demon Knight Leggings
Item Type: Armor
Grade: 1-star
Use requirements: Can only be equipped by Demon Knight Assassins
Description: These leggings were created from a unique creature found only on the Forgotten Continent
Abilities: Physical Defense+30; Magical Defense+ 30; 20% chance of remaining hidden when using skills like [hide] and [shadow masking]

Item Name: Demon Knight Boots
Item Type: Armor
Grade: 1-star
Use requirements: Can only be equipped by Demon Knight Assassins
Description: The boots of a Demon Knight Assassin. They offer a solid defense, increase speed, and aid in stealth maneuvers
Abilities: Physical Defense+20; Magic Defense+20; Speed+50; 20% chance of remaining hidden when using skills like [hide] and [shadow masking]

Item Name: The Demon Knight's Sacred Blade
Item Type: Dagger
Grade: 2-star
Use requirements: Can only be equipped by Demon Knight Assassins
Description: Forged using a long-forgotten ritual of the Demon Knight Clan, this blade grants the wielder incredible attack powers and unique skills
Abilities: Strength+40; Physical Attack+250; 50% chance of achieving critical hit; allows wielder to use the skill [blade exten-

sion]

Item Name: Demon Knight Clan Map
Item Type: Map
Grade: None
Use requirements: Only a Demon Knight Assassin can read this
map
Description: This is a map listing every hidden Demon Knight
compound in the world. However, the map is incomplete. There
are six sections missing.
Abilities: None

The armor inside was a full set and included a weapon, and all of it was far more powerful than anything she possessed currently. It was definitely more powerful than anything else anyone had in the game—save maybe Adam's current equipment. Likewise, it appeared the map showed the location of every Demon Knight Compound, but it was incomplete. It looked like this map only showed what was compounds located on the Moon Continent. Sadly, she was on the Sun Continent, so this map was currently useless.

She quickly equipped all of the new equipment and checked out her stats.

Name: Lilith
Class: Demon Knight Assassin
Lvl: 14
SP: 0
AP: 15,020
Experience: 197,150/614,400
Reputation: 38,000
Strength: +105
Constitution: +60

Dexterity: +125
Intelligence: +5
Speed: +100
Physical Attack: +1,090
Health: 220/220
Hit-Rate: ???
MP: 75/75
Movement: +200
Physical Defense: +405
Magical Defense: +405
Dodge-Rate: 5,000%
Magic Attack: +10

Skills:
Skill Name: Hide
Description: A skill that allows Assassins to hide their presence.
Current lvl: 5 MAXED
Ability: Makes Assassin invisible to everyone 10 levels above their own
Skill breaks if Assassin moves
Ability lasts indefinitely
MP Cost: 5
Cooldown time: 5 seconds

Skill Name: Throat Slit
Description: Coming up behind an enemy, the Assassin slits their opponent's throats.
Current lvl: 5 MAXED
Ability: Causes 400% damage
Has a 25% chance of causing instant death
X4 critical damage dealt if enemy is unaware of your presence
MP Cost: 10
Cooldown time: 10 second

Skill Name: Slash

Description: A basic skill where the player swings his or her
sword and attacks the enemy!

Current lvl: 5 MAXED

Ability: Causes 150% damage to enemy if it hits

MP Cost: 1

Cooldown time: 0 seconds

Skill Name: Counter

Description: a skill that Lilith learned because she was already
naturally predisposed to using it. Allows user to counter enemy
attacks.

Current lvl: 5

AP required to reach next lvl: 48,000

Ability: Redirects attack from enemy and strikes with counterattack

Does 320% damage

Requirements: Users must have precise timing when countering.
If your timing is off, the one who suffers from the critical damage will be the user.

MP Cost: 5

Cooldown time: 15

Skill Name: Shadow Masking

Description: Uses the shadows to remain unseen even while
moving.

Current lvl: 1

AP needed to reach next lvl: 4,000

Ability: Offers complete invisibility against opponents 10 levels
higher until MP runs out

MP Cost: 10 MP per second

Cooldown time: 60 seconds

Skill Name: Pinpoint Strike

Description: Everybody has a weak point. This skill shows you
your enemy's weakest points.

Current lvl: 1
AP needed to reach next lvl: 4,000
Ability: Shows the weak points of your enemy. Deals 400% damage when weak point is struck.
MP Cost: 30
Cooldown time: 10 seconds

Skill Name: Dual-wielding
Description: This passive skill allows users to wield two weapons at the same time. Demon Knight Assassins can only wield weapons of the dagger class.
Current lvl: 1
AP needed to reach next lvl: 5,000
Ability: Wielder deals 110% damage if the weapons being wielded are the same
MP Cost: N/A
Cooldown Time: N/A

Skill Name: Blade Extension
Description: Channeling mana into your dagger causes the blade to extend in a surprise attack.
Current lvl: 1 MAXED
Ability: Blade can grow up to three yards long
MP Cost: 60
Cooldown time: 10

Lilith was impressed by how much higher her stats were with the new class and better equipment. This sort of boost was like the difference between heaven and earth, like the sun and the moon. With her new skills, abilities, and improved stats, she would be much more useful to Adam.

Before leaving, Lilith used the remaining +15,000 ability points to upgrade her new abilities. She chose to upgrade [Shadow Masking], [Pinpoint Strike], and [Dual-Wielding].

Lilith only had +2,000 ability points left after upgrading her skills. Since she no longer had a reason to remain there, Lilith turned around and marched back the way she came. She hoped Adam would be impressed by her increased power.

RE-PLEDGE OF LOY-ALTY

Adam's internal clock told him that he and the others had been waiting for Lilith to finish her trial for at least three hours now.

They had begun this session at 8am this morning, and it had taken maybe two hours to reach the cave, which meant they had been playing for at least five hours, give or take. Of course, three of those hours had been spent standing around in this cave.

Susan kept glancing at him out of the corner of her eyes. She looked like she wanted to ask him something, but he could just be imagining things. It was possible she was only curious about him because of their shared association with Fayte. But even if that was the case, she was too shy to come over and satisfy her curiosity.

Fayte was talking to Titania, asking her questions about the Forgotten Realm. She was mostly asking about things like the infra-structure of human cities and what kind of races existed in this world. While Titania did not know anything about human cities (she had been sealed away for five thousand years), she could at least tell Fayte about the races.

"There are four Races of Light: Humans, fairies, beastmen, and dwarves. Humans are the most populous of the four. They aren't very strong, but they are the most balanced. My Fairy Clan has the lowest birth rates and therefore the least amount of people. To make up for that, fairies have near eternal life. Our magic is incredibly powerful, but we are physically weaker than the other races and most of our magic is geared toward healing and buffing spells. The beastmen are the strongest of the five physically speaking. However, they are also the most varied. There are many different types of beastmen like wolves, lions, cats, panthers, oxes, elephants, and so on. Among the beastmen, I would say the ones with the strongest attack power are the lions, and the ones who have the strongest defense are the rhinos."

Fayte stared at Titania in fascination as the woman spoke of the Races of Light. Her eyes were sparkling. Adam listened to the conversation with only half an ear. It was interesting and could prove potentially useful later on if he ever met one of these races. Now that he was thinking about it, he had not seen a beastman yet since Kureha didn't count on a technicality.

"What about the dwarves?" asked Fayte.

"The dwarves make their homes in the mountains. They aren't exactly what I would call peaceful, but they are great craftsmen. Many of the best weapons in the Forgotten Realm were created by the dwarves. However…"

"However?"

Fayte stared at Titania, whose frown had only grown prominent.

"However, nobody knows where the dwarves are right now," Titania admitted with a shrug. "About five thousand and five hundred years ago, the dwarves suddenly disappeared. Nobody knows why. Some of my clansmen believe the dwarves went into hiding because of the other races' greed. I do remember that humans and beastmen were engaged in a fierce war at the time, and both sides had enslaved and forced the dwarves to make weapons for them. I cannot say much more about that, though. My Fairy Clan was in the process of sealing itself off, so my knowledge on what happened to the dwarves is limited to heresay."

This time, Adam finally paid more attention to Fayte and Titania's conversation. He turned around with Kureha in his arms and stared at the woman.

"What do you mean you 'sealed yourselves off?'" Fayte asked.

"I mean just what I said." Titania crossed her arms, long hair swaying as she fluttered her wings. "About… I want to say six thousand years ago. Yes, six thousand years ago, the four Races of Light lived in harmony, but something happened that caused the humans and beastmen to begin fighting. They tried pulling both my Fairy Clan and the dwarves to their side. When we told them we would not take sides, they tried to force us. The Fairy Clan made the decision to seal ourselves off from the world. We no longer trusted the humans or the beastmen, who treated our kinsmen like slaves and murdered each other with little regard for the bonds of friendship we had all forged centuries prior."

Adam crossed his arms. Yet more in-game lore. It seemed like a lot had happened during the twenty or fifteen thousand year history of this world. Ten thousand years ago, the continent was split into five after the Four Goddesses who currently ruled the Forgotten Realm betrayed their older sister and sealed her away, according to the soul fragment he met. In between that moment and now, the Forgotten Realm had been plagued with demon lords, monsters, and infighting between the Races of Light.

What really got to Adam was not how much history this world had, but the fact that someone had gone through all the trouble of creating so much lore. Age of Gods was a video game. At the end of the day, this was all just virtual reality. The creator could have gotten away with simply making this the most realistic game ever. Yet they had spent so much time creating a world with at least ten thousand years' worth of history.

It was absolutely ridiculous.

"Are there any other races?" asked Fayte.

"Well... I wouldn't call them races, but there are divine guardians," Titania said.

"What are those?" asked Susan. She had been paying attention ever since Titania began speaking, but she'd not had the courage to talk until now.

"The Four Divine Guardians are the four most powerful divine beasts in the entire world," Titania lectured. "They are the Azure Dragon, the Vermillion Bird, the White Tiger, and the Black Tortoise. Each one was charged with guarding a specific continent." Titania crossed her arms for a moment, lips pursing in thought. "The one who guards the Sun Continent is the Vermillion Bird. It's the representative of flames, a creature said to have been born from the sun itself, so it only makes sense for it to be located here."

"Where are the others located?" asked Fayte.

Titania opened her mouth to answer, but before she could say another word—

Ding!

[Attention all players! We have an international announcement to make! As of 1:35pm, a fifth person has received a hidden class. Because five people now have hidden classes, the class rankings have been made available to anyone who wants to view them. The class rankings are ranked from most to least powerful. Each person who has earned a hidden class will also be given +5,000 Reputation as a reward. We hope this knowledge will inspire others to reach new heights.]

Adam understood the moment the announcement went off that Lilith had succeeded in completing the trials and acquired a hidden class. He hoped that meant she'd come back soon. While they were waiting, Adam decided to check the class rankings.

Class Rankings:
#1 Adam (Seven Forms Spearman)
#2 Lin Akamine (Sword Flash)
#3 Spear God (Spear Dancer)
#4 Lilith (Demon Knight Assassin)
 # Little_Su (Fairy Archer)

So aside from Lilith and Susan, the other two who received a hidden class were Lin Akamine and the Spear God. He should have guessed. Both were ranked first and second respectively on the International Power Rankings. If anyone aside from his party was going to get a hidden class, it would be them.

At that moment, just as Adam closed the window showing the class rankings, the door that Lilith had walked through lit up. The brightly glowing glyphs preceded the door opening. As rock ground against rock in a grating sound that made Kureha whimper, a figure walked through the now open entrance.

Lilith was dressed in different clothes than when she had gone in to face her trial. The black pants she now wore were skintight and showed off her magnificent hips and long legs. Lilith was a woman whose sexy legs appeared to go on forever. Her small feet were encased in tabi boots. They were black boots where the big toe was separated from the little toes. Her arms were covered in long sleeves, and a sleek chestplate made from something that looked like obsidian leather covered her torso. Drawn over her head, hiding everything except her eyes from view, was a hood and face mask. A single dagger was strapped to her right thigh.

"It looks like you successfully completed the trial," Adam said.

"Congratulations, Lilith," Fayte said with a kind smile.

"Y-yes! Congratulashums—ack! My tongue!" Susan placed a hand to her mouth, tears in her eyes as she bit her tongue.

Adam was unable to resist the urge this time and placed a hand on Susan's head. The girl stilled. He jerked his hand back and raised it to the back of his hand.

"Sorry," he apologized.

"N-no. It's okay," Susan said in a soft whisper, cheeks flushed.

"Thank you," Lilith said as she stopped in front of them. "Now that I have this new hidden class, I should be able to help you a lot more."

While anyone else would have assumed Lilith was talking to Fayte, with whom she had been partying alongside since she began playing *Age of Gods*, Adam understood that she was really talking to him. Although she faced Fayte, her eyes were locked with his.

The unwavering intensity in her eyes made him feel like he'd been struck by lightning. There was something new in her gaze. He couldn't quite place it, but it was like she'd suddenly come to a decision, or like she'd had some kind of epiphany.

Adam tried to shake her gaze off and addressed everyone. "It's pretty late. I think we should all stop here for the day. I'm sure some of you have things you need to get done in the real world as well."

"I know Susan has an appointment she can't afford to miss," Fayte said.

At those words, Susan seemed to withdraw into herself, like she wanted to become as small as possible. Adam noticed, but he said nothing. Whatever was happening in her life was not something he had any business getting involved in.

"Then we'll stop here. What time should we meet tomorrow?" Adam looked at Fayte.

"Hmm…" Tilting her head, Fayte pondered the question for a moment before coming to a decision. "I believe we can meet up the same time we did today. Eight in the morning sounds good."

Adam nodded and looked at Susan and Lilith to see if they agreed. Neither of them said anything.

"So you four are leaving for your world once again?" asked Titania with an impressive frown. "I have not said anything thus far, but do you really intend to leave us here in this cave?"

"Ah?" Fayte made a confused noise like she didn't understand, but Adam recalled a conversation he'd had with Titania a few days ago.

Whenever Adam logged off, she and Kureha were left alone at the spot where he logged off, which meant if he logged off right here, they would be stuck right here until he logged back on.

"Are you unable to move when I log off?" asked Adam.

"It is not that we are unable to move," Titania corrected. "It is more a question of where we should go. You realize where we are, correct? The Suncrest Mountain and its surroundings are littered with monsters who are level 40 and above. How can you expect us to make it back to Solum under such conditions? What's more, say we do leave after you return to your world. What do you think would happen to us if we ran into one of those monsters?"

Adam and Fayte glanced at each other. Neither of them had any idea how to answer that question. *Age of Gods* was just a game, so they had never once questioned what happened after they logged off. When a person logged out of a game, what usually happened was the game shut down. There was no need to worry about the NPCs because nothing happened until the player logged back on.

But *Age of Gods* was different. Time didn't stand still. If they logged off and Titania and Kureha were attacked in a place like this, they could easily be killed.

Now what should they do?

"If we ignore every enemy that attacks us and just run away, we should be able to reach Solum in maybe two days," Fayte said at last. She glanced at her small friend standing right beside her. "However, if we did that, then Su…"

"How about this," Adam proposed. "You three can log off now. Then I will escort Titania and Kureha to Solum. I don't need much sleep, so I can travel through the night and arrive in Solum early tomorrow morning. Then tomorrow, I'll log on earlier than everyone else and make my way back here. Sound good?"

It would be a hassle for him to do this, but he couldn't think of any other way to avoid dealing with this issue. They couldn't leave Kureha and Titania in such a dangerous area like they had been doing now that Titania had pointed out the dangers. The same went for Fayte, Lilith, and Susan. Lilith might have a new class, but she still wouldn't be able to dominate a level 40 monster on her own.

"I will go with whatever you decide," Lilith said quietly.

"It seems we will have to trouble you," Fayte added.

"Um… I'm sorry for causing so much trouble." Susan clasped her hands together and bowed to him.

Adam waved Susan's apologies off, then watched as she, Fayte, and Lilith disappeared. He then proceeded to travel with Titania and Kureha to Solum. It would normally take four days—four hours of travel each day plus four hours of fighting monsters. Adam decided to ignore every monster and cut a path straight through the valley to cut down the time as much as possible, reducing the travel time from sixteen hours to just six.

However, while he was traveling with his fairy companion and the little fox yokai, Adam could not help but think about Susan and how she kept apologizing for everything even when she wasn't at fault.

***

Levon Pleonexia sat behind a desk inside of a large office. Sitting before him were several screens filled with information, all of which pertained to *Age of Gods*.

As the Pleonexia Family heir, Levon was in charge of anything and everything pertaining to the virtual world, which had become politically, financially, and economically important to every major family in the world. Levon would even go so far as to say the virtual world had become more important than the real world. That was why it was imperative to remain on top of any new developments within the virtual world.

That was also why his current lack of information about certain key players in Age of Gods was so disturbing.

"I expected Lin Akamine and the Spear God to gain a hidden class eventually… but the other three players are completely unexpected." Levon looked up from the three screens displaying the information on the five who had received a hidden class to stare at the man on the other side of the desk. "Have we really not discovered anything about the two called Adam and Lilith yet?"

"I'm afraid not."

The man who stood on the other side of the desk maintained a relaxed stance that made it appear as if nothing could bother him. While his height was average, his appearance was extraordinary. His eyebrows were like swords and he had sharp but arrogant gaze. The smile that adorned his handsome face was lazy and seemed lack-adaisical, but anyone who was familiar with this man would know that his smile was in no way a reflection of his true personality.

Connor Sword was not a man anybody would willingly cross without reason.

Levon frowned and leaned forward. "We really haven't discovered anything about Adam or Lilith?"

"I just said we haven't. Asking me twice isn't going to change the facts." Connor chuckled at the aggrieved expression on Levon's face. "The problem is that no one has actually seen what these two look like. While Lilith isn't a common name, there are still at least two thousand Liliths in the American Federation alone. We can't find out any information just by going off her name. It might not even be her real name, and since no one has seen what she looks like…"

If no one knew what she looked like, then they couldn't run a search on her based on appearance. As the Pleonexia Family heir, he had the clout to make the American Federation's government give him any information he wanted about people living inside of the nation, but none of that mattered if he didn't even know who he was searching for. Of course, he also had to consider the idea that the name Lilith was just an alias. Very few people used their real names in the virtual world.

"And Adam?" asked Levon.

Connor hesitated for a moment, which showed he was debating whether or not what he had to say was even worth saying, but then he shrugged and plunged on.

"Aside from what we already know about him through the international announcements, we do not know much. However, there were a few people who ranted about him in online forums and chat rooms about a day before the first announcement was made. Among them was Daniel Frost. According to his rant, Adam slaughtered an entire party of his adventures, and then slaughtered Daniel and his ambush party when they confronted him."

"So aside from the fact that he is powerful, we don't actually know anything," Levon said with an almost imperceptible frown.

"Pretty much." Connor shrugged.

Levon looked back at the information on the three screens. The first screen contained the class ranking chart, the second contained all the relevant information about Lin Akamine and the Spear God, and the third contained the nearly blank information about Adam and Lilith.

"Contact the Soul Reapers," he said at last. "Tell them I will pay any price they propose in exchange for information on Adam and Lilith."

"Will do—ah, but that will have to wait until later," Connor admitted with a lecherous grin. "I have an appointment tonight that I can't miss."

"You're meeting your future bride for the first time, right?" asked Levon.

"That's right. My cute little bride. I hear she turned sixteen this year. She's not as gorgeous as your bride to be, but she's still a looker. I've seen some pictures of her, and I can tell you, I cannot wait to taint that little body of hers."

Connor's expression in that moment had turned pretty hideous. Even Levon grimaced when he saw the blatant lust in the man's eyes. Of course, Connor and Levon had the same thoughts in regards to women and their purpose in life, but he was a lot better at hiding it than his vice-commander.

"I still can't believe she's one of the people who got a hidden class," Levon muttered.

"Me neither." Connor paused. "Want me to ask her about your future wife?"

"No need," Levon said in a cold tone. "I am well aware that Susan has been blocking my attempts to track Fayte. The last time I met Fayte was sheer coincidence. If someone hadn't alerted me to her being spotted outside of the mall… anyway, Susan's parents will be there, so you cannot afford to interrogate her. I hear that girl is quite shy and easily frightened, and her father is very protective. If he gets even a hint of your true nature…"

"Relax," Connor said with a smile. "I would never let that man know what I'm really like."

With those words, Connor bid Levon goodbye and left the room. The door shut behind him with a soft click. Now left alone, Levon turned back to stare at the blank screen.

"Seven Forms, huh," he mumbled into the silence.

***

It was early in the morning when Adam finally logged off. He took a shower, got two hours of sleep, then entered the living room. He paused upon smelling the faint but rich scent of butter wafting through the air.

Fayte was cooking something in the kitchen. She wore an apron over her jeans and turtleneck shirt, and her hair had been tied into a ponytail high on her head, revealing her elegant neck. Both the apron and the turtleneck strained against her large chest.

"What are you making?" Adam asked as he walked further into the room.

Fayte looked up from where she stood behind the stove and smiled at him. "You're in for a treat. These are my world famous beef sandwiches."

"Are they really world famous?"

"They would be if I ever decided to sell them."

Adam walked over to the kitchen and saw that she was indeed making sandwiches, but she was cooking them in a frying pan. She lathered two pieces of bread with butter, placed some beef, toma-toes, bell peppers, and onions inside along with a slice of cheese and a thick dressing of some kind. Then she placed the sandwiches onto the frying pan. The loud sizzling as the butter cooked into the bread filled his ears.

"Lunch will be ready in just a minute," Fayte said to him. "Why don't you sit down on the couch?"

"All right."

Adam acquiesced readily enough, but he didn't go to the living room right away. He grabbed two cups, filled them with ice and water, and only then made his way to the couch.

It did not take long for Fayte to finish cooking. She came in about five minutes after he left, set two plates of food onto the coffee table in front of the couch, and then sat next to him. She tucked a strand of blonde hair behind her ear and turned to him with a smile.

"Well? Why don't we dig in?" she suggested.

Adam didn't stand on ceremony. He grabbed the sandwich, which was warm and had a crispy golden brown texture on the outside. The scent was very appetizing. Now that it was right in front of his nose, he realized the smell was from the combination of onions, butter, and sauce. After taking his first bite, he paused at the loud crunching sound that filled his ears.

"This is… really good," he said after swallowing. "It's crunchy on the outside, but warm and soft on the inside. You probably could make a lot of money if you ever opened a shop and sold these."

"Right?" Fayte looked quite proud of herself. "The sauce is homemade too. It's my secret recipe."

"Is it made with love?"

"Mayonnaise."

"That's disappointing."

Adam couldn't stop himself from chuckling when he saw the expression on her face. Fayte was always calm and polite, constantly wearing a refined and elegant smile—at least, she was like that when they first met. He assumed it was her politician face. When they were at home, she was a lot more relaxed, more willing to show her prideful side. Adam wondered if anyone besides him and Susan had ever seen this side of Fayte before.

Susan…

"Hey, Fayte? Do you mind if I ask you about Susan's circumstances?" he asked.

"Are you curious?" Fayte's expression changed. She was still smiling, but it was different from her normally relaxed or polite smiles. This one was strained. "I'm sorry, but while I really would like to tell you, Su's situation is not something I can talk about. It's her private affair. If you really want to know, you should ask her yourself."

Adam nodded and changed the subject. He didn't want to intrude on Susan's private life since they were not very close. Even asking out of curiosity seemed rude to him, but he could not get the image of her despairing face when she logged off out of his mind. It really seemed like whatever was happening to her was causing a lot of stress.

He sighed and wondered what was happening to him. Since when did he care about other people?

After lunch, Adam cleaned the dishes, then played video games with Fayte for about an hour. Then he went into the room with Aris's cryobed. He was pleased to see that around 85-90% of Aris'

Mortems Disease appeared to be cured, according to the monitor near the foot of the bed. Give it another week, and he was certain she would ready to wake up.

Later that night, Adam lay in bed, debating whether or not he should head into the game. He wanted to do some grinding on his own, but if he did, Titania and Kureha would be with him, which meant he couldn't just log off. He would have to go to a town or city and get an inn. There was a strong chance they could be attacked by enemies or players if he didn't find a place where they would be safe after he logged off.

"I'm only now realizing how much danger I put them in when I logged off all those times before," he sighed. "I wonder why Titania never told me until now?"

Maybe she had expected him to figure it out on his own after she mentioned how she and Kureha remain where they were after he logged off. It was obvious they were in danger whenever he logged off in a dangerous location, now that he was thinking about it, but his thoughts were still about how this was a video game and therefore not real. He needed to change that mindset from now on. Think about the game as if it was real life.

As he was lying there, a very light breeze brushed his face and bare chest. It only lasted for a second. Then it disappeared.

Adam opened his eyes. He glanced at the window, which was closed, the curtains rustling just a little. Turning his eyes away from the window, he looked at the figure kneeling by his bed.

A figure that had not been there seconds before.

This figure had skin so pale it looked like she never went outside. Her gorgeous body was covered in black clothing. Black boots. Skin tight black pants. The black shirt she wore was backless, revealing an expanse of beautiful white skin. Her long dark hair was tied into a braid that descended to the floor. Several bangs framed her beautiful face, which reminded Adam of the moon, mysterious and ephemeral. Her dark eyes were cold but contained an intense passion as she stared at him.

"Lilith," Adam said, sitting up in bed and staring at the woman kneeling with furrowed brows. "What are you doing here? If Fayte sees you here, she will know about our relationship."

"She will never see me unless I want her to," Lilith said, and the tone in her voice made him stop talking. "Master... this servant would like to re-pledge herself to you."

Adam clutched the bedsheets and closed his eyes. "You don't need to do that. I already said I don't need your loyalty. You are free to do whatever you want."

Lilith didn't speak for the longest time, but how could Adam not see the way her shoulders were trembling, the way she her lips became a line behind the thin fabric of her mask? He already knew the moment he finished speaking that he had said something he shouldn't.

"Sorry," he whispered.

"This servant... is perfectly aware of what you told her. She knows you are just looking out for her well-being and want her to make her own choices." The subservient manner of speaking that Lilith displayed made Adam uncomfortable, but he didn't stop her from speaking. No, he couldn't, because at that moment, she had looked up and held him in place with her impassioned eyes. "But Master, did it never occur to you that this might be something I want for myself? Maybe you do not need this servant's loyalty, but did you ever think that perhaps this servant wishes to pledge herself to you regardless?" Lilith paused, then lowered herself to the floor, pressing her forehead against the carpet. "Master, please let this lowly servant once more pledge herself to you. Everything that I am, everything that I ever will be, and everything that I was, I will give all of it to you. My body, my heart, and my soul are yours to do with as you please."

Adam closed his eyes and struggled with an internal battle. What should he say? How should he respond? Lilith was earnestly pledging herself to him. He didn't delude himself into thinking this was something she had done on a whim. She did it years before. Back then, he had accepted her, but then he left her to find Lexi, and after despairing over Lexi's death and subsequently being saved by Aris, he had further distanced himself from this woman to whom he owed so much.

He had told her that she should find her own path. At the time, he told himself that he was doing this for her sake, that she shouldn't force herself to serve someone who wasn't going to appreciate her, but that had been a lie. It was mere self-justification to drop her in favor of Aris.

Could he do that again? Could he leave her wanting once more? After everything she had given him?

The answer was very simple.

Of course not.

"I accept your loyalty." Adam opened his eyes and gazed at the woman. "But you should know… there are some things I cannot give you."

"I know." Lilith lifted her body once more, looked at him, and smiled. It was a smile that stole his breath and made his heart trem-ble. "So long as you accept me and use me how you see fit, I will be happy."

Lilith did not remain after saying this. She stood up and, much like the wind, disappeared as though she had never been there. Adam stared at the window as it slid shut without a sound, feeling the weight of Lilith's life, which he held in the palm of his hands.

It was, indeed, a very heavy weight.

~To Be Continued…

AFTERWORD

Hello, everyone! Welcome to my afterword. This is Brandon Varnell speaking. I sincerely hope you all enjoyed Man Made God 002. If you did, I hope you will do your best to help this series grow and reach more readers by writing a review. Books live and die by their reviews. Of course, I'm mostly just happy you are reading, and I hope you had fun.

Man Made God 002 is the second volume of my first real LitRPG series. I once again found myself struggling with the in-game stats, though I like to think I did a little better in this volume than I did my last one.

If you bought yourself the paperback, I am sure you've already noticed the first difference between 001 and 002. I changed the in-game stats from tables to simple centered text. When I first began writing this, I wanted to make the stats look super cool and went with tables because I felt it made them look more game-esque. Then some of my readers complained about how hard they were to read, so I changed it. I hope the new manner in which the game stats are presented is easier to read.

There is a lot going on in this particular volume. Adam has made a new friend, met Fayte and the others in-game, and has been going about searching for hidden classes so his team can have a leg up on all the competition.

I'm sure everyone has noticed how overpowered Adam is; there is a reason for that beyond me just wanting an overpowered protagonist. Some of you might have already figured it out. If you haven't, worry not, everything should be made clear as the series continues.

There's not much happening on the romance front right now. With Aris still sealed away in stasis, Adam is focusing mostly on becoming stronger in Age of Gods and helping Fayte, Susan, and Lilith become stronger too. I've made it so that he is very dedicated to Aris. While this series will eventually become a harem, I don't want it to just happen. I am a fan of natural progression as opposed to instant gratification.

Before I leave you all, there are some last minute thanks I must give.

I first want to thank my editor and proofreaders. My stories are always such a mess before they come along and help spruce it up. While my manuscripts are never perfect, they are as close as I'll be getting thanks to their help.

Another big thank you must go to Lonwa_A. He's my artist for this series, and he does such an incredible job with the art. I really like the more realistic art style and think it suits a gamelit series like this better than the anime-style I normally prefer.

My last big thank you goes to my readers. You guys rock. I honestly can never thank you enough for sticking with me, and I hope you will all join me in Man Made God 003!

~Brandon Varnell

BRANDON VARNELL IS WRITING STORIES AND CREATING COMICS ON PATREON!

HAVE YOU EVER EXPERIENCED ONE OF THOSE LIFE-CHANGING INSTANCES? AN EVENT SO MOMENTOUS THAT, YEARS LATER, YOU'RE STILL MARVELING AT HOW IT CHANGED YOUR LIFE?

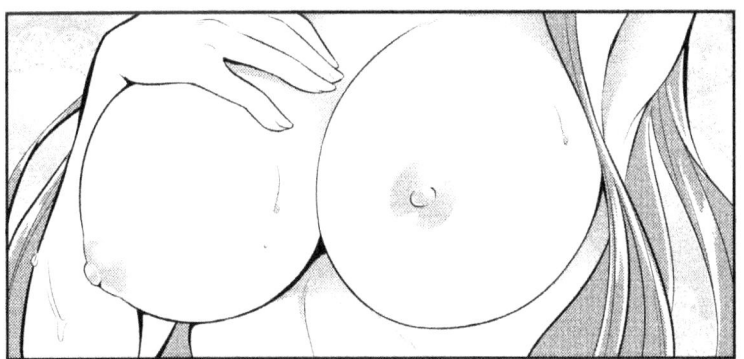

I HAD ONE OF THOSE. IT HAPPENED A WHILE AGO

EVEN TO THIS DAY, THROUGH ALL THE CHANGES THAT HAVE HAPPENED, THROUGH ALL THE EXPERIENCES THAT I'VE BEEN THROUGH, I STILL CAN'T BELIEVE HOW THIS ONE MOMENT CHANGED MY LIFE FOREVER.

NO MATTER WHAT CAME AFTER, OUR FIRST MEETING IS SOMETHING THAT I'LL ALWAYS REMEMBER.

ESPECIALLY SINCE, AT THE BEGINNING OF THIS TALE, I THOUGHT SHE WAS NOTHING BUT AN ORDINARY FOX WITH, UNORDINARILY ENOUGH, TWO BUSHY RED TAILS.

LIFE

.

.

.

.

.

.

.

.

.

.

IT HITS YOU WHEN YOU LEAST EXPECT IT TO.

COMING SOON!

AMERICAN KITSUNE

volumes 1-12
are available now!

Volumes 1-4
available on Amazon and Kindle

WIEDERGEBURT
LEGEND OF THE REINCARNATED WARRIOR

catgirl doctor

NOW AVAILABLE ON PAPERBACK,
KINDLE, AND KINDLE UNLIMITED!

Volumes 1-8
are available now
on paperback, kindle,
and Kindle Unlimited!

A
Most
Unlikely
Hero

Volumes 1 & 2 are available on paperback,
Amazon,
and Kindle Unlimited

Swordsman
Of the
Ritt 2

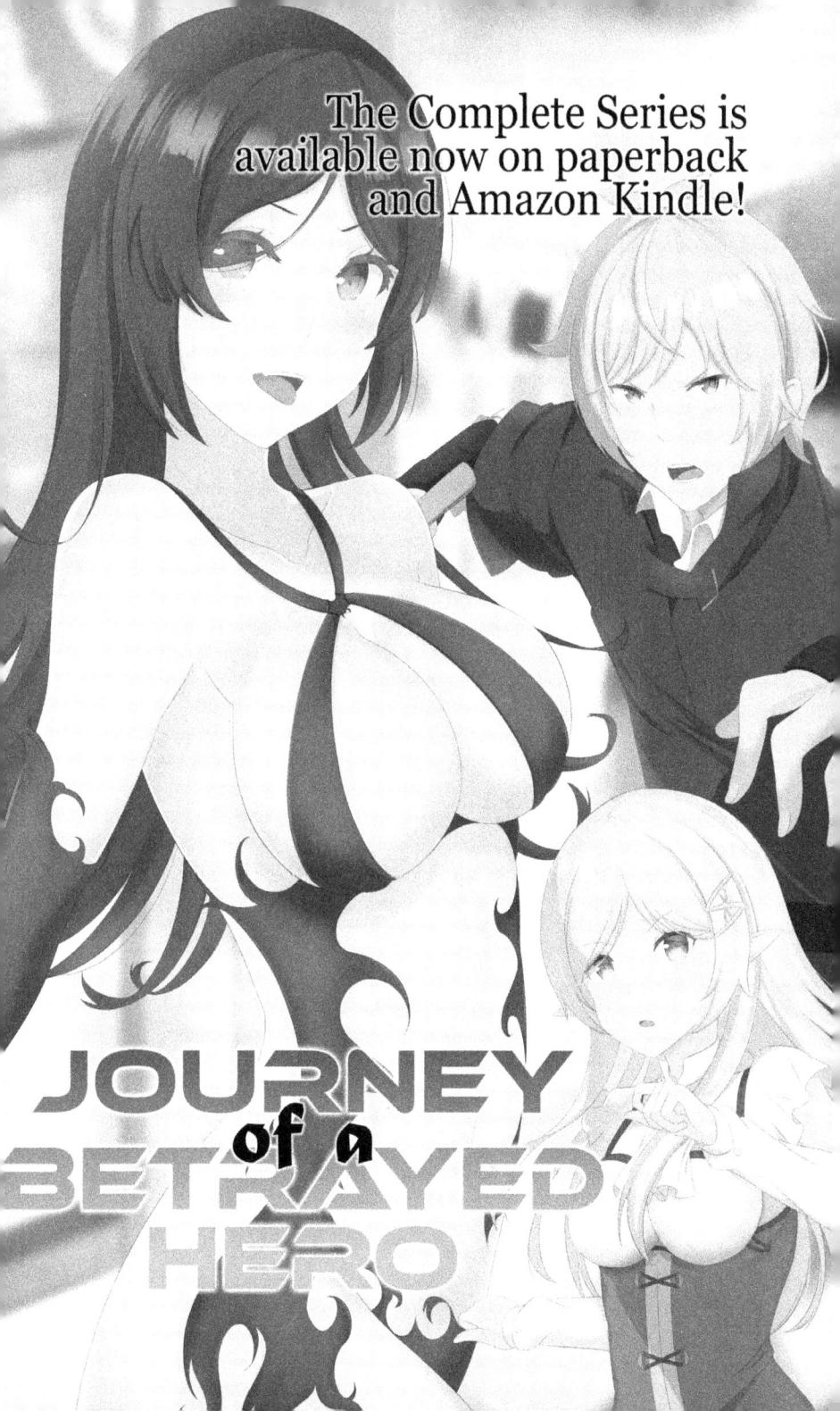

The Executioner Series

The complete series
is available now!

Want to learn when a new book comes out?
Follow me on Social Media!

 @AmericanKitsune

 +BrandonVarnell

 @BrandonBVarnell

 http://bvarnell1101.tumblr.com/

 Brandon Varnell

 BrandonbVarnell

 https://www.patreon.com/
BrandonVarnell